My IMMORTAL

ERIN McCARTHY

JOVE BOOKS, NEW YORK

THE BERKLEY PUBLISHING GROUP
Published by the Penguin Group
Penguin Group (USA) Inc.
375 Hudson Street, New York, New York 10014, USA

Penguin Group (Canada), 90 Eglinton Avenue East, Suite 700, Toronto, Ontario M4P 2Y3, Canada
(a division of Pearson Penguin Canada Inc.)
Penguin Books Ltd., 80 Strand, London WC2R 0RL, England
Penguin Group Ireland, 25 St. Stephen's Green, Dublin 2, Ireland (a division of Penguin Books Ltd.)
Penguin Group (Australia), 250 Camberwell Road, Camberwell, Victoria 3124, Australia
(a division of Pearson Australia Group Pty. Ltd.)
Penguin Books India Pvt. Ltd., 11 Community Centre, Panchsheel Park, New Delhi—110 017, India
Penguin Group (NZ), 67 Apollo Drive, Rosedale, North Shore 0745, Auckland, New Zealand
(a division of Pearson New Zealand Ltd.)
Penguin Books (South Africa) (Pty.) Ltd., 24 Sturdee Avenue, Rosebank, Johannesburg 2196,
South Africa

Penguin Books Ltd., Registered Offices: 80 Strand, London WC2R 0RL, England

This is a work of fiction. Names, characters, places, and incidents either are the product of the author's
imagination or are used fictitiously, and any resemblance to actual persons, living or dead, business
establishments, events, or locales is entirely coincidental. The publisher does not have any control over
and does not assume any responsibility for author or third-party websites or their content.

MY IMMORTAL

A Jove Book / published by arrangement with the author

PRINTING HISTORY
Jove mass-market edition / September 2007

Copyright © 2007 by Erin McCarthy.
Cover design by Rita Frangie.
Text design by Laura K. Corless.

ISBN: 978-0-515-14348-5

JOVE®
Jove Books are published by The Berkley Publishing Group,
a division of Penguin Group (USA) Inc.,
375 Hudson Street, New York, New York 10014.
JOVE is a registered trademark of Penguin Group (USA) Inc.
The "J" design is a trademark belonging to Penguin Group (USA) Inc.

PRINTED IN THE UNITED STATES OF AMERICA

10 9 8 7 6 5 4 3 2 1

For my sisters,
Kelly and Tracy

ACKNOWLEDGMENTS

I would like to give a special thank-you to Barbara Satow, who kindly read the beginning of this book five years ago when I was a brand new NEORWA member, and who then spent hours last year helping me plot this new version after I threw out everything but the prologue. Thanks for the friendship and the great ideas.

Also, a huge thanks to both my agent, Karen Solem, and my editor, Cindy Hwang, for being so encouraging when I said I wanted to explore a darker story. Your support is invaluable to me.

Prologue

❦

Rosa Francis was a demon.

She was a spirit, a chaotic blending of French restlessness, Spanish mores, and the pride of the *gens de couleur*. She was the fortitude of a mixed people heedlessly building a city in a tropical swamp at the mouth of the Mississippi, as well as the foolishness.

The father had told her she was the spirit of greed, the result of a ludicrous lifestyle reminiscent of the French Court that had no business among the cypress and the mosquito. It lived inside her, this desire for more, for extravagance, for rich and delicious foods.

For the lusty, erotic company of human men.

Some believed in her, feared her, particularly the slaves who lived in their squat wood houses on the plantations that were cropping up along River Road with increasing regularity. They understood the need to placate her, keep her ravenous appetite satisfied, and catered to her desires by leaving out their best food for her to steal and by offering her their bold men as a sacrifice to her complacency.

The Creole plantation owners, as well, believed in her,

though with no fear. Their wealth, their breeding, the arrogance in their own worth, led them to view her as entertainment. Some had seen her when she'd felt the urge to show herself, had widened their eyes in amazement, then laughingly run off to tell their friends. She had on occasion flooded a field or burned a crop to let them know that, while amusing, she could still be dangerous.

Their *joie de vivre* aside, they understood, and faithfully followed, the slaves' example of leaving out food and clothing, though they reserved this generosity for only one day per year. On the summer solstice, they created a feast for her and let her roam through their yards taking all she wished.

Tonight was that night, so long anticipated that she shivered in expectation, her sister Marguerite padding softly along beside her. Rosa preferred to glide, hovering slightly above the wet swamp as they passed through the Bayou St. John. The swamp was never silent, particularly at night. It was alive with the voices of thousands of living creatures humming in harmony—insects, snakes, and gators weaving in and out of the reeds and living under the protection of the mighty cypress watching paternally from the shore.

"Slow down," Marguerite complained, "I can't keep up with you."

"Then fly." Rosa was too excited to let Marguerite sour her mood. She knew her sister resented Rosa's slim body with long limbs, having been given a round and stout figure. Father had said Marguerite was the spirit of gluttony, the embodiment of the Creole love of money and objects, food and wine. Marguerite said her body was nothing more than the love of cake.

"I won't." Her sister's feet slowed even further.

Rosa laughed. "Fine. I'll go without you. *Au revoir.*"

She couldn't slow down for Marguerite or for anyone. She could practically smell the salmon, the roasted duck, the wild peas and rice, the café au lait penetrating through the moist hot air, enveloping her and urging her on. The hunger burned inside her and had to be satisfied.

She was stopping first at Rosa de Montana, a thriving plantation belonging to the equally thriving du Bourg family, for the simple reason that she felt it brought her good luck to begin her feast in a place of the same name as herself.

Phillipe du Bourg had been a generous man—with his money, his food, his favors—and as such had been wildly popular in the exclusive circle of planters in New Orleans. He threw lavish parties, had guests living with him for years at a time, and was known to have fathered a good dozen or so children on his slave women. He laughed, he danced, he gambled, he drank, and he lived a full and privileged life that had suddenly ended when he'd ridden off on his horse, wildly drunk, and had hit his head on the low-hanging branch of an oak.

His son, Damien, was not nearly so admired. He had returned from France upon his father's death, a vicious, pampered man of twenty-four, with a pasty-faced smidge of a wife who stood four foot nine and weighed eighty-five pounds in her skirts. Damien had been quite the favorite at court and as such had been given Marie, with the blessing of her titled family, who thought nothing of her health in the disease-infested wilderness compared to the one-million-livre fortune the du Bourgs possessed.

Rumor had that Damien had been making enemies left and right, was penurious with his money, and thought no boudoir beyond his reach, including that of the mayor's wife.

Rosa left Marguerite completely behind and sailed furiously, the wind rushing through her black hair, her wispy red sheath neither gown nor shift but more an extension of her long narrow body. She could see the gas lamps illuminating the house, the doors of its upper galleries open to allow the breeze entrance. Its white pillars stood in the shadows, racing right and left, wooden balustrades in between, an impressive structure in defiance of the soft ground on which it was built.

There was nothing in the yard. Fury ripped through her exuberant mood with the force of a cyclone. There were no lamps lit along the drive, no food, no clothes, no giggling partygoers watching from the front porch. There was nothing.

Hitting the ground with more force than was required, she sank three feet into the soft soil and stepped out in a haze of anger. The rumors were true. Damien du Bourg was not the man his father had been.

He was also standing in front of her.

Leaning on a pillar at the top of the stairs, he watched her as he smoked a cigar, pulling on it tightly before blowing out a wreath of pungent smoke. He was attractive in a way few men could claim. Rosa studied the strength of his jaw, the long cheekbones, and the haughty tilt of his head. His sandy blond hair was pulled back in a short queue, white loose shirt open at the chest, revealing a breadth of shoulders that caused her to shiver in feminine excitement. He wore no jacket, but had tight-fitting suede breeches that showed his thighs were as muscular as his arms, and his fawn-colored top boots were expensive, though well worn.

He held a flask in his other hand, which he put to his lips and drank deeply from. His expression was arrogant, rich green eyes drinking her in as his lips did the liquor.

"Do you know who I am?" Her anger returned tenfold at his bold, sweeping assessment of her.

"Since you have just stepped out of a three-foot hole, I imagine I do."

His nonchalance was creating a maelstrom inside her, pushing and bubbling and popping. "Where is my food then?"

"I don't have any for you."

Her anger boiled over, and before she could stop herself her fingers had spasmed, causing a crack of lightning to flash above their heads and a torrential rain to pour down, flattening her hair to her head and soaking into her dress.

"That wasn't very smart." He stood dryly under his porch roof, the corner of his mouth twitching upward. "All you did was make yourself wet."

Rosa blinked to clear the water from her eyes and frowned at him. "I want some venison or duck before I'll leave."

His foot propped up the column and he took another swig. "You come here and eat my food, and what do I get in return?"

He was missing the point entirely. He'd been in France too long, where the mysteries of the bayou held no sway. She quickly sailed through the ten feet between them, up the steps, and stopped inches from his face. "I don't ruin your crops, your plantation, your life."

As she brought the rain to a slowing, misting stop, he didn't blink, nor try to move away from her. She could see there was no fear in his eyes. His gaze dropped to her lips. "No one told me you were so beautiful."

Her other vice, her womanly desires, surfaced with the rapidity of the storm she'd created. It was a painful throb deep inside her, this need to feel a man's body wrapped around her own, an all-encompassing and voracious appetite that she indulged less than she did her need for food. The roasted duck was forgotten, as were his arrogance and overbearing manners. She decided that while Damien had set out no food, he was offering to feed her other ache.

Confident of her charms, she smiled slowly, floating above the porch step, while mosquitoes buzzed around the lamplight. The starkness of his statement caused a sheen of feminine pride to set her skin aglow. She was beautiful, with the exotic look of a Spaniard, and she could have whatever she wanted. She wanted him now.

Rosa laughed deep in her throat, a sensual promise. "Yes, I am."

His answer was to close the inches remaining between them and press his hard lips to hers, the taste of the whiskey droplets on his mouth sinking her into a spiral of pleasure. The wetness of his tongue pushing urgently into her mouth filled her with the masculine tastes of cigar smoke and whiskey, hot passion and urgent need.

Her hands gripped his head as she tasted thoroughly, enjoying his hard grip on her arms, the quick mating of his tongue with hers, his lustful willingness to succumb to sexual attraction. Beyond them on the porch she sensed movement. A small, pale woman was clutching her hands to her chest in horror, her brown hair unbound, her white nightgown prim and demure.

She belonged to the delicate French-designed house, with its long louvered windows and sweeping galleries, and its wide front steps leading from the swampy jungle to the civilization of the drawing room. But her delicateness, her fragile bloom, did not belong with this virile man whose appetites were as urgent and questing as Rosa's own.

"Your wife is watching," Rosa whispered in his ear now, sucking gently on the lobe.

"Is she?" He turned, still clutching her, and smiled. "Good evening, Marie. Care to join us?"

When the woman turned with a gasp and ran into the house, he laughed an emotionless laugh. "Poor Marie, she doesn't know how to have fun."

"And you do?"

"I do." He turned back with a ferocity that stole Rosa's breath, pulling her into him and molding her body to the length of his, her wet dress clinging to her small, rounded breasts.

His kisses trailed down her neck to her shoulder, worshipful hot presses that caused her to moan, her body aching with want. As his thumb brushed across her breast, teasing her nipple, she urged him, "Yes. More."

"More," he agreed, lifting her dress past her waist with demanding hands, stroking her thighs possessively. With sure and greedy movements he went to the straps of her sheath dress, pushing them off her shoulders to expose her breasts. With a groan of his own, he took her into his mouth, sucking and pulling gently with his teeth, cupping her bare, eager flesh with his soft hands.

Working open his pants, she pulled the hot length of him into her hands as her desire swirled and churned inside her, pushing out everything but the need to be possessed by a strong, reckless, mortal man. The storm brewed inside her, hot and tight, her infrequently indulged desires sparking like kindling, and she felt rather than saw that her thoughts had actually ignited the shrubbery on either side of the front steps.

He barely glanced over, murmuring, "The bushes are on fire."

"Shh, I know." She turned the rain back on with a tilt of her head, keeping her greedy hands on him, laboring over the smooth feel of his hard shaft until his panting breath hitched and he forcibly pushed her away.

"No more."

His ragged groan was her triumph, her glory in bringing a man to the edge of his control.

The gentle drops of water spattered across her arms, rolling down to her fingertips, and a fine swirling mist rose around them as she delicately poised herself over him. His back was flush against the solid column for support and he urged her body downward with his hands, spreading her thighs and easing her toward him until she hovered in breathtaking anticipation.

"I would ask you for something." His muscular arms

held her hips tightly, keeping her still, his hardness teasing her softness as he denied her.

"What's that?" She let her eyes flutter shut, not caring in the least what he wanted. There was only her need, her rolling, throbbing desires seeking to burst forth out of her in a cascade of gloriously delicious sin.

It wouldn't be difficult to take control, drop herself down onto him and force the hot joining they both wanted, but he was whispering in her ear, distracting her, asking . . .

Her eyes flew open in surprise. She'd had humans make requests of her, beg for mercy, for more, for release. But this human, this Damien du Bourg, was asking boldly what no one had requested of her before. He looked serious, his eyes filled with lust, yes, but also a cold, calculated determination. She shivered under the onslaught of raindrops, her body just far enough out that the porch roof offered no protection. "How do you know I can give you what you ask for?"

"I know who you are. You can do this." His face shined from the rivulets running down his cheeks, the lamplight reflecting off of his empty, joyless face.

She tossed her sodden hair back over her shoulder, pressing her bare breasts against the softness of his damp linen shirt. It was a foolish request, one he would live to regret, but Rosa thought Damien was deserving of regret. He had a black heart, cold and arrogant, and she was attracted to the idea of him being indebted to her.

This wasn't the normal way of things, but she was young and impulsive. She thought it would be satisfying to see this proud man forced to serve her and the father, as he would have to if she granted him the escape from death he requested.

She hesitated long enough to warn, "If I do this, I can't undo it. Do you understand?"

Though his eyes darkened, he nodded. "Yes, I understand. Do it for me."

With a shrug, she told him, "It's done."

And with a soft groan, he moved, slamming her onto him, pumping up and down, exploding her mind and body with a thousand little gunshots of pleasure as she threw back her head in utter abandon.

"Thank you," he murmured into her mouth as he kissed her hotly, the porch steps creaking beneath his boots as they rocked. "You won't regret it."

Though regret was the furthest thing from her mind at the moment, she knew, with the clarity of one who can sense without seeing, that there was going to be hell to pay for this one.

Chapter One

As Damien du Bourg stood in the Liverpool Museum, iPod at his ears, and stared at *The Punishment of Lust* by Segantini, he knew he had to have that painting.

The dreamy, muted colors of the canvas showed the regret, the pain, the hopelessness that Damien knew as intimately as himself. It was his lust that had killed Marie, and his lust that had lured Marissabelle, yet they had taken the punishment for his sins.

Like the two women drifting in the empty landscape in front of him, he too was wrapped in shroudlike, clingy bonds of pain, suspended in nothingness for eternity.

"Excuse me," he said to the female security guard who had been discreetly trailing him.

"Yes?" She crossed her arms over her ample chest and eyed him suspiciously. Not an attractive woman, she looked like life had given her a reason to distrust, and he was sorry for that, sorry that she too knew pain.

"Do you know where I can buy a print of this painting?"

"The gift shop might have it." Her shoulders relaxed a fraction. "Do you know where the gift shop is?"

Damien smiled, knowing the effect it would have. "No. Perhaps you could point me in the right direction?"

"I guess I can walk you over there."

"*Merci*. Thank you, I appreciate it."

She gave an unexpected smile in return, and a plain face became almost pretty. It was a rationalization on his part, that random acts of sexual kindness could make up for what he had done, but it was the only way he could live with himself, and he had a long life to live.

Damien readjusted his plans for the evening to include the suspicious security guard and her Rubenesque body.

⚜

From: Busylizzie
To: Marley Turner
Subject: Hey, sis!

Hey Marley miss you lots. Would say wish you were here but if you were here I guess we wouldn't be having any fun because this is definitely not the place for a prude like you. LOL. Parties every night and the hottest most amazing guy I've ever met in my entire life. I swear, I am going to stop at **nothing** until I have married this guy, Mar. His name is Damien du Bourg, isn't that the most sexiest name ever? And Louisana (sp?) is sexy too, it's hot all the time and all the guys are sweaty, it's like a hunk calendar 24/7. Damien lives in this totally weird huge mansion—hello, it even has a name, Rosa de Montana, isn't that cool??—and it's like his ancestors house. Did I mention he's totally rich? <g> He won't let me poke around upstairs or anything but I know how to change his mind, but I won't tell you how because maybe a nun is reading this over your shoulder and I don't want to shock a sister. Just my sister.

When is your retreat thingie done? We may have a
wedding to plan. ;-)

Hugs, Lizzie (in love)
Lizzie in love, I like that!
*document attached

"Oh, Lizzie." Marley gave an exasperated laugh and
reread her sister's e-mail three times. It was hard to pinpoint what was the most ridiculous thing about it. There
was the juvenile enthusiasm for a man she'd just met.
And overuse of the word *like*.

But maybe more absurd than anything Lizzie could
ever write was that Marley felt an unpleasant, swelling
jealousy, an envy for her sister's carefree selfishness.
Intellectually, Marley was appalled by the reckless
lifestyle Lizzie lived. But at the same time she resented
the ease with which Lizzie leaped into new situations,
relationships. Marley didn't want to be Lizzie—she was
too stable and cautious to willingly jump on a train
wreck—but she wanted a piece of Lizzie's exuberance.
Marley wanted to be the one who made a mess, just
once, and then walked away and let someone else do the
cleaning up.

She wouldn't, of course.

But she couldn't hide from her growing sense of dis-
content, as spending the summer on a retreat at the Bene-
dictine convent had proved. It had been an attempt to
escape the needs and wants that swirled around her, peck-
ing away at her emotions, leaving her worried and dissat-
isfied, but her strategy had completely failed. Her desires
clamored even louder for attention. There was literally no
peace, no retreat from her problems, her fears about her
family, and her loneliness, so she was going home.

"Bad news from home?" Sister Margaret asked.

She glanced over at Margaret, who was charting her

family's genealogy on the other computer in the lounge. Marley was leaving the convent the next day on a mid-morning flight, but she had asked permission to check her e-mail and to let her family know she was returning home earlier than expected.

"Maybe. I'm not sure."

"You sighed."

"Did I?" Marley stared at Lizzie's smiley faces, perky and bouncing, just like Lizzie. "My sister, Elizabeth, she's 'in love.'" Marley made quote marks in the air. "But she just met this guy, and there is no mention whatsoever of my nephew, her two-year-old son. She's left him with my cousin again while she's off with this guy. I worry about her."

Marley hadn't spoken to any of her family in over two months, since she'd arrived at the convent, which had been a painful attempt to distance herself from their problems, to stop trying to play savior for everyone. It had been the hardest thing she'd ever done, and now she felt doubt, guilt rising up from that well of worry her family always filled. The e-mail from Lizzie was dated mid-June and it was already late August. Marley had spent the entire summer in prayer and reflection, and by the end of her time at the convent had realized her ache to be a mother was coloring all her thoughts, all her actions, driving her unhappiness.

It had led her to the decision to adopt a child and become a single mother.

What had Lizzie spent the summer doing?

Marley was almost afraid to ask.

Especially when she replied to Elizabeth and her e-mail immediately bounced back.

Her sister's account had been closed.

Marley frowned and opened the attachment.

❧

The Punishment of Lust looked good on his wall. Damien's first instinct had been to frame the print in stark, sleek black, to mirror the austere nature of the painting, the bleak landscape. But then he had decided it was a better visual reminder to surround the image in a rich, gilded, ornate frame that echoed the France of his youth, the days when he had romped at court with Louis and Marie. Not his Marie, but the king's Marie.

It was that early life which had brought him here, to now.

He hung it in his private room, the refurbished former *pigeonnier*, so that it could remind him of who and what he was.

The woman on his sofa moaned in distress at his distraction, and he shifted his gaze from the painting, refocusing attention back on her as he slid his tongue smoothly between her hot, wet thighs.

As if he could ever forget what he was, what he had stupidly asked for, what he was chained to for eternity.

There was no forgetting, and there was no escape.

Chapter Two

Mme. Damien du Bourg
River Road, St. James Parish
Louisiana

Father Francis Montelier
Sacred Heart Church
Lyons, France

November 19, 1790

Dear Father Montelier,

Bless me, Father, for I have sinned. It has been nineteen
months since my last confession.

I understand, Father, that my confession here is irregular
and that it may not be within your power to grant a sacra-
ment via the post. But I hope that given my family's long-
standing relationship with you, and the personal affection
I had for you as a child under your holy tutelage, you will

approach my confession with a measure of understanding
for the circumstances I find myself in. There is no priest here
at Rosa de Montana, and my husband does not permit me to
travel the distance to the local parish, so as such, I am alone
with neither counsel nor religious influence.

However, neither loneliness nor lack of guidance can ex-
cuse nor explain the things I have done, and I ask you and
God for forgiveness. My egregious sins are as follows:

> *Taking unseemly pleasure in marital relations.*
> *Willingness to overlook my husband's improprieties.*
> *Envy of those improprieties and their beauty.*
> *Self-loathing for my lack of control.*
> *Interference with the purpose and sanctity of marriage.*

Sin is rampant here in Louisiana, vice wrapping around
us as oppressively as the heat, but that is no excuse for my
unspeakable actions, and I ask very humbly that, in what-
ever way is possible, you grant me a measure of comfort and
cleanliness, with your forgiveness from a loving God.

I am yours most sincerely,
Marie Evangeline Theresa Bouvier du Bourg

⁂

Marley watched out the window as the taxi turned into a
deeply rutted drive, nearly consumed by low-hanging
branches and lush foliage.

"Are you sure this is it?" It looked abandoned, and
there was no sign, no address marker. Just thick, oppressive trees that formed a heavy canopy, blocking out the
relentless sun.

"Sure it is," the driver told her, dark eyes glancing at
her in the rearview mirror. "Everyone here 'bouts knows
Rosa de Montana. Lots of people coming and going all
the time."

"Why?" This didn't look the kind of place anyone would be eager to just dash off to on a regular basis. They were miles from anything resembling civilization, and Marley thought most funeral homes were cheerier than this isolated entryway. The two dilapidated posts on either side of the drive screamed *Texas Chainsaw Massacre*, *Amityville Horror*, *The Seventh Sign*.

"Parties."

"Parties? Like cocktail parties?" Maybe Damien du Bourg was the Jay Gatsby of the bayou.

Her driver gave a little laugh and smiled at her over his shoulder. He was in his fifties, his hair a bristly gray, and he wore an ear bud for his cell phone. "Not exactly. Word is they're more like sex parties."

"Sex parties?" Marley adjusted her canvas summer purse on her lap and contemplated the concept. "What do people do at sex parties?"

Okay, so that came out wrong. Of course she *knew* that sex had to be involved, somehow, but she was having a little trouble visualizing exactly how these things played out in a crowd. It seemed to defy logic that a large gathering could dissolve into intimate hedonistic sexual gratification. Were there hors d'oeuvres? Alcohol? Did they start off mingling over dinner, cocktails . . . and then what? Someone rang a bell? Were there rules? Who did you hook up with? Was it *in front* of other people?

Yeah. She had a hard time visualizing it.

The driver gave a real hearty belly laugh, the guffaws cutting in and out each time the taxi hit a rut in the pitted driveway. "Sweetie, you sure you want to go on up there?"

"I have to. My sister is there." She hoped, anyway. No one knew where Lizzie was, and Marley was more than a little worried, fear starting to replace her earlier irritation.

So Lizzie was unreliable. So she had run off before and always resurfaced. But never had she cut herself off from her family for over eight weeks. It was too long, and

the only place Marley could think to look for Lizzie was
here, at the plantation house she had mentioned in her
last e-mail.

"She know you're going to visit?"

"No." But Lizzie would be glad to see her. Her sister
was always glad to see her, even when she pouted and
told Marley she was a fun-sucker, ruining all Lizzie's
good times.

It was true. She was a fun-sucker. She couldn't help it.
Someone had to be rational, even if it was boring.

They slowed to a crawl, the taxi turning into the circular drive that abutted the impressive mansion. It had definitely seen better days. The once white paint had softened
to a dirty gray and flaked aggressively in all directions.
The shutters clung to the house precariously, like novice
mountain climbers with white knuckles, knowing if they
relaxed just a little, they'd be down on the ground.

"She ain't much to look at," the driver said.

"No. But it's still gorgeous." It was massive, its long
galleries sweeping left and right from the front door, a
grand reminder of the days when conversation was an art,
the French owned New Orleans, and sugar was the road
to riches.

In the closed chill of the car, the air-conditioning blast-
ing next to her shoulder, Marley was puzzled. This type of
crumbling house, with the past struggling to remain in the
present, the musty whispers of history wafting out from it,
was Marley's brand of pleasure, not Lizzie's.

Marley loved history, the past, anything vintage or antique. A progressive Jesuit priest in college had told Marley that history and religion were the most effective means
of avoiding the present, and she suspected that was true.
She had certainly used both as a means to that end from
time to time, though she felt no guilt for it. Every day she
was firmly grounded in reality as an urban teacher and
designated Sane Person in her dysfunctional family and

was entitled to an occasional respite. She found that escape in antiques, and in old houses, with the stories they breathed, and how they sparked her normally dormant imagination.

On the opposite end of the spectrum sat her sister. Old made Lizzie itch. She wanted new, shiny, clean, the next big excitement, the latest and the coolest. This wasn't the kind of place her sister would enjoy staying in, yet Lizzie had claimed she was here.

Marley had spent the last three days trying to track down her sister, with no luck. None of Lizzie's friends knew where she was, her cell had been disconnected, and her last landlord had evicted her in June. Doing Internet research on this plantation and Damien du Bourg had revealed only that he did in fact own the property and that it was a Louisiana historic landmark, but closed to the public since it was privately owned. The house had been in the du Bourg family since its construction in the late eighteenth century, and that was the extent of what she'd been able to determine.

There had been no way to know if Lizzie was here, so Marley had hopped on a plane to find out for herself.

She handed the driver fifty dollars. "Can you wait for twenty minutes or so? I just want to make sure someone is here before you leave."

It didn't look teeming with activity. The whole house gave the feeling of having been abandoned.

"Sure. You okay going up there by yourself? I can park and walk you up." The driver suddenly looked worried, his head leaning toward her paternally.

"No, thanks. I'm fine." Maybe. She forced a smile. "I'm the well-adjusted sister. I'm just going to go in there and haul her out." She'd done it before. Marley had never had Lizzie's looks or her confidence, but when it came to protecting her sister, she would do whatever it took, and she doubted anything Lizzie did could shock her.

"You do that then." He nodded in approval. "This isn't the place for a nice girl like you, you know what I'm saying?"

What bothered her was knowing that Lizzie wasn't a nice girl, hadn't been one in a long time, and that she couldn't fix her sister any more than she had been able to fix her mother. So she just smiled at the well-meaning driver. "I know, thanks."

Marley opened the door and felt the heat hit her, heavy and invasive, filling her lungs and pricking her skin. The porch gave low moans of protest as she climbed the steep steps, her sandals making slap, slap sounds as the rubber hit the wood. Worried but optimistic, she knocked and waited. Knocked again. Waited some more. Peeped in the window and saw nothing but shadowy hulks of furniture.

Walking to the end of the porch, she leaned over, trying to see more of the property. How the heck her sister had ended up in such an obscure corner of Louisiana was a total mystery to her, and she would have doubted it was even true if it hadn't been for the letter Lizzie had attached to her e-mail. It had been a letter from one Marie du Bourg, a resident of Rosa de Montana, and a confession to her priest two hundred years earlier.

Whether it was real or fiction was almost irrelevant. Why had Lizzie attached it to her e-mail, with no explanation? And the plaintive yet polite tone of the letter had disturbed Marley, had her rereading the words several times. She sensed Marie's agitation, but she didn't know why Lizzie would have wanted her to read it. Bottom line, why had Lizzie been here and how had she gotten that letter in the first place?

"Hey," the driver called to her, the passenger window down as he looked up at her.

"Yeah?" She didn't want to leave, but she couldn't see anything but weeds and, soldiered behind the trees, a row of tiny wooden buildings slowly deflating with age.

"There's a man coming round the other side of the house. He came out of the *pigeonnier*."

Marley didn't really know what a *pigeonnier* was, but she was relieved that at least there was someone on the property. She started back across the porch, wiping her forehead with the back of her hand. She was sweating from the heat and from her nerves, and she was sorry she'd worn jeans. A loose skirt or shorts would have been a better choice in this climate.

When she reached the top of the stairs, she spotted him. The man coming from the other side of the property walked with strong, graceful strides, his MP3 player dangling around his neck, like he'd just pulled it from his ears. He was tall, he was broad-shouldered, he was gorgeous. Even from a distance it was easy to tell he was a complete hottie, which was irritating. Marley didn't do well around hotties. Normally articulate, in the presence of male physical perfection she tended to make strange gurgling sounds and blush like a Victorian virgin.

Six-year-olds she worked wonders with. Men baffled her.

"Damn," Marley muttered. He was almost at the bottom of the steps and there was no way for her to run down them quickly and meet him before he noticed her. Acutely aware that this was not her best angle, she started down the stairs anyway, walking slowly so nothing on her body would jiggle. It was a futile attempt. She was a bit—okay, a lot—curvier than Hollywood standards dictated, and from down there, her thighs probably rivaled the porch columns for width.

"Hi," he said as he stopped and smiled up at her, hands going into the pockets of his jeans. "Can I help you?"

It was a brilliant smile, full of charm and wit and promise, and Marley sucked in a breath before responding. With total clarity, she saw the appeal of Rosa de Montana to Lizzie if this was Damien du Bourg.

"Hi." She tucked her hair behind her ear and moved faster down the steps. Good-looking or not, he might know where her sister was, and that was more relevant than his broad shoulders and her body defects. "My name is Marley Turner and I'm looking for my sister Elizabeth Turner. She goes by the nickname Lizzie and I got an e-mail from her saying she was here."

The smile quieted, the charm cooled, and he casually shrugged, looking unconcerned. "I'm sorry, I don't recognize that name. And there is no one here at the moment except for me. I'm Damien du Bourg, the owner of this relic."

"It's beautiful," she told him, meaning it sincerely, digging into her handbag.

"I'm glad you think so."

She got out the last picture of Lizzie she had, from the previous spring when they had taken a four-day jaunt to Cancun, her gift to Lizzie for her twenty-fourth birthday. It showed Lizzie at her best, wearing a tiny yellow bikini, belly button ring flashing, her blond hair loose and flowing over her shoulders. She was smiling, her arm around Marley. It was truly regrettable that the one picture of Lizzie that Marley had to show around also had herself in it wearing a bathing suit, but at least she was holding Lizzie's son, Sebastian, who blocked most of her stomach and thighs from view. That tankini had been a serious error in judgment.

"This is Lizzie . . . do you recognize her?" It didn't surprise her that Damien du Bourg hadn't reacted to Lizzie's name. It was just like her sister to fall in love with a man she didn't even know. Sometimes Marley thought Lizzie was like a perpetual thirteen-year-old.

He took the picture, studied it, glanced up at Marley with curious eyes. "No, I'm sorry, I don't. But she might have come to one of my parties. I entertain frequently. Which night was she here?"

"I think in June." Marley swallowed her disappointment,

a sick churning suddenly starting in her gut. God, Lizzie really was missing. She hasn't realized how much she had been counting on arriving here and discovering Lizzie, oversexed and perky as usual, happy to see her.

But Lizzie wasn't here. And no one knew where she was.

His eyebrows shot up. "So long ago? I'm not sure I can remember who was here in June, but I can ask around if you'd like. Maybe someone will recognize her." He looked at the picture again. "This is you, yes?" He tapped her face in the photo, half hidden behind Sebastian's round apple cheek and her own sunglasses.

She nodded absently, wondering what she needed to do next. Call the police and file a missing persons report. Then what?

"Your son?" His eyes were unreadable, unemotional.

"No. Lizzie's son." And Marley felt guilty even looking at him in a picture. She knew he was happy and healthy staying with their cousin Rachel and her husband. They had three kids under the age of eight, and Sebastian was benefiting from a stable home environment where he was loved and well cared for. But Marley still felt ashamed that from time to time she had resented that it was Lizzie who had a child, when she herself wanted one so desperately.

That had been the only rift in their relationship, when Sebastian had been born and Marley had offered to raise him. Lizzie had balked, angry, offended, but here it was two years later and she had dumped her son with Rachel. Sometimes Marley wondered if that was meant to be a slap to her.

"You look a more natural mother than your sister," he commented, handing the picture back.

Marley bristled as she tucked the picture back into her purse, her need to defend her sister greater than her own personal resentments. "Lizzie tries to be a good mother, she's just young."

"I'm sure. Is the child missing too?"

Damien didn't sound worried, just mildly curious. Marley found herself disliking him, even as she acknowledged she was being unfair. If he didn't know Lizzie, he had no reason to feel the same concern that she did. "No, her son is fine. He's with family."

"That's good." As he spoke, he glanced down at her chest, she was sure of it. She hadn't imagined that, and he actually lingered, really studying her breasts in her tight T-shirt, making her shift her feet in discomfort. It was absolutely the wrong time for him to behave like that, and even worse was that her own body reacted positively to the attention. Marley bit her lip and shifted her purse in front of her chest.

"Do you have a child, Marley?"

The way he said it, his faintly accented voice hypnotic, his eyes caressing, made her cheeks grown warm. It was none of his business, but she found herself answering. "No. I'm a teacher, first grade."

He laughed softly, the sound unexpected and not pleasant. "That doesn't surprise me in the least."

It sounded rude; it felt humiliating. Maybe he meant nothing by it, but all she could hear was a good-looking man saying it was totally obvious to him that she would be a spinster teacher, a dried-up cliché, a woman afraid of herself and her own sexuality. That wasn't true at all. She hadn't found a man she really connected with, that she could love, and that was nothing to be embarrassed about.

Which didn't explain why her cheeks got hot and she fought the urge to explain herself. "Look, will you just call me if you find anything out about Lizzie?"

"Of course. Give me your card and I'll let you know if I hear anything."

"I don't have a card." She'd just told him she was a grade school teacher. She didn't walk around passing out pencil-border business cards. That was not in the budget. "Do you have some paper?" She started digging in her purse for a pen.

"Just come into the house and I'll put your numbers in my PDA."

"Okay, thanks," she started to say, but he was already walking away, moving across the lawn in the opposite direction of the house. She scrambled down the steps and followed him, wondering where he was going.

In a second it became apparent he was headed to the round, white towerlike structure. The *pigeonnier*, she had to assume. He opened the door and stepped inside, not really waiting for her. Marley hesitated in the doorway. The round room was a living area, complete with a thick couch slip-covered in white cotton, blue pillows tossed on it, and, set at a prominent angle from the one window, a modern steel desk with a laptop computer. The walls were stark white painted bricks, and the décor was sleek, focusing on texture instead of color. Except for a very prominent piece of art, framed in gold, its somber blues and grays a splash of cloudy color on the otherwise blank wall.

Damien tossed his MP3 player down on the desk and lifted a PDA out of its charger. "Phone number? Cell? E-mail?"

She rattled off the necessary info and watched him quickly and efficiently enter it. He glanced over at her, dark eyes expressionless. "I'm sorry, what did you say your name is?"

"Marley. Marley Turner. My sister is Elizabeth Turner." Not that she believed for one minute this man could help her. He said he didn't know who Lizzie was—and he didn't really care.

But she was too worried not to push a little harder. "Do you think someone might remember her?"

He studied her for a second, then shook his head

slowly. "Maybe, but to be completely honest, I doubt it. People don't come to my parties to remember anyone or anything. They're here to forget, to hide in the dark with total strangers."

There were so many questions she could ask. Like why did he encourage that kind of behavior in his own house? What was *he* hiding from? And what could anyone possibly achieve or gain or forget by having sex with strangers they didn't care about and were only using for selfish, distracting pleasure?

But that wasn't any of her business. All she was concerned with was finding her sister and hauling her back home where she belonged. Where Marley was determined to keep a better eye on her in the future.

Knowing all of that didn't prevent her from wondering what exactly Damien did at his parties, wondering if he participated or if he was just an observer, a perverted ringmaster.

"I appreciate you trying at all," she said, annoyed at her crude thoughts, wanting out of the small room, away from this man with the dark green, charming, sinful eyes. He could have sex with three women at once and it was totally irrelevant. People were depraved, and she couldn't change that, not even in her own sister.

"You know I can't help you, don't you?" He suddenly pushed a button on his organizer and tossed it roughly on the desk, scattering some papers resting there. "I want to help you, but I can't. I'm sorry, I really am. But we can't always do what we'd like, and we don't always get what we want."

Didn't she know it. If everyone got what they wanted, Marley would be sitting in a house back home in Cincinnati with a husband and children. Lizzie would be a nurse and their mother wouldn't have tried to kill herself three times. She didn't need this guy giving her a lecture about regret.

"I just want to find my sister. I'm sorry I bothered you. I'll just leave now."

"You do that." His nostrils were flared, jaw clenched, words low and tight. "It won't work, you know. I won't do it, no matter how tempting it is. So yes, you should definitely leave."

Marley frowned, suddenly sorry she'd given him her phone number and e-mail address. She had no idea what he was talking about, he looked annoyed, and she wasn't getting anywhere. She backed toward the door. "Fine. I'm sorry." Her fingers passed over the printout of Lizzie's e-mail she had tucked into the outside pocket of her purse. She had also printed the letter Lizzie had attached and had put it in the middle compartment of her purse. Bracing herself for a brush-off, she paused in the doorway.

It might tick him off even further to ask, but if he knew anything, anything at all . . . she had to hear it. Had to know. "I'm leaving, but . . ."

"But what?" He leaned against his desk, pinning her with a passive stare, his arms across his olive green T-shirt.

"Do you know who Marie du Bourg is? My sister, she gave me a letter from Marie, and I just thought it was odd . . . it was quite old, a confession apparently . . ."

Marley stopped talking when Damien stood straight up, his fists clenching, jaw dropping, voice angry and confused. "What the hell do you know about Marie?"

"Nothing. Just that she lived here. I don't know why Lizzie had her letter."

"Give it to me," he demanded sticking his hand out. He moved toward her, and Marley instinctively shifted her purse slightly behind her back.

It occurred to her then that maybe he had lied. Maybe he did remember Lizzie and maybe he did know something that could help Marley find her sister, and he was just choosing not to tell her.

And he wanted the letter from Marie du Bourg for whatever reason. This could work in her favor if she played it right. She took a deep breath, gathered her courage, and stood her ground.

"Find my sister and I'll give you the letter," she told him, impressed with how cool and confident she sounded. Blackmail wasn't exactly her forte, but she was feeling a little desperate.

Damien stopped walking, eyes narrowing. "Well, Miss Marley Turner, I was truly not expecting that. You're much more devious and bold than I gave you credit for. But I don't know where your sister is."

"But you can help me find her."

"I doubt it."

"Do you want the letter or not?"

"Oh, I want it."

"Then find Lizzie."

"That letter belongs to my family. Your sister is a thief."

"I don't have the original. Lizzie just copied the letter into an e-mail. That's not a crime."

He smiled, a slow, charming smile that made her stomach flip over. Damien leaned closer to her. "I admire your loyalty to your sister," he said in a low voice. "Give me the letter and I'll let it be known that I'm entertaining Friday evening. If your sister is in the area, I imagine she will show up. Does that satisfy you?"

Marley was acutely aware that he was standing only a foot away, that he was tall and broad and very masculine, tension ripe in his taut muscles. "I'm not satisfied that easily," she told him, lifting her chin and locking eyes with him. He wasn't going to intimidate her with his sensual persuasion.

The smile became a wolfish grin. "That sounds like a challenge."

"No. Just a warning." Marley took another step back,

not wanting to turn around so close to him, not wanting that feeling of vulnerability that not having an eye on him would bring. "I'll be here on Friday for the party and I'll bring the letter. If Lizzie is here, I'll give it to you."

"If that's your requirement, then be back here tomorrow. I need some more information about your sister so I can make sure she arrives on Friday."

Marley debated the wisdom of that. "Why can't I give the info to you now?"

"I have an appointment that I am already late for."

It went against her better judgment, but she nodded. "Fine." In the morning she'd rent a car, since she'd be staying in the area until at least Saturday. And being able to drive away from this man on her own whenever she couldn't tolerate him anymore felt absolutely essential.

"Excellent. Just one question before you leave. If Lizzie has been missing since June, why are you just looking for her now?"

It was a direct hit. Guilt sliced through her, agonizing and raw. "I didn't know she was missing. I've been in a convent all summer in solitude."

The look on his face was sheer horror. He pointed an accusing finger at her. "You're a nun?"

"No. I went on a religious retreat." And discovered that in many ways, she had lost her faith.

Some color returned to his face, but he still shook his head slowly, his eyes disbelieving. "Oh, this is priceless."

On that note, she turned around and just left. There was something so volatile and disturbing about him, even when he was being polite, that she felt cornered, vulnerable. It wasn't a good feeling and she cut across the grass, taking big purposeful steps.

"See you tomorrow, Marley," he called from the door, amusement in his voice. "I'll be waiting for you, with bells on."

How Lizzie could have ever thought for one second that she loved this man was beyond Marley.

He did nothing but disgust her.

And fascinate her.

Chapter Three

Damien watched Marley Turner walk quickly across his lawn toward the waiting taxi. He hit number two on his cell phone and listened to it ring three times.

"Hello?"

"I'm not amused," he said, leaning in his doorway.

"Damien, sometimes your cryptic remarks are adorable. Sometimes they just piss me off. Today is the latter." There was rustling, like Rosa was rolling over in bed. Then the click of her lighter, and he heard her suck in a drag of her cigarette.

"The girl showed up." Or more accurately, woman. Marley Turner had been an intriguing little package, obviously scared but gutsy and determined. When he had tipped his hand and shown how eager he was for Marie's letter, she had seen an advantage and taken it, and he respected that kind of quick intelligence.

She was also clearly disgusted with her sister's behavior, but defended Lizzie fiercely in the next breath.

"Your latest ploy to tempt me." Usually the bait Rosa shoved in front of him didn't interest him—or did, but was easy enough to resist. This time, though, she'd found a woman who was going to prove a challenge. Marley was gorgeous, with thick, lusty brown hair with golden streaks in it and flawless skin, pale for August, a small dusting of freckles across her nose. Her body was lush, curvy, with thighs that Damien had wanted to grab on to and thrust into, and her dark hazel eyes met his straight on. Not with boldness, but with determination. She had been attracted to him, like all women were. After two hundred years, that was often more wearying than arousing, but what had intrigued him about Marley was that she had the willpower to resist the pull, the lure, the charm he had been given along with his immortality.

She wasn't exotic or a blond bombshell. She was dangerous because at first glance she seemed so ordinary, just an average-size woman in her mid to late twenties. But then she had stared him down, and Damien had felt the first niggling of concern.

Marley had gotten into the back of the taxi, and as it pulled away now, she turned and glanced back at him, eyes wide. Damien felt a very painful kick of lust even as she disappeared from view down his pitted driveway.

Her innocent sensuality appealed to him, and he wanted for the first time in a very long time.

"I don't know what you're talking about and I don't care." Rosa sounded like she was about to drop back to sleep.

"She knew about Marie. She couldn't have known that without a little help from you. But it won't work, you know. I won't do it, no matter how many carrots you dangle in front of me."

"She knew about Marie?" Rosa was more alert. "Damien, I didn't, I wouldn't . . ."

"You're a terrible liar. Just let it go, alright? I'm not so easily manipulated."

Disgusted, he hung up the phone and concentrated on the retreating taxi.

He would resist her. He had to. It was the only way to save himself.

࿊

November 11, 1790

Dearest Sister Angelique,

I have debated the wisdom of penning this letter to you, but have found myself unable to resist the compulsion to sit down and write to you. I miss France dreadfully. I find myself quite steeped in nostalgia these days, missing the quiet companionship of the other girls at school, the way we laughed and talked and dreamt of our respective futures. I miss my youth.

I imagine that is melodramatic, and you would scold me something fierce for not appreciating the good fortune bestowed upon me by my most advantageous marriage. But I shall tell you, Sister, the secrets of my marriage, because I cannot keep my lips sealed any longer. If I do not expel it all from me, I shall burst forth in hysterics upon my maid, or a complete stranger, perhaps even one of the neighborhood ladies—I shall tell them every last dreadful, seductive, scandalous, horrifying moment of what has happened here at Rosa de Montana, and that, of course, I cannot do.

I arrived in Louisiana in May of last year, as you know. What you don't know is that after the three-month-long oceanwide journey, I already knew what was in store for me in my marriage. It was destined to be a loveless match, of course, based on politics and business. That I understood when I took my vows. It was what I expected, and I knew my duty. What I did not anticipate was the callous disrespect my husband showed me. Damien is a fantastically attractive man, with a physical form and features that are unflawed. Would that I could say the same for his character. But I am muddling this, not making sense.

Our wedding night—I should not even speak of this, I should be ashamed of my indelicacy, but the truth is, Angelique, I will never post this letter. Damien reads my mail before it goes out, and generally speaking, begrudges me the post. Also, even without his interference, I have neither the courage nor the time to actually send you this missive. It is as if I am talking to you, taking comfort from you, yet I do not have to witness your sadness, your judgment, your pity when you discover how far into sin I have fallen. I daresay I drank too much wine tonight as well, so it is best if I write all of this out, purge myself, then dash the whole sheaf into the fire.

That is precisely what I shall do.

So I can tell you the truth of that night.

I spent my wedding night alone. Yes, I did. After that whole day of anxiety, of smiling falsely, of feeling Damien's hand upon my elbow as he led me around the room greeting our five hundred guests, I was deposited in my bedchamber in his town house in Nantes. I donned the appropriate white nightrail and camisole, tied with pale blue ribbons, straight from Paris, exquisite and fabulously expensive, as Maman deemed only appropriate to wear when sealing marriage to one of the wealthiest men in France.

I confess to nerves, and allowed myself to spin certain fantasies about the tenderness of my new spouse as he assuaged my fears. But there was also a bit of anticipation, as my husband, as previously noted, is a very attractive man, and I felt certain if any man could bring pleasure to a marriage bed, it was him. I was to be disappointed on both accounts.

Damien did not enter my chamber at all that night, and the next morning, after I had dried my tears and the maids had snickered behind their hands at me, we boarded the ship for our passage to New Orleans. My husband, who had left me alone the night before to what purpose I knew not, was distant and aloof. I can tell you the whole of what he said to me that entire day.

As we departed the house: "You have entirely too many trunks, Madame."

Port side: "Wave good-bye to France, Marie, as you'll not see her again."

In my cabin, adjacent to his, long after sunset: "Do you know what it looks like that my brand new wife cannot trouble herself to attend a dinner with myself and the captain one day after our marriage? Sit up."

The latter came eight hours after the initial two sentences, when I was feeling the ill effects of the sea. Never having traveled by boat before, I was unprepared for the devastation of the constant motion, and it was in this state of extreme mortification that my husband found me.

"I apologize, Monsieur, but I'm feeling unwell." I tried to pull myself to a sitting position, but the room spun most dreadfully and I leaned against the cabin wall, bilious and suffering.

He gave a snort of disgust, sat on my trunk, and pulled his boots off. I was too ill to consider what he was about. You know I have never been of the most reliable health, and at that moment it was all I could do to keep from disgracing myself. His anger was not readily apparent to me, preoccupied as I was, though I sensed he was displeased.

When he approached me, I thought it was to offer me comfort. To assist me. I laugh now, a bitter laugh of pain at my utter naïveté. What a foolish, young, innocent child I was, with no notion of the depravities and cruelty of men. I know now. Damien had not my comfort in mind.

"Cease your playacting," he said, sitting on the bed next to my waist. Having already peeled off his coat, he unbuttoned his vest and yanked his shirt loose. "I allowed it last night, but tonight I am of a mind to taste exactly what I've bought."

"I am not playacting. I feel quite ill." Behind the nausea a prickle of panic rose. Surely not. He wouldn't. He hadn't before, so he wouldn't now.

"And I suppose last night you did not lock me out of your room?"

"No!" Such a thought had never even occurred to me, and had it, I wouldn't have even known where to secure the key. But I never would have locked him out, even if the key had been placed right into my palm. In those days, I was honest and dutiful, lacking in manipulation and deviousness. I looked up at him in astonishment. "My door was open to you."

His green eyes were hard, dull with alcohol. "It does not become you to lie to me." When he leaned closer, I could smell the whiskey, and my stomach churned violently. His fingers brushed my hair back, causing me to tremble. It wasn't a tender touch, that I knew. It was possessive, angry.

"I understand marriage was not your desire—that if it were left to you, you would have taken the veil."

I gave a slight nod. I could never let him know what it had cost me, how it had broken my heart to leave behind the convent, my sisters, the Church. "But I will endeavor to please you always."

He gave a slow, charming grin. "Will you, now?"

"Yes."

"Then lie back, Marie, and let us lift your skirts."

Do you know the feeling you have when a horse throws you and you land hard, air slapped out of your lungs? That is how I felt when Damien spoke. My shock was sufficient that I couldn't say anything in return, could only blink up at him, heart racing.

"I am sorry that this marriage was not your choice, I truly am. But you were a gift to me, from King and country, to increase the blue in my offspring's blood. For such a gift I paid most handsomely to support Louis' latest building endeavors. I do not expect affection from you, but I do expect you will satisfy your duty to me."

I nodded again, not trusting myself to speak. It seemed much, much wiser not to argue with him. His chest blocked out the light from the candle behind him, and the room felt

*close, stifling. The boat rocked relentlessly and I felt small
and scared, like I did when I was a child and I was momen-
tarily lost in the shop from Maman. I was alone, no one to
care, no one to save me. I was now Madame Damien du
Bourg, my life would never be the same, and this harsh
stranger owned my comfort, my days and nights, my destiny.*

*I suppose he tried to include me. To engage me. But I felt
so cold, so ill, so detached, that I could only lie there stiff, still
as a stone. His mouth on mine was suffocating, his hands invasive. He kissed me over and over, in unimaginable places,
wrinkling and tugging my skirts and my bodice, and tears
rolled down my cheeks, dropping behind my ears onto the
bed. I felt a great rocking wave of fear, shame, and sadness,
that overwhelmed me as surely as my seasickness did.*

"I grow impatient," he murmured once. "Kiss me back."

*I tried, but I failed. My stomach, it hurt ever so much, and
I felt the cold, hard eyes of a stranger on me, his hands
touching me, his body pressed against mine, crushing bones,
muscle, heart, and lungs.*

*The pain shocked me, took my breath away, set a little
yelp tripping off over my lips before I could stop it.*

*Then it was done and he was standing up, buttoning. He
wiped his bottom lip, head going back and forth. His scoff
was disgusted. "That most definitely was not worth my ten
thousand livre."*

*When we arrived in the port of New Orleans, the brack-
ish water clinging to the ship, a fetid smell rising up our
nostrils, and grasping water foliage swaying and reaching
for us, Damien gave a grim smile and said, "Welcome to
Louisiana, Marie."*

He might as well have welcomed me to Hell.

⚘

Marley had grown up in Cincinnati, had spent her whole
life on the banks of the Ohio River, knew the mystique
surrounding paddle boats, and was aware of how vital the

rivers had been in the history of United States commerce. But Cincinnati was nothing like New Orleans. Cincinnati was just as hot and humid in the summer, but it lacked the wild, wet growth of the Louisiana waterways. Her hometown was careful, family-oriented, one foot in a northern climate, one foot in the southern mores of church and chatting.

New Orleans had a wildness inherent to it that Marley didn't understand, that made her uncomfortable, even as it drew and pulled on her. She wanted to go back to Rosa de Montana—to encourage Damien du Bourg to help her find Lizzie, no question about it, but also because she wanted to see the inside of his plantation house. She was curious whether he had done to it what he'd done to the *pigeonnier*—blended old-world architecture with modern style. And she was curious about Damien, she had to admit, way more than she was comfortable with.

The night before, she'd rented a car, extended her stay at her hotel until the weekend, and had made a last-ditch effort to find Lizzie by calling their cousin Rachel to see if she'd checked in. Lizzie hadn't called Rachel, and Marley had spent a restless night staring at the textured ivory hotel ceiling, the light in the sprinkler head flicking on and off as she worried. In ten days she had to be back at work for the start of the school year, but how could she possibly go home without her sister?

It wasn't possible, that was the problem.

In the morning, she made herself maps using her laptop and the printer in the business center of the hotel, and drove to the police station. They were polite, but unconcerned, especially since she had no real proof Lizzie had been in New Orleans. She filled out the necessary missing person forms, then headed out to River Road, past half a dozen other plantation houses. If she'd been there for pleasure, she would have stopped at each and every one and explored.

But this wasn't about pleasure, and she was going to stay alert and smart. If Damien knew anything about Lizzie, she was going to have to convince him to tell her.

When she reached the end of the drive and parked in front of the house, Damien came out of the *pigeonnier*, which she thought he used as an office. He was wearing jeans, a T-shirt, and hiking boots, but not the rustic kind. When she looked at him, she didn't see an athlete going climbing, or a workman on his way to fix something. What she saw was wealth, confidence, and a slight European flavor that was the influence of his French ancestry.

Marley had never attracted a lot of men, good-looking or otherwise. That had been Lizzie's specialty, and Marley had never minded her sister's popularity. She herself had never fantasized about or coveted the cream of the social crop. Her goal had always been to find a nice guy who was intelligent and kind and respectful. Never once had she wavered in that desire, that conviction, that certainty. No bad boys for her.

Which didn't explain why the sight of Damien du Bourg made her mouth go dry, her palms sweat, and her inner thighs pulse with interest.

He didn't look upset or surprised to see her, or anxious to get Marie's letter from her. Unconcerned described him best. And he looked tousled, sexy, hair wet, like he'd just stepped out of the shower. His smile was casual, relaxed, as she got out of the car.

"Good morning, Marley."

"Hi." He wasn't wearing bells as promised, but he still looked pretty darn chipper. Marley felt hot and sticky, and her night of tossing and turning was catching up with her. Patience was not going to be her word of the day.

"Would you like to come in? Have a drink? Give me the letter?"

Marley glanced over at him, not sure if he was joking or not, and irritated either way.

"No?" He shrugged with a smile. "Well, it was worth a try. And just so you know, it's very possible your sister won't show up at my next little gathering. There's nothing I can do about that."

"Then why am I here?"

He gave her a mocking frown of disapproval. "So negative this morning. You're here so I can gather facts about your sister, so I can be accurate in what I'm telling people. In order to find someone, we have to know whom we're looking for."

"What do you want to know?" She got the sense he was toying with her, and it made her frustrated and angry.

"Let's get inside, relax, have a seat, and we can talk. Did you bring Lizzie's picture? I'll scan it and send it to some friends."

"I have it but you'll have to cut Lizzie out. I don't want Sebastian's picture shown around." Or hers, for that matter.

"Whatever you say, Miss Marley Turner." He opened the door and swept his arm out to let her enter.

While he was polite and cheerful, Marley suddenly wondered if she was making a huge mistake. It slammed into her consciousness that she was being remarkably trusting. No one knew where she was. They were completely alone on God only knew how many acres. Damien could kill her, toss her in the swamp, and she'd never be found. Maybe that was precisely what he had done with Lizzie. The thought about made her heart stop.

She couldn't believe that the idea of Damien being guilty had never occurred to her before. But it did now, with a glaring Technicolor horror film hugeness, and she came to a complete halt in the doorway. This was a stupid girl move waiting to happen.

"You've stopped walking," he commented from behind her. "In case you hadn't noticed."

"I just had a thought . . ." That he might be a murderer. Marley couldn't think how to finish the sentence in a way that wouldn't raise his suspicions. She just stood there, heart pounding, grappling with her purse. She'd feel better if she had her cell phone in her hand. Instead of her phone, her fingers landed on the snapshot of her with Lizzie.

"Here's the picture." She turned around and shoved it at him.

His eyebrows went up. "That was your thought?"

"Well, yes, and also . . ." Turning had been a mistake. She was way too close to him, close enough that she could see a faint caramel-colored stubble on his chin, like he'd forgotten to shave. She could smell him, hear his breathing. He was so incredibly attractive, so sexy, so . . . arousing, and yet he could be sick, twisted, violent, evil, for all she knew.

"Yes?"

He was waiting for an answer and she had no clue what to say.

"Damien, who's your friend?" A woman's voice came from outside, behind Damien.

Marley relaxed, relieved to have his attention distracted from her.

Damien, on the other hand, winced when he heard the new arrival. "Rosa. What a surprise." From the tone of his voice, it wasn't a happy one.

A head of black curly hair popped out from behind his shoulders. The woman had deep dark eyes, coffee-colored skin, and an uncertain ethnicity, her features exotic and striking. She was smiling. "Hi. I'm Rosa." She slid around Damien, putting her hands on his elbows and squeezing through a nothing of a space when he didn't move out of her way.

"I'm Marley. Nice to meet you," she said automatically, as her heart rate attempted to return to normal. Damien couldn't murder her with someone else present. She didn't think. God, this had been such an idiotic thing to do.

"So what brings you to this dump?" Rosa asked cheerfully, plopping down onto the sofa and crossing her legs. She was thin, with legs probably longer than Marley's whole body, and she was wearing a flowing cotton skirt with espadrilles.

"She's looking for her sister," Damien said. "What are you doing here?"

"We had plans, remember?"

"No, we didn't."

Rosa smiled, her mouth full of perfect, sparkling white teeth. "Yes, we did. You said you were going to take me car shopping."

"Over my dead body."

Rosa seemed to think that was funny. She laughed and swung her leg back and forth. "You're not going to die anytime soon, Damien."

"Precisely my point. I'll see you later, Rosa. Thanks for stopping by." He gave her a pointed stare.

Marley stood uncomfortably just inside the door, debating the merits of bolting. She could probably make it to her rental car before he could catch up with her. She patted her pocket for the keys.

"Fine, I'll leave since you're in such a lousy mood." Rosa sighed and stood up, smoothing her tight scoop-neck shirt across her nonexistent belly. "I hate this painting," she commented as she straightened the framed piece of art above Damien's sofa. Rosa took her time crossing the room, a sly little smile on her face.

"I'm sure I'll see you around, Marley," she said. "Maybe we can chat when sourpuss isn't here to ruin it."

Marley ripped the photo she'd brought back out of Damien's hand. "Do you recognize my sister? She's missing and I think she was at one of Damien's parties."

Rosa looked at the snapshot, then shook her head. "No, I'm sorry. I've never seen her before."

Then she went to the door and put her hand in Damien's.

Marley watched in surprise as Rosa gave him a full kiss on the mouth, her lips lingering so long that he finally set her away from him.

"Bye." She gave a little wave and left.

Damien grimaced. "Sorry. That's . . . Rosa. She loves to irritate me."

"Is she your ex-wife?"

He looked startled. "No. Why?"

"You look like you have a past." Despite Damien's annoyance, they were clearly comfortable with each other. Rosa's mouth had covered his with no awkwardness, no hesitation.

"Well, that is certainly true. We've known each other a long time." Damien leaned against the wall.

Marley nodded. "I can tell." She glanced back at the painting hung so prominently on the white wall. It was hauntingly beautiful, two women suspended in nothing, a cold, barren landscape behind them. It seemed to echo the ache she was feeling, the worry she felt over Lizzie. "I actually like the painting."

"Thank you." Damien moved in next to her and studied it alongside her. "It's called *The Punishment of Lust*. Do you understand punishment, Marley?"

The question was too obscure for her to answer. But it suddenly saddened her to hear the pain in his voice, to feel the way he stood next to her, stiff and isolated. She wondered about him, about how he lived his life, why he seemed to be alone despite his notorious parties. While she couldn't answer the question, it seemed Damien knew punishment—she suspected he was castigating himself for something.

"I understand that punishment is necessary. And that the punishment should fit the crime. Is that what you mean?" Maybe Lizzie should be punished for running off and worrying her family. But Marley knew Lizzie punished herself enough on her own with her violent mood swings, her highs and her extreme lows. Marley would always forgive Lizzie for her flaws, and she would never abandon her.

"It seems to me that most often the one who pays for the crime is not the criminal." He moved his finger in a slow half circle, tracing the women. "This painting is from a series on bad mothers. They've abandoned their children because of their lust . . . they placed carnal desire, their own pleasures, above the needs of their children."

A chill went through Marley. That sounded too personal, directed at Lizzie. But it was just a coincidence. He wasn't trying to make a statement to her—it was just a painting.

He was much closer to her now, and when he turned and spoke, she could feel his breath on her cheek, hot and inexplicably arousing. A shiver rippled over her skin.

"Do you understand lust, Marley?"

It was meant to rattle her, clearly, but it had the opposite effect. His probing yet somehow casual flirtation irritated her and made her bolder than she normally would be. Jerking her head to the side, she met his gaze head on. "No, I don't. I'm not a lustful person."

His finger came out and traced her lip, the same way he had outlined the painting. The touch was warm, erotic, invasive. Appealing. "I think you are wrong, very wrong. I can feel the lust in you, Marley Turner."

For a second, one small tiny blip, Marley forgot who she was. In that brief splash in time, she almost believed Damien's words, and followed her instinctive urge to shift into his touch, spread her legs around his. Give in to the desire to live like Lizzie did, for a short shallow moment.

But she didn't. Moving her head away, she said, "That's heat stroke, not lust."

Damien burst out laughing. "You're very amusing."

"I aim to please."

His finger tapped the end of her nose. "I shouldn't

have asked you here, to the plantation. This was a mistake. Let's drive into town and get some lunch and talk there. You can follow me in your own car and go back to the hotel from there."

Separate cars, a public restaurant. That worked for her. "Show me the way."

Chapter Four

❧

"Where are the letters?" Rosa didn't bother to waste time with a greeting. She hated the nasty little house, with its old-person smell and suffocating heat, and she didn't want to hang around, even if they were only out on the porch.

"Why?" Anna stared at her from her habitual spot in a white plastic chair next to the front door, her tired brown eyes still sharp and alert.

Rosa tried to quell the discomfort that seeing Anna always brought, the reminder that if Rosa wasn't who she was, she too would grow old like that, her body shrinking and sagging and wrinkling until she was nothing more than vein-peppered skin and brittle bones.

"A woman showed up today. He was talking to her in the *pigeonnier*."

"So?" Anna rolled her rheumy eyes and gave a snort that irritated Rosa. "Lots of women show up here, and have for as long as I've been alive."

"This one's different. He wants her."

That got Anna's attention even as she scoffed. "That's your wishful thinking," she said, arms crossing over her chest in skepticism, though she sat up straighter. "You've always been a dreamer."

"And you've always been too quick to assume the worst." Rosa watched a fly buzzing in front of Anna's face. With speed that belied her age, Anna reached for a fly swatter, arched, and swung, bringing the fly down in mid-flight.

Rosa lost patience. She had never liked being forced to deal with Anna, and liked it even less now, when she was feeling more desperate than she'd like. "Just give me the letters."

"What? You're just going to hand them to her? That doesn't make any sense."

"What do you suggest I do? I can't leave them for her to find. She's not staying in the house like others have in the past." It was a little dig, a reminder.

Anna wasn't offended. She laughed. "True, true. But what makes you think she'll care about any of this?"

"She's oozing compassion. I can see it, feel it. It's all around her, like an aura. The martyr who takes care of everyone, that's who this is. And he likes that in her." That baffled Rosa, but there it was. Damien had gotten strange over the centuries, preoccupied with redemption, inflated with pity, and this one appealed to him.

Slowly nodding, Anna said, "I can see that. You might be on to something"

"So give them to me. I'm going to make friends with this girl."

But Anna shook her head. "Just send her to me. She'll trust me more, the sweet old lady."

"Good point."

Not that there was anything sweet about Anna. Or herself.

"You're as devious as ever, Anna. It just warms the cockles of my heart to know that."

꧁ꞏꞏꞏꞏ꧂

"What did your sister say about my plantation?" Damien asked, gazing at Marley curiously over a cracked laminate tabletop in a worn diner.

Marley wanted to be truthful, wanted to mention anything that could help Damien find Lizzie, but at the same time she wanted to protect her sister, wanted to keep to herself just how childish and delusional Lizzie could be. It was embarrassing to Marley that Lizzie had declared herself in love with Damien when he didn't even remember her. Not that Lizzie would ever be embarrassed by that herself—but Marley had enough embarrassment, guilt, shame, and repression for both of them.

"She said that she was staying there. That there were really cool parties and hot guys . . . she said it was like being in a hunk calendar. She mentioned you as the owner, said you were, uh, totally amazing."

She would have expected Damien to be smug about that last part, and waited for his reaction, but he just looked troubled.

And he didn't even acknowledge the compliment. "I honestly don't remember her. I wish I did. I can see how worried you are."

"I am worried. Lizzie has left before . . . she's kind of a free spirit. But she's never been gone this long without contacting someone. So what can I tell you that will help? How can you be sure she'll know that you're having a party?"

Damien had ordered black coffee, and when the waitress placed the mug in front of him, he smiled at her. She was a plain woman, heavyset and wearing her hair pulled back in an unflattering ponytail. When he smiled up at her, her hand paused with the coffee, and she blushed a little.

"Anything else I can get ya right now?" she asked, beaming back at him.

"No, we're fine, thank you so much." He glanced at her chest where her nametag hung crooked on her cotton uniform. "Ruby."

She blushed again, clearly flustered. "Just yell if you need something, alright?"

"I will, thank you."

Marley wanted to ask what the hell that was all about. Ask if after she was done dishing on Lizzie, he would tell her who exactly Damien du Bourg was and why he flirted with random women. And then he could just provide a nice little explanation for why he hosted sex parties on a regular basis. Instead, she sat across from him and fought impatience, irritation. She wanted to hear what he had to say about Lizzie and then she wanted to leave. Because to her complete and total irritation, she understood why Ruby stammered and blushed at Damien's smile. Marley felt the same way.

There was something irresistibly attractive about him. She couldn't pinpoint it, but it radiated from him, and she absolutely did not want to respond to it.

He took a deep drink of his coffee, than sat back with a sigh. "Do you understand what kind of parties I have?"

"I have a vague idea that they're adult parties."

"That's a very polite way to put it." He looked amused. "My parties are definitely adult parties, and they are by invitation only. You won't find drug addicts or prostitutes, anyone underage or participating against their will. My parties are for sophisticated, successful adults who want to engage in discreet, anonymous entertainment. Your sister was not someone who would have been extended an invitation. Therefore, she must have attended as a guest of someone who did get an invitation."

Marley wasn't sure if that was helpful or not, and detected an insult to her sister. "So, you can ask everyone who got invitations in June if they know Lizzie?"

"No." He shook his head. "It doesn't work like that.

We don't use names, only e-mail addresses, and my guests are assured that their attendance is not kept on record. So if I were to contact them all asking if they know your sister, they would assume that I have records of their attendance, which I don't. And mentioning Lizzie's real name will immediately close mouths anyway. Even if they don't mind being singled out, they're going to know that if a girl disappeared during one of my parties, there could be a major scandal. And if they're the one who brought Lizzie, they're certainly not going to admit it now that she's missing. These are people in important positions in the community—these are doctors, lawyers, ministers."

"Ministers?" Marley almost choked on her soft drink.

Damien smirked. "Yes. It's not porn stars who want complete anonymity, Marley. It's people who are doing what they shouldn't be doing."

He might as well have added a "duh" at the end of his sentence.

"Do they pay you?" Maybe it was none of her business, but she was pretty sure she could alter her attraction to disgust if he arranged these parties for a fee. Bad enough he did it at all, but for profit? That was more than she could handle.

"No." Damien's expression was closed, inscrutable. "I do it as a community service."

That was a novel way to put it. Most people just stuck to working the soup kitchen and tutoring at-risk kids when they felt the urge to help their fellow man. But whatever. "And for your own entertainment?"

"Of course." He shrugged carelessly, but his eyes told a different story. When Marley looked at him, she saw it clearly, so obvious she couldn't believe she hadn't seen it before. Damien's eyes were burning, with both anger and a raw, agonizing pain.

The emotion took her breath away, stripped her indignation, stirred her compassion. Marley found herself reaching forward, putting her hand over his, wanting to comfort him. "Damien . . ."

She stroked his hand, and he glanced down at it, looking startled. The moment hung between them—his pain, her sympathy, his reluctant help, her fear. Then Damien shifted his hand, slipping it over the top of hers, and held her still. His thumb moved, stroking across her skin, sliding under to circle over her palm. She sucked her breath in at the sudden change in his eyes. The pain was gone, replaced by desire, a raw and powerful lust, and she snatched her hand back.

Touching him had been a mistake. It had taken her gesture of comfort and flipped it on its side, shifted control over to him, and made her feel vulnerable, needy. As though when he had caressed her hand, he had seen inside her, where she was hungry to be the center of attention for the first time, desperate to have someone love her, focus on her, be strong enough to let her lean on them just once. Whatever truth there was to that, none of it was relevant here with him, and she wasn't about to let Damien muck around in her insecurities.

She sipped her soft drink, then said, "So if you invite the same people, you're hoping Lizzie will show up with whoever she was with last time? What about her picture? I thought you were going to show it to some people."

"Just a few close friends. My hope is more that she'll arrive with the same people as before, which is why I wanted to hear about her. I need to know the type of man she is usually drawn to and where she was before she arrived in Louisiana. Maybe I can target the invitations based on that, since we don't know what night she was here exactly."

"She made it sound like she was here for several days."

"That's helpful. I had a three-day event in mid-June."

The word *event* made Marley want to snicker, but she

held it in. "I think she came here straight from Cincinnati. She was definitely home for Memorial Day, because I left the following week, and I saw her before I left."

"What type of man does she normally go out with?"

Any man with two legs that had at least a smattering of English language skills. But that would sound snarky if she said it out loud, which it probably was. Marley shrugged. "Lizzie doesn't have a type—she's gone out with construction workers and a doctor. Tall guys, short, thin, built. I've never seen her date a guy much older than thirty, thirty-five though. And generally speaking, they're white."

"What about the child's father? Could she be visiting him?"

"I don't know who Sebastian's father is." Another source of contention between her and Lizzie. "She wouldn't tell me. She just said it didn't matter because he wasn't in the picture anymore."

Damien shook his head. "This isn't much. But I'll do what I can. I'll invite the largest group possible without arousing suspicion. Given the short notice, we should get a nice attendance . . . most like the challenge of rearranging their busy work and social schedules to attend a last-minute party. It adds to the stimulation. With a little luck, your sister will show up."

"What time should I be there?" Marley's mouth went dry at the thought of going to Damien's party, but she would just station herself near the door as a coat checker or something and look for Lizzie. She had no intention of actually seeing any of these people doing whatever it was they did.

"You're not going to be there at any time."

That made her spine straighten. "Yes, I am. I have to be there to recognize Lizzie."

"No. For one thing, I don't think this is your sort of party, Marley. Second, people are going to notice you charging through the rooms staring at them. While most of them enjoy voyeurism to a certain extent, they're not going to appreciate your marching up and shoving Lizzie's picture in their faces."

"I wasn't going to do that!" Much. "I can be discreet. I have to be there, Damien."

"No."

"Yes. I'll check coats or be the caterer or something."

"No."

"Isn't everyone masked? How are you going to recognize Lizzie?" He was being irrational and she was getting frustrated.

"Yes, everyone is masked. I think we'll do a pirates of the Caribbean theme. Appropriately over the top, which is what people are expecting. Men as pirates, women in as little as possible. Bikinis should do nicely. That will help me recognize Lizzie, since you won't be there."

Marley felt her face go hot. The thought of Damien wandering around a room full of bikini-clad pleasure seekers, studying their bodies in detail, was an image she just didn't want in her head.

Especially because if Marley wanted to get in to that party, which she had to do to ensure Lizzie didn't escape Damien's notice, she was going to have to blend in with the crowd.

Which meant she was going to have to wear a bikini and a mask and be scrutinized by men.

Damien in particular, help her.

Just the thought of his eyes roving over her bare, bathing suit–clad body made her want to pass out stone cold and wake up when it was all over.

❧

Damien's reasons for the bikini theme were legitimate. But he also was very much looking forward to witnessing Marley half naked trying to go incognito through the party. Which was foolish on his part. Playing with the fire of his self-control.

He knew she intended to sneak in and look for her sister herself. It was there, written in the determination in her eyes.

He didn't doubt it for one minute.

What he did doubt was his ability to maintain the detachment from her he needed.

With this one, it would have to be look, but never, ever touch, and that was not going to be easy.

In the beginning, I will own it was tolerable, Angelique. Even though the thick heat of the bayou wrapped around me like wet linens, and I frequently felt fatigued and ill, it was not unbearable. The neighbors came to call, there were dinners and an occasional ball, and the quiet social niceties with the other ladies of River Road. These comfortable moments of tea and sewing, inane chatter and talk of fashion, were pleasant distractions from the stress of my marriage.

Damien was polite and all that was proper in public, but in private we went on as we started. He had little tolerance for me, and I had no conceivable notion of how to please him. No one taught me how to satisfy a man either in bed or out, how to anticipate his wants and needs, or how to strike that proper chord in conversation with him. I was taught to pour, to powder, to dance, to curtsy, but none of those served me in the slightest in the company of my husband. Damien wanted something, it was quite evident to me, and I didn't know what it was or how to give it to him. The shame, the failure to please my husband, made me even more nervous in his presence, so that I dropped things, averted my eyes, turned my face against his kisses.

In retrospect it was not surprising I suppose that his disgust of me increased, and I began to notice the way he smiled at the servant girls, the way he charmed every lady

*who came to call, how he would disappear for several days
into the Vieux Carré. At home he began to dance with several young widows on a regular basis whenever there was
music at large gatherings. The widows got his charm, while
I got his impatience, his grimaces, his sarcastic barbs that
confused me and left me mute, which further annoyed and
antagonized him. It seemed as if Damien enjoyed the company of everyone but me, and for the first time it occurred to
me that perhaps if I did not satisfy Damien as a wife, he
would look elsewhere for his pleasure and companionship.
Perhaps he already had. Perhaps that was the appeal of
town, those women of ill repute who would please a man for
a few coins. Maman had whispered about such things to me,
warned me that a wife must be biddable and accommodat-
ing at all times so as not to force a husband to seek comfort
from another woman, but that was the extent of her instruction. In considering the matter, I conceded that while I might
be disgusted, I could ignore a dalliance of Damien's in town
with a paid companion, but I could not abide a liaison with
a lady, one of our neighbors, right under my nose in the
country.*

*Now fear was added to all my other concerns. What was
tolerable would surely become intolerable if I had to be sub-
jected to the disrespect of a faithless husband. My acquain-
tances were merely that, new superficial friendships that I
could not confide my fears to, and our society was limited to
a few close neighbors. Damien prefers that I stay here on the
plantation, so there is no ability to attend Mass, and I was
growing increasingly lonely, with nowhere to seek advice.*

*The house, while lovely and sizable, is stuffy and close at
all times because of the Louisiana heat, and the foliage, the
swamp, the insects, all seem to close in around the house and
press down upon it. It is a marvel, an elegant manse in the
midst of such wilderness, but the household fights nature daily
to keep its encroaching fingers away. With neither my maid
nor I equipped with the knowledge to deal with the unfriendly*

climate, the constant damp made my hair an uncooperative disarray, and mold raced along the walls of my wardrobe with little provocation, ruining several costly gowns.

When I fainted in July, I credited the heat, but Damien insisted a physician be sent for. I must confess I was pleased by this show of concern and took to my bed readily, allowing the maid to plump my pillows and fuss about me. Through the open gallerie windows of my bedchamber, I heard the hooves of the horse heading down the drive to summon the doctor, and I was suddenly, childishly glad for my weak disposition.

There, I thought, now he shall be forced to pay positive attention to me. Damien will worry, will come to realize what I mean to him, and he will write my family back home and they will be shamed for sending me to this awful, suffocating, primitive country. Mean-spirited and juvenile though it was, I couldn't help but feel it, and I hoped the physician would diagnose me with an ailment that would garner sympathy yet would not kill, maim, or disfigure me. An inflammation of the lungs would do quite nicely.

But when the man took his leave, and spoke to my husband in the hall, Damien returned with something of a smile on his face.

Damien's smiles were never genuine, never loving or affectionate or wondrous. They were charming, insolent, coaxing, provocative, sly, and haughty. The one he gave me then was sly.

"Why, Marie, I had no idea you were such an accomplished actress."

I cannot adequately express to you how apprehensive this made me feel, how his one short sentence robbed me of all hope, smugness, childish savant, and filled me with fear.

"Whatever do you mean?" I sank back into my bedding.

"The doctor tells me you are enceinte. *Were you planning to tell me anytime soon?"*

"What?" A baby? I'd had no notion that I was expecting, none whatsoever. "Is he certain?"

Damien nodded, stopping at the foot of the bed with his arms across his chest. "Yes, he is certain. Are you saying you didn't know?"

"No. How would I know? I've felt nothing . . . oh, my." I put my hands on my cheeks. A baby. I was truly overjoyed at the thought. "Is he absolutely certain?"

"He is certain. And I think this is the most emotion I have ever seen you express. It would seem you are pleased, yes?"

"Yes," I whispered, too excited at the prospect of a baby, my baby, to give much thought to his insulting words. I touched my flat stomach. A child would fill my long days, would give me companionship and a sense of purpose, create a vessel for all the love I had to give.

Damien came around the side of the bed. He smoothed my ruined coiffure, destroyed by the faint and the humidity. I looked up at him, cautious, yet unable to prevent a smile of satisfaction. I was a good wife. I had conceived within a few months of our marriage and he could surely not find fault with that.

"The baby should arrive in January or February."

"That is a long time to wait," I said.

Damien laughed and leaned over and kissed my forehead, a soft quick press of his lips. "It will be here before you know it. And in case you are wondering, I am pleased too."

My heart swelled with pleasure, gratitude, and excitement, as my husband caressed my cheek, my lips.

It was, in retrospect, perhaps the purest moment of happiness in my marriage.

When Friday rolled around and Marley's frantic phone calls resulted in no news of Lizzie back home in Cincinnati, she donned the black bikini she had bought the day before. Black was supposed to be slimming, but her thighs didn't seem to realize that, so she had also bought a ridiculously long tan raincoat to toss over the bathing suit.

Extra clothes, in case the theme had changed and she could cover the stupid bikini, were shoved into her beach bag along with a mask. She was wearing sandals with the bikini and trench. She'd drawn the line at heels, and had stuck to flat leather sandals.

Feeling like a cross between a Bond girl and a psychiatric patient, Marley got in her rental car and drove to Rosa de Montana to attend her very first, and please, God, very last, sex party.

Chapter Five

It was a flawed plan from the beginning.

The only thing that propelled Marley forward was the need to find her sister. She didn't want to let the opportunity slip by, and she would recognize her sister and her sister's voice under any circumstances, she was positive. Attending this so-called party might be her only opportunity to find Lizzie and drag her inconsiderate butt home.

But what Marley knew about flirtation, seduction, and swinging could fit on the head of a pin—and there would still be room to spare. She knew she was going to have to lie low, hang in the shadows so no one would notice how completely uncomfortable she was baring any flesh from neck to knee.

She sort of figured Damien would spot her. After all, she'd be the only one sweating and whimpering. Or to re-phrase that, she'd be the only one sweating and whimpering from fear and nerves as opposed to ecstasy. It was expected she'd stand out. She was a first grade teacher with mud brown hair and a stubborn thirty pounds that refused to disappear no matter how many carbs she cut.

She had nary a tattoo anywhere, and sensible sandals. It wasn't going to be easy.

What she didn't expect was that Damien would be on to her less than five minutes after she walked in the door.

Parking the car down the drive, she had gone up the steps of the big house, simple black mask on, and had stopped to compose herself. There were twenty cars already parked out front, and she could hear voices, music coming from the house. She wasn't sure she could do this. Her heart was racing and she had perspiration in icky places.

"Going in?" a voice asked from behind.

Marley turned around, both terrified and relieved. "I was thinking about it," she said to the man who was bounding up the steps in his cheesy pirate outfit.

There were no lights on the porch, and only two torches illuminating the impromptu parking lot, so she could only see the man's outline, his white shirt, his eye patch. He was on the short side, thin, very unthreatening in appearance. He moved until he was standing next to her and she could see him smiling in reassurance.

"Your first time?"

"Yes."

"Come on. You can go in with me." He opened the front door, and with a hand lightly on the small of her back, he urged her forward. "Remember, only do what you want to do. But it's about having fun, so what you want, take as much as you can handle."

Marley's brain was too terrified to fully understand even what he was saying. She just nodded and walked into the house, pausing in the foyer and taking in her surroundings. The house was lit by candlelight, and the flames danced on the faded wallpaper, over the worn Aubusson carpets, and softened the tears in the blue fabric of a pair of Louis XIV chairs sitting silently on either side of a French occasional table. The smell was a mix of the old musty, stale air, and the newer scents of candles burning and a vase full of flowers. The latter struggled to freshen the house, which the pervasive odor of rot still clung to.

There was a lack of symmetry to the rooms on either side of the foyer, their doorways not aligned, as if each salon was declaring she was elegant all on her own, and chose not to mirror the other. Well worn, but well preserved, proud and slightly haughty—just like its owner— the Creole mansion fascinated Marley.

"The house is beautiful," she said softly.

"It's also hot in here," her companion said, tugging at the neck of his white shirt. "No air-conditioning in these old museums."

Marley thought it was warm, but not stuffy. All the windows were open, and a warm breeze shifted through the foyer. She was straining to see up the staircase, to see the portraits hanging along the right side wall, when she felt hands on her.

"You're overdressed anyway." The short, seemingly harmless guy undid the belt on her jacket and had it stripped off her before she could even blink.

Marley grabbed for the sleeve, trying to keep it on, but he had the element of surprise on his side. The raincoat was gone, tossed behind his back, and she was standing in the stupid black bikini, suddenly realizing what a huge, huge mistake this had been.

"Much better," he said, his eyes widening as he stared at her breasts. "You looked more like a spy with that coat on. And while that could be sexy in its own right, I really prefer this."

His finger stroked across her breast, lightly squeezing her nipple. "Nice."

Marley smacked at him, disgusted, shock turning to anger. "Hands off."

Mr. Nice Guy smirked and took a step closer to her.

"Not ready yet? Going to play shy? Or do you like a guy who takes it anyway, even when you say no?"

No, she definitely didn't like that. Marley clenched her fists and inched backward, ready to either knee him in the nuts or flee into the living room, whichever seemed more appropriate. There were low voices everywhere, surrounding her, hinting at many partygoers, yet she could only see shadows, not people. The house was dark, too dark.

"I'm not playing games," she said. "I really mean hands off."

"Okay," he acquiesced, more readily than she had expected. "I was just making sure you're weren't trying to start up a little roughhousing. But this is your first time, you're not ready yet, I understand. Let's go get a drink and we'll take it slow, watch some of the other couples for a while. It's good for me to have to wait."

Marley tried to formulate some kind of response, but her mouth was stuck shut like she'd eaten an entire jar of peanut butter.

"Actually, she is my special guest this evening."

Marley turned and saw Damien standing in the doorway, looking casual as usual. The pirate look suited him better than it did the skinny breast-grabber. Damien wore tight black pants, knee-high boots, and a white shirt only half buttoned up. He looked comfortable in the clothes, very masculine, like he'd just stepped off ship into the Port of New Orleans. She was thrilled to see him for a whole giant number of reasons.

"Hi," she managed, unable to prevent herself from shifting just a little closer to him. "Sorry I'm late."

His hand slid around her waist, and his gaze pored over her body, lingering on her chest. Marley struggled not to blush, knowing he was doing it just for effect.

"You're here now, that is what matters."

"We were going to go get a drink," the other guy said. Damien shook his head. "No. She's only meant for me. She likes to watch the others, but she only wants me to touch."

Ho, boy. Marley struggled not to squirm. Damien was saving her behind, but she was embarrassed nonetheless.

"For real?" the guy asked.

"Yes," she said, trying to sound firm.

"That's too bad," he said, but he shrugged and walked away, heading into the room Damien had emerged from.

Marley sighed in relief.

Damien gripped her waist harder and leaned toward her. "Marley, what the hell are you doing here?" he said in a low, angry voice in her ear.

Marley tried to pull away, uncomfortable at the way his warm hand gripped her bare skin, his breath hot and rough on her cheek. "I needed to make sure you could recognize Lizzie . . . what if she's dyed her hair or something? If you had just let me come as a waitress I wouldn't have had to do this."

"So this is my fault?" He sounded amused, his thigh brushing hers.

"Yes." She turned her head a little to give him a defiant stare. He wasn't looking at her face. His eyes were down on her chest again. Marley glanced down herself, and swallowed hard. Yikes. She really shouldn't have worn the bikini. Her D cups were straining, the triangles being dragged low by the sheer force of gravity. There was a lot of skin showing. She needed that raincoat back on and pronto. She pulled away from him to retrieve it.

"Where are you going?"

"I'm putting my coat back on." She bent over and grabbed it off the floor.

"Not if you want me to escort you through all the rooms so you can look for your sister."

"You'll escort me?" She hadn't expected him to agree to that. She thought he would toss her out on her bikini-covered behind.

Marley shoved her arms through her sleeves even though he had just told her not to. She felt way too vulnerable half naked. Generally speaking, she wasn't all that comfortable in her own skin, even with clothes on. Forget clothes off. Her sexual experience was mostly limited to college, when she'd had what she'd thought at the time was a grand love affair. Later they'd both realized it had been more of an enthusiastic case of puppy lust.

Damien crossed his arms over his chest. "Well, I'm certainly not going to let you stroll around on your own. I can't even imagine the kind of trouble you'd get yourself into."

He was probably right, but it was still kind of insulting. "Like I said, I wouldn't have had to resort to this if you had just cooperated with me."

"Alright, I'll accept full responsibility. This is all my fault." He came toward her, hands landing on her shoulders. Damien's fingers shifted under the coat, caressing her skin, skimming down her arms, forcing the sleeves of the coat to give way. He caught it, while her breath hitched, goose bumps rising on her flesh. His mouth was right in front of hers, his legs pressing against her bare thighs. Turning casually, as if he had no idea how nervous she was, he stripped the coat off of her, folded it, and set it on the Louis XIV chair.

Then he rounded on her, shoulders set, voice firm. "So, since we are in agreement, I have created this rather precarious situation, and to make it right, I'll take you around so you can look for your sister. But you have to stay right next to me. You will not speak to anyone, you will not touch anyone, and you will leave the mask on at all times. Do you understand?"

"Yes." She had no intention of disobeying. She was going to stick to Damien like white on rice, keep her mouth shut, and not make eye contact with anyone, since apparently that could be misconstrued as an invitation to touch her nipple.

"If you see your sister, you will whisper delicately in my ear, and then I will handle it."

Marley said, "Fine," but couldn't quite prevent an eye roll. She wasn't totally clueless. She wasn't going to grab Lizzie by the hair. She could be discreet. Her whole life was about discretion, about not rocking the boat, about settling everyone back down.

Attention was not her friend. She much preferred to observe than to be observed.

Damien laughed softly, taking her hand and lacing her fingers through his. "That was quite a smart-ass look on your face. Now don't let go of me. You look very rich and decadent in that bikini and there are plenty of men here who'd love to eat you for dessert if you give them the slightest encouragement."

Marley just nodded, pondering his word choice. She kind of liked the sound of that. She wasn't overweight, she was decadent.

Damien pulled her into the living room, moving along the right wall, behind the sofas and tables, slowly around the perimeter of the room. There were people talking, the light from the candles bouncing off various pirate costumes ranging from crisp, just-out-of-the-bag discount-store quality to a very authentic, shabby-looking outfit on one man who had broad shoulders and the legs of a professional athlete. He glanced at her, his lips on the neck of his companion, and Marley shifted her gaze away.

The women were all dressed in the requisite bikini, some retro, some tiny scraps of nothing, others perky and colorful. Two women she saw were already out of their tops, both with men lavishing attention on their breasts. The blonde was stuck to one dark-haired guy, the brunette actually had two men, one on each breast. Maybe it felt fabulous, but Marley thought it looked weird, just a little too mammalian for her tastes. So busy staring, just a little shocked, Marley ran into Damien's back.

He had stopped walking, and she grabbed his shoulder with her free hand to steady herself. Her heart was pounding, adrenaline high, and she felt like she had when she was sixteen and she'd let Lizzie talk her into sneaking into a cemetery. Like then, she knew now what she was doing was a bad idea, and the fear of discovery, of getting in trouble, of punishment, was added to the little jolt of excitement that she was doing something she shouldn't, something just a bit naughty.

She'd never, ever seen someone else engaging in this casual foreplay. She'd never even seen *herself* engaged in foreplay. As she clung to Damien's back, she marveled that everyone looked so relaxed, so unconcerned, so disinterested in what was going on around them. A quick count showed twelve people in the room, including the skinny guy who had escorted her in. He was talking to a very thin woman with dark hair, his hand on her knee, stroking.

"Looked at everyone?" Damien whispered over his shoulder.

"Yes. She's not here."

Damien moved out of the room, through the doorway with a transom window above it, into what looked like a library, the thick mahogany built-in bookcases filled with row upon row of books.

"That wasn't so bad," she whispered, glancing back over her shoulder. Inappropriate, but not entirely a porno flick.

Damien startled her by turning completely around and looking down at her. She was suddenly very aware all over again of how nearly naked she was. Why did the men get pirate outfits and she was stuck in a bikini? She was sure she could have really rocked a nineteenth-century ball gown. That would have been so much better.

She couldn't see his eyes, but his expression looked enigmatic in the candlelight. "Not bad enough for you, hmm?" he murmured. "That was only the reception room, Marley. No need to be disappointed."

"I wasn't disappointed!"

His finger landed on her mouth. "Shhh," he whispered, lips brushing against her ear. "Don't disturb the guests."

And he stepped back to show her the inside of the library.

When Damien had been standing in front of her, she had only been able to see the bookshelves. But when he moved, she saw two couches and a desk in the cozy wood-paneled room.

On the first couch was a thin woman with small breasts lying sideways, a man between her thighs, her fingers in the back of his hair tugging and gripping, her teeth gritted against the pleasure.

The second couch had a more voluptuous woman reclining on it, her hands cupping her breasts, a pirate on his knees in front of her. Marley couldn't see specifics of what he was doing, but the soft moans, the motion, the ripe, tangy scent in the air told her very clearly what was going on.

She swallowed hard and shifted her gaze quickly, embarrassed to be watching, ashamed that she felt a little jolt of jealousy.

Turning didn't preserve Marley's modesty. Instead, she was given a full frontal of a third woman on the sturdy antique desk, sitting facing them, heels up on the wood, legs spread, arms resting on her knees, showing quite clearly what was hidden from view with the other two. Marley could see everything the woman had and then some, including the man's tongue sliding along her pink swollen flesh, up and down with slow, deliberate movements.

It was the most shocking thing she'd ever seen, the position haughty and erotic, showing a woman who was confident in what she wanted, and ready to receive it. Marley must have made an involuntary sound, because Damien's hand moved into place over her mouth again.

"This room is for pleasuring women," he whispered in her ear. "It is all about worshiping the female figure, coaxing ecstasy from her, going and going until she thinks she can't take anymore, licking and sliding and making love to her with your mouth until she is begging to be taken, begging for a man to complete her."

"Oh," she said very eloquently behind his hand, unable to rip her eyes off the woman on the desk. The woman's back was straight and proud, her eyes half closed, straight dark hair sliding in her face. Marley was taken aback, still amazed that people did these things together in anonymity with total strangers, but aside from that, this woman's confidence fascinated her. When had Marley ever sat straight, legs apart, and demanded she get what she wanted?

Never. She didn't even *ask* for what she wanted, sexually or otherwise, let alone demand it.

There was something very, very appealing about that.

"What are you thinking?" Damien murmured, hand stroking around her waist, thumb playing with the band at the top of her bikini bottoms.

His touch didn't feel sexual necessarily, just intimate, his breath hot on her cheek, his face close in the dreamy, muted candlelight, the room warm and small and filled with the soft sounds of passion.

"I was thinking that she looks like a queen . . . and that he is paying homage to her."

"That is a beautiful description. Are you picturing yourself as the queen?"

"No," she said truthfully, resting her hand on Damien's arm so she wouldn't lose her balance as she leaned to look around him. She could never picture herself as the queen. "I would be the faithful lady's maid watching from around the corner."

Like she was now, vicariously aroused, intrigued, fascinated, and yet surprised by that. Curiosity overcame shame, desire raced ahead of her manners, and she stared, the couple's intensity locking her out, yet drawing her fully into their passion.

"Then perhaps the lady's maid needs to find a footman to worship her."

"Maybe." Wasn't that what she had been searching for for the last ten years? Her footman/Nice Guy? Her own Joe Average, the wealthy and gorgeous need not apply.

"Though I think you could be the queen if you let yourself."

Marley didn't know how to let herself be anything other than what she was. She was a caregiver, not a queen, and she couldn't change that, didn't want to. But once, it would be amazingly freeing to have that kind of entitlement.

And as they watched, the queen broke, her head snapping up, her nails digging into the flesh on her knees, her thighs tensing. No sound came from her, but she rode out her orgasm, powerful, in control, owning herself and her pleasure.

Marley couldn't look away, had to follow the climax to its satisfying end, the woman's legs relaxing, her wiping her upturned lips, running a languid finger through the man's hair. There was something beautifully intimate about that.

Marley's own breathing had hitched a little, her nipples hardening, body reacting to what she was seeing. Dampness crept along her inner thighs, and Marley blushed under Damien's scrutiny, suddenly realizing he was watching her, not the woman on the desk, and she was sure he knew she was turned on, if only just a little.

It was just that the idea of embracing her own sexuality, taking what she wanted with no apologies, the heady thought of selfishness, had her interest, excitement, stirring to life. A wondrous shiver whispering, *What if you did?* crept over her.

Damien leaned toward her, his body brushing against hers from hip to chest, and for a second she thought he was going to kiss her.

She was appalled to realize she would have welcomed it, with open lips and wet inner thighs.

But he didn't kiss her. He stopped just short of her mouth and said, "Maybe you just need a king to take your queen, *ma cherie*."

❧

After quickly guiding Marley through a succession of rooms, each one more graphic and boisterous than the last, Damien deposited Marley in the music room on the first floor. It was a refreshment area, sexual activity off-limits, meant for guests to regroup, to talk, to settle on what would be their next pleasurable pursuit.

It was a reasonably safe place to leave Marley for five minutes. "Do not leave this room," he told her roughly.

"Fine," she said, looking too shocked, overwhelmed, aroused, to protest.

"I'll be back in five minutes." Damien left the room, re-tracing his steps to the hall and making his way to the back of the house. He shoved open a door that led to the back garden and sucked in some fresh air.

It had been a mistake to let Marley into the party. He should have locked her in the *pigeonnier* the minute she appeared. But he had felt sorry for her, her concern for her sister so palpable and intense, and he had given in to temptation. He had wanted to see her reaction to the en-tertainment, he had wanted to see her in that damn bikini.

The view hadn't disappointed. She was lush, curva-ceous, her full breasts straining against the ties on the top, her backside perfect for grabbing on to, gripping, as a man pushed himself between a woman's receptive thighs.

And the way she had watched the guests . . . her eyes wide, glazing over, her cheeks pink and her breath tumbling out over plump lips . . .

Damien swore, leaning against the wall, the foliage in the garden wild and overgrown, the vines and branches and leaves rushing in a hundred different directions, consuming the path, the bench, the house, the once elegant brick wall.

Marley had been aroused, and so was he from watching her. Damien pulled his cock out of his tight pirate pants and stroked viciously, urgently. He was angry with himself for putting himself in this position, angry with Rosa for sending Marley to him, angry with Marley that she was so innocent in her sensuality, so ripe and ready to be plucked, so giving and kind and in need of a good, hard, hot fuck from a man who knew what he was doing. Angry with Marley that she was in fact the very temptation Rosa had thought she would be.

Squeezing hard, he brought himself to a quick, tight completion, body tense, heart sick, thoughts jumbled and furious. Breathing fast, he shook the result of his efforts off his hand into the dense bushes and shoved himself back into his pants. He was not going to touch Marley.

And under no circumstances whatsoever was she to touch him.

"Well, that was a total waste."

Hitting his head back against the bricks of the house, Damien wiped his sweaty forehead with his shirt sleeve. "Rosa. Why am I not surprised? You're like mold. No matter how hard I try to get rid of you, you keep coming back."

"Oh, come on." Rosa stepped out of the back door to stand next to him. She was wearing gold stiletto heels and an orange string bikini that could double as dental floss. "Don't be so dramatic. And why are you out here jacking off when there are twenty women inside willing to do it for you? *I* would even do it for you if you just asked nicely."

He gave her a mocking smile. "No one is as good at it as I am."

"Funny."

When he wanted to be, which wasn't often. "Your question was stupid. You know why. You know I haven't let a woman touch me in a hundred years."

"I know, but that doesn't mean I understand it any more than I did a hundred years ago." She put her hands on her thin hips. "You'd be so much more relaxed if you were getting some."

"I thank you for the concern but I'm fine." As fine as he could be.

"If you were fine you wouldn't be splitting your time between working yourself over in the garden and dating the most unattractive women imaginable."

Damien would never tell Rosa that he gave pleasure to plain women because he felt compassion for them, that he took his own pleasure just from watching them revel in his attention, from seeing them grow in confidence. When he put his tongue between the thighs of a shy, inhibited, insecure woman, she bloomed for him, and that was the only sexual gratification he would allow himself.

"Beauty is in the eyes of the beholder."

She snorted and rolled her eyes. "Does she know what you are?"

"Who?" He played dumb. Let Rosa spell it out.

"Marley Turner. Does she know what you are?"

"Oh, you mean the fact that I'm immortal, servant to the Grigori demons?" He gave her a mock bow. "At your service, as usual. But no, Marley has no idea exactly who she is dealing with. And I have no intention of telling her. I'm going to help her find her sister, get that letter from her, and then send them both on their way."

Without having ever tasted a single inch of Marley's flesh.

Rosa scoffed. "You've never been at my service. But I'm willing to overlook that for now. And in case you hadn't noticed, the girl is attracted to you."

"She is also incredibly innocent."

"Which would explain why she is drinking a martini that has been spiked with a hallucinogenic drug."

"What?" Damien pushed away from the wall. Marley wouldn't be that stupid. "Are you serious?"

"Very. I saw the guy do the drop. And for some weird reason I felt compelled to find you and tell you, because she clearly doesn't have a clue."

"Damn it." Damien pushed his hair back off his damp forehead.

Then he went back into the house to find Marley and assess the damage.

Chapter Six

Marley felt like she was floating. Like even though she was still sitting on the couch where Damien had left her, her body was rising up, up, up, into the hot bright light of the candle flames.

Something was wrong. She felt like she'd had six martinis, not just sipped off one—like all the blood had rushed out of her limbs, and now her arms were useless, numb hunks of flesh. There was a man sitting next to her, talking, but she couldn't seem to focus on what he was saying. She frowned, tried to concentrate, but his face seemed sharp, too close to her, his words floating in and out of her consciousness.

To be polite, she nodded from time to time. It made her feel bad that she was doing such a poor job of carrying her end of the conversation, and it was that guilt, that sense of manners, that kept her from protesting when he moved in closer still, his leg brushing hers, his arm sliding around her back.

She took another sip of her martini because she was thirsty and it tasted so good, like apples and cinnamon sugar, like a big, wet lollipop. With the edge of her tongue she licked the rim, and a warm, tingling sensation rolled through her, settling between her legs.

Suddenly black pants were in front of her and hands grabbed at her drink. Startled, Marley held on. "Oh, it's spilling!" And it seemed very important not to lose it.

A glance up showed Damien staring down at her, frowning.

"Hi," she said, giving him a big smile. He was so very cute, and he had been so nice to let her stay. They'd been through the whole party, and no sign of Lizzie, but it had been very, very nice of him to help her.

Damien gave another tug at her drink, managed to take it, and dumped it into a potted plant next to the couch.

"I wasn't done with that," Marley said, frowning, surprised by his behavior. She was amazingly thirsty. He had just wasted that tasty drink, still half full.

"I'll get you a new one." Then he turned to the guy sitting next to her. "Leave. I want you out of my house in the next sixty seconds."

Confused, Marley glanced at the guy who had given her the drink. When had he put his hand between her legs? And why didn't she feel it? Without hesitation, the guy pulled away from her bikini bottoms, stood up, and left. No good-bye, no anything. That struck Marley as a little bit rude.

Damien took her hand and pulled her up. "Can you walk?"

"Of course I can walk," she said, though she had to admit something strange seemed to have happened to her legs. She couldn't feel them at the moment, which was really very funny. She giggled when she stood and the whole room swirled. Whoa. Psychedelic.

Damien pulled her, and she stumbled along behind him. They went out the door, through a dizzying maze of hallways and doors, up one set of steps, then up the big, curving staircase, and down a very long hall. They moved in slow motion, her legs heavy, head lolling, but at the same time with so much speed that Marley couldn't follow where they were going.

Candles lit the way, and the upstairs was hushed and empty. Her feet stumbled and tripped over the carpets, her mouth felt dry, and her thoughts bounced from here to there, never really staying long enough to land on anything in particular.

She turned right and left, trying to see the furnishings in the hall, the portraits, the chandeliers. It was a mosaic of colors and sensations, and right in the middle was the stark white face of a woman. Marley pulled free from Damien and moved toward it.

"Who is she?" she asked, captivated by the eyes staring out at her. The painting shimmered in the light, undulating like they were on a ship at sea, that drawn, solemn face reaching out and arresting her. Marley lifted a hand, wanting the world to stop moving and shifting, wanting to touch that sorrow that was so clearly etched on the portrait, wanting to soothe and comfort.

"That is Marie du Bourg, wife of the first Damien du Bourg," Damien said, pushing her hand down so she couldn't touch. "This was painted in 1790."

"Oh." Marley felt tears in her eyes, without explanation or warning. "She looks like her letter." That made no sense in words, but she knew it was true. The woman was dark-haired, very petite and delicate, her fair skin ethereal, lips and cheeks tinted with a blush of pink. "She looks like she could cry."

"That is possible. She was very unhappy here."

"How could anyone be unhappy in such a beautiful place?" Marley asked, stomach sick, tears swelling, throat closing off. She wanted to weep for the sorrow she saw in Marie. For herself. For her sister.

"There are many reasons to be unhappy. Perhaps Marie knew them all."

✾

It is taking longer than I thought to write this, as it is now two days since I originally sat down, quill in hand. I have much more vitriol to dispose of than I realized, and I find myself reluctant to toss this into the fire until I have finished what I have begun. I need to write it, Angelique, to see it on the page in front of me, to acknowledge what I have done, who I have become, what went wrong so quickly.

The first few weeks after I fainted, Damien and I had a new understanding, though unspoken. He was more courteous, he spent more time at home and less in New Orleans, he watched what I ate and urged more on me when I picked. He discussed plans for a nursery with me, and expressed a preference for the name Phillipe, which had been his father's. A trip to town was sanctioned for more appropriate clothing for me, as well as linens and lace for the nursery. A delicate rosewood cradle was purchased and brought home, displayed proudly in the room next to mine, and I visited it frequently to run my fingers over the shiny wood, to contemplate a baby resting in it.

Those days were spent in happy anticipation, a tentative agreement to be pleasant between us, any anxieties quickly thrust aside by the feeling of my child slowly growing inside me, by the knowledge that I would be a mother. Mother of the heir to the du Bourg fortune, mother of Damien's firstborn, mother of a child who would look to me as his entire world.

In the oppressive heat of the past summer, I was a satisfied woman, pleased to enter the hallowed halls of the club of motherhood.

It helped also that Damien stayed in his bedchamber, that he no longer felt inclined to make frequent nighttime sojourns to my suite and push his body into mine in a way I thought I could never get used to, could never enjoy. If I found him in the back hall, leaning a little too close to a giggling chambermaid, I was prepared to pretend I had seen nothing. It was a flirtation, nothing more; of course he was not acting upon it. Not in my house, not in my presence, not when I was enceinte. *Men, attractive men like Damien, flirt as a matter of course. It means nothing. I was mistress of Rosa de Montana, I was Damien's wife.*

I was stupidly naïve, is what I was.

In late September I was dressing for dinner, as we were to entertain the Spanish mayor and a few other government officials and their wives, when I felt a cramp in my abdomen. A twinge, I assured myself, nothing more. My belly was rounding quite nicely, necessitating less restrictive stays, and I urged my maid to leave the laces bound as loosely as possible.

"Madame?" she asked. "I cannot make them any looser without it falling off."

The pain that came at the moment was so sharp, so sudden, that I bent over and sucked in my breath. Fear made perspiration bead on my forehead. It was nothing, of course it was absolutely nothing out of the ordinary. Just the normal stretching and discomfort, but I knew immediately I was lying to myself. The pain had been too severe, too agonizing to be anything but bad tidings.

"Madame!" she exclaimed, touching my back as if to assist.

"Never mind, Gigi," I said as I stood up, the pain subsiding slightly. "I'm fine. Just help me into my gown."

But by the time she was finished dressing me, and the emerald necklace that had been a wedding gift from Damien lay across my pale, powdered chest, I felt the dreaded warm, moist sensation down my thighs, now expected and so very unwanted. "That will be all, Gigi, thank you," I said tightly, wanting to be alone.

"Yes, Madame."

She curtseyed and left and I carefully descended to the edge of the bed, hand on my belly. A quick lift of my skirt revealed what I had feared—I was bleeding, quickly, violently, great torrents of red careening down over my thighs and knee. The front of my shift was blooming scarlet, the stain growing with each second. I was terrified to move, frightened that I would make it worse, knowing without a shadow of a doubt that it was too late, that for whatever reason, I would not be having this child, that my baby, my hope, my heart, was no longer alive.

The pain robbed me of breath, the cramps angry and convulsive, sweeping over me in great rolling waves, and I began to feel dizzy, my tears blurring my vision, my sorrow clogging my throat. I do not know how long I was there, but long enough for my husband to knock sharply and enter my room, long impatient strides moving him quickly inside the door.

"What in hell is taking you so long?" he demanded. "We have guests in the salon wondering where their hostess is."

I tried to speak, tried to say something, anything, but only a tight, small sob made its way out of my mouth.

Damien stopped and took in the sight in front of him. His face changed, his shoulders dropped, his eyes lost their coolness. "Oh, Marie, no." He moved over to me, went down on his knees in front of me, took in all the red, now staining my white dress itself, shifted my skirts, and swore violently at what he saw.

My tears came faster. His hands went into his hair as he stared between my limbs, his jaw set, nostrils flaring in anger. Then he got control of himself, unclenched his fists, and said carefully, "Let me help you out of that dress."

"I shouldn't move . . . maybe the physician . . . perhaps . . ." I couldn't express what I feared, what I hoped, but Damien knew.

He shook his head and glanced up at me. "No, darling, it's too late for help. I see the baby."

"Oh!" I put my hands in front of my face, my grief threatening to pull me under in a faint.

"Stay with me now." Damien squeezed my knees and reached for the pull.

When my maid entered the room, Damien already had me out of my evening gown, and it lay crumpled and ruined on the floor, the violent red blood appearing a rich violet on the blue overskirt. Gigi gasped.

Damien glanced back at her. "Send for the physician and inform our guests that Madame du Bourg is indisposed this evening. I'll be down shortly, but have dinner served now. Then send someone up to run a bath for Madame."

Gigi had been curtsying, bobbing up and down rapidly as she is wont to do, but at his last words her head snapped up. "Monsieur, I don't think putting her in the water . . . it is not healthy for a woman who . . . it is not the best course . . ." She trailed off, unsure how to convey what she meant without being impolite.

I recognized her intent. A woman bleeding heavily should not be put in the bath, and I appreciated her care and concern.

But Damien did not. He turned and roared at her, "I do not believe the master of this house asked for the opinion of his wife's chambermaid. Now do as I told you!"

"Yes, Monsieur," she said, eyes wide, feet scrambling backward.

Damien took his handkerchief out of his pocket and wrapped it around something. My stomach clenched, the pain still searing my belly, but that in my heart greater. I leaned forward, wanting to know, wanting to see.

"Don't look, Marie," he said. "It will only upset you more." He quickly covered the bundle with the voluminous folds of my discarded and bloody dress.

"The priest—can you ask the priest to come and bless our baby?" I asked, unable to look away from my gown, not caring that I was still bleeding, only vaguely aware that the room had begun to spin, that my head was hot, mouth thick and dry.

"If it will make you feel better," he said. "But I see no point. A priest can't bring him back to life."

"But he can pray for his soul." I tried to reassure myself. "And our baby will be in heaven, Damien, with a God who will love him."

My shoe suddenly went flying across the room, slamming into the silk brocaded wall next to my armoire. I was startled by his violent burst of anger. Damien hurled the second slipper after the first.

"Oh, Marie, don't you understand? There is no God. There is only Earth and Hell, and sometimes the line between the two is very, very small."

❧

Marley tumbled back onto the bed Damien pushed her toward. "Whoa." She giggled, staring up at the thick curtain hanging over the bed, dropping her mask to the floor. "You could have warned me."

"Why? So you could have protested?" Damien pulled her sandals off her feet.

That confused her a little. It seemed an odd place to start a seduction, at her feet. Regardless of his methods, she should say no, of course. There was Lizzie to consider. And Damien was more man than she could handle, she was positive.

But somehow, she couldn't bring herself to protest, stand up, leave this antique bed, this plantation house. It felt like she was dreaming anyway, like she was floating in a cloudy haze of sensations, and she was really aroused, really just nice and wet already, and it seemed like such a good idea for him to fill her up, ease that ache.

He dropped her sandals on the floor. Then he turned and pulled something out of the armoire. The room was dark, the only light the moonlight flooding in from the tall windows. A breeze danced over her, warm and humid.

Damien unfolded a sheet by snapping it crisply in the

air, then letting it float down over her. "Close your eyes, Marley. Go to sleep."

"You want me to go to sleep?" That didn't make any sense to her, and she shoved the sheet aside. It was too hot for that anyway.

"Yes, *ma cherie*, go to sleep."

"Oooh, is that French? Are you French, Damien? That's sexy." She lay on her back, resting her hands on her stomach. She'd forgotten she was wearing the bikini. She should be embarrassed—she could only imagine how huge her thighs looked smashed down and spread out—but she felt too languid, too relaxed to care.

"Technically I'm Creole, of French descent. But you're not closing your eyes."

"If I close my eyes, will you make love to me?" Marley was a little startled that her thoughts came out as actual words, but it was what she wanted after all. Damien was so appealing and she was so aroused.

But he shook his head. "I cannot. It wouldn't be right." He stood at the bottom of the bed, arms crossed over his chest.

The rejection hurt her feelings, felt like a slap to her dignity, her femininity. "Never mind. I shouldn't have asked . . . you have all these women to choose from . . . why would you choose me?" And when the tears dribbled out of her eyes, she didn't bother to wipe them, just let them cascade down her cheeks in fat, quick drops.

It hurt. Everything hurt. No one loved her, Marley. They only loved what she did for them, loved that she was their housekeeper, cleaning up after them. Her mother, her father—who buried his head in the sand—Lizzie. No one cared about Marley except for how she cared about them.

"Oh, but I would choose you. I would choose you above any other woman." Damien climbed onto the bed, moving alongside her as the mattress adjusted to his weight, propping his head up with his arm. "But you're flying high on drugs right now and I will not take advantage of that. You would regret sleeping with me tomorrow."

Marley didn't think she would regret that, honestly. Not when she felt the way she did, hot and bothered and fizzy inside. But she was surprised to hear she was on drugs. "I'm on drugs?"

"Yes, there was something in your drink." Damien pushed her hair back off her forehead. "I don't think you had much, but enough to impair your judgment."

"Oh." That explained the way she felt, like she was drunk inside a never-ending orgasm, her body hot and excited, mind floating and wondrous. "I haven't had sex in five years," she told him.

His eyebrow rose, but he gave no other reaction. "Is there a reason for that?"

"I've been waiting for Mr. Right. But he's late. Very, very late." She started to giggle, but wasn't really sure why. Most of the time it didn't seem funny that she was still single. "I think he forgot to ask for directions, just like a man."

The curtain on the top of the bed looked soft and shiny. Marley stared at it hard. "My mom, she's bipolar, you know. Between taking care of her, cooking and cleaning for my dad, working with my students, helping Lizzie with Sebastian . . . well, I haven't had a lot of time to go looking for him either. And he just hasn't rung my doorbell. Nobody rings the doorbell but the UPS man and the guys who try to sell me doorknocker polish and magazines."

"Doorknocker polish?" Damien frowned.

Marley undid the tie at the back of her neck. The strain of holding her breasts up had the nylon strings digging deep into her flesh. It hurt, was giving her a headache. "I think Lizzie is bipolar too. But my mom, she's always on the down side. She gets depressed to the point where she doesn't bathe, won't dress herself. Lizzie's the opposite.

She's high, all this nervous energy, crazy optimism . . . she wrote that she was in love with you, but you don't even remember her."

"It's wonderful, Marley, how you take care of everyone. But you need to make sure you take care of yourself too."

"That's what a vibrator is for—taking care of myself." Marley laughed again, pulling the bikini top off altogether. It was irritatingly tight, itchy and distracting.

Damien sat up and started unbuttoning his shirt.

Now this had possibilities. Marley licked her lips, getting the last bits of cinnamon sugar from the corner.

But when Damien stripped his shirt off, revealing a very impressive, muscular chest, he took the shirt and laid it across her own bare chest, his eyes averted.

"I thought men liked big breasts," she said, offended, even as she snuggled into the well-worn, soft, warm fabric of his shirt. It smelled like him, rich and strong.

Damien smiled, that charming, smooth smile she'd first noticed on him. "You have beautiful breasts, Marley. So beautiful that if I look, I'll want to touch."

"So touch." What was so hard about that for him to figure out?

But he made a sound of frustration. "It's not that simple. Nothing is what you think it is, and to touch you, make love to you like I want to . . . it would be wrong. It would be a sin."

"A sin?" Marley frowned. Damn it. This wasn't supposed to happen. She was here, half naked, at a sex party, and this was a golden opportunity to throw over all her responsibilities, all her frustrations, all her reservations, and indulge in a night of pure sexual hedonism.

But the man she wanted to guide her through the freedom of debauchery was telling her that it would be a sin.

She sighed. This was very disappointing. "That's the most depressing thing I've ever heard."

Marley bunched up Damien's shirt and tucked it under her head like a pillow. She rolled up on her side, pressed the palm of her hand on his chest. His flesh was hard and warm, his heart pounding beneath her touch.

"Are you going back down to the party?"

"No. I'm going to stay here with you."

Marley smiled, head spinning again. Sleep was starting to sound very appealing. "Thank you. It's so nice to have help for a change." His face went out of focus, so she closed her eyes.

"You're welcome," he said.

And Marley spiraled off into the darkness of her dreams.

Chapter Seven

Damien watched Marley sleeping, her lips parted, chest rising and falling laboriously. Help her? That was ironic. He couldn't even help himself. He definitely couldn't help someone else, especially not someone as completely tempting as Marley.

When she had removed her top, it had taken every ounce of his willpower to prevent him from reaching over and cupping her warm, lush body.

It was his job to promote sin, to encourage lust, obsessive and selfish sexual desire. For that, he was given eternal life, and there was no way out of the bargain he had stupidly struck. But he could no longer take personal pleasure, wouldn't be able to live with himself if he did, knowing that women found him irresistible, that his powers of seduction were demon-induced, that he was nothing more than a vile snake charmer.

He gave pleasure to women who benefited from his attention, who grew in confidence from their dalliance, who were empowered by it. It was the only way for Damien to reconcile what he was with doing a small measure of good. Marley was different. It wasn't compassion he felt for Marley, but intense desire, interest, longing. There was no way he could touch her and stay in control, and that was a risk he simply couldn't take.

Rosa was the child of a Watcher, a demon sent to look after human welfare, who instead had embraced his lust for human women, one of two hundred Watchers who had done so. For Rosa and her father, who had given in to temptation and sin, it was a game to tempt Damien to do so as well. To them it was inevitable that he would give in, become just like them in their proud, evil mischievousness, and over the last one hundred years they had sent many, many women to him to achieve that ultimate triumph.

Yet Damien knew he had made many mistakes, and he didn't want to repeat them. What he had done back in his mortal youth and his early days of demon servitude, how he had pulled Marie down into his moral sewage, then manipulated Marissabelle to save himself, all fed his convictions, his self-loathing.

Long ago he had come to terms with who and what he was, and accepted responsibility. This was how he had to live. He would provide an atmosphere for those already eager to immerse themselves in their sexual appetites.

But he would not take the innocent down with him this time, not when Marie's dark, agonized eyes still haunted his dreams, showing him that for all his long life, he had never been a man of worth.

⁘

When our baby died, and I lost so much blood, my dislike of Damien's plantation grew. It was this place, I told myself as I sat on the porch, staring endlessly out at the overgrown drive, at the pigeonnier *flanking the west of the house, at the new slaves' quarters marching in a solemn row down by the indigo fields, this place was the reason my baby had died.*

Nothing is healthy here. Disease is rampant, the air unbreathable, my constitution compromised by the lack of adequate care.

I refused to dress, refused to powder, but spent many, many weeks sitting aimlessly in my most comfortable mourning gown, the extent of my activity to move from the porch to the salon, to the garden, to bed. Have you ever been swimming, Angelique? Do you know how it feels when your limbs are underwater, how you have to push harder to make them move? That is how I felt, as if my every movement required more effort, as if my world had slowed to a turtlelike crawl, where it hurt to breathe, was fatiguing to walk, was beyond my ability to think.

At first, I believe Damien tolerated my behavior, though I saw little of him. But I think, to give him proper credit, he was allowing me to indulge in my grief, and perhaps needed time to deal with his own. At the time, however, I had little notion of him or what he was about, as I couldn't seem to wrap my mind around anything other than my own pain.

But I believe that as fall shifted into winter, he grew weary of my invalid state. Just before Christmas, he approached me in the salon where I was listlessly watching the fire.

"You will be dressed this evening. We have dinner guests."

"But . . . ," I said in alarm. "I cannot."

"You will." His green eyes were hard, completely lacking in patience and concern.

When Gigi dressed me that evening, I was startled to see that I had lost weight, that my breasts no longer filled the bodice of my gown, that the waist was too loose to be flattering.

Gigi clucked. "Madame, you must eat! Men like women who are soft and round."

But I didn't care. I didn't care about anything. I went to dinner, I forced vague smiles and spoke only as much as was necessary. I did my duty and I did not once look at my husband.

I could not. I couldn't bear to see disgust, distaste, disappointment on his face. I had failed to complete the one task I had been brought to Louisiana to do, and my shame, my guilt, my grief were stones around my ankles, weighing me down completely.

There was pity in the faces of those around me, that night and on many others that followed. The men looked at me uncomfortably, and as if they felt sorry for Damien. The older women patted my hands and murmured that I was too refined, too delicate to be living in the swamp. Clearly I belonged back in France. The younger women expressed concern for my health, but behind the words was the smug satisfaction that despite my enviable marriage, their beauty was greater.

It was true that I was losing my looks. The looking glass revealed a gaunt face with dark shadows under eyes that suddenly appeared too large for my head. My hair was dull, skin so pale it had a purplish cast in places, looking bruised and unhealthy.

But I didn't care.

Not even when their comments grew more and more direct. Not even when Mademoiselle Delerue looked me straight in the eye and said, "My goodness, Madame du Bourg, I had no idea you were still so ill! Should you be out of bed? You look just absolutely awful."

This was in the salon one evening after dinner, and Damien overheard. Before I could respond, he did.

"My wife is fine," he said. "Just not vain. But we thank you for your concern, Mademoiselle Delerue, and would you be willing to indulge us and play the pianoforte? It is my understanding that you are an excellent player and I would love to hear your skills for myself."

She twittered as he bowed low, too low for an unmarried girl.

I knew his patience with me had completely run out.

That was further confirmed when he appeared one night

in my bedchamber. I was asleep, but woke when he pushed the coverlet back, sending cold air racing over my back and shoulders. It was dark, and I could smell liqueur on his breath, hear him breathing as he settled onto the mattress beside me.

"Damien?" I whispered.

"Yes, it is your husband. Were you expecting someone else?"

"No, of course not." I stiffened when his hands landed on my backside, fondling my body and working my chemise up. "Damien, please . . ."

"Please, what? More? Please, Damien, yes, that feels so good? Damien, please, yes, I've missed you so much?" His voice was mocking, harsh. "Don't bother to ask me to stop, Marie. I've waited long enough. I have been more than patient. I have been a fucking saint."

I winced at his language, as I wince even now writing it on paper. It was blasphemous and crude, which perhaps sum up large portions of my husband's character.

His mouth moved along my ear, nuzzling me, speaking in a hoarse, raw whisper, his hot flesh sending a shiver down my spine. "It is a cruel irony we face. We must do what you hate to give you what you want, but there is nothing for it. You will do your duty and I will do mine, no matter that you are the one woman who seems averse to my touch."

What could I say? What could I do? My wishes had no place in my marriage, and there was no recourse. I was a wife, this was my husband, and I would do what I had been raised to do, what was my duty, to respect the sacred vows I had taken to honor and obey.

Speaking would have been a waste of breath, worth neither the time nor the effort, and would have achieved nothing.

So I said nothing, did not utter one cry of protest, not even when in his drunken roughness, he bruised my wrists, tore at my tender flesh with his urgency, pushed my head into the hard wood of the bed.

I simply stopped speaking altogether from that moment.

When company was present, I managed the necessities, but with Damien, alone, I ceased talking.

It no longer felt worth the effort, and I had nothing to say anyway.

⁂

Marley woke up with a headache and the realization that she was virtually naked in a bedroom at Rosa de Montana. Alone, which was a minor blessing.

"Oh, God." Unfortunately, she remembered everything from the night before. The party, getting aroused by the woman on the desk, wishing she could experience that kind of liberation. Having a martini, coming upstairs with Damien, taking her top off.

Throwing herself at him and crying when he said no.

It was a complete and total nightmare. It was mortification in capital letters. Embarrassment with a whole bucketful of humiliation tossed in along with it. She was going to have to sneak out a back door and get the hell away before Damien discovered her. Showing him what a needy loser she was had not been in her plans, and there was no way on planet Earth she could ever face him again.

And had she really blathered on about her family? Her mother's illness, Lizzie's problems—those were private. She didn't tell *anyone* what went on in her family. It was no one's business. Yet she had told Damien.

The shame flooded over her in a hot, sticky wave.

Marley forced herself to sit up, the room spinning slightly, her mouth dry. With shaky hands, she reached for her bikini top, folded at the bottom of the bed and sitting on top of a white T-shirt and a pair of basketball shorts. Apparently Damien had anticipated her embarrassment and had given her some clothes to wear. She was grateful for the gesture, because she had no idea where her raincoat had ended up, and she could not drive back to New Orleans and walk into the hotel in a bikini and a pirate shirt.

And actually, the pirate shirt was missing. She had been lying on a regular pillow and was covered with a light sheet, the floral pattern faded with time and washing. The night before, she had shoved this sheet off when Damien had tried to cover her, but apparently after she had passed out, he had persisted.

"Oh, Marley," she whispered, fumbling with the bikini top, trying to tie it around her neck. "What the hell were you thinking?" Why would a man like Damien du Bourg—gorgeous, rich, clearly sexually experienced—want to have sex with her?

Duh. He wouldn't. Doing her would scream entanglement, and she was sure he wouldn't want messy morning afters where women assumed too much.

The knock on the door made her jump. Marley knew her cheeks were burning, and she couldn't see Damien again, she just couldn't. There was nothing either of them could say that would erase her embarrassment.

The knock came again. "Marley? It's Rosa . . . Damien's friend you met the other day. Can I come in?"

Marley hesitated, than relented. Maybe Rosa could show her the quickest way out so she could avoid Damien. "Come in."

Rosa entered wearing a yellow sundress, her hair pulled back off her face. "Good morning. How are you feeling?"

Like an idiot. "Fine. Just a bit of a headache." And she couldn't get her strings tied around her back. Stretching her arms, she tried again.

"Damien feels really bad that you had something slipped in your drink. That sort of shit isn't condoned at his parties. He wanted me to check on you."

"I'm fine."

Rosa raised an eyebrow and moved toward the bed. "You don't look fine. You look like you'll start bawling if I say boo." She climbed up onto the bed and reached for Marley. "Here, let me get that. You need to cage those babies in pretty tightly or your ties will blow when you least expect it."

That had Marley giving a watery laugh. She did feel like crying. The whole situation was ridiculous, and she hated her oversized breasts. She'd like to give them away and be done with it.

Rosa's fingers made swift work of the ties. "Look, don't let it hurt your feelings that Damien has bugged out of here on you. He's a dog, like all men are. And he never stays long with women he sleeps with."

That Marley would have understood. That she could have lived with. But his rejection was too much. "I don't want to see him." Rosa had moved away, the bikini top securely in place, so Marley reached for the T-shirt. "I was actually going to ask you where he is so I can avoid him. Is there a back door or something?"

"Yeah. I'll show you. Damien is in the *pigeonnier*, so we'll go around the other side." Rosa got off the bed. "You didn't find your sister, did you?"

"No. Can you please tell Damien to let me know if Lizzie ever shows up here? He has my contact information." Marley took a shaky breath and pulled the shirt on.

"Sure."

In another minute, she had the shorts on over the bikini bottoms, and had her feet in her sandals, which had been lying on the floor by the bed. She really couldn't get out of there fast enough, despite the queasiness in her stomach. They were in the hall heading for the back stairs when Marley realized the keys to the rental car were in the raincoat.

"Shit. Have you seen a coat, tan, a trench-shaped raincoat? I think it got left in the foyer."

Rosa shrugged. "I don't know. But we can go that way." She turned and headed down the long hallway toward the main stairways.

"This house is huge," Marley whispered, awed in spite of her need to escape her humiliation.

"It's big, moldy pile of bricks. I don't know why Damien hangs on to it."

Marley was a little astonished at that kind of attitude. This house breathed history. It had been in Damien's family for centuries. She caught sight of Marie du Bourg's portrait on the wall. The same sorrow reached out to her, just like it had the night before. That hadn't been a drug-induced hallucination. Marie's eyes had called to her, pleaded.

Remembering the letter in her purse, the printed e-mail from Lizzie, Marley slowed down. "What do you know about Marie du Bourg?" she asked Rosa, pointing to the portrait.

Rosa stopped. "Damien's wife? She came from France, a fragile French flower, got her portrait painted, then died."

Marley was startled by the disdain in Rosa's voice. "That's it?"

"That's it. But if you really want to know more about Marie, or anything else about this place, you need to ask Anna. She is about a million years old and knows everyone and everything that has ever happened here."

"Really? Where can I see her?" Marley should let it go, but she wanted to know, hear all there was to hear.

She also needed to e-mail Damien the letter from Marie. He had done his part to find Lizzie, and she couldn't ask for any more than that. The letter did belong to his family and he was entitled to see it. Fortunately she had his e-mail address from the other day when they'd had lunch together and he'd given her his card. There was no reason to subject herself to a face-to-face encounter.

"Anna lives in a crappy little house that used to be the

overseer's place. I can point you in the right direction. It's a ten-minute walk from here. Anna loves to get visitors. And she has such an eagle eye it's possible she might have noticed your sister. She watches everything that goes on here. Binoculars."

"Really?" So there was no chance of pretending she wasn't a party guest if this woman had watched her arrive the night before. That was somewhat embarrassing, but since the whole week was a series of uncomfortable moments, Marley was willing to risk one more to gain any information about Lizzie. "Great."

She followed Rosa down the stairs and into the foyer. There was no one around, the house hushed except for the distant sound of a vacuum. "Damien?" she asked Rosa, tilting her head toward the sound.

But Rosa snorted. "Damien running the sweeper? That would be the day. There's a cleaning crew here picking up after last night."

"Oh, of course." Duh, Marley, she told herself. Like rich people needed to vacuum their own mansions. Her raincoat was still sitting on the Louis XIV chair, and a quick check revealed the keys still in the pocket.

She jingled them. "I'm ready. Do we drive to Anna's or walk?"

"Walk. Do you want to say anything to Damien before we go? We could pop in to the *pigeonnier*."

What could she say? Apologize for throwing herself at him? "No." Just the thought of seeing Damien made her cheeks go hot. "I have nothing to say to him."

❧

Rosa abandoned Marley twenty feet from the house. "She'll be on the porch. That's where she always is. See ya."

"You're not going with me?"

"Nope. I have to get my nails done."

And Rosa bolted back the way they'd come.

Marley stared at the weatherworn house and gathered some courage. She was in desperate need of a shower, hot from the hike over through the tall grass and humidity, wearing Damien's T-shirt and basketball shorts, which, horrifyingly, were a little snug in the waist. She didn't need a mirror to know that her hair was snarled and sticking out in six directions, and she would lay down cash that she had a couple of big old dark circles under her eyes. Hopefully the old lady had cataracts, because Marley was probably downright scary.

But since she couldn't fix that, she'd just forge ahead.

When she came around the corner of the house, the woman was sitting on the porch, like Rosa had said. She looked old, petite, her body enveloped in a pink knit top and shorts, her feet tucked into crisp white sneakers.

"Good morning," Marley said, smiling as she went up the walk. She stopped at the bottom of the steps. "My name is Marley Turner. Rosa said you wouldn't mind speaking to me a bit about the history of the plantation. Am I interrupting you?"

"Come on up here, child. Have a seat. The only thing you're interrupting is me waiting to die, and most days that's damn boring."

Marley laughed at the wry humor in the woman's voice. She went up the stairs and sat gingerly in the rocker next to Anna. She put her hand out. "Marley Turner."

"Anna." She shook Marley's hand very delicately. "And you're a Yankee."

"Probably. I'm from Cincinnati."

"What brings you to this old place? You don't look like the usual type we see round here."

Marley was going to try not to read anything into that, positive or negative. "I'm looking for my sister. Lizzie Turner. She was here early in the summer, at one of Damien's parties."

Anna nodded. "She young?"

"Twenty-four."

"These young ones, they don't understand what they're getting themselves into. It's fun and exciting for a while. Then it's not, and they're alone."

"Rosa said maybe you had seen Lizzie. That you know what's going on at the big house."

Anna gave a laugh, her hands folded in her lap. "Rosa gives me too much credit. I see things, sure, but just people coming and going. The past is more my expertise, not the present. I don't leave this old porch very often."

Marley felt tears in her eyes without warning. "So you wouldn't recognize my sister?"

"No, child. I'm sorry." Anna patted her hand. "But she'll turn up."

Wiping at her eyes, Marley tried to get control of her emotions. She felt like ice, slowly cracking from the edges in, the split racing faster and faster into her center. "I hope so." Taking a deep breath, she quickly spoke again before she totally lost it. "I also wanted to ask you about Marie du Bourg. What happened to her?"

Anna frowned a little. "Why do you ask about Marie?"

"My sister sent me an e-mail and it had a letter by Marie attached to it. It was a confession to her priest, dated in 1790. Then upstairs, in the house, I saw her portrait. I want to know what happened. Her words, her eyes . . . I can feel her pain."

Recrossing her crisp sneakers, Anna stared at Marley. "Marie married Damien du Bourg in France in 1789, right after the death of Damien's father, Phillipe, who built this plantation. It was said that Marie hated Louisiana, that she was of too delicate a nature, her husband too wild in his ways. But that is the way of the du Bourg men."

Given the current Damien's nocturnal gatherings, Marley could believe that. Not that Damien had been wild with her. He'd been perfectly restrained, damn him.

"How did she die? They couldn't have been married very long. Was it yellow fever?"

"No." Anna studied her. "Tell me, Marley Turner, do you understand what it is like to be trapped in your life?"

Yes, she did. She was trapped inside her family, held there by her love and worry.

"I'm trapped inside this body that is too old to be any good to me. Marie du Bourg was trapped inside this plantation, in a marriage that had no love. Can you understand that?"

"Yes," Marley said, her throat tight.

"I believe you." Anna stood up, startling Marley with the quick movement. "That's why I'm going to give you Marie's letters to read. Not the pretty letter she meant for her priest, but her real thoughts, her account of her time here."

"You have a journal?" Marley was stunned. Why did Anna have something like that?

"Of sorts. Can you read French?"

"Yes." It made sense the letters would be in French.

"Old French?"

Marley nodded. She had majored in Education, with a dual minor in French and Theology. All three had suited her shy personality, fueled her love of history and religion. "I can actually read it much better than I can speak it."

"Okay, give me two seconds then."

"Can I help you?" Anna was shuffling to the door, so Marley jumped up to assist.

"I'm fine, but thank you. You sit on down and I'll be back before you can blink."

It was a little longer than that, but Anna came back, with a stack of letters inside a ziplock bag. "Now, I expect you'll have a care with these. They're damn old."

"Of course."

Anna sank into her seat with a sigh. "And the other rule is that you can't be running off and telling Damien about these letters. I can see in your eyes when I bring him up that you've got that crush on him all the girls get."

Marley dropped her mouth open, ready to protest. She did not have a crush. That was preposterous, high school, unfathomable. Even if she found him mildly sexually attractive, she would not under any circumstances call that a crush.

"No, don't bother denying it. I can see it. It's none of my business. I'm only bringing it up because I won't give these letters to you if I don't think you can follow the rules. For over two hundred years no man has ever read these letters. They're passed down through the women here, and they are for the eyes of women only."

"Why?" Marley's already dry mouth felt raw and scratchy.

"Because there are some things only a woman can understand. There are desires, wants, pains that no man can feel, and only another woman knows a woman's heart. Marie's thoughts should be read with the respect she deserves."

"I can do that." Marley wouldn't have it any other way. "I'd be honored to read her letters."

Anna nodded and handed her the bag.

"Marley!"

Marley jerked in her chair and gripped the letters tighter. "Shoot, that's Damien." He was yelling her name from some distance away, but he was clearly getting closer. They could hear his feet crushing the grassy brush.

"Damien du Bourg, don't you set foot in the front of my house," Anna roared, with surprising volume for such a tiny lady.

Marley was shocked silent.

"Anna?"

"You know it's me. Don't you do it, Damien. We have an agreement. Now get yourself back to that big house."

"I just want to speak to Marley for a moment. Is she there?" Damien's voice sounded charming, conciliatory.

Anna clucked in disapproval and muttered under her breath to Marley, "Chasing you like a dog after a bitch in heat. Never change, I'm telling ya. They're all the same. You make him work for it, honey."

Marley almost laughed. Damien wasn't going to be working for it. He didn't want it, not even when she had offered it free and clear with no effort on his part. "Don't worry about me. I can take care of myself."

"Marley?" Damien called again. "I need to talk to you. Can you come back to the house?"

"In a minute. I'm having a nice chat with Miss Anna here. You go ahead back and I'll be there soon." She winked at Anna, who gave her a wide grin back. "Let him wait," she whispered, irritated with him for making her feel undesirable, vulnerable.

"Five minutes. I'll be on the porch," he said, sounding frustrated.

"Great."

They heard him moving away and Marley felt immense satisfaction. "So why can't Damien come into your house?"

"Because he's a pig and I don't allow livestock in the house."

Marley laughed.

Chapter Eight

Marley couldn't avoid Damien forever, but she did dawdle on the walk back to the big house, hoping maybe he'd given up and moved on to more exciting activities, like telling the maid where to mop. Unfortunately, he was standing on the front steps, pacing.

Her sandals suddenly became very interesting to her, and she studied them intensely as she approached the steps he was already heading down.

"I see you found the clothes I left," he said, stopping on the third step.

Nothing like cutting right to the heart of it. He might as well announce she'd been virtually naked.

"Yes, thank you." She stopped at the bottom of the stairs, and crossed her arms over her chest. Eye-level with his knees, she spoke to them. "I'll send the clothes back after I wash them."

"You don't have to bother. It's not a big deal." He moved, coming lower.

Marley already felt her cheeks heating. But she sucked in a breath, pulled herself and the shards of her dignity together, lifted her chin, and faced him. "It's not a big deal to send them back."

Shrugging, he took the last step and stood next to her. "I wanted to see you this morning because I want to apologize for last night. I can't tell you how terrible I feel that you were drugged. I don't like that kind of behavior at my parties and I try to police it, and that it would happen to you of all people . . ."

What the hell did that mean? She brought her arms in tighter.

"I am very sorry."

Damien looked and sounded sincere, and Marley couldn't really find any reason to fault him. He wasn't the one who had doctored her drink. "It's okay. You told me not to come to the party and I didn't listen. I accept responsibility for my role. And thanks for taking care of me. I was a little, uh, out of it." That was as close to the subject as she was willing to skate, but Damien suddenly covered his mouth and coughed a little. She realized in shock he was amused. She wasn't. "You think that's funny?"

Despite the shake of his head, his eyes told her the truth. The bastard was on the verge of laughing.

"Yeah, it was just hilarious that I took my top off in front of you."

His eyes darkened. "That was not amusing, no."

Now that hurt. Marley was already raw, feeling bruised, battered. She was worried about Lizzie, worried about herself, wondering why exactly she had done the things she had the night before. Was she really so needy, so vulnerable, so sexually repressed?

Damien's reminder that he did not find her attractive was the last drop in an overflowing cup of emotion. "Can we just forget that ever happened, please? I'm leaving, you'll never see me again. Can't you just let me walk out of here with at least a shred of my dignity intact? I got the message last night—you're not interested in me, and I can live with that. I never would have thrown myself at you anyway if I hadn't been loopy, because I realize my limitations. But it would be nice, polite, if you could stop pointing out that you would not have sex with me if I were the last woman in Louisiana."

Okay, that was a little dramatic. Marley clapped her mouth shut and mentally winced. She was losing it. She was on the edge of some kind of meltdown and she needed to go back to the hotel, regroup mentally, pack her bags, and get the hell out of there.

Thinking to do just that, she brushed her fingers over the T-shirt, reassuring herself the bag of letters tucked in her waistband wasn't going to fall out, and turned to go.

Damien grabbed her elbow. "Marley."

She jerked free. The last thing she needed or wanted was to see pity in his eyes, compassion on his gorgeous face. But he was stronger than she was, and he stepped in front of her and took both her wrists in a viselike grip.

"Why do you see yourself that way?" he asked in a low voice. "Why don't you recognize how stunning and alluring you are?"

She sighed and stared over his shoulder. "You don't have to do this. I'm not insecure and I don't need you to make me feel better. I'm just having a really bad week. I want to find my sister, and I want to go home."

"Let me try one more time. One more party to lure Lizzie."

"No." She couldn't do that again, couldn't see all those people, couldn't stand next to Damien and pretend she didn't want him so much her body ached. She couldn't take the heartache of picking through room after room of partygoers reveling in sexual oblivion and still not finding her sister, wondering in the back of her head if Lizzie was dead.

"I'll let the police look for her. Maybe I'll hire a private investigator if I can afford it."

"You should do that. But one more party won't hurt." Damien bent over, trying to get her to look at him.

Marley kept her eyes averted.

"Unless you're afraid."

"Afraid of what?" she asked with disdain, giving in and looking at him.

"Afraid of what you want."

Her heart started to hammer loudly in her chest. He was picking through her fabrications, wandering too close to the truth. "What do you think I want?"

"I think you want to be the queen. You want to stand up for once and have everyone bow to you." Damien stroked her wrists with his thumbs and leaned over, his lips suddenly brushing her cheek, her temple, her ear. "Or at least have one man bow to you."

She could deny it, but he wouldn't believe her. And it would be a lie. She did want that liberation, just once, that kind of confidence, that courage to demand what she and her body wanted. Marley crossed her arms tighter but let Damien rub and nuzzle against her, until he was kissing her neck, her ear, the corner of her mouth, caressing her flesh with his mouth. Making him stop would be the right thing to do, but she was afraid if she stepped away, had to be strong just one more time, that she would cry.

Tears never came easily to her, and they were a failure, a display of emotion she couldn't afford the luxury of having, and after last night, she refused to cry again. Which meant she had to stay put, had to let him play his game with her, let herself unbend just a little and indulge in his touch, whatever his motives. He was certainly good at what he was doing, and her body was stirring to life, appreciating the attention.

"Let me bow to you." Damien flickered his tongue across the corner of her mouth, his hand gently pulling her arms away from her chest, forcing them to her sides before returning higher to cup her breast.

He found her nipple easily and toyed with it, rolling and rubbing over the peak until Marley was breathing harder, head starting to slide back. His hands were here, they were there, they were stroking and caressing and moving, big and demanding, yet graceful and fluid.

"I like seeing you in my clothes. They're workout clothes, functional, yet on you they hug and tug and make me think all sorts of things I shouldn't."

Now there was a hand sliding over the satin nylon shorts, right along the apex of her thighs. Marley shivered as he found her clitoris, even through the layers of clothes. He pressed lightly, circled, pressed, circled, pressed. "What things?" she asked, swallowing hard, desire thick and hot in her mouth.

"Hot and sweaty things. Sports imagery, like you in this shirt with no bra, soaked from a Gatorade dump. Sitting on a basketball, legs spread. You hitting the showers, me assisting . . . I can keep going if you'd like."

That was plenty to keep her fantasies rolling for months after she got home.

"I absolutely love your body," he added. "I want to lick you from head to toe."

His mouth closed over her breast and Marley bit back a moan. That thing he was doing, the way he sucked, then pulled—she was going blind with pleasure. Desire was dragging her in, emptying her mind, stirring and rising, her body screaming yes, this was what she wanted.

Then she heard the crinkle of the ziplock bag under her shirt.

Marley jerked back, startled. She wasn't supposed to let him see the letters.

And if he was the one bowing to her, why did she feel so out of control, so pushed and led and coaxed?

"What's the matter?" He reached for her again.

Marley retreated backward. "Nothing." She put her hand on his chest to stop him when he would have taken her into his arms again. "But if I'm in charge, then we play it my way. And I don't want to do this in the driveway."

The corner of his mouth tilted up and he looked aroused, excited. If she had doubted his interest ten minutes earlier, she didn't now. He couldn't be faking that tightness in his jeans, that lusty look in his eyes.

"Are you teasing me? Going to make me work for it?"

Marley didn't know the rules to these kinds of games, but she knew she couldn't let him see the letters from Marie, and she knew if she took pleasure from him, it was going to be precisely and only that. She wasn't going to open up to him, she wasn't going to give herself, her heart, or her trust, or try to take more than Damien was offering.

She was going to be in control, and she was going to stand up and get what she wanted, exactly what she wanted, for the first time in her life.

"Yes. I want you to work for it." Marley shoved him backward with the palm of her hand, knocking him off balance.

Damien shook his head slightly, a scoff of disbelief escaping. But he was smiling, a dangerous, sensual smirk.

"Then start running, Marley," he said in a low, rough voice. "Because I'm going to start chasing."

❦

The conception of our baby had arrived so quickly, mere weeks after our marriage, that I think we both assumed a second pregnancy would occur just as easily. But as the winter thawed into spring, and the spring warmed to summer, there was no baby, and I was secretly pleased.

I wanted an infant, absolutely, but I couldn't help but feel a vicious sort of triumph that whereas Damien had put random effort into conception the first time and succeeded, he was denied again and again now. He seemed to take it as an affront, as if I were doing something to prevent it, and he showed up night after unpleasant night, reeking like whiskey and climbing into my bed with a grim determination.

One night he said, "Are you preventing a babe?" Then before I could even shake my head, he laughed, a cold, empty sound. "Of course not. As if you'd know how to do such a thing. No, we'll just have to keep trying."

I didn't answer. I never did. I never spoke.

Another time he complained bitterly about that very thing. "Don't nod your head! Use a goddamn word. I want to hear you say a word."

He was unbuttoning his breeches, and he looked sufficiently angry that I forced myself to say, "Yes," to his original question, which had been to inquire if I was eating when I first awoke in the morning, a suggestion from the physician to build my strength back up.

"What?" He put his hand by his ear in a mocking gesture. "Did you hear that? I thought I heard something. It sounded like my wife, but she speaks to me so infrequently I'm not sure I'm right. She'll repeat it now so I can verify that is what I heard."

"Stop," I whispered, wondering if I had finally pushed him too far.

"That's another word! This is astonishing. This brings us to a grand total of eight words you have spoken to me in the past two weeks. I have been tallying them, you know. I was hoping we might achieve double digits before we reach week's end."

I sat up in bed, suddenly ashamed of my behavior. "Damien."

The candle flickered on the nightstand, the shadows playing across his face. "You know, I believe I have changed my mind," he said. "I'll leave you alone in your misery tonight."

He left, slamming the bedchamber door behind him. I could hear his boots stomping down the front stairs, and his anger was sufficient enough that I even heard the front door shut behind him, the windows rattling.

Unable to return to sleep, I paced the floor in front of my open windows. There was a soft breeze stirring in the June night, and I stepped out onto the gallerie, not caring that I was in my nightrail. I was suddenly worried. I had resented and despised Damien's visits to my bed, but it came to me for the first time that the cessation of those visits would in fact be worse. At present, it appeared my husband wanted relations with me, wanted a child. I had that, such as it were.

If he lost the desire for me or for an heir, what would I have then? Nothing. I would be thousands of miles from home, the despised and deposed wife of a wealthy man, the talk of the neighborhood, the unenviable little nothing of a social whisper, shut behind the doors of this plantation for the rest of my life. No baby of my own.

Damien could live his life as he chose, with or without me. But I, without the care, concern, or support of my husband, for all intents and purposes, would be nothing. Less than nothing. And everyone would breathe a sigh of relief when I succumbed to the climate and finally took myself off into eternity. I would receive a small stone marker in the du Bourg mausoleum, beside my child, and that would be that.

I found, quite vehemently, that I didn't want such a fate. I wanted a husband who respected me. I wanted a child, then a second, and a third. But I needed to acknowledge that I was going about my marriage in an entirely wrong fashion.

Which was confirmed at that exact moment by the realization that I could hear my husband's voice floating up from the front steps. He was speaking to a woman, voices too low for me to hear exactly what they were saying. Neither could I see, not even by leaning as far over as I dared, so I found myself, with neither thought nor direct purpose, heading down the stairs and pulling open the front door.

I'm not sure what I expected to find. A part of me had to have known that any business my husband was conducting at midnight on the front porch with a woman when he had been drinking was undoubtedly inappropriate. Yet I confess myself still shocked to see the vicious truth of it directly in front of me. My husband was embracing with a woman, his hands on her backside, hers digging into his hair. They were flush against one another, mouths entwined, legs entangled.

She whispered in his ear, while I stood there, frozen in shock. Her thick black hair trailed loosely down over the back of her bold red dress, which had a Grecian line to it and a high waist, no stays. It clung to her everywhere and I was suddenly inexplicably jealous of her health, her vitality, the clear sensuality she exuded, the way she sank her teeth into my husband's ear and smiled a delicious little satisfied smirk.

Damien turned then, looking unconcerned to see me. "Good evening, Marie. Care to join us?"

What to say? What to do when forced to face his clear insouciance? I could only think what my behavior had been, my disgust at his physical attentions, my lack of concern for my appearance, my all-consuming grief and refusal to speak, and how for all my ladylike pretensions, breeding, and notions of self-worth, I was now jealous of a raven-haired harlot.

I fled back into the house.

But here is where I shall shock you, Angelique. I did not return to bed. Instead, I hesitated inside the foyer, then found myself moving to the first window to the left of the door. From behind the glass of the morning room, hidden by the drapery, I watched them, together under the gaslight of the porch lamp.

My interruption was clearly of no import to them. In the time it had taken me to tiptoe softly to the window, they had resumed their former activities, more aggressively than before. My husband had the front of that shocking red dress pulled down, and I saw quite clearly the roundness of her breasts, the darker circle of her nipples, before his mouth covered them.

What amazed me, what seemed so extraordinary, was that they were standing up locked together, that they both looked so violent in their pleasure. There was jerking and tugging and heads tilted back, eyes rolling in ecstasy. She had her hand clasped around Damien's manhood, moving up and down with slow, languorous strokes, and I found myself resentful that doing such a thing had never occurred to me.

What Damien and I did—it was quick and efficient, conducted in the dark with little conversation.

What they were doing was totally different, and it was oh so utterly wicked, wrong in every sense of the word, but for the first time I saw the appeal, for the first time I felt an awakening in my own body, a heavy, tingling sort of anticipation as I watched. When Damien sucked hard on her nipples, my own ached beneath my nightrail. When she moved over him, faster and faster until he pushed her away, my own heart rate increased until I could hear the quick rushes of my panting breath.

Even when the rain began to fall, soaking her dress, his shirt, forcing linen to cling to taut breasts and rippling muscle, they did not hesitate, did not stop. Damien shook the rain from his face, and she tilted her head back, as if she exalted in the mist that flowed cool over her hot, aroused body.

I felt that I should stop watching, that I should leave them alone in their debauchery, but I couldn't look away. I couldn't tear my eyes from their explosive passion, from the connection that flowed between them, the whispered murmurs that I couldn't hear, but could see, in the form of their lips moving urgently.

Then her dress was around her waist, legs wrapped around his, Damien's back against the porch post. They surged together. It was not him solely pushing into her, nor her sliding onto him, but a total collision of the two, and *even from my hiding space behind the glass and wood, I could hear their mutual moans of pleasure.*

Clinging to the curtain, a novel heat pooling between my thighs, I breathed hard, watching my husband thrust himself into that woman, over and over, while I wished most shamefully that it were me.

Chapter Nine

Marley jerked on the bed when her cell phone rang. She dropped the letter she'd been reading and moved quickly to the desk, hoping it was Lizzie or at least Rachel calling with news.

It was from a local area code. "Hello?" she said, her mouth thick, eyes dry from poring over Marie's letters.

"Are you hungry?"

Damien's voice was low, charming, seductive. Marley rubbed her damp palm on her jeans. He hadn't waited long. She'd only left him late that morning, after she had promised to show up next Saturday for another party. And yet he was already pursuing her, just as he had threatened.

"Why? What are you suggesting?" Marley was stiff, her neck and back sore, her thoughts jumbled and muddled, her heart filled with worry and sorrow for her sister and for the long-dead Marie.

Damien laughed. "Dinner. To start with. Unless you have a better idea."

While Marley had basically decided to have sex with Damien, and soon, she had also decided it would be on her terms, for her reasons, for personal empowerment and liberation. Having him come up to her small hotel room wasn't appealing or arousing in the least.

Neither did she think she wanted to be alone. Marie's pain, the tragedy of losing her baby, reached through the centuries and ate at Marley. She understood that burn, that ache to be a mother, to feel a child growing within her, to anticipate holding a baby in her arms. She had mourned with Marie, felt her anguish. It made her own longing rise again in great tumultuous waves, a craving so fierce and earnest that she felt stunned, melancholy, a bit desperate.

Heaped onto her concern for Lizzie, Marley felt knots of tension forming in her temples, her forehead. She needed to get out of the hotel room, away from her own thoughts and feelings. "I guess that's fine. Do I have to get dressed up?"

"Your enthusiasm is flattering," he said, though he sounded more amused than irritated. "No, you don't have to dress up. We'll go somewhere casual."

"What time?"

"Five minutes. I'm right outside your hotel."

Marley flushed. He hadn't been kidding when he'd said he was going to chase. "Oh, okay. I'll meet you in the lobby."

"Perfect."

They hung up and Marley chanced a glance in the mirror. Yikes. She'd returned from Rosa de Montana and had showered, but she hadn't spent much time with the blow dryer. Now her hair was frizzy, her skin pale, and she still had black circles under her eyes from the martini incident. In an effort to distract attention from her facial flaws, she threw on the one skirt she'd packed, a floral cotton, and paired it with a sleeveless white knit top that clung tighter than most of her T-shirts. For Marley, allowing anything to delineate her breasts was a major concession, and she hoped Damien would appreciate exactly what the effort cost her.

The closest thing she had to lipstick was a dessert-scented lipgloss, so she slid that on, stepped into sandals, grabbed her purse, and went downstairs, leaving Marie's letters tucked safely in her suitcase.

Damien was already waiting in the lobby. She saw him the minute the elevator doors opened and she exited. She wasn't sure what she'd expected—maybe him pacing anxiously, or at least standing there looking impatient, or even lounging in a chair drinking coffee and reading the paper. Instead, he was talking to the desk clerk, a pale blonde whose laughter could be heard all the way across the lobby.

Unfamiliar, unpleasant feelings reared up and threw Marley. God, she was jealous, and she hated it. Yet that didn't stop her from strolling up to him and announcing, "Sorry I took so long. I'm ready to leave. Now."

The desk clerk looked startled, but Damien only pulled his elbows off the desk, turned, and smiled. "I didn't mind the wait, you were hardly a minute." He turned back to the blonde. "Thank you so much for your help, Renee. Have a great day."

She took the business card he was pushing over the desk to her. Her cheeks were pink, eyes sparkling. "My pleasure."

Annoyance made Marley speak without thinking as she strode down the steps to the front door. "Inviting her to the party? Or lining up your next conquest for after I'm gone?"

Damien didn't react to her obvious anger. He just put his hand on the small of her back and leaned closer to her. "Green is not your color."

That he'd seen right through her made her irritation that much more annoying. "I don't know what you're talking about."

"Renee expressed interest in Rosa de Montana. I offered her a tour."

"How nice." She could have stopped right there. But her mouth opened again. "You've never offered me a tour." Now why the hell did she say that? She sounded like the insecure, jealous woman that she was.

Damien moved in front of her, cutting her off. He slipped his hand lower down her back, to the first hint of the curvature of her backside, while his eyes locked with hers, dark and determined. "Marley. I'll give you whatever you want. Just ask for it."

He wasn't talking about the tour, she knew that. But she wasn't ready for this yet, knew that it was too easy still for him to tip the balance in his favor, that she wasn't in control, didn't own the situation.

"Thanks. I'd love a tour of the plantation." She glanced around his shoulder, striving for casual. "Did you drive or are we walking somewhere?"

"We can walk." His tone matched hers for nonchalance as he opened the front door to the hotel for her, nodding pleasantly to the bellman. "I just thought we'd go down the street and pick a place. Your choice. There's a dozen restaurants within walking distance. The French Quarter is at your service."

"Sounds good." The day was cooling down, but it was still hot. Marley pulled a band out of her purse and yanked her hair back. She twisted it up into a bun, figuring the frizz would only get worse in the humidity. "What kind of food do you like?"

They had passed a rather innocuous looking café and an antique shop.

"Anything. I'm easy. If you're up for trying the local cuisine, there's a place on the corner here that's good. Silly name, good food."

She nodded, feeling warm in the fading heat, distracted.

"So why did you choose the Hotel Monteleone?" he asked. "It's a very nice hotel, a bit expensive for a trip such as yours."

"The first three hotels I called didn't have rooms available on such short notice. And I didn't have time to look for any more. I needed a place to stay and I really wanted to stay in the French Quarter." Though she had to admit, the hefty room rate was preying on her. She was going to rack up a couple of grand in bills between the hotel, rental car, and food by the time she got Lizzie home.

"Teachers are notoriously underpaid."

Marley carefully watched where she was walking. The sidewalks had random holes in them that would have her down on her knees in a flash if she weren't careful. "That's true. But I love my job."

Damien pointed to the corner. "That's the place I was talking about. We can sit in the courtyard if you'd like."

"Sure." Though how he could look so fresh when she felt sweaty and wilted was truly a gender injustice. "Have you always lived here, on the plantation? Did you grow up in the big house?" Maybe that would explain his being so unaffected by the heat.

"Actually, my school years were spent in France at boarding school. I lived in the *maison principale* as a child, but now I mostly stay in the *pigeonnier*. It's compact and convenient."

"It's small though. I can't imagine living there when you have that whole huge intriguing house you could be in." She could wander for weeks and never get tired of exploring it.

Damien stopped to open the door to the restaurant. He glanced over at her. "It's too big for one person."

There seemed to be a world of information in that sentence if Marley wanted to play shrink.

"Besides, I need Internet access and electricity, and it was difficult enough wiring the *pigeonnier*. It would cost millions to update the house to modern standards, and it doesn't seem worth the expense."

Marley didn't answer because a cheerful hostess was greeting them. A minute later, they were seated outside on the patio and Marley was shaking her head no to wine. Just the thought of drinking any form of alcohol made her stomach lurch. She wasn't completely recovered from her first unplanned foray into drugs the night before.

"I am sorry about last night," Damien said after the waitress left, like he understood where her thoughts had gone. "I hope you're feeling okay."

"I'm fine. Just a little leery of drinking tonight. But don't let that stop you from ordering whatever you want."

But Damien shook his head. "I don't drink much anymore. Not even when I'm entertaining."

Marley snapped open the menu, not sure if there was censure in his voice or not, but definitely not wanting to revisit the sex party and all the confusing feelings it had aroused in her. "So what do you do for a living, Damien? What did they teach you at that French boarding school?"

She meant it to be light, a change of subject. But it sounded a little sharp. Like she thought he was a rich snob. Damien had a hell of a poker face, though, because he didn't react at all. He just smiled.

"I learned the usual. Literature, math, world history, French, how to do as little as humanly possible and maintain average grades, and how to sneak out of my room at night to meet girls. But in the end I must have learned something, because I make my living designing websites. I own a design firm."

"And you enjoy that? It's successful?" Marley was thinking about how many webpages you'd have to design to pay the taxes on the plantation.

"I consider it successful. We don't do individual designs, we only do major corporations who need a multitude of functions and applications on their site. Our designs start at ten grand and quickly go up from there."

"Oh, wow. I'm impressed." She was. He wasn't the lazy playboy sponging off family money the way she had assumed. "And you work at home most of the time?"

"Yes. I am more productive that way, working on my own terms, by myself." Damien eyed her steadily. "I don't play nice with others."

Marley laughed. "You like everything to be your way?"

"Yes. And so do you."

"What?" Marley set down her iced tea, forgoing a sip. "I do not!"

"Of course you do. You want your mother, your sister, your father, to do exactly what you want them to."

Well, that was rude. And totally untrue. Marley's cheeks went hot with anger. "I want to help my family. I want to take care of them, not dictate to them."

"But essentially you're telling them the way they are doing it is wrong and they should do it your way. But I would guess your sister is happy living her life the way she does."

"But she puts herself in danger, she does things and they're stupid, and she ne—" Marley stopped speaking, took a breath to calm herself. "She doesn't make wise choices for her son."

"It seems to me the wisest choice she made was to leave her son with your cousin. The rest of the mistakes are hers and hers alone, and I bet she doesn't even consider them mistakes. Only you do."

His words rang true to her, and she resented it. Why was she the bad guy here? She was the one who just wanted Lizzie to have a happy, healthy, productive life. Why did that make her a control freak? "Would you let your sister disappear for two months with no word and not try to find her? Is that what you're suggesting? That I just assume she's fine and living it up and go about my business?" Because she couldn't do that. She had to know that Lizzie was alright. She couldn't ignore the foreboding feeling that had taken up permanent residence in her gut.

"Of course not. I know how worried you are. But chances are, she is off having fun, stripping on Bourbon Street or something, and will be surprised to find out that you've wasted one minute worrying about her, because if your roles were reversed, she wouldn't. If it were my sister, I would do exactly what you're doing, but then I admit I'm controlling. Or I try to be. And if there's one thing I've learned, it's that you cannot control someone else." Damien raised his wineglass in a mock toast. "Most of us can't even control ourselves, let alone someone else."

Was he talking about himself? Marley had no idea what he could or couldn't control. But she did know she didn't agree. "Maybe I can't force Lizzie to do what she doesn't want to, but that doesn't mean I shouldn't be there to support her."

"I respect that. I admire you, Marley, for your love and loyalty to your family. But are any of them grateful for the sacrifices you make? You're spending, what, like five hundred bucks a day while you're here trying to find your sister, bleeding yourself dry financially and emotionally. Would any of them do it for you?"

No. She knew the answer as clearly as she knew her name. But she didn't need him to tell her she was wrong, to mock her choices. "I don't do it for gratitude. I do it because I love my family, because it's the right thing to do. It's not about me."

Though hadn't she just spent the whole summer wondering why it was never about her? Pondering if her role as family martyr was the right thing to do, or if she was merely denying herself a full and complete life at the same time she played enabler to her screwed-up relatives?

"It should be," Damien said, his shoulders stiff, voice firm. "For once, just once, it should be."

"Is it about you, Damien?" All her anger had deflated. God, he was right, and she was so tired. Just so absolutely bone-deep tired. She had spent twenty years trying to fix people who didn't want to be fixed, but how the hell could she just walk away? It felt wrong, too selfish.

"When I was younger, it was about me. Always about me. I was a spoiled rich kid, I'm ashamed to admit. I was thoughtless and selfish, but I made a huge mistake, one that I've been paying for ever since. And that mistake taught me it's not about me. Ever. I fight every day to remember that."

He looked sincere, eyes burning with agony and passion for his convictions. Marley had known all along there was more to Damien than what he showed the world, she had seen that pain, sensed that desolation, but now, it pulsed from him in a great ugly wave of raw emotion.

"I'm sorry," she whispered, because it hurt to see his hurt.

"Let me do the right thing now. Let me take some of that burden from you."

It was so tempting to slump her shoulders and give in. To let him field some of her worry, her pain; to take their mutual burdens and share them together, or better yet, push them aside and just enjoy each other. Marley wanted something so desperately, and she didn't even understand what it was.

His hand covered hers, and stroked her warm flesh. "Stop fighting me and let me focus on you."

It was a gesture meant to comfort, she thought, but the touch was more sensual than comforting. Marley felt desire spark to life, felt the vibration between them yet again and recognized it for what it was: sexual tension. They both wanted to have sex with each other, that was blatantly obvious, had been from the minute he had touched his lips to her skin that morning. And it suddenly occurred to her what he was doing. This was all part of the chase. This was a very skilled and sensual man gaining her confidence, manipulating her.

The waitress sashayed over right then and plunked down their plates. Marley waited impatiently through the waitress's ketchup/soft drink refill/napkin speech, grateful when the server moved on to another table with a final parting smile for Damien.

Marley leaned forward, ignoring her entrée. "Is this about sex? Some kind of game?" she said in a low voice, conscious of the table next to them with two older couples eating their dinners. "Last night I offered it and you didn't want it. This morning you wanted it and I said no. If you think I'm going to give in and have sex with you because you proclaimed it should be all about me, forget it. Nice try, but if I want to have some Me Time, I'd rather have a spa day."

She was lying. She was almost positive having sex with Damien would be better than a seaweed wrap, but she had a point to make.

"I'd be happy to give you a spa package, because you certainly deserve it. But I don't know where you got the idea I was talking about sex. I was just going to ask you if you wanted to stay in the big house so you weren't getting killed with hotel costs."

Her jaw dropped. She was surprised she didn't actually break it on the patio bricks. Oh, damn, he was good. And he was digging into his food like he didn't have a care in the world, at the same time he dug around in her head, picking through her emotions like a fork through rice. Marley gritted her teeth. "That's very generous of you."

He shrugged. "You seem to like the house. It's big and empty, so no one would bother you. You're waiting for the party on Saturday and I feel guilty that you're spending so much money. It makes sense."

"So you're just Mr. Nice Guy looking out for me?" Marley didn't bother to hide the sarcasm.

"No. I'm a selfish bastard who likes to think he's reformed, and who relies on other people to accept his easy gestures so he can ease his guilty conscience."

Damien popped a shrimp into his mouth and winked at her.

Damn it. He had her. He'd chosen the right angle to play her. She couldn't resist the idea that she would actually be helping him by letting him help her.

"Okay. I'll stay in the house. Thank you."

Both the house and the man lured her, more than she wanted to admit.

❧

Damien hadn't lied to himself in 150 years and he didn't want to start now. He wasn't inviting Marley Turner to stay in his house solely out of altruism, though he did legitimately feel bad that she was spending so much of her hard-earned money on a hotel. But he could admit he also wanted her near him, he wanted her to be in his house, in his space—he wanted her to come to him on her own terms, and he wanted to show her all the power of taking pleasure for herself.

When she had tried to leave his house that morning, defeat in her eyes, a tremor in her voice, looking rumpled and sexy and insecure, Damien had lost the will to resist. If he'd ever really had it. He had denied himself much in the last century, and despite knowing it was wrong to take advantage of the attraction she would inevitably feel for him because of the demon influence, he wanted to do just that. Wanted to enjoy the beauty of desire on her face, total capitulation to the pursuit of her own pleasure.

She was sitting across from him, eyeing her plate with suspicion. He had convinced her to order alligator and now she was poking at it, frowning. She moved it around and around, breaking the nugget of meat into three pieces, leaning closer and closer to it like she could ascertain its taste purely by her stare. She stabbed a tiny piece with her fork, lifted it, licked it. Her face cleared a little and she put it in her mouth. She chewed slowly, reflectively, then commented, "Not bad."

A whole piece went in her mouth and she smiled. "Pretty good actually. It tastes like chicken."

He had the sense that's how she approached everything—with caution, then when she was ready, when something had earned her approval, she gave that approval wholly and without hesitation. He wanted that from her for himself, a confident, trusting approval, and it shocked him, scared him, aroused and intrigued him.

Here was a woman who could actually say no to him, who could resist the lure of the demon. She could shatter his resistance, disassemble the carefully constructed life he had created for himself, and show him that his compromise was merely that—a halfhearted, cowardly attempt to distance himself from his inescapable reality.

She had the compassion of Marie, the strength of Marissabelle, and together the combination was beautiful and potent.

He had already given in to it.

"Only chicken tastes like chicken," he said.

And he could only be what he was.

He was Damien du Bourg, servant of the Grigori demon, and ultimately selfish. He had spent a hundred years giving to women, fighting against his own passions, certain he had been changing, evolving, growing as a human being.

Yet with one woman, in the space of three days, he had been shown he hadn't changed one iota. He was still selfish, and all the rationalizations about exposing Marley to the pleasure of her own sensuality formed an honest layer covering the deeper truth—he wanted her, and he would chase, with all his powers of persuasion, until he got her. It was still about him, and he truly was a bastard.

She laughed at his comment and ate another piece.

He was going to catch her, of that he was certain. There was already acquiescence in her eyes, though she had possibly a few more days' resistance in her.

When she came to him, she would think it was her idea. She would think she was in control.

And very possibly, she would be.

※

I wish that I could say that I held my head up with a demeanor and dignity befitting a woman of my rank and breeding. I wish that I could tell you that from that moment on I devoted myself to acts of charity and self-improvement, that I expended my energy in spreading the word of God to the slaves, or other such noteworthy efforts.

I did not.

Instead of using the moment as a lesson on the entrapment of sin, how the tendrils of lust can grasp you, entwine you, and pull you further into a dense jungle of sinful conduct, and walk steadfastly away, I did just the opposite. I felt the tug of sin and I went toward it. I found myself looking at my husband through new eyes, through the vanity of the coquette, through the interest of a woman who is curious to understand what makes men and women disregard all sense of morality for the privilege of sexual exploration.

Whereas before I had been content when my husband ignored me, I now coveted the very idea of his attention. There were secrets of seduction, and I wanted the answers.

So I turned to my maid.

"Gigi, my appearance has taken a turn for the worse," I said the next morning as I stood in front of the full-length looking glass. "I need to correct that."

"Oh! Very good, Madame." She bobbed.

"How should we go about this?"

"Well ... what exactly are you trying to achieve, Madame?"

I could have been subtle. I could have said that I wished for better health, to look less fatigued, for an edge of sophistication in dress and hair.

Instead I revealed exactly what I was thinking. "Monsieur du Bourg has lost interest in me. I need to seduce my husband, Gigi."

Her dark eyes went wide, then she smiled broadly. "Oh, yes, Madame, I think that is an excellent plan. Monsieur du Bourg will be most pleased."

"So I need your help. What should I do?" Staring at myself with critical eyes, I knew that at the moment I was not a woman who could seduce a man, nor was I a woman a man would desire. I looked small, pale, fragile, and as if mere breathing were an effort for me. The woman on the porch had not been voluptuous at all, but she had what I lacked— strength, confidence, passion.

Gigi was taking my question seriously. Her eyes narrowed and she tapped her finger to her lip. "Pudding. That is where we start."

"Pudding?"

Gigi's plan, it seemed, revolved around avoiding Damien for several weeks while she overfed me rich, creamy foods and took me for long walks along the river to increase my strength. Then, with my hair dressed, a revealing gown, and a flirtatious manner, I was to approach Damien, shocking him with my transformation.

He would be unable to resist, Gigi assured me.

I had my doubts, but I had no better plan, so I took to tromping about on long walks that put a flush to my face and fatigued me, and I forced myself to swallow significantly more than I was used to eating. Those first few days were a struggle, but after two weeks the walks had become easier, and the bodice of my gown didn't gape so appallingly. I spent a great deal of time darting into doorways whenever I saw my husband approaching, so he wouldn't see me.

It was pathetically easy to avoid him, and he never

sought me out, which fueled my jealousy, my determination. There were loud parties more nights than not, parties I was not invited to hostess, parties that lingered on long into the night. I had glimpses out the windows of games on the front lawn, laughter and clinging gowns on women who were clearly not ladies. It seemed we had male house-guests, friends of Damien's from town, and he was entertaining. Gigi whispered to me that below-stairs they told her these were the sort of parties Damien's father had thrown before his death, and that the master seemed to be following in his predecessor's footsteps. The servants said that Damien had different female companionship every night, the latest being a rather well-known widow who had fallen into a dissolute lifestyle.

Perhaps I should have taken that as a sign that my husband was irrevocably lost to sin, and that by my present course of action, I was merely following his example and allowing my base emotions to guide me. Even as jealousy, vanity, and selfishness fueled my determination, growing and spiraling faster and deeper inside of me, I did not note the warnings. I did not look upon Damien's behavior and judge it with the disgust and contempt it deserved. I thought nothing of his salvation, and therefore, not of mine.

I merely wanted attention, wanted to know the secrets of femininity that other women had perfected, and I wanted to understand the power of seduction.

It was with this poisonous, inappropriate attitude that I went to my husband, susceptible, eager, in fact, to be coaxed into pleasures of the flesh.

This is where I blush, where I feel the keen prickles of shame as fully as if it were yesterday, Angelique. The guests had left, according to my helpful eyes and ears, Gigi. I had been dressed for hours, waiting for such an opportunity. Damien was in the garden, taking a cigar alone, so Gigi hurriedly pinched my cheeks, fussed with the bustle on my gown, and sent me on my way with an excited little wave of her hand.

For three weeks I had worried and wondered and antici-pated Damien's reaction to seeing me, and more impor-tantly, my reaction to him. I knew nothing of the ways of the coquette, had no experience simpering and flirting. So when I slid out the back door into the garden, my heart was pounding, my breathing hard and fast, cheeks hot. I expected to feel embarrassment on seeing Damien.

I did not anticipate what stole over me when I paused on the path and took in his figure, legs spread, back partially to me, one boot up on the perimeter of the brick fountain, chest bent forward over his knee as he smoked and stared into the dark water. What I felt then was a warm anticipation, a physical attraction, a desire to move in nearer to him. I mis-took this for tenderness, for a baffling realization that per-haps I'd grown fond of my husband during our self-imposed absence from one another. Perhaps I even cared for him, could grow to love this man who was to be my companion for life.

This was yet again the naïveté of the young innocent mis-reading her response. I know now that what I felt was lust, new and unexplored, and not identifiable to the inexperi-enced, but very much a sexual desire springing to life.

"Pardon," I said, *gathering my courage and inching forward. "Am I interrupting your solitude?"*

"Indeed you are." Damien turned his head, inspected me. *"But I shall endeavor to forgive you."*

Everything in me screamed to return to the house, to slink back to my chamber and accept who I was and how little I mattered to my husband. But a heretofore unknown pride stiffened my spine, forced my chin up, led my slippers over the pavers toward the fountain.

"Have your guests returned to town?"

"Yes." Damien stared at me, clearly curious. His eyes ran

up and down over me, the dim light from the house casting a shadow over his face. "You are looking rather well this evening, Marie."

It was enough of a triumph to bolster me, to coax a smile to my lips. "I thank you most kindly."

"Do you?" He sounded faintly amused. He drew on his cigar and blew smoke over the fountain in a pungent cloud, his attention shifting from me back to the water.

That was it. Nothing but a cursory inspection of me, then . . . disinterest.

"I have missed you of late," I said with a boldness born of desperation. The burn, the ache inside of me demanded that I proceed, desired and clamored for his touch, his experience, his understanding of me as a woman.

But he merely laughed at me, a soft, deep rumble in his chest, the sound rolling over me, more terrible than a slap, more shocking than a slice to tender flesh.

"What is it that you want, Marie? More gowns? More pin money? No, that is not what you desire. Do you wish to return to France? That I cannot allow. There is trouble stirring in France, you know, and it is not a good time for you to abandon me and our marriage."

"That is not what I want. I want you to . . . to return to me," I whispered, throat tight, cheeks burning.

"In your bed? Is that what you mean?" Damien smiled, a cool, harsh smile. "I am shocked, my dear."

I said nothing. I could not. I merely stood there, heart racing, breath rushing in and out, and waited.

"Ah, I understand. This is because you wish for a child, yes? While I would like that too, I find myself displeased with you of late. I believe before we resume proper spousal relations, you owe me a most pretty apology for your unpleasant behavior."

Do you see what he was doing? The humiliation he was putting upon me? I believe he enjoyed my discomfort, and the position of power he held over me.

If I had been myself, the woman you raised, who had a firm understanding of right and wrong, a solid grip on her convictions, I should have walked away then and allowed him to wallow in his dyspeptic and cruel emotions. I did not.

All the vices that claim and coax and cajole us into sin were working upon me, and I was willing to debase myself in order to achieve my goal. I did not know it then, but at that moment I lost myself.

"I am sorry, Damien, if I have displeased you. That has never been my intention and I will try to be a more satisfying wife."

His eyebrow rose. He noticed the emphasis I put on a particular word. "That was not so hard, was it? And I accept your apology."

I could not prevent a sigh of relief.

But then he continued. "However, I will not return to your chamber tonight or any other night. If you wish a babe, you will come to my chamber." His voice was relaxed and even, but his eyes glittered sharply, his jaw stiff. "You will come to me, and you will climb into my bed and you will tell me exactly what it is you want. Then I shall be pleased to give it to you."

My mouth moved, but no sound came out. I was shocked, appalled, frightened. If it had taken all my courage to come out into the garden dressed as if for dinner, how could I ever presume to go to his chamber?

"No? You don't wish to? Well, that is somewhat disappointing."

He reached out and drew his finger along my décolleté. The touch made me shiver, my nipples hardening with a foreign discomfort.

"You look rather fetching tonight. Your maid has worked wonders with you."

I confess I was offended. "She has done nothing. I have simply regained my appetite."

"Oh, I see I have pricked your pride." Damien leaned

closer, tilting my chin up. "How interesting to know that vanity exists within you after all. Come upstairs and show me that you have regained, or rather developed for the first time, all of your appetites."

It could have been a tender touch. I wanted it to be. I wanted him to assure me that all was well between us. That if I came to him, we would start afresh, and have a true and sacred marriage. There was no such reassurance, of course. No smiles, no promises, no loving embrace.

Instead he moved away from me, crushing out his cigar with his boot. "I won't wait for you but I will be in my chamber. Do as you please, Marie. You always do."

Chapter Ten

Marley followed behind Damien in her rental car and wondered if she'd lost her everlovin' mind.

Yes, Damien lived in the *pigeonnier*, and she would be staying in the main house, but who was she kidding? Just the two of them until Saturday? She might as well strip naked now and save them both the aggravation of her futile resistance.

She hadn't had sex in five years. Even then, it had been a brief, less than stellar performance by her high school crush, whom she'd run into at the park. All those years of daydreaming over Brian in sophomore algebra could have been spent more productively if only she could have had a glimpse into the future and known he was a sexual dud.

But maybe she was the dud. That was a very real possibility.

If Damien was a dud, she'd eat her skirt, one flower at a time. He looked like he could bring women to orgasm just by suggesting it.

That was part of the reason she'd clung to her rental car. She needed a way out, fast, if being around Damien for the next few days had her in over her head, which she suspected it would. She also had the niggling little fear at the back of her mind that she was being stupid, that she had no reason to trust him. But she always managed to wrestle that fear into submission by reminding herself that he'd had ample opportunity to take advantage of her, sleep with her, dismember her and toss her in the swamp the night before when she'd been half-dressed and drugged. If his motives were evil, she'd have been dead already.

Cheerful thought.

Damien came and opened her car door when she parked behind him in the driveway. He smiled at her and bent toward her. Marley backed up instinctively, then mentally groaned at her weird reaction when he pulled the button by her ankle to pop the trunk. He was just getting her luggage, and she'd been afraid he was going to put the moves on her in the Ford Taurus. Jesus, she needed to get a grip.

"So where are your parents?" she asked as she got out of the car and followed him around to the trunk. "Did they retire to a condo or something?" He couldn't be more than thirty. His parents would be the right age for golf and traveling around the globe.

Damien lifted out her suitcase. "My parents have passed. My mother when I was a child, my father when I was twenty-four."

"Oh, I'm so sorry." No wonder he didn't live in the big house. He truly was alone, and that overwhelming square footage must be a constant reminder.

"Don't do that," he said, cupping her cheek with his free hand.

"Do what?" she asked, amazed at how breathy she sounded. But there was something so inherently sensual about having a man's large hand cover her face like that, and she felt so bad for him.

"Feel sorry for me. I can see that softness in your eyes,

that pity. I don't deserve it, Marley, I truly don't. Save your compassion for someone else."

He didn't sound angry, just earnest. Marley shook her head. "Everyone deserves my compassion."

"You should protect yourself more. Someone is going to take your goodness, that compassion, and they're going to hurt you. They're going to shred you, make a mockery out of your trust and kindness, and they will walk away without a single drop of guilt or shame, and leave you bleeding."

His words were soft, but harsh, his fingers stroking over her skin. Marley shook her head again. "So I build steel armor around myself and never care about anyone? Never let anyone in? That sounds lonely as hell to me . . . I'd rather risk it."

He jerked back and yanked her second bag out of the trunk.

"You're not going to shred me, are you, Damien?" she asked, even as she was sure of the answer.

"No. No, I'm not."

"I know. That's why I'm here."

Pushing the handle back down into the suitcase, Damien turned and slammed the trunk shut. "That doesn't mean you won't regret the day you met me."

Marley slipped her purse back onto her shoulder and pulled up the suitcase handle before he could grab and carry both bags. She started rolling it over the gravel. "Oh, come on, don't be so goth. You sound like you're auditioning for vampire tour guide, all ominous and brooding."

He glared at her, but there was amusement in his eyes, and he struggled to keep a smile off his face. "Fine, but don't say I didn't warn you. I know I can be difficult."

"You've never seen a six-year-old lose his recess privileges. It's ugly. I think I can handle you." She hoped. Playing cat and mouse with Damien was a little different than handing out color-coded behavior cards to students.

"Now show me the house, please. I didn't have any time to look around last night."

Because she'd been too busy taking her bikini top off for him.

"By the way, why do you call the *pigeonnier* the *pigeonnier*?"

"Because pigeons used to be kept there."

"Oh." Duh, Marley. "I guess I figured that, but I meant why did they need a whole building to keep pigeons? Did they eat them or what?"

"Back in France, in the Old Regime before the Republic, only landowners could own pigeons. So building an elaborate structure to house your pigeons was a sign of wealth and class. And yes, they were eaten." Damien urged her to start walking again by pushing his hand lightly on the small of her back.

Marley marveled at the money, the heritage that belonged to Damien. Being just a nice, Midwestern, middle-class girl of unknown European ancestry, it was awe-inspiring to think about Damien's lineage.

"Just to warn you," he said, "there's no working plumbing in the house."

Marley stopped on the first step. "Then, uh, how do you bathe, et cetera?" It was the et cetera that really worried her. She didn't hang with the idea of peeing behind a bush. Flush toilets were her friend. That alone was worth three hundred bucks a night back at the hotel.

"I turned the old kitchen into a bathroom because it was the easiest way to manage it without digging under the foundation of the main house. You'll have to share it with me." He took her suitcase from her slack hand and moved up the stairs to open the front door. "And it's out the back door and across the garden, so you won't be able to dash to the bathroom naked. Unless you really want to. I don't mind."

"Despite my secret yearnings to be a nudist colonist, I

think I'll be fine." She rolled her eyes. "Hey, you know what I've been wondering?"

He raised an eyebrow. "I can't even imagine."

"Why is the front door on the second floor? I mean, you have this big dramatic staircase that essentially leads to the second floor, which is really the first floor because you have all first-floor stuff on it, so what's really on the first floor since you're not using it like a first floor?" Okay, that made no sense. Marley stopped in the foyer and clamped her lips shut.

"When the house was built in 1777, the ground-level floor was used for storage only, in case the river flooded. Water could pass through the bottom floor and not damage the structure of the house or the furnishings. Later it was turned into the rooms I have now—the music room, a living area, a weight room."

"You have a weight room?" Something about the image of Damien sweating with his shirt off did strange things to her insides.

"Yes. Feel free to use it."

Marley snorted. "Do I look like I work out?" And even if she did, she would not do it in front of Damien. "But how do you work out without electricity?"

"I open the gallery doors. It lets plenty of light in."

They were still standing in the foyer, and Marley realized Damien was patiently waiting for her to stop gawking at the chandelier and stop touching random candlesticks and the mirror over the nineteenth-century table. "Sorry. Just smack my hand if I touch something I shouldn't."

"You can touch anything you want. I don't believe the past should be carefully preserved as if the world has never moved forward. If I cared enough to take the time and spend the money, I would shock the purists and make this house a home by mixing antiques with comfortable contemporary furnishings."

"You should. You could move back in." Marley thought

it would be an amazing thing to do, to restore the house to its former glory by appreciating the past while living in the present, and carefully blending the two.

"I don't think it would be worth the effort. Now let me take you upstairs to the second floor where the bedrooms are."

"You mean the third floor." Marley followed Damien up the stairs.

"If you want to be that precise, sure. But my family has always called it the second floor. The floor with the bedrooms. Where you'll be sleeping."

She was not going to read anything into the way he phrased that. Glancing into the first room on her right, Marley was intrigued by the white shroud around the bed and the simplicity of the furnishings. It was less ornate than the room she had stayed in. "Can I have this room?" It would be embarrassing to walk into the room she'd been in last night with Damien. The poor man might have flashbacks of her thighs rolling around.

"If you want. But I should tell you this was the mourning room."

Marley stopped just inside the doorway. She glanced at the cross on the dresser. "What do you mean?"

"I mean, this is where dead bodies were laid out on the bed for mourning before burial."

No thanks. A shiver rippled up her back. "Never mind. I'm sure you have another room I could use, right?"

"How about the one you were in last night?"

"Alright." Damn it.

When they walked in, Marley tried not to blush. Instead, she threw her purse on the dresser and said, "Thanks for showing me around. I shouldn't keep you. Have a good night."

He frowned. "Let me show you the bathroom. And the refrigerator is in the *garçonnier*."

"Oh, I'm sure I can find everything."

"No, let me just give you a quick tour. I don't want you to feel uncomfortable."

She'd feel more comfortable if he'd leave her the hell alone, but Marley put on a smile and followed him down the stairs and out the back door. "What's a *garçonnier*?"

"It's the sleeping quarters for teenage boys, traditionally. Once a son turned fourteen he moved out of the big house, even though he took all his meals with the family."

"Why did he get his own place?" Marley twisted her ankle on the gravel path and swore under her breath.

"To allow him to experience independence and to grow into manhood. Which I think means, in essence, allowing him freedom out from under the watchful eye of his mother to grow into manhood with the servant and slave girls."

Of course. It always came down to the penis. "Or maybe it had something to do with the mother wanting his stinky feet out of the house. Have you ever smelled a fourteen-year-old boy? It's not a pretty thing."

Damien laughed. "Maybe. But I live here now and hopefully I don't smell." He opened the door to a white square building with a porch, fifty feet from the *pigeonnier*. "This is where I sleep, and I have a small kitchenette in here. I don't really cook much so it's not extensive."

The building was small, though bigger than the *pigeonnier*, and it was decorated in a similar eclectic way, with a modern tubular bed and ornate, gilded portraits on the wall. The refrigerator was stainless steel and stood directly across from an antique mahogany armoire.

It struck Marley that if Damien had redone the kitchen as a bathroom, the *pigeonnier* as his office, and the *garçonnier* as his bedroom, he was avoiding living in the big house. It almost seemed like it would have been easier to convert the whole bottom floor of the big house into an apartment for him, instead of his hodgepodge of random buildings.

"I'm sorry everything is so inconvenient," Damien said. "Maybe you should stay in here and I'll sleep in the big house."

Sleep on his sheets? Stare at his clothes hanging in the armoire? That was a seriously bad idea. "No, you don't have to do that. It's fine. I like the big house."

"I have to work tomorrow during the day, I'm sorry to say, so I won't be able to entertain you, but there is food. Feel free to come in here whenever you want. You should be able to fix yourself something for breakfast and lunch if that's okay with you, or you can go to town, of course." He pulled open the fridge to reveal some very clean shelves loaded with staples before he slammed it shut again. "Feel free to explore the big house, the attic, outside. Just don't go into the swamp."

"The swamp monster might get me?" He was amusing her. He looked actually nervous about having a guest. It was obvious that while he had his infamous parties with a certain regularity, he didn't seem to have traditional houseguests.

"Either that or a gator." He stuck his hands in his pockets. "If you need anything just come over to the *pigeonnier*. At any time. My work is easily interruptible, and I want you to be comfortable. Though sometimes you might have to just poke around to find what you need . . . I don't really pay attention to where the maids put things."

"Damien, relax." Marley pulled her ponytail tighter. "I'm an easy guest. And I'm used to taking care of myself. Everything will be fine."

"Okay." He nodded. "Good. It's just, I'm not used to having anyone stay over. My wife was an excellent hostess, but I'm much more comfortable writing a check for the caterer and the cleaning crew."

Hello. Marley barely heard a word past *wife*. "You were married? For how long?"

He winced. "Eighteen months. She hated this moldy plantation."

"I'm sorry it didn't work out. I think the house and the property are stunning." Small consolation, but it was true.

"Thank you. I'm sorry she died too. Very, very sorry."

"She died?" Marley was horrified. She had just assumed divorce. "When?"

"Two years after my father died." Damien rubbed his hand over his jaw. "Just forget that I brought it up, alright? I didn't mean to say anything in the first place and I can see what's it's doing . . . you're getting that look again."

"What look?" Marley wanted to cry. How could one person know so much tragedy? Damien was wealthy, but he had no one to share his material fortune with. That made her profoundly sad and ashamed. She had no reason to resent her family. While they were flawed, they loved her, and they belonged to her.

"The look that says you want to cuddle me and make shushing sounds in my ear." He gave her a wry look. "I don't need to be cuddled, I promise. I am perfectly fine."

"That's the problem with men," she said, a lump still in her throat. "They turn down good cuddling for the sake of pride."

"If you're going to be in my arms, it's not going to be from pity."

"No? What will it be?" She knew what he was going to say. Passion. Desire.

His nostrils flared. "Lust. It will be from lust. I don't want you feeling sorry for me, I want you begging me for more."

Oh, shit. Marley backed up. For some crazy, wild reason, her eyes darted down to his crotch. He had an erection in his jeans. Nothing to be sorry about there.

"I think I'll just go to bed. Bathroom's out here

somewhere, you said? Thanks. For everything. I'll see you tomorrow. Good night."

She turned and fast-walked out the door onto the wooden porch, hoping she would recognize the bathroom when she stumbled on it. Her cheeks were hot and her inner thighs likewise. Nope, she wasn't feeling sorry for him. She was feeling sorry for herself. Sorry that she was too much of a chickenshit to just stroll up to him and start begging.

"Good night, Marley," he called after her. "Turn right—you'll find the bathroom at the back of the garden. And sleep well."

Like that was going to happen. Marley yanked her ponytail out. Her brain hurt.

⁂

Lead us not into temptation, but deliver us from evil.

Oh, Angelique, if only I had remembered to pray. I feel very fatigued this evening and have not written since this morning. Besides, I ran out of paper and had to fetch some from Damien's desk. It was unfortunate in that I was discovered by my husband leaving his library, sheets in hand, and he would exact payment.

I am so lost to all that is proper. I know not myself any longer.

You must anticipate that I went to Damien that night in July. It was a course of action I had set myself upon and could not alter. I wanted too badly both the reassurance that my marriage still existed in some measure and I was not to be socially and physically cast off, and as well, to know whether, if I shifted the initiative to myself, I could discover the satisfaction of pleasure.

These new feelings of curiosity, of desire for Damien, led me to follow him into the house. Led me to disrobe with the maid's assistance, and head down the hall to his chamber in nothing but chemise and wrapper, the carpets shocking and intimate on my bare feet, my hair unbound, air swirling around my exposed ankles and calves.

I knocked and Damien bid me enter. Though embarrassed and nervous, I can't say that I hesitated. I slipped inside and shut the door behind me. Damien was sitting in a plush damask upholstered chair by the window, his shirt off, whiskey glass in hand. I had never been inside his chamber, and it was stately and large, very masculine, with dark furnishings and thick carpets. The papering was done in a rich blue, and the linens likewise. It smelled different than my room does, with its powders and perfumes. Damien's space smelled like soap, leather, liqueur, and tobacco. Like him.

"Well done, Marie," he said, raising his glass to me as he stood. "I was laying odds at three to one that you'd retire to your own chamber and wish me to the devil."

I can never predict what is going to come from Damien's lips, and I do not understand his wit. I realized that this was a source of irritation to him, so I knew I had to speak or risk his ire. "Why ever would I go to all this trouble to dress and pursue your company in the garden only to wish you to the devil?"

Damien laughed. "Alright then. Come closer and tell me what it is you want." He sank back into the chair, stretching his legs out. "There is no other chair near the window, but here is a seat for you." He patted his lap.

A fissure of excitement tripped through me. Damien looked very, very attractive, so powerful, so naughty, so sly. I wanted to experience that sort of confidence, arrogance.

I walked over and descended onto his legs, my hands carefully on my knees. Our bodies made contact, his legs hard beneath my soft bottom, my shoulder brushing against his bare chest. It felt strangely intimate, curiously wicked, especially when his hand spread onto my waist, helping to balance me. I turned to look at him, to study his hard jaw and his equally hard green eyes. My confidence grew. "I want you to make love to me."

"This is a curious turn of events, but again, I must re-mind myself that you desire a child." He stroked his thumb along my back. *"And perhaps it's jealousy. I don't imagine it pleased you to see me on the porch with Rosa."*

No, it hadn't. And my jealousy had been twofold— jealousy that my husband had sought out another woman, and jealousy that she knew pleasure at his hand.

"Is that her name? Who is she exactly?"

Damien just shrugged. "A whore, nothing more. Don't trouble yourself overmuch."

❧

Marley reread Marie's handwriting three times, swore, then finally stuffed her feet in sandals and headed out of the bedroom Damien had put her in.

Something wasn't right with these letters. She understood why Marie's husband was named Damien. It was a family name. Okay. The first Damien du Bourg had built the house, and Marie was his wife from France. Sure, fine, whatever. But how in the hell could the woman Marie saw her husband cheating on her with be named Rosa?

She ran down the stairs, her footsteps echoing in the empty house. It hadn't bothered her to be alone here the night before when she had retreated from Damien to the big house, but suddenly she was aware just how vast and shadowed the structure really was, even in the strong sunlight of mid-morning. With a shiver, she jogged out the front door.

So the Rosa that Marie had described didn't really sound like the Rosa that Marley had met twice, but she still thought it was an unusual coincidence. One that made her uncomfortable.

Avoiding the side of the house with the *pigeonnier*, since she didn't want Damien seeing her out of the window and questioning her destination, Marley ducked around to the north side of the house and hoped she could remember the way to Anna's cottage. Since she was practically running, five minutes later she burst out in front of the house, winded and sweaty.

Anna was on the porch. "Mornin', Marley. Didn't expect to see you today, but it's a pleasure. Come on up here and have a chat."

Wiping her palms on her denim shorts, Marley sucked in her breath and climbed onto the porch.

"How are you, Anna?" she forced herself to ask.

"Still here. That's something. How about you? I thought you left, thought you were heading back north."

Marley shook her head. "I decided to stay in the house until Damien's next party . . . I'm hoping my sister will show up."

"Mmm-hmm." Anna raised an eyebrow. "Was that Damien's idea?"

"Yes." She would not blush, would not blush . . . Too late.

"He's hard to say no to, isn't he? All the du Bourg men are like that."

"Actually, I wanted to ask you about Marie's letters. She mentioned a woman named Rosa, a woman that her husband was, well, you know, with." God, how old was she? She couldn't even bring herself to say *sex* out loud. "Don't you think it's strange that the current Damien du Bourg knows a Rosa too?"

And who was the present Rosa exactly? But Marley supposed if she wanted the answer to that, she should ask Damien.

Anna just shrugged, her lilac T-shirt slipping off her bony shoulder. "Not so much. These families round here all use the same names, generation after generation. The du Bourgs only have two names: Phillipe and Damien. They just switch them out."

"For two hundred years?"

"Yes."

"What about when they have girls?"

"They don't have girls."

"Ever?" How was that genetically possible?

"Never. They're not a real fertile folk."

"Why do you live here, Anna?" Marley kind of thought Anna was a retired nanny or housekeeper, but it occurred to her she had no reason to assume anything.

"My great-grandmother was the quadroon mistress of one of the Damiens. He gave her this house in 1834. My family has lived here ever since."

"Oh. Well, that was nice of him." Marley was embarrassed. That was a really stupid thing to say, but it had just slipped out, Anna's explanation shocking her.

Anna laughed, the sound trailing off into a cough. "Suppose it was. But I'm sure my great-grandmother, Marissabelle, earned it. It's not easy to keep a du Bourg man pleased and satisfied."

Great. Just what she wanted to hear. Like Marley didn't have enough anxiety over sleeping with Damien, now she had to hear it was in his genetics to be unsatisfied. "Because they're rude and arrogant? Or because they're, you know, always wanting attention?"

"All of the above. And Marissabelle wasn't an obvious choice for that Damien . . . she was too old to be innocent and fresh, too young to be a jaded sophisticate, both of which might appeal to a man like that. Instead, she was right in the middle, twenty-five years old, the daughter of a mulatto slave and her white master, not much loved by either. But while they were never the most caring of parents, her father did pay for her to receive an education and for gowns, and the usual frills for a young girl."

"How did she meet Damien?" Marley pulled her shirt off her sticky back and leaned closer to Anna. Her voice was soft and soothing, but hard to hear, genteel Southern, and Marley wanted to know the story, hear what had happened between Anna's ancestor and yet another Damien du Bourg.

"That's a long story."

"I have time."

Anna stared at her for a second, then made a sound with her teeth. "Well, when Marissabelle was eighteen, her father planned to marry her off to some white man he knew who didn't mind her black blood, and who welcomed the money her father offered. Since an interracial marriage would have been illegal, they planned to pass her off as white. But Marissabelle had fallen in love with a slave on the plantation she had grown up on, and he got her with child. When the baby was born black, her father beat her for ruining her chances to make something better out of herself. She ran to the baby's father, the man she loved, but he turned her out. He wasn't going to risk trouble just for a woman he'd taken a tumble with."

"God, that's horrible."

"Yes, it was." Anna glanced over at her. "Picture a young girl, raised to think she was beautiful, a bit spoiled materially, knowing nothing about the hard truths in life, not understanding the brutal reality of racism. She didn't understand that no matter her father being white, she was still a black girl. Her mother wasn't going to stand up to her father, and her father wanted her to abandon the baby, pass it off as belonging to another one of the slaves on his plantation. Her man had broken her heart. And when she went to her father's friend, the one who had thought to marry her, he told her he could tolerate marrying a quadroon, but he'd never marry a slut. However, he had a deal for her. He'd find her a place to stay, let her keep her baby, pay for all her and the babe's needs, if she would just spread her legs for him whenever he asked her to."

Marley looked at Anna in horror. For some reason, she had not seen that coming. "Men are disgusting."

"And women are practical. She took the offer, of course, so she could keep her child." Anna closed her eyes briefly. "Have you ever loved a child, Marley? Do you understand why she did what she did? She couldn't leave that baby at the mercies of anyone else, couldn't imagine life without her flesh and blood in her arms. She would have done anything to keep her son with her."

Marley swallowed hard. "I know how she feels, even though I don't have a child. I'd do anything to protect my sister, and even more to keep my nephew happy and healthy. I can't imagine giving up my baby."

"The man was decent to her. He kept his word, finding her a nice place to live, a shotgun cottage in the French Quarter, getting her a housemaid to help with the baby. And he taught her what her impatient first lover hadn't— how to draw out pleasure, how to pull your heart right out of the bedroom and let your body be all of you. No love, no emotion, just eye-rolling ecstasy. You can have that, you know, pleasure just for the sake of pleasure, and you can learn each other's bodies, be comfortable together and still never feel anything for the other."

Marley wanted that too, just once, wanted to have an affair that felt good, that pleased her but meant nothing. That's what she wanted from Damien, just selfish sex.

"She never loved that man, but she learned to welcome his attentions, learned to look forward to his visits. Learned to take for herself what she wanted, and manipulate him by turning his desire for her against him. Yes, Miss Marley, she learned a lot about how to tease and coax and please a man, and how to please herself along the way. She had two daughters with that man because she loved children and he was decent to her son. He brought all three of them toys and sweets, and he'd play with them, toss them up in the air, and tickle their bellies to make them laugh."

The way a man treated children said a lot about his character. And yet that long-ago man hadn't married Marissabelle. Had called her a slut. Marley felt the injustice, at the same time her heart longed for the happy ending she knew wasn't coming. "Did he love her?"

Anna shrugged. "It seems unlikely. I know that's not what you want to hear. It's written all over your face, child. You want to hear they were in love and everything worked out just fine. But it didn't. And I'm sure that in the telling on down from Marissabelle, over all these years, some of the details have gone missing, but I'm telling you as I remember it. The man got married three years into their relationship and Marissabelle knew about it, knew the wife had big money, knew she resented the time he spent with his quadroon mistress. He used to tell Marissabelle his wife ranted and raved and cried over it, but he kept coming anyway, because a man wants to do something, or give a gift freely and of his own will, not because his wife asked or demanded it. Men are stubborn, proud, spoiled."

"Not just men. I know women like that too."

"True. But Marissabelle used that to her advantage. She became his forbidden fruit, and that meant that at a point in their affair when he might have been getting bored with her, his wife's fussing only made his mistress all that much more appealing to him. She was his independence, his defiance, his control."

Marley adjusted in her plastic chair again. The sweat on her neck, her armpits, her shoulder blades, slid and shifted and made her skin itch. She wondered if Lizzie felt that way—if the men she jumped into bed with were ways to display her independence, her way of proclaiming she could do whatever she wanted and no one could stop her. The thought made her feel hopeless. If that's how Lizzie felt, Marley would never be able to help her change her life, get grounded. Lizzie didn't want to be grounded, and Marley had never been willing to accept that.

"So what happened? Did the wife kill him or something?"

Anna gave a soft chuckle. "No. Never would have thought of that. You got yourself a bit of a morbid mind, Marley Turner. No, he didn't die, and if she had known what he was planning, Marissabelle would have killed him herself. It turned out his wife couldn't have children. So because she held the purse strings in their marriage, and because he wanted a child to hold on to all that money, they took his two daughters by Marissabelle, moved to Alabama, and told everyone they were his legitimate children with his wife. He didn't want the boy of course, because he was half black and not his own blood. So it was just Marissabelle and her son left to fend for themselves. Again."

"Oh, no." Marley pulled her knees up to her chest, sick to her stomach. "How could he have done that to her? How could he live with himself?"

"I expect he thought he was doing the right thing for all of them. He knew he couldn't keep Marissabelle forever, and the girls were only an eighth black, so no one would ever know the difference. He could give them a home, an education, and keep his wife happy. He gave Marissabelle enough money to keep her and her son out of poverty for a fair while, and everybody's happy, right?"

Marley didn't think he could have really believed that.

"Well, Marissabelle wasn't happy, didn't want to give up her girls, but what was she going to do? No court was ever going to take her side, and she knew he did love his daughters. There just weren't any choices for a woman like her, and so she took the money, gave him her babies, and wished him a slow, painful death in hell. Then she swallowed her pride, took all her talents of seduction and manipulation, and started attending the quadroon balls in search of a new benefactor."

"What's a quadroon ball?"

"They were very popular around that time in New Orleans. Rich men came to the balls to find mistresses. The women were all half- and quarter-black women, and the balls were nights of debauchery between French and Irish men who had too much time and money, and women who were taught from birth to lure these men and to look at themselves as better, a class above their slave and freemen counterparts. You can imagine these weren't bingo nights." Anna gave a laugh and grinned at her. "These were like the parties the current Damien has."

"I am so naïve," Marley said, pulling her T-shirt off her breasts and yanking it down over her knees. "I can't fathom how men decided to start having actual balls with these women in order to shop the market for a mistress. It's just so mercenary. And creepy." So had these guys just been sitting around the gentlemen's club one day lamenting the ability to pick over all the hot mistresses at one time and decided to throw a party to do just that? Did they line them up, rate them according to cleavage, auction them off to the highest bidder? "I can't imagine standing around with all those men checking me out. It must have been so degrading."

"You're talking like one of those feminists."

Marley heard censure in Anna's voice. "So? What's wrong with being a feminist?"

"Nothing, except you're not standing in those girls' shoes. This was 1833, Marley. These women didn't have choices like you all do now. Being at a ball, wearing a nice gown, dancing with men, flirting, eating elegant food, was a hell of a lot better than slavery."

"Yeah, but it's still slavery, just in a pretty dress. The man who becomes your benefactor owns you just the same as a plantation owner does a slave."

"So either way you're owned, but one keeps your hands out of the dirt."

Marley figured she'd rather dig in the dirt than give oral sex to an obnoxious rich guy, but she didn't say it out loud. Marissabelle was Anna's relative, and truthfully, what did Marley know about it? She'd never done back-breaking manual labor or been destitute.

"Most of those women considered themselves lucky. You ever go hungry, Marley? You ever live on the streets? That's what Marissabelle was protecting herself and her son from, and it was a position that had its drawbacks, sure, but it had some perks too. Parties, gowns, pretty manners, and believe it or not, there are some women who like sex, like the games they can play with men, like the pleasure they can take for themselves."

"I can't imagine enjoying sex when a man is paying you for it."

Anna stared at her, her eyes dark as granite. "Then you don't understand the power of sex. You don't understand power itself. And you definitely don't understand the freedom of letting yourself do what your body was designed for, without worry, without fear, without restraint. Just diving in and doing it."

Marley hugged her knees harder. "No," she whispered. "I don't understand that." She didn't do anything without fear, without restraint, without weighing the pros and cons and stressing over the outcome, the future, her feelings, and everyone else in the universe's feelings about her, her actions, their actions, and why the Earth was round. Freedom? She had no idea what that was.

"So Marissabelle met Damien at a ball?" She could see it in her mind's eye, the beautiful women, the candlelight, fluttering fans, flirtation, men moving confidently and arrogantly, sure of their place in the world, their worth.

"Yes, but not for a while. First she was one man's mistress for six months, but he was fickle and lost interest.

She wasn't sorry to see him go because he was quick with his fist. Then she was with another man for near a year and he was nice enough, if a bit boring in the bedroom, but he dropped dead one day and she was back at the beginning, back to the balls."

"It sounds scary, to always have to rely on someone else for your security, never really knowing if you'll wind up with a nice guy or not."

"I suppose so." Anna grinned at her, her dentures shifting a little in her mouth. "But not so different than dating. You're taking a mighty big risk of being annoyed or bored when you say yes to a man asking you out."

"That's true." Then again, Marley didn't even date anymore, so what could she claim to know about it?

"Marissabelle had heard about Damien du Bourg, and she had avoided meeting him. It was said he was strange, eccentric, reckless to the point of suicidal. He had volunteered to bury the dead in the last cholera epidemic the year before, and they said he worked nonstop, burying bodies all day for two months. They said he stank like death, like dirt, and he never once seemed afraid he'd catch the sickness. He never complained, never asked for payment, just stood side by side with working men dealing with all the bodies that stacked up higher and higher every day. They started to call him Death's Door because it seemed he was always knocking on it and yet never took that last step. He drank heavily, he raced his horse, his carriage, he wrestled alligators in the swamp, and had a collection of cottonmouth snakes. Marissabelle thought he sounded strange, a bit off. Not quite right in the head."

"I would have to agree with that. He definitely sounds a little strange." And creepy. Though she supposed there was something to be admired about a man who risked his own life to bury dead strangers.

"But one night she accidentally caught his eye, and he asked her to dance. He didn't say much, didn't give her all that flattery, some real, some false, that the other men did. He just held her, just stared down at her, unsmiling, just let her see that he was a man who could match her, pride to pride, passion to passion, wit to wit. She wanted him physically, was drawn to him in a way she didn't understand. It was like being reeled in on a hook by an expert fisherman, and when the dance ended and he said, 'Come home with me,' she didn't hesitate. She just said yes. There are some men like that, you know, or sometimes it's just that one man with that one woman . . . the two together are combustible. Irresistible to each other."

While it was a stretch to think she was irresistible to Damien, Marley certainly understood how Marissabelle had felt. She was flopping around like a fish on a hook herself. "So her time with him was passionate?"

"Very much so. Their relationship was passionate, angry, demanding, sweaty, powerful, lusty. The rumors were true. He was strange and reckless, but that excited her, challenged her. She was an enthusiastic lover, and he gave her a house."

"And?"

"And that's it. End of story."

"That can't be the end of the story. Did they stay together forever? Did they have children? Were they in love with each other?"

"No, no, and no." Anna sighed. "But I'm tired now, Marley. If you have any more questions, maybe you could come on back tomorrow and we'll chat again."

Marley looked at Anna, saw how pale and drawn she was, and felt terrible for not noticing sooner. "Oh, I'm so sorry. Do you want to take a nap? I can help you into the house. I didn't mean to push, Anna."

"Not your fault I get tired so damn easily." Anna shifted in the chair and grimaced. "Do yourself a favor and never get old."

Marley laughed. "Okay, I'll work on that." She stood up. "Is there anything I can get you? Water?"

"Just go on back to the big house and I think I will take a nice nap. You come on back tomorrow and we'll talk." Anna stood up and tugged her shirt down lower. "And you can gossip to me and tell me what sex with this Damien du Bourg is like."

This wizened old lady was way more liberal than Marley was used to. Her cheeks were burning. "I'm not sleeping with Damien."

"But you will be. You will be."

❦

Suddenly I understood that if I wanted to gain that which I sought, I had to let Damien know what I was seeking. With heart racing and palms damp, I sat on his lap and said, "Rosa appeared to be enjoying your attentions."

He studied me. "Perhaps she was faking her desire, as whores are wont to do."

I remembered her face, thrown back to the rain. "I do not believe that. And I . . . I want to understand . . . I want to feel that pleasure myself."

Bracing myself for laughter, for sneering criticism, for mockery, I straightened my spine and met the steady gaze of my husband. He did none of those. Instead he shifted me on his lap so that my thigh made contact with his arousal.

"If it is merely pleasure you seek, I can certainly give you that, Marie." His hand moved up my back, petting very lightly, very relaxed. "So what did you see between Rosa and myself that appealed to you?"

I considered, then gave my answer. "That you seemed to be on equal footing."

"Your answer fascinates me." Damien brushed his lips over mine. "You are fascinating me."

Then he lifted his glass to my lips and tipped it. "Have a sip so that we may be on equal footing."

The liquid slid into my mouth, cool and hot at the same time, burning my throat and fanning out into my limbs like fiery fingers. I felt warmth most acutely between the thighs, and I shifted, anxious, uncomfortable, ready for whatever was to come next.

"Now take off your chemise, since I am not wearing a shirt, so we are further on equal footing."

I struggled out of my sleeping jacket, Damien not moving to assist me. When it was pooled around my waist, I took a deep breath. How to describe the anticipation? The realization that somehow, this time, it was completely different. My body had awakened, was clamoring for the attention of my husband.

When Damien's mouth touched my lips, my neck, the top of my bosom, it generated a wholly different reaction than previous times. Whereas before I'd felt only fear, discomfort, and embarrassment, now my skin tingled, my nipples beaded, my mouth went hot, my breath rapid. My hands found their way to Damien's chest and pressed against his firm, warm flesh. The strength there excited me, intrigued me. I stroked all around and down even lower while he continued to administer his attentions to me for long and luxurious minutes.

Damien set me on my feet, and when he demanded I remove my shift, I did so with a shocking pride for the desire I saw in his eyes. I peeled my clothing right off, letting it drop to my ankles, and stood at excited attention while he took in my appearance, eyes rolling up and down.

"Since we are on equal footing, you must do to me as I do to you, wouldn't you agree?" he asked as he removed his trousers.

I nodded in consent. I had never seen Damien completely without clothing, and the sight of him, standing in front of the windows, bathed in summer moonlight, limbs strong and sleek, manhood rising toward me, set me speechless. He was astonishingly handsome, and I felt a greedy pride, a vanity, a triumph that he was my husband.

On the bed together, Damien's touch was slow and easy, as if we had no particular destination in mind, as if strolling along the lane and partaking of the view was as pleasurable as arriving. His mouth, his hands, his tongue, moved with agonizing slowness over me, caressing and teasing and pleasuring me in the most intimate of manners. My body succumbed to the assault most cheerfully, with a total surrender that astonished me. I was restless, eager, unfulfilled, suffering in my ecstasy, and when he did that which he had never done before, I came to the full and complete understanding of how pleasure can shatter and drown and drive all reason from your head.

Do you know that sensation, Angelique, when a man slides his tongue into that hot, eager space between your thighs? That is what I am talking about, that is the way a man can draw a woman down into his carnal oblivion, with an acute sensation so tight and furious that it catapults you face first into sin, where the only concern is physical fulfillment.

Perhaps I should not say this to you, even in a letter I shall never post. Perhaps I am, only because I want to shock you like I have shocked myself. This is further evidence of my moral decline, as is the very real and moist arousal I am experiencing right now just from the memory of that night. I should feel shame, yet I am thinking of my actions then not with disgust, but with longing.

Equally wicked and yet so very titillating is the memory that after I had clawed myself back to reality, I went down with quite eager anticipation when Damien guided my head and asserted that it was my turn to express my support of equality.

You know, of course, what I did the following day, don't you? You are cringing, Angelique, wishing I had remembered myself. But the plain and unembellished truth is that I liked what my husband had done to me well enough that I went back to his chamber the next night for more. Not once was conception of a child on my mind. No, I went simply for the sheer pleasure of it.

Damien smiled when he saw me pass into his chamber. "It is quite early. I just retired," he said.

"I'm accustomed to keeping early hours." Can you imagine that I stood there and lied so coolly, so easily?

He didn't believe me, though. Damien laughed. "So you wanted to speak to me before you sleep? Perhaps you wish to discuss your wardrobe needs or the dinner menus?"

I moved in front of him and his hand went into my hair, wrapping around and around with a possessiveness that I enjoyed. "No. I wanted to see if I might join you in your bed again this evening. That is, if it isn't entirely too soon and my performance last night wasn't too vexing."

He kissed my earlobe and whispered, "I do believe you are flirting with me, and I confess I find it arousing. Trust me, ma cherie, it is not too soon, and your performance was of a fine quality. You were very eager to explore, and open to instruction. I couldn't ask for any more than that, and I do believe if you remove that shift, we can further your education."

That he did, that night, and the many that followed. Damien showed me that pleasure need not be found only in bed lying supine with a man in the position of domination. That as many ways as the body could shift and twist and bend, we could be joined. He showed me how very much might occur before the actual act of copulation, with skilled fingers, mouth, and tongue, and how delicious it all could be.

He even had a looking glass brought in to show me what I looked like astride his masculinity. It was a shocking, tantalizing image of myself, cheeks blooming with color, hair loose and wild, wet strands stuck to my forehead. My eyes were bright and feverish, skin pink with exertion, nipples rosy and taut, my shoulders rolling back, thighs spread on either side of him.

"*You are beautiful,*" *he told me, catching my eye in the reflection of the glass.* "*Absolutely stunning.*"

And I saw that he was right, that I looked like a woman very well pleased with herself and her husband, and it made me shatter in ecstasy over him.

Chapter Eleven

Damien knew that Marley was in the bathroom. He'd been waiting close to an hour for her to emerge, but the door stayed closed. It was dark outside, and when he walked around the perimeter, he moved in and out of the glow of light from the half dozen windows, listening for the sound of the shower. He didn't hear anything, and he was starting to get concerned.

He had the feeling she'd spent the afternoon with the old woman, since he'd seen her returning to the house from that direction. God only knew what tales Marley had heard, what twisted falsehoods and exaggerated dramas she'd been entertained with. Marley didn't strike him as the unpredictable or hysterical type, but he couldn't imagine what she was doing in there, and the windows were all shielded with plantation shutters.

Except for the transom.

Damien eyed it. It was a good eight feet up, over the door. Striding back to the garden, he grabbed a rusty chair and hauled it over. He climbed up on it and looked in the window, which was dusty and warped, but not completely opaque. It gave him a muted view, but he could still see everything inside the bathroom.

What his roaming gaze landed on nearly made him fall off the chair. Marley was naked in the bathtub, her hair piled up on her head in a messy heap, her nipples breaking the surface of the water and deflating bubbles, her toes clenching the bottom rim of the deep soaker tub. She had pulled a little table over next to the tub and had put a bottle of water on it. There was something in her hand, a letter or a manuscript, and she was obviously reading it, her lips moving slightly.

Damien felt punched with desire, smacked in the chest, the gut, the groin, an erection springing up painfully and aggressively. Marley looked pink and lush and warm, and he wanted to slide his hands over her water-slick skin and dip his fingers into her moist inner thighs. He wanted to take his hard cock and shove it inside her, joining himself with her, watching her eyes roll back, listening to her cries of delight.

Her eyes always watched him too closely, filled with compassion, confusion, pleading. He wanted to rip those emotions out of her and replace them with hot, eager, selfish lust for him.

He couldn't penetrate her, of course. To do that would be to completely lose himself in the Grigori curse, his servitude. But he could pleasure her. Could relieve Marley of all her worries, her burdens, for a few minutes.

Damien climbed down off the chair, shoved it aside, and reached for the doorknob.

It twisted open when he tried it.

※

Marley was feeling relaxed, languid, aroused. The bath water was warm and silky on her skin from the bath oil she had poured into it. The claw-foot tub was deep, and curved so that she could rest in the perfect reclining position. Damien hadn't prepared her for the reality of the bathroom. He had made it sound like he'd thrown a water closet together out of a dilapidated old kitchen. In truth, it was a twenty-by-twenty luxury bath, complete with a four-head tiled shower, a dressing area, four sinks, and the impressive tub she was soaking in.

There were baskets with towels, trays full of bath beads and oils, bottles of water, and even a wine rack. If a house was only going to have one bathroom, this was the kind to have.

Pushing her sweaty hair back off her forehead, she took a sip of her water and sighed. She hadn't felt this calm since before she'd gotten the e-mail from Lizzie over a week earlier. The water was lulling her, the scented candles that she'd lit on the counters soothing.

And the latest words written by Marie were intriguing her, and to be honest, arousing her. The newly awakened passion in the wife of the first Damien du Bourg leapt from the page, shocking Marley at the same time it stirred her own body to life. Thoughts of Marissabelle, of Damien's party, of her own sense of sexual repression, together with the triumphant tone of Marie's words, had Marley's nipples hardening, her breath quickening. Her desire was climbing to levels she could not ignore, aching needs so acute she could no longer pretend they didn't exist. They did, and she wanted to explore and appease them one by one.

If Damien made any sort of overture toward her, she would give in, embrace what Anna had spoken of—sex for the sheer pleasure of it. The idea had a smug sort of boldness to it as she rested naked in the warm tub. Setting down Marie's letter, careful to place it on the table away from the water and cover it with the plastic bag, Marley closed her eyes and pushed the last bit of bubbles up to her chest, brushing them over her nipples.

The ache was unbearable. It had been so long since

she'd had an orgasm, so long since she'd allowed herself any sort of release. Her palms moved again over her tight beaded nipples, and her thighs clenched against the answering echo from her swollen clitoris. Her skin felt slick, and it was easy, so easy to just shift her hand around, cup her breasts, tease her nipples, glide down through the warm water, and maneuver her middle finger into her curls.

She was shocked at herself, waiting for the self-consciousness to arrive, waiting for the desire to deflate, leaving her embarrassed and reaching for a towel. Masturbation had always felt shameful to her, and she had tread lightly around it, acted quickly in the dark when she couldn't resist, then hurried to cover up what she had done, but this time those feelings weren't arriving. She felt excited, her body felt good, and she explored for the first time with a slow curiosity, amazed at how a little shift here or there could change the whole tenor of intensity.

With her free hand she gripped the side of the tub so she could fully slide her finger inside herself, gasping at the sensation of cool in hot. Her breath was coming faster, and she picked up speed, in and out, discovering that the base of her finger could tease her clitoris, tripping off hot shocks of pleasure with each stroke.

Her back arching against the porcelain, Marley spread her knees farther and tested and teased, exploring and pleasing. Her body responded, tightened, ached, escalating swiftly and confidently, enjoying the attention. Breathing hard, she yanked her finger away, her thighs trembling, free hand white-knuckled on the tub. Amazing. She was already skirting the edge, and it felt good, too good to reach the end so quickly, and she wanted to draw it out a little, see how mindless she could make herself, see how desperate and aching she could become by her own touch, her own understanding of her body and desires.

She was reaching for her nipples, wanting to test them with squeezing and brushing, when she heard him.

"Don't stop."

Marley shrieked, her eyes flying open, legs jerking together, water sloshing over her chin. Damien was standing in the bathroom, four feet away from her, watching. His eyes were dark green, his jaw and shoulders rigid, a very obvious erection in his jeans.

Mortified, heart thumping wildly, Marley rolled onto her side, pressing her breasts and pelvis against the tub so he couldn't see her body. "What the hell are you doing in here?" she said, her voice high and shrill and shaking with embarrassment.

He started walking toward her and Marley gripped the tub tighter, wishing more than anything she weren't naked. With her right hand, she tried to gather bubbles to cover her butt. Maybe he hadn't been able to tell what she'd been doing.

"I'm watching you touch yourself."

Shit. "Well, stop it! That's rude." And humiliating, embarrassing, mortifying, Drano-drinking-suicide inspiring.

Damien picked up the little table and moved it out of the way. He crouched down next to her, face close, voice low and raspy. "No, I'm not going to leave because you look absolutely beautiful, and I have to watch you finish."

Marley gasped. She must look like a hooked trout, bug-eyed and mouth gaping, but he was on crack if he thought she was going to just keep going with an audience. "I don't think so."

"You have a choice. Either you can finish, or I'll do it for you."

No response came to mind. Marley wanted to tell him to get the hell out, that neither of them was going to be finishing her, but the words never formed. It seemed like she should be completely yanked out of the mood, that her arousal should have cooled, frozen out by mortification. But she was naked, her inner thighs were still wet, her hot nipples were pressing against the cold smooth tub, and Damien du Bourg was staring at her with a healthy dose of lust in his eyes.

She was still turned on, no doubt about it. But that didn't mean she could swallow that lump in her throat and give him an answer.

"You don't have a preference?" he asked, running his finger over her bottom lip. He gave her a light kiss, the pressure teasing, the tip of his tongue flitting in and out, before he pulled back. Marley gave a sigh of disappointment.

"If you can't, then I'll choose for you." He pushed on her shoulder, rolling her back into the water, the limp bubbles sloshing over her belly, clinging to her pubic hair. Marley grabbed the side with her right arm so she wouldn't entirely lose her balance and look like a rolling whale.

She tried to cover up, tried to fight panic, tried to shift so he couldn't see everything, but Damien gripped her arm and lifted it so she was exposed to him. Her breath caught, and she ignored her hair when it won the fight against her hairclip and oozed down her neck and into the water.

The moment strolled on and on, the only sound in the room her ragged breathing, Damien's steady breathing, the lapping of the water against the tub.

Then, still watching her, Damien took her hand and covered her middle finger with his mouth, burying her in the hotness, his tongue slipping and flicking along her skin. She shifted, startled, heat flooding her womb, wanting to pull away, wanting even more to stay. He took her now wet finger, his own over the top of it, and caressed around her nipple, down her belly, and without preamble, sank them both together into her moist body.

Instinctively, she clamped her legs closed. She couldn't do this. It was too much, too arrogant, too defiant for her and her natural, cringing modesty. With a force borne of desperation, she managed to free her finger from under his and grip the edge of the tub. "No, Damien, I can't."

The words were barely out of her mouth when his tongue laved across her nipple, nearly making her leap out of the tub. The hot taste of desire mingled with embarrassment in her mouth, and she fought the panic, wrestled it aside, so she could enjoy the pleasure he was bringing to her. His finger worked inside her, stroking with just the right speed, just the right pressure, just the right attention given to her hard clitoris, while his mouth did delicious and skilled things to her breasts. He licked and sucked, bit and tugged, until she was moaning, throwing her head back, letting her eyes drag half shut.

"If you can't, can I?" he asked.

"Yes," she said, not even hesitating. It was her choice, that was clear, and she was choosing to take what he was offering.

"Thank you," he said, before his mouth covered her nipple again.

That made Marley smile, that he acted like she was doing something for him instead of vice versa. But her grin dissolved into a groan when he pressed his thumb inside her.

"Oh, God," she said in utter delight, then was appalled at herself for using the name of the Lord in vain. Not just in vain, in sex. Her cheeks flushed, and she tried to back up, tried to move away, because this was wrong. It had to be wrong.

But his strong arms held her down as he leaned over her, his T-shirt brushing over her shoulder, his head bent to pleasure her breasts, his hair tickling her warm, sensitive flesh. He moved slowly, torturously, touching her everywhere, stroking and coaxing until she couldn't remember why she shouldn't do this, why she couldn't embrace the feelings he was stoking in her.

The room was humid, the candles sending thin ribbons

of smoke up because she hadn't trimmed the wicks, their flames casting a flickering light over Damien's face, over his stern jawbone, his straight nose, moist lips. A drop of water clung to his chin and she reached out, swiped it off, amazed at how gorgeous he was, how perfectly masculine, hard and fierce. Her gesture caught his attention, and he turned from her breasts to give her a searing kiss, hot and reckless, while his finger stopped gliding politely and instead thrust hard and demanding inside her.

While his mouth controlled hers, his free hand lifted her leg, hooked it over the edge of the tub. It lifted her backside and belly automatically, spread her thighs farther for him, and Marley gasped, grabbing at his shoulder. She wanted to tell him how that pressure felt, how his touch had her insensible, how she felt each stroke in every inch of her body, but there were no words. Her mind was wrapped up in pleasure, foggy and drunk with desire, and she clenched her legs, forced herself higher to meet him, to make his thumb go deeper.

But he pulled it out entirely and Marley yelled an involuntary, "No! Don't stop."

His answer was to bend over, cup her slick backside with his wet hands, and bury his mouth in her. The first touch of his tongue sent her jerking in ecstasy, nearly bucking him off, but he held on. The second touch, where he swirled over her clitoris, made her shudder, and the third, when he sucked, shot her into an orgasm.

It was a good one, the kind that hung on and on, clinging like the moss outside the window, digging in and staying, long after it could have dropped away. Marley heard the sounds that came from her mouth, saw the top of Damien's head, felt the hard tub against her shoulder, but it was through a haze, her mind separated from her body.

She swallowed hard as her cries petered off. Relaxing her legs and back, her butt automatically dropped down into the water. Damien got a faceful of water and she laughed, feeling exhilarated, bubbly, light-headed. "Sorry, my legs are like rubber. I couldn't hold them anymore."

He shook the droplets off and smiled at her. "That was worth getting a little wet."

Not sure what to say, Marley pushed the heavy, moist hanks of hair off her forehead and smiled. She let her body float a little in the water as she watched him watch her. He was stroking her knee, looking lazy and content, his forearm resting on the edge of the tub.

"Let me get you a towel."

"Thank you. I'm starting to shrivel." Marley was contemplating how courageous she actually was. That orgasm had bolstered her, made her feel less self-conscious, but she wasn't sure she could just stand up naked and climb out of the deep tub. That required lifting her leg a good bit higher than could possibly be attractive.

Damien opened one of the walnut built-in cabinets and removed a thick, fluffy towel and a terry cloth robe.

"This is a beautiful bathroom. It's like a spa in here."

"Complete with towel boy." He gave her a little bow and held the oversized buff-colored towel out to her.

Marley stood up and quickly grabbed the towel and wrapped herself in it so he couldn't see any personal parts. "You do that well, the bowing. I had no idea you could look so deferential. Or maybe it's more . . . lordly."

He bowed again, with a huge arm flourish. "If I can be of further assistance, I am yours to command, Mademoiselle. Otherwise, I will bid you *bonne nuit*."

That knocked the grin off her face as she struggled to slip the robe on over the towel. "You're leaving? You're not . . ." *Going to put it in?* was what she was thinking, but there was no way to say that without sounding tacky.

Damien shook his head. "No. Not tonight. That was all you needed."

She finally got the robe belted and yanked the towel out from the bottom, dragging it through the water before dropping it on the floor. "Oh." His frankness embarrassed her, but she also knew immediately he was right. She couldn't have handled any more at the moment. Sex would have been too intimate, too reaching, too emotional.

"Thank you."

"Pas de quoi." Damien took her hand and kissed the back of it.

"You're feeling very French tonight."

"Oui."

She laughed. "Do you really speak fluent French or are you just trying to impress me?"

"I learned French before English."

Marley stepped out of the tub, taking the hand that Damien offered to assist her. "You'll have to speak French sometime and make me swoon."

"Voulez-vous couchez avec moi?"

"Very funny." She rolled her eyes for effect, but his playfulness pleased her. It made her feel more comfortable with what he had just seen, what he had just done to her.

Damien laughed. "You seem to be the only person who ever finds me amusing."

Marley was touched by that and not sure why. But something about him spoke to her, went to places inside her soul he shouldn't, and she knew she was already slipping, already forgetting that she had to stay disconnected, that this was about freedom, not emotional entanglement.

"Maybe they don't see what I see." She lightly touched his chest, knowing she was too late. Just looking at him made her feel all gooey inside, an emotional hot fudge sundae.

His smile disappeared. He looked alarmed, and he grabbed her hand, pulled it down and away from him. "Or maybe you see what isn't there. Don't do it, Marley. Please don't."

"Don't what?"

"Feel sorry for me. Develop feelings for me. I can't return them."

She hadn't meant to go there, didn't want to ruin the evening by getting deep, but she couldn't resist asking, "Can't? Or won't?"

"Can't."

It wasn't a surprise, but it still pricked. "Okay. Duly noted. Now you can rest easy that I know the score. Whatever I do from here on out is with my eyes wide open."

Her assurances sounded defensive and she knew it.

Damien sighed. "Maybe this was a mistake."

The words sliced and burned, humiliated her. She was not some grasping, needy woman. She wasn't an obsessive stalker type imagining elaborate relationships that weren't there. Just because she liked him, and wanted to sleep with him, did not make her a risk to his perfectly structured world of superficial hedonism.

"Just leave, Damien. I'll see you tomorrow." Marley turned, scooping up the towel, staring hard at the tile floor as she tried to collect herself.

"I've upset you."

Um, hello? Give the man a gold star. "No, you've annoyed me, so go before I say something I'll truly regret."

He opened his mouth, then seemed to think better of it, which was a smart move on his part. If he said something stupid, she would be tempted to stuff the towel in his trap.

Instead, he just turned and left, closing the door softly behind him.

Marley sat on the edge of the tub and sighed.

Why did it feel like in trying to find her sister, she was slowly losing herself?

❧

Rosa was sitting on his couch when Damien got back to the *pigeonnier*, angry with himself, frustrated with his body for wanting Marley, for throbbing and pulsing with the need to take her. And he was frightened, scared at the look he had seen in Marley's eyes, and even more terrified by the way he had wanted it there, how he had felt a strange tremor of an echoing feeling in his own chest.

That was an absolute catastrophe.

He glared at Rosa, sitting cross-legged on the sofa, watching a DVD on his portable player. "Go away. I need you here tonight like a fucking hole in my head."

"Nice hard-on." She glanced at his jeans. "Why do you torture yourself like this? I could hear her moaning from fifty feet away but you don't allow yourself to participate? You need counseling. You're going to burst or something."

He did feel like with one false move his entire body might explode, but so far he had a lid on it. The body he could handle, the heart he wasn't so damn sure about. "Then you'd better leave. You don't want to get hit when I go off."

Tossing the DVD player aside, Rosa stood up. She was wearing shorts and a blazer and she actually looked worried about him. If Damien didn't hate her for the lying, conniving demon she was, he'd be touched by her concern.

"Stop this, Damien. You're going to make yourself insane. Just let me help you." Her hand skimmed over his thigh.

"Help me how?" He knew what she meant and he was too exasperated to dance around it. "You think we should have sex? I think you say that about once a month."

"And you always say no, which is stupid. Come on, we know each other inside and out, and I can just take the edge off for you."

"What you want is to control me."

"So what's wrong with that?" She smirked at him.

Damien suddenly wanted to yank that smugness off

her face. "Fine. You want to help me out, you can go down on me. That would be a huge help and I really appreciate the offer."

Her jaw dropped. "You want me to give you head?"

"Yes." He moved to undo his jeans, taking a sick delight in the confusion and alarm on her face. "You're better than nothing, and like you said, we do know each other well."

She pulled away and made a face at him. "Oh, gee, thanks, that's real flattering. Forget it. I'm not going to do it if you have that kind of an attitude."

He'd thought so. Damien felt a certain smugness of his own. If Rosa wanted to play games, he could play them right back.

"Go ask Marley to do it, I'm sure she'd jump at the chance. She's totally hot for you."

That ruined his triumph at besting Rosa. "Leave Marley alone," he said through gritted teeth.

Rosa stared at him, then burst out laughing. "Oh, this is too precious. You've fallen for her, haven't you?"

It was hard to shrug casually when his heart was pounding and he had broken out in a sweat. He refused to fall for Marley. He absolutely would not allow it. "Don't be ridiculous. We both know I'm immune to selfless feelings."

"That's true," she said cheerfully. "You are pretty much a gigantic bastard. I like that side of you better than this weird self-flagellating Damien you've turned into. I admit, when I met you, I thought you could use a good smack of humility, but I never wanted you to become a boring exercise in self-restraint. You're like a poster child for suffering. The father doesn't like it."

Damien clenched his fists. "I'm doing what I was told to do. I create an environment of sin for others. Women take their clothes off for me. That's all I agreed to do, and that's all he's getting from me."

Rosa crossed her arms and stared at the wall, at his

painting of *The Punishment of Lust*. "And every time you thumb your nose at the Grigori, every time you stand up in defiance and refuse to accept what you are, I get a stripe on my back for the mistake I made."

Damien felt the blood drain from his face. She couldn't be saying what he thought she was. "What do you mean?" He was hoping he was wrong, very wrong in how he was interpreting her statement.

But Rosa turned to him, her chin lifted defiantly. "I mean I get beaten when you disobey. I am the one who made you, you are my mistake, and I'm not allowed to forget that."

The guilt dropped onto his already heavy burden and Damien felt sick, his hand shaking, his gut twisted and gnarled as he realized how truly vile he was and how much pain he had caused in his lifetime.

"Rosa . . . I didn't know. I'm sorry."

She bristled. "I don't need your pity, any more than you want mine. It's the way it is, and it's the way it always will be until you accept who and what you are."

That was what he was afraid of, his biggest fear. That someday he wouldn't be able to fight, to resist, to bear the burden any longer, and he would give in to what he was, what he had become. "Why don't I get punished? I've never even met your father, and he's definitely never punished me."

"How do you know?" she asked, grabbing her beaded purse off the sofa and sticking her hand through the circular handle. "You don't know anything."

"Explain it to me. Let me understand so I can help you." He'd never liked Rosa, but sometimes he suspected that was because they were so very alike. And he didn't want Rosa to take any more punishment on his behalf. Hiding behind a woman's skirts was cowardly, and while he was a bastard, he wasn't a coward.

"Oh, fuck off, Damien. I don't need your help." She

whirled around and stomped toward the door. As she blew past his desk, the wastebasket erupted into flames. The white ceramic bowl he dropped his keys into went spiraling off the end table and crashed on the wood floor. And as she passed through the front door, a crack of lightning illuminated the yard as punctuation to her anger.

Damien poured water on his wastebasket and marveled at how quickly his evening had gone downhill.

He'd offended Marley and pissed off Rosa. Two for two. He wasn't just a bastard, he was an accomplished bastard.

Raucous laughter filled the room. Damien glanced over at the movie Rosa had been watching on his DVD player. *Dangerous Liaisons*. That was ironic.

❧

Rosa flew across the yard, angry tears blurring her vision. She had always had a fondness for Damien, had always been bothered by the fact that he didn't take what she offered so freely. But she had shrugged that off.

Pity could not be disregarded. She didn't want him to feel sorry for her, ever. That look he'd given her had changed her mind. She had been about to tell him the truth, that her father's plan to punish Damien was already in play. That it involved Marley and her sister, the very stupid and slutty blonde Rosa had met back at the beginning of the summer.

Rosa had been planning to warn Damien, risk herself yet again for him, but now she hoped he'd choke on his pity. He had never appreciated her enough, and now he was going to pay for that serious error in judgment.

Chapter Twelve

Within a matter of a few short weeks, I was with child again.
We celebrated that fact with an excess of wine, food, and
conduct inappropriate for the dining room. But as we were
alone, and the walnut table was so very large, Damien
didn't see that it mattered ever so much.

I was inclined to agree, as I would have agreed with
nearly any suggestion of his during that time. I was drunk on
his attention, giddy with anticipation, heady with the freedom of loosening all my moral and personal constraints and
embracing my lust. I reveled in pleasure, morning, noon,
and night. I could not get enough of Damien, and could be
coaxed by him into all manner of misconduct. He could tug
me out onto the balcony of his bedchamber sans clothing,
tease up my skirt in the drawing room midday, bend me over
the bed for a hearty good-morning, disrupt my bath with
soapy, helpful hands. I allowed it, liked it all.

It is astonishing to me how quickly I was altered, how
attention from my husband and exploration of our mutual
physical fulfillment could arouse such pride, such vanity,
such haughty self-assurance. I was a different woman than I
had been when I married Damien—now I was triumphant,

*quite pleased with myself, with my husband, with my place
in the world.*

*We were entertaining again as well, and I gloried in it,
smiling and reveling in all the comments on how my looks
were much improved, and the felicitations for my renewed
health. For the first time since my arrival in New Orleans, I
sensed jealousy from some of the women, and it thrilled me.
I was proud, pleased, feverish, my sensual joy bounding up
and spilling out of me in laughter and dancing, my conversations with the ladies verbal sparring matches that I often
won. For the first time I partook of the gossip, delivered my
own barbs and sallies, and enjoyed the admiration I re-
ceived for my cruel wit.*

*It seems now almost as if I took on my husband's person-
ality as my own, that his attentions overtook me, consumed
me, infected me with his moral flaws. Or perhaps he merely
drew out whatever defects a quiet life in the convent school
had hidden. It certainly did not take much for me to embrace
passion and to become infected with the petty feelings of
envy, jealousy, and loathing.*

*At one of our dinner parties during this period in our
marriage, I slipped into the hall to confer with the cook and
stumbled across Damien and Mademoiselle Delerue, her
hand on his chest, her mouth close to his as she giggled.
Damien looked over at me, a smile on his face, his eyebrow
rising. His expression looked bemused, as if he had found
himself cornered by the enterprising miss and hadn't yet
managed to extract himself.*

*He didn't look guilty of an indiscretion and he was not
embracing her in return. All anger and disgust I felt was directed at her, and yes, at myself. Had I been a better wife, I
would have dissuaded this type of behavior long ago. But my
inattention had practically invited other women to try their
hand at dalliance with Damien.*

"Oh," she said with a giggle. "Madame du Bourg. Your

husband was just kind enough to show me the ancestral portraits."

"Those are upstairs," I said flatly, overcome by the sudden urge to yank every last one of her golden curls from her youthful and stupid head. "A part of this house you shall never see."

"Well." She sniffed a little, her white silk gown rustling as she drew back. "How ungenerous of you."

"Perhaps. But I don't share well with others, so if you would kindly keep your interest fixed on what's occurring in my drawing room, I would be much obliged."

She did not even pretend to misunderstand. "Oh, what do you care? The servants talk and we all know you don't even have a relationship with your husband."

Clearly, her information was old, dating back from the time after I had lost my first child. How dare she imply Damien didn't desire me? Anger made me indiscreet. "Apparently your servants should not serve as spies, as their information is simply inaccurate. If you disbelieve me, my husband and I would be happy to give you a demonstration of our relationship right here."

She gasped, and Damien let out a loud laugh. Mademoiselle Delerue lifted her chin. "You are vulgar and I refuse to listen to this anymore."

"Then keep your designs and flirtations away from my husband, and I will not have to offend you with my vulgarity any longer."

She made a miffed sound through her nose and returned to the drawing room.

Damien grinned at me, putting his arm around my waist. "You are quite commanding when you wish to be. I find it highly arousing."

I pretended to show disdain. "Really, you find everything arousing, so this is hardly a compliment."

He nuzzled my ear, starting a slow burn that burst into

flames inside my body. *"I find everything about you arous-*
ing, wife, and if you want compliments, steal away to the
music room with me for a few minutes and I shall compli-
ment you profusely from your head to your toes."

"They'll notice we're gone!" I protested, while secretly
thinking it was rather a marvelous idea. It was always
pleasant to know that Damien desired me, that he could not
resist me even during a dinner party, that he no longer had
to seek out women such as Rosa of the red dress for his gratification. I, his wife, could be everything he required.

"Not for five minutes. They'll never miss us. Come now,
you can be commanding, ordering me about, and I shall
shower you with pretty words of devotion."

"You are shameful," I said, with so little censure that I
was already smiling, and kissing him in return.

"Absolutely. Never doubt that."

He pulled me to the music room and I confess I followed
most eagerly, assisting him most obligingly by lifting my
skirts before bracing my hands on the pianoforte.

Mademoiselle Delerue is a conniving young thing, no
better than she should be, and I was certain she had cornered Damien largely against his will. Yet the same could
not be said for our scullery maid.

I was walking along the path that cut between the kitchen
and the house, inhaling the thick, heavy scents of baking
bread and jasmine. The air was humid and I felt warm, but
not unpleasantly so. The cruel heat of August had given way
to September, and I was inclined to forgive the climate its
vagaries for once.

When I turned the corner and came into the back garden,
my contentment fled. Damien and the fleshy maid were in an
embrace, her cap askew, her dress down around her waist,
showing plump, heavy breasts. Damien's mouth was on one,
suckling, his hand grinding into her bottom.

Anger such as I'd never experienced before exploded in

me, shattering like a champagne flute tossed on a stone floor.
"Forgive the intrusion," I said in a shrill voice.

The maid jerked back, cheeks flushing. "Oh, Madame . . .
oh."

I stepped forward, and without thought, without hesita-
tion, I struck my hand across her cheek, slapping her soundly
for her insolence. She let out a startled cry and stumbled
backward, hand on her cheek, eyes pooling with tears, bosom
bouncing in her tawdry half-dressed state. I felt no sympathy,
no remorse.

"Get back to the kitchen. If I ever see you with my hus-
band again, I'll turn you out and you'll be forced to hawk
yourself on the streets of New Orleans."

With increased sobbing, she turned and ran up the path,
fussing to fix her dress as she went.

Damien wiped his bottom lip. "That was rather harsh,
my love."

"Do not speak to me." I whirled, intent on going back
to the house, my fury forcing tears into my own eyes. I had
foolishly thought that since Damien and I had entered
this new period in our marriage, he had been content with
me. That he enjoyed my attentions and needed no other.
I thought, perhaps, even that he and I were starting to care
for one another. That we laughed together and chatted
together and shared great pleasure together and that
it meant something. That we were husband and wife, to-
gether.

Now he had taken that notion and spat on it.

Damien caught me by the elbow. "Do not tell me you are
jealous. That was nothing, Marie, it meant nothing. She is
such an ugly plump thing, I felt sorry for her."

I drew up short. "There are other ways to show compas-
sion for one you pity!"

To my mortification, the tears were escaping and rushing
down my cheeks. Damien wiped my face and tried to kiss

me. I raised my hand to slap him away, irrational and volatile. He of course simply grabbed my hand and held it.

"You don't want to do that."

"Yes, I do." I yanked my hand hard, struggling to free it, my slippers sliding on the bricks, unbalancing me.

Damien grabbed me to prevent a fall. "Don't be angry. She is nothing, but you, you are my wife."

I struggled, but he merely held me tighter, his embrace strong, his will unbendable. "Listen to me. You have my name, my heir, and I believe, a piece of my heart. She is nothing, while you are everything."

Then he was kissing me and I let him. Do you understand? I let him. I heard his words, reveled in their meaning, embraced them and their implications with greedy, defiant selfishness. Desperately I wanted to believe him, to feel secure in my position, his affection. I felt his touch, welcomed it, and my anger blended with passion as he kissed me. But my haughty pride, so very much increased of late, still stinging from the sight of the unattractive maid, compelled me to fan the flames of our argument by attempting to jerk back once more.

I believe I knew what I was doing. I believe a certain small part of me knew he would not let me go, and I wanted that confirmation. I wanted him to fight for me, to feel the anger that I did.

He didn't disappoint. Damien held on, tighter, and walked me backward, almost shoving, until my back hit the wall of the house. His hand went in my hair and he kissed me harshly, fervently, hotly, and his fingers curled around the careful arrangement Gigi had created. With rough yanks and tugs, he disassembled the coiffure while his mouth raced over my neck. I leaned against the wall, assaulted with my own desire, my own eagerness.

"My wife," he said, looking into my eyes as he tore down the front of my gown. "My Marie."

My head was smacking into the house, my breasts

pinched from the gown, my leg twisted awkwardly on the bricks, and Damien's touches were rough, demanding, his kisses deep and smothering. But it excited me, aroused me, heightened my awareness of each touch, left no time to recover before the next kiss or suckle or pinch assaulted my senses.

When he lifted my skirt, shifted aside my pantaloons, and surged into me, I welcomed his roughness, enjoyed his possessive pounding.

"I own you," he said, thrusting me against the wall, my shoulders scraping and my head colliding with the solid structure. I cared not. I was tight and tense with pleasure, consumed by him, of him, for him.

"And you own me, Marie. Never forget that. I am yours."

I reached my peak as his hot seed exploded inside of me, our bodies, our lives, sinfully and passionately entwined.

That night I awoke with the moon high and my linens soaked with blood.

⁂

Marley spent the day wandering around the French Quarter, taking a walking tour of St. Louis Cemetery #1, browsing antiques, and snapping pictures in Jackson Square after grabbing a trio of beignets at Café du Monde. She hadn't planned the day out, but when she'd woken up, she knew she had to get away from Damien, or more accurately, away from her own feelings about him.

He had warned her not to fall for him, but the ugly reality was that Marley was sure she already had. If he could only see his face when he talked about his wife, about his home, his parents, the way he hid the pain in his eyes with a careless smile, he would understand how it had happened. She looked at him and she wanted to soothe him, to hold him, fix him, make him see that the rewards of love were worth the risk of being hurt.

She was the hopeless optimist, he was the jaded cynic.

Not a good combination, but an obvious one.

Staring through a window at a display of elaborate Mardi Gras masks, Marley marveled at the intricacy of the feathers, the beading, the rich and vibrant colors. They were beautiful, extravagant, expensive. All designed to hide your face, to allow the wearer to become someone else for a few hours, to say and do anything without regard for the consequences.

Her cell phone rang in her purse, and Marley reached for it, hoping it was her cousin Rachel. The number on the phone was a local number, so she flipped it open, steeling herself for an uncomfortable conversation with Damien. "Hello?"

"Hey, Mar! What's up?"

"Lizzie?" Marley gripped the phone tighter, her heart dropping into her stomach. "Are you alright?"

"Of course I'm alright, why wouldn't I be?"

Her sister sounded puzzled, and Marley's overwhelming relief quickly gave way to frustration. All this time, all this fear made ridiculous with one careless sentence from her thoughtless sister. "No one knew where you were. Have you called Rachel? We were worried about you."

"Oh. Sorry. But why would you be worried about me? I'm fine. In fact, I'm fabulous. I met this guy . . . he is amazing. He's perfect, and I've finally figured out who I am, you know what I mean? It's like I can define myself in him." Lizzie gave a dreamy sigh in Marley's ear.

Marley felt slapped. All the months, all this worry, and Lizzie had just run off with another guy? Her voice sounded sharp and shrill, even to her own ears. "Why haven't you checked on Sebastian? Let someone know where to reach you?"

"He's fine with Rachel. God, you sound so pissy. I haven't talked to you in months and you're already yelling at me."

"Because I was worried about you! I thought you were dead in a ditch and you're just off playing house with the flavor of the week? What if something had happened to your son?"

"Nothing happened, obviously," Lizzie said with annoyance. "Give me a break."

Marley closed her eyes and prayed. She had never been so angry with her sister in her entire life. This was too much. This was beyond what she could tolerate. "Where are you, Lizzie?"

"Shreveport. Where are you, Miss Piss?"

"New Orleans."

"No shit? Wow, that's cool. Let's get together this weekend. Alex and I are going to a party at a plantation on Saturday. Where are you staying? I'll ask Alex if he minds dropping me off at your hotel so we can have dinner together. I'm so impressed, Mar. You never go anywhere. Are you actually sightseeing by yourself?"

Marley looked out on Royal Street, her temples throbbing, neck tightening. As a matter of fact, she was sightseeing. But she wanted to throttle her sister six ways to Sunday. How could she not miss her son? "I came down here looking for you at Rosa de Montana when we didn't hear from you. I'm staying there."

"You're staying there? Ohmigod, that's so hot. Now I will definitely see you on Saturday, because that's the party we're going to. So what do you think of Damien? I can't believe you managed an invite to stay in his house. That is so cool. Has he gotten in your pants yet? I know you have like a vault door over your zipper, but if anyone can get past your security, it's Damien du Bourg." Lizzie giggled.

Marley wanted to throw up, forehead clammy, stomach hot and roiling. Lizzie thought Marley was a joke, her prudishness a challenge to a man like Damien.

Maybe she was right.

Damien had barely put any effort into the chase—one dinner and an invitation to stay at the plantation—and she'd already let him touch her.

But worse than any of that was her realization that Lizzie didn't really care about Marley's feelings. Nor did Lizzie care about her son, and a piece of Marley's love for her sister shriveled up and died.

"I was spending a lot of money on the hotel, and Damien was nice enough to offer me a place to stay," she said, crossing her arm over her stomach. She suddenly felt cold, despite the balmy evening warmth.

"Whatever." Lizzie snorted. "If you believe that, you are so dumb."

Dumb was exactly how she felt. And numb. "Call Rachel, okay? Give her a number where she can reach you."

"Fine." There was a rustling, than Lizzie said, "Gotta go, sweetie. See you Saturday. Love you!"

"I . . ." Marley wasn't sure what she was going to say, but Lizzie didn't wait for her answer anyway. She had already hung up.

There was a row of tables inside a bakery across the street, the gallery windows and doors thrown open to the fresh air. Marley walked over, ordered a cup of coffee, sat down, and fought the lump in her throat. The sounds of the cars, the people, all rushed around her, but she felt disconnected, goose bumps on her arms, a hard icicle of pain stabbing into her chest.

She sat there for an hour, noiseless tears creeping down her cheeks, until the coffee she hadn't touched was cold and the counter staff started giving her curious looks. They didn't know what she was doing. Marley didn't either.

The sobs came in the car during the hour-long drive back, ugly loud tears that shook her shoulders, blinded her, took over so violently that she parked at the gates of

Rosa de Montana and let them have their way with her. Ten minutes later, when she pulled around by the house, Damien came out of the *pigeonnier* and opened her car door.

"Marley. I didn't expect you to be gone so long. I was getting worried about you."

She stepped out, knowing she looked like hell, knowing she'd never be able to hide the puffy eyes, splotchy cheeks, and sniffling nose. She didn't care.

"What happened? What's the matter?" He took in her appearance, put his hands on her shoulders and pulled her into his chest. "Marley . . . did the police find Lizzie?"

Did they find Lizzie's body? She could hear the unspoken words as clearly as if he'd yelled them. In some ways, she'd been better prepared to hear that horrible conclusion than what she'd actually heard.

The strong arms around her were comforting, and his chest was hard, solid, smelling like cigar. "Do you smoke?" she asked him, surprised by that. She'd never seen him smoking, but the rich tobacco scent seemed right on him, and she wanted to bury her nose in the cotton of his shirt, absorb him into her.

"On occasion. When I'm worried or thinking hard." He squeezed her waist. "What the hell's going on, Marley?"

She pulled back and looked up at him. "Lizzie called me. She's fine and can't imagine why I was worried about her."

"Oh, shit. I'm sorry . . . I mean, I'm glad she's alright, but I'm so sorry that . . ."

"That's she's a selfish bitch? Yeah, me too." Marley felt tears pooling in her eyes again. "She didn't even ask about Sebastian. How can she not wonder about him? Miss him? I don't give a shit what she does to me, but when she neglects him, she hurts that little boy. He's just a baby, for God's sake. I'm so . . ." She shook her head, pulling away from him.

"Disgusted? Angry? You have every right to be."

"You said it would be like this, that Lizzie was just off screwing around, and you were right. Lizzie said I'm dumb, and she's right too. I am. I'm dumb enough to keep thinking that she'll start caring about something other than herself." When he reached for her again, Marley backed up, tears gushing again, blinding her. She twisted her hair into a bun and looked away, out toward the green hill that hid the river. "I hate feeling like this, so stupid, so ashamed."

"Why the hell should you feel bad?" Damien asked, his voice rising. "You haven't done anything wrong here. Lizzie should feel ashamed, not you. But you know she never will, and you can't blame yourself for her flaws. You said yourself you think she's bipolar. She probably needs medication. That is not your fault, Marley, and you can't fix what's wrong with her."

Marley let go of her hair, all the rage inside her scaring her. She had never felt this intense, red, wet anger, this consuming, head-splitting furiousness, and she was ashamed, no matter what Damien said. Everything felt out of control, wild, insane. "I'm jealous of her," she said, amazed she had the courage to say the words out loud.

"Why? You are a thousand times better a person."

"But . . ." Marley swiped at her tears and clenched her fists. It was getting dark on the driveway, the night dropping down on them, gravel and shells under her sandals making noise as she paced back and forth, back and forth.

"Just say it."

"I am jealous of Lizzie. Because she is a mother and I'm not. If I'm such a good person, why does that little boy belong to her and not to me?" Marley had never admitted that secret thought out loud. Maybe hadn't even admitted it to herself. It felt horrible and wonderful all at the same time to purge its smallness out of herself. She wanted a child and she was angry that her sister, her flawed and selfish sister, had one she took for granted, casually treated like a pair of jeans that fell in and out of favor depending on her mood. It wasn't fair, and it made Marley angry.

"Because you follow the rules and Lizzie doesn't. Because she doesn't think about anyone else but herself and you do. Any woman can be a mother by accident, but you'll be a mother by choice, and your child will be very fortunate."

He was trying really hard to be sweet and patient, even as he looked like he'd rather smack some sense into her, and Marley suddenly felt like laughing, an embarrassed giggle actually erupting from her mouth. She must sound like a complete and total lunatic stating the absolute obvious.

"God, thank you, Damien. I'm sorry all of this has been dumped in your lap. You're probably regretting the day I showed up. I've got a whole department store full of baggage and I'm spilling it all over your driveway. I'm jealous of my sister. I admit it. Jealous because I want to have a baby and yet I have no clue how to go about finding a husband."

"First of all, I don't regret you showing up here. In fact, I'm very glad you did. I was feeling sorry for myself, you know, and you showed me I was being an ass. But if you want a baby, have a baby. Who the hell says you need a husband?"

Marley gave a watery laugh. He made it sound so easy, so simple. "I had actually decided to adopt a baby when I realized Lizzie was missing."

"See? That sounds like a perfect solution. Stop taking care of your sister, who obviously doesn't appreciate it, and start taking care of you."

The lure of that was fantastically attractive. Marley took a deep breath, wiping her eyes on the sleeve of her shrug. "Why does it smell different out here at night? It smells damp or something." The sounds of the insects were alive and buzzing all around her in the moss and trees.

"That's the swamp, back on the other side of the sugar cane."

"Take me into the swamp, Damien. Show me your property." Marley suddenly felt reckless, desperate to do something, anything, unwilling to sit down and be alone with her ugly, unpleasant thoughts.

"Right now?"

It was stupid, insane, and he was going to say no, of course, but it felt good, wild, demanding, to ask for it. "Yes, right now."

"Okay. We can take the boat out."

Marley stared at him. "Are you serious? You'll actually take me out there in the dark?"

"Sure. I have headlights on my boat and I've been out there in the dark plenty of times. I know my swamp." He tilted his head. "You thought I'd say no."

She nodded. "I thought you'd politely tell the good girl who's fallen off her rocker to go in the house and take a Valium and go to bed. That everything would seem better in the morning."

"Don't you watch talk shows? That would be repressing your feelings. Sometimes you need to reach out, step outside of what makes sense, and let everything out. I understand that. God, do I understand that." Damien reached for her hand. "You're safe with me. Get as wild as you want, Marley."

Chapter Thirteen

For the first time in her life, Marley understood the allure of danger, of speed, of accepting a thrilling dare and rushing off into the dark with it. On acting with utter impulse and not questioning it, doubting it, worrying it, or picking it apart.

Lizzie had never been tormented by her choices. She dove headfirst into random waters that looked sparkling and warm, and occasionally actually were. More often than not Lizzie crashed on the rocks, a violent splat on hard, unforgiving boulders, but she always dove again.

Marley had always wanted to dive, just once, arc up into the air like a dolphin and hurl herself off into oblivion, but she never had. Riding in the swamp with Damien felt like she had leaped off that cliff.

It was reckless, heading out into total darkness with a man she really didn't know all that well. The motor drowned out the sound of the swamp, and it was too dark for her to see anything. Marley felt the humid spray of the water being tossed up by the boat cutting through the reeds and wondered how Damien could even see where they were going.

"If you look over the side you can see the reds of the gators' eyes," he said, leaning back toward her to talk, one hand still on the motor.

Marley gripped the bench she was sitting on. "Are you serious?" The concept of red-eyed alligators was fascinating and frightening all at once. She hooked her feet under the bench, gripped the seat, and leaned toward the side, peering into the darkness. The first thing she saw made her jump back into the middle of the boat. "Holy crap, there's one right next to the boat."

It was smaller than she expected, but the red eyes glowed, staring at her, mysterious and strange, watching her pull back, judging, like he knew she was afraid, knew she was a fraud, that she would always be a doormat, never wild, never fun. Marley scooted closer to the edge, defiant, locking her gaze onto his. She wouldn't be afraid, she was tired of being afraid, tired of being safe and boring and lonely.

"What are you looking at?" she asked the gator. "I can be here if I want to."

Damien laughed and killed the engine. The boat glided, cutting through the water smoothly. "I don't think he cares if you're here or not."

"Then he can quit looking at us." Marley swiveled around and stuck her tongue out at him in the dark as they moved past him.

"That's not all there is in the water . . . Legend has it this swamp is haunted."

Wonderful. Marley tried to sound skeptical, but her voice cracked. "Haunted by what?" Glancing around, she couldn't help but think that if any place was going to be haunted, this murky swamp would be it.

"By the spirit of a slave, passing through on his way north after escaping from a plantation down the road."

Damien paused and Marley was sure she didn't want

to know the rest. Yet she found herself saying, "So he died here? How?"

"He was eaten by a gator, just torn to pieces and scattered around. Yet they say he didn't die right away, but suffered, lying there with no legs and a missing arm, just bleeding to death, slowly and painfully."

"That's horrible."

"Yes, it is. And they say while he was dying he called up the powers of voodoo and cursed the swamp, cursed the gator, cursed his master, and all white men. Now, in . death, he appears to men, so hideous that the very sight of him causes instant death to those who look at him."

"Really."

Damien gave a half smile. "Really. At least four men have been found dead in this swamp over the past hundred and fifty years, with no explanation for what happened to them. Was it Old Jacques? Let's hope we never know."

Goose bumps ran up her arms. He had a creepy voice when he wanted to. There was an edge to it, a wildness, that almost thrilled her as they floated in the dark.

A soft thump distracted her. "What was that?" It sounded like something had hit the boat, and her heart was starting to race. Damien had told his story too well, and she was envisioning the dead slave dropping down onto the bench next to her in the dark.

"Just sit still for a minute, Marley," Damien said in a low voice, shifting closer to her with slow, calculated moves.

"Why?" She froze in place, sudden fear sending bile up into her throat and her heart doing a frenzied crescendo. "What's wrong?"

Damien shot forward, his hand reaching out and grabbing something off the bench next to her. Marley gave a startled yelp. "What the hell is that?"

"Cottonmouth." Damien extended his arm over the side of the boat and flung the snake back into the swamp. They heard it splash into the water. "They're poisonous."

Marley grabbed the top of her cotton shirt and pulled it off her neck, her throat tight. "Jesus Christ." She shivered, feeling like something was brushing across her chest, her arms. "How did you know it was there?"

"That sound. It dropped out of the tree. I'm used to them."

Her eyes had adjusted to the darkness and she could see Damien shrug, returning to the bench in front of her. He was wearing a dark T-shirt that blended into the night, but she could see the outline of his body, see his face lighter and brighter above his shadowy shoulders. The story Anna had told her rose in her mind. She could picture Damien's ancestor, his Damien predecessor in the nineteenth century, out here in the swamp, gathering up his cottonmouth collection.

There was no fear from Damien, instead a nonchalance, a total simpatico with his surroundings.

"Death's Door," she whispered.

His head turned slowly. "What did you say?"

"Death's Door. That's what Anna called the Damien who gave her great-grandmother that house. She said he got the nickname by defying death, that he was reckless and unafraid, and buried bodies after a cholera epidemic." Marley loosened her grip on the wooden bench. "I was thinking that he must have looked like you."

"Perhaps."

"What's it like to know this is yours . . . that your family has been here for two hundred years?" She found herself envious of that sense of tradition, that total understanding of who and what you were.

"There is pride, and yet there's a sense of hopelessness. That I can't hold on to this forever, that eventually the house will collapse and the land will have to be sold."

Marley hadn't thought the future was so precarious for the plantation. She had assumed Damien would keep it, nourish it, pass it down to the next generation. "But why? Don't you want to give it to your children?"

Damien gave a bitter laugh. "Do you see any children, Marley? There's only me, and a big empty house."

"You're not happy, are you?" Of course she had known that, she had sensed it from the first day, felt that his pain surrounded him, kept him cut off from everyone else. Now she knew that his wife had died when he was way too young to have known so much loss and she knew it was a stupid question to ask. He obviously wasn't happy.

"Not particularly. But then most people aren't. And by the way, you should sift through whatever Anna tells you. She loves to tell a good story, and it's not always true."

"Are you telling me Death's Door didn't exist?" At the same time he was very smoothly changing the subject.

"No, he existed. And he did some truly insane things. I think that he wanted to die. But he didn't. No matter what risk he took, he didn't die."

Marley suddenly understood why Damien threw his adult parties. It kept him firmly standing in that careless existence, defiantly selfish, living only in the moment, never having to face the future.

"You'll have children someday," she told him. "And they'll be grateful you kept this house."

He gave a soft laugh. "Marley Turner, you are bleeding compassion again. Maybe I don't want children. Maybe I think they're all time-sucking, whiny brats who grow up, throw you in a nursing home, and steal your money."

"And maybe I think you're a lousy liar."

"And I think if you had to drag me into the swamp at eleven o'clock at night the very least you can do is make it worth my while."

That was a tone she recognized, and a fissure of excitement raced up her spine. "How could I do that?"

"You could give me a kiss."

As the last word left his mouth, his lips covered hers, with that dominating, dauntless possessiveness he had used on her before. That confidence, arrogance, that she would like what he was doing, would welcome his touch. He was right, of course. His kiss took her in, dragged her under, lifted her up and out of herself to where the only thing that mattered was her, him, and the way he made her body come alive with desire.

Damien's tongue moved deftly across hers, his fingers in her hair, his knee pushing hers open, out, so he could move between her legs. He didn't try to touch her anywhere else, and they blended their mouths together for several hot, thrusting minutes. Marley marveled at his restraint, at his skill in waiting, waiting, building the tension between them higher and higher. She was already growing clumsy in her technique, mouth slipping in her desperation, fingers grasping at his chest, hips pushing forward trying to gain contact.

Instead of appeasing her, easing her ache, taking them to the next logical step, Damien pulled back, wiped his lips. "That was worth coming into the swamp at eleven o'clock. Thank you." He settled back on the opposite bench with perfect nonchalance, even if his breathing was a little labored.

"That's all you want?" she said with no attempt to hide her dismay. Okay, there was teasing, and then there was just insanity. He couldn't get her all revved up like that and then not take her for a spin.

"Are you offering more?" he asked, voice silken, erotic, forearms on his knees, expression dark and dangerous.

"Yes." That was why she was out here, to forget about Lizzie, forget about responsibilities, to just do what she wanted to do for once. And she wanted to do Damien.

"Good. But maybe we should head back. I don't think a boat is the best place for what I think we both have in mind."

"Why, what could happen?" Granted, it might be hard to maneuver on a wooden bench, but doing it in a boat seemed sufficiently wild to satisfy her feverish need to be free of constraints.

"We could capsize. We could float into the reeds and get the motor tangled. We could drift too close to the bank and get stuck."

"Couldn't those things happen anyway?" Marley glanced around, but she couldn't see the shore. It was too dark to see much of anything.

"*Mais non,* not when I'm in control. But if I'm on the floorboards with you, I'm not in control."

That sounded kind of pleasing. "So if we get tangled up and stuck, do we languish out here indefinitely, shriveling up and dying of dehydration?"

Damien gave a soft laugh. "No. We use my cell phone and call for help. Or if we're close to shore, we get out and walk home."

"Hmmm." Marley slipped her butt down onto the floor of the boat to test stability. It rocked ominously from her movement. She looked up at the midnight sky, inky black and dotted with stars. "I guess we'd better go back then. All this thinking about it has spoiled the moment anyway."

He didn't say anything, but he didn't move to start the motor either.

"Do you ever wonder if any of this is real, Damien?" Marley stared up and up, her neck straining as she looked past the leaves of the trees, the dripping Spanish moss, to the endless expanse of sky. She stretched her arms to the sides of the boat. "How do we know we're really here?"

"*Je pense, donc je suis,*" he said, leaning forward, forearms on his knees.

"What?"

" 'I think, therefore I am.' Descartes. Your existence is confirmed by the fact that you can ask the question in the first place. We are all very real, Marley. Painfully real."

Somehow she felt bright and shiny and hard and real, and yet at the same time so odd, so strange, so dreamy, so outside of her normal life that this all could have been a sleep-induced fantasy. "If a tree falls in the woods and there's no one there to hear it, does it make a sound? I guess no one knows but the tree."

Damien shifted onto the floor, the boat listing left, then right, with his movement. He was on his haunches, leaning toward her, his face stark and close. "If a woman is pleasured in the swamp and there's no one there to hear it, does she make a sound?"

Marley laughed. "Hmm . . . good question. I guess *she* hears it."

"And the man who pleasures her."

"True."

"Let's test the theory." Damien's fingers landed right on her nipples with amazing accuracy.

"I thought you said we should go back."

"And spoil the moment? I don't think so."

She understood then that he was going to give her what she had asked for, a wild ride into licentiousness, an abandonment of convention, even if it wasn't logical or comfortable or safe.

Damien popped the snap on her shorts, yanked down her zipper. His hand cupped her panties as his lips traced over her breast. Need rose in her fast and hard, startling her with its speed, its velocity. When he bit her nipple, tweaking it sharply between his teeth, she let out a cry, not of pain, but of pleasure.

Then he had her shirt up and over her shoulders, her head, and down on the floor of the boat. "Sit on the seat," he demanded.

It was a command, and she didn't hesitate to follow it. Marley scrambled backward, pulling herself up with trembling hands, curious what he had planned, wondering how they could do this. As she was rising, he tugged down her shorts, so quickly and efficiently that she barely had time to blink before the warm air rushed over her bare thighs. She found herself standing straight up in a rocking boat in her bra and panties, shorts around her ankles, afraid to move and set the boat rocking. And afraid to shift the mood, ruin his plan, allow her fears and insecurities to seep in. She wanted to stay, just like that, desired and in desire, for as long as the moment could draw out.

Damien pulled his shirt off and brushed past her legs to lay it out on the bench. "Sit down."

Even as she was bending her knees, he was skimming her panties down past her thighs, exposing her sex to him in a way that could have embarrassed but instead only excited her. She sank to the bench, her bare backside touching the soft warmth of his cotton shirt. He had the shorts and panties off her ankles and her bra unhooked and likewise disposed of in about thirty seconds, his movements swift and sure, demanding. Marley sat naked in the dark, breathing hard, her skin tingling and prickling from all his brushes and touches and yanks.

There was something about the position, the night air, the knowledge that she was completely naked and he was fully clothed that had her exhilarated, nervous but excited, the experience new and fascinating.

"You have a beautiful body," he whispered, running his lips over her nipple, hands on her thighs.

It was on her lips to say something apologetic, disparaging, to critique her thighs, her breasts, that appalling stomach doink that wouldn't go away no matter how many sit-ups she sweated through, but she stopped herself. If he thought she was beautiful for whatever reason, in whatever way, she was going to accept it, appreciate it, revel in it. "Thank you." She put her hands on his shoulders and tossed her hair back away from her face. "Right now I feel beautiful sitting here like this."

And she did. She felt a little anxious, a tinge embarrassed, but also aroused, pleased with herself. Anticipating what he was going to do.

What he did was torture her breasts. He licked and sucked and tugged, first one, then the other, until Marley was gasping, tossing her head back, digging her fingers into his thick hair. "Damien."

It wasn't enough, it was too much. She inched her legs apart, shifted restlessly on his T-shirt, shivering when the breeze drifted over her slick nipples. "I . . ." She wasn't sure what she was going to say, but it was probably going to be some form of begging.

Damien cut her off, his mouth trailing over her shoulder, his fingers sliding inside her. "Shh. Don't say anything. Just feel."

That she could do.

He moved over her, everywhere, tasting her flesh, teasing and coaxing her into delicious sighs of delight with his fingers deep inside her, stroking confidently. The single-mindedness with which he approached her pleasure made her feel decadent, indulged, selfish, like she was entitled to his attention, deserved his expert loving. But as he plucked and stroked and moved over her, and the minutes drew out, and her body burned with a fierce wet tremor, she wanted more, she wanted to own all of him, to take that intensity he was turning on her and pull it inside her. She wanted to see Damien, to feel him, to touch his naked flesh like he touched hers, and to know the sensation of him deep inside her body, thrusting out that ache she burned with. When he moved down onto his knees, between her legs, when he pushed them apart, far and wide, she was ready and reaching for his jeans.

"You sit on the bench," she said. "And I'll be on top."

He had her too close to the edge, and she knew that an orgasm brought about by his fingers wasn't going to be enough this time. She wanted everything.

As she grappled with the front of his jeans, trying to find the zipper pull, she suddenly realized that he was shifting out of her reach. "Get back here," she said with a laugh, feeling a little bossy and demanding herself for a change.

"Marley, we can't do that on the boat, so don't tempt me."

"Will we capsize?" She knew nothing about boating. His erection was hot beneath her fingers, even with the barrier of his jeans. Her mouth went dry in anticipation. She was willing to risk a dunking in the swamp for a chance at that.

Damien grabbed her hand, stilled it. "It's possible. But more importantly I don't have a condom."

Well, that was an ugly dose of reality. One she didn't want to face. "You're not going to catch anything from me, I promise. And it's the wrong time of the month for getting pregnant."

"Marley."

There was a world of meaning in that serious, soft-spoken but steely voice of his. Marley sighed, feeling a flush rush up her cheeks. No wild sex on a boat for her. "Sorry. That was a stupid thing to say. Here I just got done telling you how much I want a baby and then I'm suggesting we skip birth control. I didn't mean it to sound like that. I'm not some obsessive woman trying to con you into coughing up your sperm. I just was being greedy . . . I don't want to wait to have sex with you."

"We are having sex, or we were a minute ago."

Marley twisted her fingers in his hair and tugged a little to emphasize her frustration, bumping his thigh with her knee. "No, that was me sitting here stark naked, while you are totally clothed and giving me pleasure."

"I don't have a shirt on." He brushed the edge of the T-shirt she was sitting on as he hunched down between her legs.

"That doesn't count."

"Why are we talking about this?" He tried to slide his thumb down between her thighs, over her clitoris, intending to push in, take his way again.

Marley shifted away. "No."

"No?" His voice took on an edge of annoyance, of authority. "I say yes. Let me in, Marley."

"Okay," she agreed, heart pounding, an idea forming in her head. Let him think he was in charge, but she was going to give back to him whether he liked it or not. She was being greedy for once, that was true—that was what the night was all about, and she had decided she wanted to pleasure him like he was her. "Sit on the other bench and I'll stand in front of you. This position is too awkward for you."

He sucked in his breath. "Very good suggestion, *ma cherie*. Just watch your balance when you stand."

When Damien was seated on the other bench, she carefully stood and closed the distance between them. His mouth was almost level with her pelvis and he wasted no time in wrapping his arm around her waist, drawing her flush against him, and kissing her, dusting light feathery touches all around her pubis, high, low, random presses of heat against her overstimulated body.

It was distracting, and she allowed herself a moment of indulgence while his tongue traipsed over her swollen flesh. It felt so damn good, her standing position bringing her closer, tighter to him, his hands on her backside, the carnality and intimacy appealing. Her low moan scattered out over the water, hands digging briefly into his thick hair, and she burst with a quick, tight orgasm. Wanting more, wanting him, she didn't even let him finish stroking her through the last tremors before she quickly dropped down to her knees, taking him by surprise.

"Where are you going?" Damien tried to pull her back up, but Marley resisted, reaching for his pants. "You didn't even finish . . . I was only getting started with you," he said.

Ignoring that, she undid his button, his zipper, while he made a growling sound low in his throat.

"Marley. Don't try it."

"I don't mean what I suggested before. Don't worry about the condom. I just want to . . ." She pulled him out of his jeans and closed her eyes at the feeling of all that rock solid heat. "I just want to taste you a little."

"No." He hooked his hand under her chin and tilted her head upward. She couldn't really read his expression in the dark, but he shook his head firmly. "No, you don't have to do that."

"I want to." Marley was already stroking him, the fascinating feeling of him growing even harder under her touch eradicating the discomfort of kneeling in the boat.

"No." Now he was holding her forehead, preventing her from bending over, his other hand working its way over her breast, trying to distract her attention away from him.

Marley got angry. "Don't tell me what I can and can't do." If he could give it, he could take it. This was not going to be charity orgasms for Marley. This was both of them doing and sharing together.

Yanking away from his hold, she shifted and slid her mouth over him before he could stop her again, taking him deep. Damien moaned, trying to pull back, his voice rough and tortured. "Marley . . . I don't let women . . . not since . . ."

His thighs were tense around her shoulders, his stomach muscles clenched, his breathing tight and quick.

Even without the rest of the sentence, she thought she understood what he was saying. That he hadn't let a woman do this since his wife had died. That it was an intimate act he had denied himself. That she could give him that, be the first in a long time, aroused her and renewed her determination.

"You need to stop," he said, but he had stopped fighting, was no longer shoving at her, attempting to pull away.

As she moved slowly up and down the length of him, his fingers wrapped around and around in her hair, like he was going to jerk her head right off him with the slightest provocation. But she wasn't going to stop, was intending to keep on going, for him, for her, for the freedom they both needed to reach. Marley slid back, flicked her tongue over the tip of him, tasting his hot, salty flesh.

"Marley." It was a warning, his fingers tugging harder.

He was going to dig in, find his willpower, set her away. She could sense it, so she took him deep, sucking in the hollows of her cheeks and opening her throat, gripping his jeans, rocking him in and out. It had been a long time since she'd done this, longer than she wanted to reflect on, and in the past, she'd always felt that oral sex obligation. He did her, she had to reciprocate, it was only polite and the right thing to do, but honestly, the quicker the better. It was never awful, per se, but she'd never taken any personal pleasure from it.

This was different, a whole new experience. When Damien tensed, when his breath came out in strangled little grunts, when his fingers yanked violently in her hair, she felt pride in his pleasure, felt his reaction drive her own, spurring her on, making her more aggressive, eager, aroused, driving her motions more frantically, which circled back around to arouse him even more all over again, until they were both gasping.

"Marley."

He'd given in, she could hear it, in the raw way he spoke her voice, with no warning, no threat, with only a desperate sort of passion, a vulnerability that tripped a feeling of triumph in her. "Yes?" she asked, lifting her head, testing him, knowing he'd groan at the loss, glad when he did. Before he could react further, she went down again, covering him, rushing her thumbs along the underside of his testicles.

It was instinct she was going on, the need to gauge his different reactions, find the angle, the motion, the combination that did to him what he did to her with his tongue. She didn't have the technical experience, but she was good at listening. It was what she'd spent her whole life doing.

This position, the fingers, her hair sliding over his thighs, her rapid in and out, seemed to hit the jackpot.

"Fuck, that feels good," he said, gripping her head, thrusting her harder onto him.

He had a point. It felt pretty damn good to her too. Marley let him take over the rhythm, let him fill her rough and frantic, the control she normally saw from Damien nowhere in evidence.

She knew when he was going to come, felt his body tense, his testicles tighten, felt his last thrust, then his feral yank back so he could explode outside of her. It was a courtesy she didn't appreciate and Marley didn't let him go, followed him back, tightened her hold on his pants.

"No, damn it," he said.

But Damien was already pulsing into her, his hot liquid bursting into her mouth, over her tongue, as she held on, eyes closed, reveling in the feeling that she had done that, given that to him. And when he pulled back, she swallowed when she didn't have to, just because. Because it wasn't the expected thing to do, because he wouldn't think that Marley Turner would, and because she wanted him to see that she had enjoyed it too.

Damien expelled his breath, relaxed his thighs. With

slightly trembling hands, he cupped her cheeks. "You didn't have to do that. Any of that."

"I wanted to." Marley shifted in the boat, her knees suddenly making it known that it was painful to be pressed into dry wood. She was stiff, her own tense muscles finally relaxing, but she couldn't have cared less. It wouldn't have mattered if she'd popped out her kneecap in the process, she wouldn't have stopped. That had been hot.

Damien reached out, lifted her up by the armpits, and she smiled at him, stretching her legs a little, anticipating a healthy dose of appreciation, praise.

But he just wiped his forearm over his sweaty brow and shook his head. "Damn. I need a drink."

Marley waited for him to say more, but he didn't, and she cautiously sat on the bench across from him, her confidence fizzling. He tucked everything away, zipped back up. Her own nudity became instantly awkward, and she bent over, her breasts brushing her knees, and retrieved her T-shirt and pulled it on.

It was harder to be casual about putting on underwear in a rocking boat, but Damien didn't seem to notice her jerky movements, and it was too dark for him to see the red stain of embarrassment she could feel on her cheeks.

Why did she always do this, let this dissolve into awkward insecurities? Why couldn't she unglue her mouth and say something, tease him, kiss him?

She didn't know why, only that she remained silent, groping around for her shorts, her sandals, staring out at the shadowed trees as she slid her shorts on, trying to lift her butt no more than was absolutely necessary to get the damn things on.

Damien turned on the motor and they cut back through the swamp, Marley shivering from the cool air, from the way he turned his bare back to her, his shoulders taut and tense in the moonlight.

When they docked, she said, "Don't forget your shirt," just to say something.

"Thanks." He just picked it up, threw it over his shoulder, stepped onto shore, and turned to give her a hand out of the boat.

Marley took it, knowing her palms were clammy, and tried to move past him without touching his skin. His hand slid away from hers. This was awful. She had pushed it, and she had ruined it. Whatever it had been.

"You go on in," he said. "I'm going to have a smoke. I'll see you in the morning." He gave her a brief, distracted smile, then left her at the edge of the garden.

She watched him walk away. Just stood there and watched his back as he left, retreated, without any of the words or touches or intimacy she wanted, craved. God, she'd been a fool. She could never have sex simply for the sake of sex. That wasn't her, and she would never have freedom, that independence she craved so desperately, until she came to terms with who she really was.

Marley went into the *maison principale* and up to bed, with the scent of him still on her skin, her clothes, in her mouth, with her body still moist from want, and her heart sick with desire for what she could never have.

Chapter Fourteen

It was amazing to Marley that she'd actually slept at all, yet she must have, because she jerked out of a dark, suffocating nightmare when the door to her room opened.

God, if it was Rosa, she was going to scream.

Maybe if she pretended she was dead, Rosa would leave her alone and Marley could attempt to slink back off the property for the second time.

Or she could get her butt out of bed, thank Damien for the night before, and leave with her head held high like a big girl. Like a queen.

"Good morning."

It wasn't Rosa. It was the man himself. Marley forced her eyes open, but didn't bother to lift her head from the pillow. She must have slept with clenched muscles, because every inch of her body ached, and her butt felt like she'd taken on a marathon with no previous training. Watching Damien cross the room, a smile on his face, she wasn't sure if she was grateful or not that his mood from the night before seemed to have passed. It was easier to stay angry than to forgive and expose herself all over again.

"Hi." Let him read anything into that. Marley dug into the corner of her eyes, wiping a stray lash out of the way. "What's up?" She'd prefer to still be attempting to sleep rather than lying there worrying and wondering why he'd turned his back on her after coming in her mouth. Though she supposed she knew why. He hadn't been ready and she'd forced the issue, taken his desire and used it against his emotions.

It hadn't been fair of her, and she was sorry for it.

He stood next to her, striped button-up shirt undone, black pants on. "I need to go into town for a meeting. They refused to do it online."

"Okay." A note to her explaining would have sufficed as far as she was concerned. Marley yawned and pulled the sheet up higher, covering the thigh that had been exposed.

"And before I went, I wanted to make something clear."

Not sure what to say, knowing an apology wasn't right, determined not to sound needy or weird or clingy, she kept her mouth shut, flicking her hair out of her eyes. She needed a haircut.

"I don't want you to leave. I know I was an asshole last night and I'm sorry. There are things about me you don't know, can't understand, but I want you to stay. I want you with me."

"That's it?" Marley watched him, the way he stood straight but not rigid, expression remorseful yet still confident. She mostly felt wary, displeased with her own reactions to him. If they were going to do this, she had to be honest, she had to remember the goal was her pleasure, not her attempting to heal him.

"I can't give you any more than that."

"I didn't ask for any more than that." Marley rolled onto her back, ran her eyes up and down the length of him. He was so damn good looking.

"No, I don't suppose you did."

"No." Marley twirled a finger around a strand of hair, studying him, making him wait even when she already knew her answer. When he didn't break eye contact, but met her stare straight on, bold, she wet her lips. "I'll stay. Because I'm in control."

His nostril flared. "I think you're right."

"Now get over here and give me a kiss before you leave."

The corner of his mouth went up. "Yes, ma'am." Knee on the mattress, he crawled up the bed, pinning the sheet against her, forcing her legs apart. Damien brushed her hair off her face and descended over her, giving her a hot, deep kiss.

Marley gave herself into it, groaned, passed that control right back over to him. Or not necessarily control, but direction. This was what she wanted and he would give it to her. Damien buried his lips in her neck, back to her mouth, slipped his tongue into her ear, ran over the front of her sleep shirt. The sheet was yanked down, kicked out of the way, panties gone with fast hard jerks, his belt clanging as he undid it and his zipper.

No touching, no prepping, no easy, soft, coaxing words or teasing touches with his tongue. He just pushed into her, hard and demanding.

Marley fell back on the pillow, shocked, thighs falling open farther as the tight, thrilling pressure ripped a moan from her. Her body hadn't been ready, but now she moistened for him, growing slicker with each thrust, her hip caught by the sheet, her fingers digging into the mattress.

She meant to say something, to guide or praise or protest, but all she did was burst out with short exhalations of hot air with each powerful push, his body pounding against hers. Turning her head left and right, squirming, she looked toward the gallery, saw the sun was coming up, peeking through the silk draperies, and she gripped the sheet, mind empty and full and ferocious with the pleasure of his touch.

Damien cupped her cheek, forced her face back forward. "Look at me."

He was deep, so far inside she wasn't sure she could take it, the pleasure acute and agonizing, elemental. Heels slipping, arm up in the air, Marley was overwhelmed by the sensations, the intensity, the feeling that he was everywhere in her, from head to toe, taking her, stroking, electric. His breath blasted over her, and she returned it, their lips brushing but not kissing, his forehead resting on hers, pressing, eyes sinking into her as her own lost focus.

The entire world lost clarity, and in the hot cocoon of his body over hers, she climaxed, jerking up, silent, arching into him, a shudder sliding from shoulder to shoulder, her thighs clamping onto his.

Damien came right after her, with tight, gritted teeth, forehead grinding down into hers.

Then they were panting, sweat trickling between them, shirts rumpled and lips moist. He was heavy on top of her, but Marley didn't care. She stared up at him, with no words, but no awkwardness either.

If they both walked away right that minute and never spoke again, she would be content. That was the best sex she'd ever had in her life, primal and raw, and that was hers to keep forever.

"How was that for a kiss good-bye?" he asked, finally pulling back slightly. Whatever hesitation he'd been grappling with the night before, this was clearly his way of showing her he was over it.

"It worked for me."

"Good. Me too." Damien peeled himself off her, leaving her bare chest glistening, T-shirt shoved around her neck. "I'll be done around noon. Want to go to lunch with me?"

"Sure. Should I meet you somewhere?" Marley was impressed with herself. She sounded casual. Hell, she even felt casual. He was still in the process of disengaging his penis from her, and yet there she was having an utterly inane conversation like they did that every day, and it felt perfectly normal.

Damien kissed the right corner of her mouth. Then the left. "It seems a waste for you to drive in separately and then have to follow me right back home. Why don't you pack a bag and we'll spend the night in my city house."

"You have a city house?" Why did that surprise her? It shouldn't, yet it did.

"Yes. On Esplanade, the edge of the French Quarter. I don't go there as much as I used to."

Marley gripped his lapels and gave him a light kiss. "Sounds good. Just tell me where to meet you. And make sure you change your shirt before you leave."

"You don't think sex and sweat are good scents for a boardroom?" The corner of his mouth went up and he peeled the shirt off, pushing up on his knees.

"Probably not." He had an amazing chest, smooth and muscular. She indulged herself by squeezing his biceps a little. Nice, very nice.

"What are you going to do today?" he asked, getting out of bed and rubbing the back of his head.

"I'm going to stay in bed, just like this, for at least another hour. Then I'm going to move my right leg."

Damien laughed. "Perfect plan. You make me jealous."

If he had anything else to say, she didn't hear it, because Marley drifted back into sleep, a rich, thick sleep void of dreams and deeply satisfying.

⁂

Marley wondered if anyone looked at her and knew that she'd had earth-shattering sex just hours earlier. That she still felt that languid afterglow coursing through her. Did they know she was having an affair, that she was doing what she knew intellectually was morally wrong, a sin some would even say, yet what felt so right?

Is this what appealed to her sister, this secret satisfaction, this walking around knowing she'd been naughty, looking at people and thinking *I had sex today. Did you?*

There was no future in these feelings, no way she and Damien could go beyond that morning, but for the day, Marley wanted to just enjoy it, to remember the feeling of him over her, in her. Her skin prickled in the hot sun as she strolled down the sidewalk, having haphazardly taken a parking spot she'd seen on St. Anne's, and walked toward the restaurant Damien had directed her to.

"Out for a stroll?" an older man asked her as he watered down the sidewalk in front of his tobacco shop.

"Yes. It's a beautiful day." And she was Snow White, birds singing, bunnies blinking, squirrels chattering around her feet. She smiled at the man, content. In the next few days, she was going home and she was going to start the adoption process. But until then she was Damien du Bourg's lover, and she was going to enjoy that.

Damien was standing outside, in front of the black awning, talking on his cell phone, hand in his pocket. When he saw her, he smiled. As she approached, he was hanging up. He leaned forward, slipping his phone into a pocket, and he kissed her.

"You look gorgeous," he murmured. "Like a woman well fucked."

Marley let him nuzzle her ear, enjoying the hard, grizzly feeling of his unshaven chin on her soft flesh. "What a coincidence. Because I am."

"I should be ashamed of myself. I should feel bad for leading you into such base behavior. But I don't."

"I don't either." Marley laughed, moving out of his touch, feeling light and confident and desirable. "And I'm hoping you'll debase me again later in this city house of yours."

Damien watched Marley sashay away from him in a floral skirt, tossing her hair over her shoulder as she reached for the door of the restaurant. He had to remind himself that this wasn't real. That her attraction to him was because of the power of the Grigori, that she was allowing him to strip down her moral boundaries because of the temptation of lust.

Yet something in him kept saying it was different. Marley had been able to resist him, had been able to evade his touches and get her mouth around his cock on the boat the night before. Never had any woman been able to resist his distractions, his determination to pleasure her and avoid her touching him. It had surprised him, caught him defenseless, and he'd barely grabbed a breath before he'd been exploding in her mouth.

He hadn't handled it well, afterward. But he had needed time, away from her, to sort through what had happened. Spending the night tossing and turning and thinking from every angle possible, he had decided Marley was entirely different than any other woman he had known in the last two hundred years, because not only could she resist him, she actually appeared to like him. That was a completely unique response. Women were attracted to him based solely on the physical, the demon lure. Yet Marley liked him. Damien. As both a person and a man.

And it was that certainty that had allowed him to let himself go that morning, let him explode inside her, take the pleasure she had offered so freely, so generously. It was different with Marley, and that was damn dangerous.

Because he wasn't different. Nothing had changed, and he was using rationalization to excuse his behavior. A hundred years of conviction thrown over for a few days' pleasure, and ultimately at her expense. He should be castigating himself, but he just felt easy, content, and oddly at peace.

Marley turned back to him and smiled as they entered the restaurant. "What's their specialty here? I'd like to try something new."

"I can recommend all kinds of new specialties," he said, sliding his hand around her waist, wanting to touch her, feel her, be closer to her laugh and her smile.

If this wasn't real, he didn't care.

He'd had entirely too much reality for the last two centuries.

✥

Marley sat on Damien's balcony, a glass of wine in her hand. "This is beautiful. All these hanging baskets . . . who takes care of these?"

"There's a building manager for these condos." Damien pulled his chair closer to the railings and propped his feet up. "I give him free rein to take care of the place."

Lunch had been delicious Creole food, and Marley was sleepy from the sun, a full stomach, and the restless night's sleep. "I could take a nap right now."

"We could do that." Damien's eyes were closed and he looked just as languid as she felt. "There's a bed four feet away. All we have to do is stand up."

Like they'd actually sleep if they made it to a mattress. "Is this a ploy to get me naked?"

"No." His head tilted back, like he wanted more of the sun. "If I wanted you naked right this minute I'd just say so. Or make it so. No, I was actually talking about taking a nap. I'm dead tired."

When he stood up and took her hand, she went with him, figuring sex or sleep would be the outcome and both sounded damn appealing.

The bed was low, crisp white bedding against navy blue walls, which were outlined by thick, creamy wood-work. Silver mirrors faced each other over the dresser and bench, and a metallic nightstand bounced light from the windows around the room, casting rainbow shadows. Marley loved the order of all of Damien's furnishings, the understated elegance, how every object served a purpose.

She kicked off her sandals and climbed onto that fluffy oasis, the duvet sinking beneath her knees. "Very soft."

"Pull the duvet back." Damien had taken his own shoes off and was unbuttoning his shirt.

Marley peeled the comforter and sheet down and slipped inside, giving a sigh as her head hit the pillow. "Oh, crap, this feels good."

Damien slid in from the left and stuffed two pillows behind his neck. He lay on his back, hands steepled on his bare chest. "I think Americans should initiate the siesta. This feels amazing with the sun on us."

What felt amazing was the way everything was so comfortable with Damien. If she sat back and analyzed it, it would probably disturb her, so she wasn't going to do that. Marley rolled onto her side, trailed her fingers over his arm.

"Are you still having the party Saturday night?"

"Do you want me to?" He turned his head in her direction, studying her. "I can cancel it."

"No. I want to see Lizzie and she said she was going to be there." Besides, if he canceled the party, logically it would be time for her to go home. And she wasn't ready, not quite yet. She wanted more time with Damien.

"Okay. But let me know if you change your mind."

"Thanks."

He reached over, wrapped his arm around her, pulled her closer. "I owe Lizzie a thank you."

"For what?"

"For bringing you to me."　　　•

Marley's first instinct was to blush, to ignore his words, to not want to screw up the moment, or misinterpret what he meant. But instead she said what she felt. "I still want to strangle her, but I'm glad I came too. Glad I met you."

Maybe they were both meant to be this for each other, this warm bed and soft, unexpected comfort, for right now, right when they both seemed to need it. And it could be enough, a gift, a lovely memory.

Resting her head on his chest, she settled in closer to him, running her finger over the leather of his black belt. "I forgot about the letter, Damien. Lizzie's e-mail with Marie's confession. I need to give it to you, so remind me when we get back to the plantation and I'll dig it out. Actually it's in my purse, so I can give it to you whenever I can drag my lazy butt off this bed."

Damien stroked her back. "I need to tell you something. Something I'm not proud of, but that you should know, so you'll understand why I don't deserve your pity. I wasn't faithful to my wife. I made her so damn unhappy, and I was so selfish."

While Marley was surprised, she could hear the pain in his voice, had suspected there was something he was harboring guilt over. "Oh, Damien. You made a mistake. You must have been very young."

"Don't forgive me. I don't."

She could hear his heart beating strong and solid beneath her. "Maybe you should. Was it just once, or was it an affair?" Cheating was something that she didn't understand, but she also figured everyone made at least one mistake, some just bigger than others. A one-night stand fell into the latter category. Though on the other hand, a long, drawn-out relationship with another woman would be hard for even a bleeding heart like her to explain away.

"It wasn't an affair."

"Damien du Bourg."

"Yes, Marley Turner?" He sounded faintly amused.

"I think you and I need to make a pact to stop beating the hell out of ourselves and just move forward. Can we do that, you think? Both of us just live our lives." Marley yawned, ready to drop off to sleep. "Let's do that."

"Is it that easy?"

"Yes." She had decided it could and would be.

"Okay, *ma cherie*. I don't make promises I can't keep, but I'll try." He kissed the side of her head. "I'm falling asleep."

"Me too." Her eyes were closed, thoughts thick and hazy. And as she drifted off to sleep she felt entirely at peace with herself and her life.

❧

Damien was warm and strong next to her, his breathing steady and silent, and it felt normal, natural, right to Marley to just slide in closer to him after she woke. At first, it had seemed a mystery to her why she felt the sense of familiarity, of ease, that she did with Damien. But she didn't question it any longer. It was what it was, and she intended to enjoy it. They were together, for now, and it was freeing, exhilarating, not to question it, not to dissect or worry or contemplate the future.

There was only now, and that was a heady, satisfying feeling.

She didn't even realize he was awake until his hand moved over her thigh. Enjoying the view she had of him with his eyes still closed, Marley kissed his mouth softly, rubbing her lips over the bristle on his chin.

It was different from that morning, as they touched slowly, with exploration, lips and hands and tongues testing, reaching, tasting. They peeled each other's clothes off without urgency, not bothering to toss them off the bed, just letting them fall where they came off. Damien readjusted the thick covers, shoving the fat duvet down as their skin heated and dewy sweat gleamed on his chest.

Marley enjoyed his naked flesh, liked both the look and the feel of it, and she caressed his rock-solid backside languorously, with a lusty greed she had never felt before, had never indulged in. And while Damien's fingers and mouth played over her nipples and sank into her wet thighs, she explored his shaft, his testicles, learning the feathery movements that made him grit his teeth and his cock jump.

It didn't seem alien to touch that way, but intuitive, as if all along she had been a sensual woman, and had never understood herself. With Damien, she felt the power of her sexuality, felt the pride that came from making a strong man groan, and when he coaxed her with a gravelly, "Ride me, Marley," she didn't hesitate. Tossing her hair back over her shoulder, she pushed him on his back and straddled his thighs.

Rubbing lightly against him, she paused to swallow, to catch her breath, to take in the sight of him staring up at her, his green eyes dark with desire. For her. His large masculine hands cupped her waist, slid up her sides to tweak her nipples and cover her breasts. The ache was everywhere, the pleasure complete, full, gorgeous, alive in her the way it never had been before, and she wanted to savor, to make it last forever.

But Damien said, "Take what you want now, or I'll force it on you."

And since she wanted to own this pleasure, she sank herself down onto his erection, letting out an appreciative groan as he stretched her aching flesh. She moved her hips, pumping their bodies together, grinding herself and her swollen clit against him, digging her feet into the bed, sliding and rocking and losing herself in the sensation of him inside her. Damien held on to her hips and thrust up hard to meet her frantic movements, until they were both sweaty and hot and excited, their cries filling the bedroom, the antique bed slamming against the plaster wall.

She came first, which she expected to do. Damien didn't seem the type to give in until a woman had been satisfied. Satisfied she was, screaming with total abandon, gripping the bedsheets, and snapping her head back. Damien followed suit, but with silent, feral thrusts, eyes rolling back, hips slamming up so hard Marley bounced forward.

They hung in that moment as long as possible, until Marley's thighs shook and a funny little sensation tickled her throat from all the yelling she had done. With a cough and a sigh, she draped herself over his damp chest, stroking the hair there, content to let him rest inside her indefinitely.

"Let's spend two nights here instead of one," he said softly.

"Sure." Because lying with him brought a sense of contentment she hadn't known existed.

⁂

They spent the two days shopping in the Quarter, walking down to Jackson Square for café au lait and beignets, and getting naked together over and over again in that fluffy white bed. It was so wonderful, so easy, so delicious, that Marley started to suspect she was doing more than indulging.

She was falling in love.

Which was a mistake, but one she wasn't sure how to correct.

So their last night at the town house, as they were drifting off to sleep, she probed about his wife, his infidelity, wanting to remind herself that he had a past, and a spotted one at that. He had a significant amount of guilt, and it would be disastrous to expect more from him than he could give.

"How did your wife find out about your affair?" she asked him, snuggling up alongside his hip.

He glanced over at her, obviously startled. But he answered the question. "She walked in on us."

"Oh." That wasn't a pretty picture. "I guess she was upset."

"Yes, of course." His mouth was turned down in a frown. "Why do you ask?"

"I just want to understand what happened . . . I can tell you still feel guilt over it."

"As well I should. There was no excuse for what I did to my wife. Not anger, not alcohol. And I'll never be able to undo it."

"Which is why you need to forgive yourself," she murmured. "Because you can never undo it."

"Maybe someday. But not today."

"Who was she, by the way? A co-worker?"

"It was Rosa."

"Oh." It didn't surprise her any more than it pleased her. The last person she wanted to picture Damien making love to was exotic, thin Rosa. "I see."

But it was a full eighteen hours before Marley realized the significance of Damien's admission.

Chapter Fifteen

Treks to Anna's were starting to take on a pattern. Marley had burning curiosity, she ran to Anna, and Anna only fueled the fire of her imagination.

When she had suddenly realized what Damien had said as they were dropping off to sleep the night before, she found herself yet again on the path to Anna's. Damien was working in the *pigeonnier*, reading his e-mails, and Marley had been walking in the garden, imagining what it had looked like once upon a time, when it had been tended and controlled, when she remembered that Damien had said he'd cheated on his wife with Rosa.

And why that was significant. The first Damien had cheated on his wife with a Rosa. It was too much to be a coincidence.

In the middle of her contentment with her life, the promise of stability, hope for the future, amazing sex, her feelings of complete and utter balance with Damien, even a peaceful resignation toward Lizzie, this tidbit suddenly rocked her boat, shoving her right toward the metaphorical alligators.

Anna wasn't on the porch, and when Marley knocked, the older woman called out, "Come on in."

Marley found Anna in the kitchen taking the skin off of a peach. "I'm sorry, am I interrupting?" Two seconds earlier she had been ready to call this little old woman to the mat for making up fake letters, and now suddenly she felt guilty for even thinking Anna could be dishonest. She was just a lonely old woman who barely came up to Marley's breasts.

"Not at all. Peach?" Anna held out a fresh one to Marley.

"No, thank you." Marley crossed her arms. "I was just wondering how you got Marie's letters."

"Marissabelle found them." Anna sliced her skinned peach into thin pieces onto a paper plate. She didn't seem to think it was odd that Marley had barged in asking such a random question. "In the big house."

"Did she live there?"

"Honey, she was his mistress. She didn't live in his house. She lived in his town house on Esplanade for a while because he didn't want her regular like, just when the urge struck."

Oh, Lord. Town house on Esplanade. The very town house where she had taken an odd, intimate nap with Damien two days before. The beautiful house where she had shared take-out dinners with him on the balcony, then made love to him in that big, white bed over and over, was the very same place where Death's Door had holed up his mistress.

Something about that made her feel very uncomfortable.

"Then he gave her this house, of course, when he decided he wanted a closer reach."

"So how did she find the letters?"

Anna shrugged.

Marley wasn't sure how to dance around what she really wanted to ask. So she just said it. "Are you sure these letters are real? There are some strange . . . similarities between what happens in them and the present."

Anna sucked a fruit slice between her thin, gray lips. Those dark eyes pierced Marley, never blinking, unreadable. "Everything is real, child. Even things you couldn't possibly imagine are real. Go on and finish the letters, then come back and see me. We'll talk it all through."

There was something in the way Anna spoke that sent a shiver up Marley's spine. Marley stared at the paring knife in Anna's gnarled hand, suddenly wondering how old she actually was, where all her family had gone.

"As soon as I finish them, I'll bring them back. I'm going to be heading home soon. Sunday." It was the logical thing to do. The day after the party. She could see Lizzie and still be home in time for the start of the school year. Sensible.

"Does he know you're leaving?"

They both knew who *he* referred to. "No."

Anna shook her head. "He's not going to want to let you go until he's tired of you."

That irritated the absolute hell out of her. This wasn't about him. This was about her. It was her choices, her sister, her sex life, her liberation, her future.

"I have no doubt that he'll survive the loss."

Anna grinned, a secret, sly smile that raked Marley's nerves raw.

"No doubt," the old woman said with a laugh. "No doubt."

❧

"I am sorry," he said for the sixth or seventh time, his eyes red and bleary, shirt and jacket disheveled as he stood next to my bed.

"I know," I managed, trying not to cry again. "As am I. But it's not your fault."

"I should have taken more care with you."

"It does not signify." It had occurred to me, as I had bled and bled and bled out our baby's life during the night, that I was being punished for my behavior these past few months. I had not been a moral and upright person, not fit to raise a child, and now I would not be entrusted with such a task.

His fingers brushed over mine, softly, as if he were afraid to touch me. I knew I must look ghastly. I felt weak, heartsick, ashamed, my womb still contracting in painful spasms.

"It does. I promise you that next time, I shall exercise more caution. I will not anger you . . . I will not dally with the servants. In fact, I shall send away all the female staff under the age of fifty so you can rest easy in your trust of me. I am sorry," he said, his voice cracking.

Would you understand, Angelique, that at that moment, I knew I was completely and utterly lost to him . . . that I loved Damien, that I felt the pull of compassion, the urge to comfort, to cleave him to me, even as I barely had strength to draw a full breath? In the many months of our marriage, I had never seen what could be characterized as genuine emotion from my husband. At that moment, he was sorry, and I believed him, as I could see quite clearly it was the truth.

"Oh, Damien," I said. "Darling, if it is your fault then it is mine as well. I was a willing participant, not to mention that I have always been in exceedingly poor health. I am of a petite stature and perhaps will never be able to bear a child."

That was my greatest fear, one I had not been able to voice until now. That now that Damien and I were together, truly married, and I could see that he felt some level of affection, concern for me, I feared the cruel irony of never being able to seal our bond permanently with the glorious gift of a child.

He gripped my hand fully, entwining his fingers with mine and squeezing. "You are not in poor health. You have not been ill one day since our vows. I am completely confident that you will have many of my children and they shall all be dark-haired beauties like their mother."

"Even the boys?" I asked through a watery smile, grateful for his reassurance.

"Yes. But big and strapping like their father."

I laughed, but had to stop midway when pain shot through my lower abdomen. An involuntary gasp left my mouth and Damien looked at me in alarm.

"Gigi!" he roared over his shoulder. "Send the physician back up. He is in the drawing room."

"I'm fine," I managed, even as my doubled-over posture betrayed me. It was difficult to put on a brave face, though, and I wished to be alone. "After the doctor assures you of that, I believe I'd like to take a nap. Will you come to me in a few hours?"

"Of course." He kissed the top of my head. "I think I'll go for a quick ride, then I'll be right back."

But two hours later I was roused from a restless sleep by loud voices in the drive, a woman screaming, horses snorting, men shouting.

Gigi, who had been sitting in a chair mending, rushed to the window.

"What is it?" I asked, struggling to sit up. My body was not cooperating and dizziness rushed over me.

Gigi shrieked, then clapped her hand over her mouth.

"What?" She was starting to alarm me.

"Oh, Madame! It is Monsieur du Bourg!" Darting a quick glance at me, she burst into tears and leaned out the window again. "He is in the drive, on the ground. I think . . . I think he is dead. His head . . ." The words dissolved into hysterical sobbing and she ran over to the water basin on my bureau and heaved into it.

I didn't bother to go to the window. Instead I ran straight for the door, ignoring the dizziness, the wave of fatigue that washed over me, the way my legs felt cold and disconnected from my upper body, and the sharp stabbing in my belly.

"*Madame!*" Gigi was screaming now, rushing after me. "*You cannot! The bleeding, oh God.*" She started to pray, a Hail Mary, frantic and disjointed.

I was down the stairs, out on the porch, in the drive, and there I saw what Gigi had. Damien, on his back, his neck at a curious angle, blood streaming from his temple. It was obvious his neck was broken. Our majordomo and the overseer were down on their knees.

Even as I sank to my own knees, even as I knew he couldn't survive the injury, I felt blood rushing down my legs again, my dash down the stairs reinvigorating my body's own trauma.

"*Madame du Bourg!*" The majordomo looked at me in horror, already peeling his coat off and laying it over my shoulders. "*You shouldn't look . . . you shouldn't be out of bed.*"

"*Is he dead?*" I touched Damien's forehead even as I spoke the words. His flesh still felt warm. My hand over his mouth rewarded me with tiny puffs of breath. "*He's alive! We need to get him into the house. Take him up to his bed-chamber.*"

Our majordomo looked worried. "*Of course, Madame.*" He called for several slaves who had been watching from the corner of the house, and they ran over.

"*He can't live, Madame. He has broken his neck,*" the overseer said, his lips pulled back like he was going to be ill. "*There's no hope for it. He's probably dead already, just warm still.*"

His words sent heat rushing through my face, and I thought for a second I might faint, but I rallied. The slaves cradled my husband in their arms, waiting for instructions. I directed them to the house, where Gigi was standing in the doorway sobbing.

"*Then he shall die in his house instead of in the dirt.*" I tried to stand, but the landscape shifted and whirled in front

*of me and I fell back to my knees. A glance down showed
vibrant spots of blood on my nightrail.*

*As the majordomo lifted me into his arms, I asked, "What
happened to Damien?"*

*The overseer adjusted the jacket over me as the major-
domo walked me toward the house. "He was thrown from his
horse, Madame. That animal has been skittish for the last
three months. I can't explain it. We never had any problems
with him before, then suddenly he wouldn't tolerate Monsieur du Bourg. Good Lord, this is just like his father, only
two years' passed now."*

*My head was too heavy, so I let it loll back. I stared at the
sky, so crisp and blue, so enhanced with glorious white clouds.
"It's such a beautiful day," I said, because it was. The air was
warm and clear, the world a humming, peaceful place, and it
was my time to leave it.*

*"Why in hell would she say that?" the overseer whis-
pered urgently to the majordomo.*

"The shock."

*Shock? Yes, it was a shock that at the same time I had lost
our baby, I was also losing my husband.*

*But that shock was nothing compared to what I discov-
ered a mere hour later.*

❧

"I don't suppose I can talk you out of attending the
party," Damien said as they drank coffee in the garden at
sunset on Saturday.

Marley raised an eyebrow. "I don't suppose you can."
She stared into her cup, a black French toile pattern rising
above her sloshing coffee. "I have to see Lizzie."

"I understand. I do. But please stay with me. And
don't drink anything."

A girl drank one spiked martini and some people
thought she needed to be watched for the rest of her life.
But she'd be a liar if she said there wasn't something very

appealing about having him care enough to be concerned. She was usually the worrier, not the other way around.

"Can I at least have bottled water?"

"Don't be a smartass."

Marley pulled in a deep breath. "I love the way it smells here. Everything is thick and floral. I never thought I'd like Louisiana so much, but it's really gorgeous."

"Like you."

"Shameless flatterer. You already know I'll sleep with you tonight, you can cut the crap."

"Extra favors." He winked.

Marley laughed. God, she was going to miss him. She really cared about him, was grateful for the time they'd had together, for who he was, and how they were lonely people who'd both been able to lean on each other when they needed it the most.

"You know I should leave tomorrow. Monday at the latest."

His smile quieted. "I was hoping we could ignore that—let's say, oh, indefinitely. I don't want you to leave, *ma cherie*. Not yet."

The sadness in his voice caused a big fat lump to leap into her throat. "I can't stay. You know that. I have a career, family, my life back in Cincinnati." And she'd be taking back with her the knowledge that she was independent, strong, as sensual as any other woman. That was her liberation, her gift from him, and she would be forever grateful for it, even as she knew staying would be a mistake.

"I know." He leaned back in his chair, stared out at the garden, back to the sugarcane Marley could see way off in the distance. "That doesn't mean I have to like it. I warned you from the very beginning that I'm a spoiled, selfish man. I want what I want. And I want you."

"You're not nearly as selfish as you'd like to think you are." Marley twirled the coffee in her cup, setting it back down. "And you don't really want me to stay. Not really. Right now I'm just attractive to you because I'm different. Prude."

"You weren't a prude when you were screaming in the swamp, and in my bedroom."

"True." She was into the truth. She could own up to that. "But I'm not like your usual women."

"What does that mean? What do you think my usual women are like?"

"Look at Rosa. She's thin and gorgeous."

"You're gorgeous. And Rosa, she and I are toxic together. We bring out the worst in each other. I wouldn't want you to be like her."

"So why do you let her come around here?" Marley had wondered that ever since he had confessed that his one-night stand had been with Rosa.

"She just shows up. I can't control that."

He wasn't telling her everything. Not even close, she could just tell. But she was leaving, because that was her choice, the right thing to do, and there was no sense in getting worked up over it.

"Maybe she's in love with you." Marley could certainly understand how that could happen.

Damien burst out laughing. "Please. That is not the feeling Rosa has for me."

His cell phone rang and he glanced at the number.

"You can answer it," Marley said. "I'm going to run up and change. Thank you for not making tonight a bikini theme." She stood up and squeezed his shoulder as she walked past him. "Oh! And here's that letter I keep forgetting to give you." Marley pulled it out of her pocket and set it on the table.

Then she went quickly toward the house. She had an hour and she was going to finish those letters from Marie before this party and return them to Anna.

It was time for all the answers.

❧

"They are both going to die!"

I hovered in and out of consciousness, but I heard Gigi's agonized words floating over from my left.

"Whatever will we do? There is no family here . . . oooohhh, this is so horrible. My poor mistress, so young, so sweet."

Gigi was in full dramatics and it was comforting for some reason. I pried my eyes open to check on Damien. I had insisted they put me in bed with him, regardless of how scandalous that might be. If we were both to die, better not to divide the staff to attend us. Given Gigi's words, I knew Damien hadn't expired while I was in my faint, but I was prepared for the visual evidence that it was merely a formality that he lived.

He was still, lying on his back, but very clearly breathing.

"Get yourself into the hall," the housekeeper reprimanded to Gigi. *"Running on like that will not help anyone."*

Right as they passed into the hallway, Damien's eyes opened. With a soft groan, he turned to me and whispered, *"Marie?"*

"Yes!" I gave a sob and managed to turn onto my own side, so that we lay facing each other. I was so desperate with relief that it didn't occur to me how curious it was that he had such mobility in the face of such an injury. Gratitude rushed through me, pleasure, confidence that if Damien could speak, could move, he would recover. *"How are you feeling, Damien?"*

His answer was not as expected. He didn't sound agonized, in pain, afraid or at peace, as the dying are usually one or the other. In a firm, strong voice, this was where my husband leaned in to me, eyes locked with mine, and told me the truth.

What truth is that? That he was not going to die. That he could not die, ever. Can you imagine such a thing? Had you *guessed this would be where my letters are leading? No, neither could I at that moment.*

Yet he told me all in great detail, in urgent whispered tones, how he had bartered with a demon, and gained eternal human life in exchange for his servitude.

It sounded fantastical, a fevered result of his accident, his imagination run wild under the influence of the doctor's carefully administered laudanum. "Hush, Damien," I whispered. "You need your rest."

"It was her, you know," he said, green eyes glassy and hard. "Rosa is the demon's daughter, and she is the one who granted my request."

"The horse threw you, and when you fell, your thoughts have been jumbled." The candles flickered around us, the clock on the mantel ticking with slow, loud predictability, and the bed curtains shrouded around us, attempting to block out the late afternoon sun with little success, and I was suddenly afraid.

"No. It's the truth." Damien sat up, startling me. He moved his neck, raised his arms, shifted his hair aside to show me there was no longer a wound where his temple had been dashed open. "If I had not made this bargain, I would be dead now. No man can survive a broken neck."

I just shook my head. It was incomprehensible, what he was telling me, and I did not wish to hear it. My body was still cold and exhausted, my thoughts floating in a whirlpool, with nothing to stop their motion, no solid surface to cling to.

"And my task assigned to me by the demon father is to promote and inspire sin in others, particularly the sin of lust." Damien rested back down on his elbows, speaking quickly, urgently.

"What?" The sin of lust. The sin I had succumbed to, so eagerly and blissfully. The sin that had stripped my womb of our child—yes, that would be a sin brought forth by a demon. And I confess, I thought if anyone would willingly

strike a deal with a demon, it would be my always arrogant, always reckless husband.

"To facilitate this goal, I have been given the power of attraction. Women cannot resist me. Women will abandon their values to seek pleasure with me."

"Abandon their values . . ." So I knew it was true then, most absolutely, as I knew I could not resist Damien, and even as the horror, the shock, the disgust all warred within me, can you believe that I took pleasure and relief in learning that I was not as weak as I had assumed? Inability to resist the lure of selfish sexual pleasure was such a failure, such a demonstration of the weakness of my character. Yet here it was said to me that I'd had no choice, no hope of resisting. How could I stand firm against the satanic and immoral pull of a demon?

Sweet, sweet rationalization. Yet another tool of the devil, but I took it, I sank inside it, I wrapped it around me without hesitation.

Damien took my hand. "We must call Rosa in here, and she can grant you the same exemption from death."

"What? No!" Submit to such an aberration? I couldn't fathom doing such a thing.

"You are dying," Damien said, his voice rising. "I cannot let you bleed to death, Marie. I will not."

"Rosa is that woman . . . that woman in the red gown?" I wanted to be indebted to her for nothing, and I wanted no part of immortality. I had succumbed to so many sins, I would not compound them with giving myself over to the devil. The very idea terrified, sickened.

"Yes, she will save you."

"I do not want her to save me. It's not right." But I was glad that Damien wanted me to live. Even then, as we were, both covered in blood and feeling the pain of punishment for our misdeeds, I felt that selfish vanity, pride, greed, that Damien cared about me, wanted me with him in eternity.

Perhaps it was more guilt on his part than love, but I

chose to believe what I wished. He loved me enough to want an exemption from death for me.

"Hush," he said harshly. "You will do as I say. And we must continue to act ill, even when we no longer feel pain, so the servants don't talk. We have to let them nurse us back to health, allowing everyone to think we've made a miraculous recovery."

My own eyes focused on his green ones, so hard and determined, so desperate, their alluring depths coaxing me in, compelling me to give over everything I knew as right, as moral, as God's will.

I opened my mouth to speak, to give another refusal, as a violent, breath-robbing pain shot through my womb, fanning out with ferocious pressure. With tremendous relief I went under in a faint.

When I woke up later, Damien was out of bed. I heard him by the window, speaking in anger. With great effort, I turned my head and saw that she was in my room. Rosa. The woman in red. She was wearing a ball gown this time, bustled in back, her décolleté daring and excessively exposed, her long black hair piled in curls on top of her head.

"You are being rather impossible," she told Damien. "There are objections to your request."

"Why?" Damien, who looked quite fit, hale and hearty, paced in his blood-stained linen shirt and breeches, his feet bare, no evidence of his severe injury.

"First of all, your wife is not dying. She will make a complete recovery. Secondly, she will not consent, let alone ask for my gift, and she must be willing in her role of servitude."

I lay still, not wanting it discovered I was awake.

"What makes you think she won't consent to be with me?"

"While she is quite embarrassingly in love with you, she is still a milksop, Damien. She doesn't want the life you choose."

Despite the insult, I couldn't find fault with her logic. I would never agree to serve the devil. I might be flawed, sinful, *ashamed of my recent conduct, but I was not so far gone as that.*

"Then free me."

"What?" Rosa gave a startled laugh. "Why?"

"If Marie will not die now, and will not accept immortality, I choose to live out my mortal life with her as man and wife. I have made a bad bargain, which I regret. Release me and return me to who I was three months ago."

She fingered her necklace, the gems not visible in the dark. "You are an arrogant fool. I cannot do that and you know it. And it is not my concern if you have suddenly grown wise to the drawbacks in the bargain we made. You should have thought through all of those before you asked for my assistance, which I bestowed so graciously."

"I am asking you now most humbly to release me," Damien said, sounding anything but humble. His voice was stiff and angry. "Show some compassion for my wife."

Rosa's hands clenched in fists. Her voice rose. "What do I care for your little invalid wife? And if you cared, you would have considered her feelings prior to my joining with you on your front porch. You, Damien du Bourg, are a hypocrite, and a stupid rich man who thinks the world is his to order about. Well, the truth is as such—I am the daughter of a demon, and you are a demon's slave. This is what you asked for, and this is what you've been gifted with, and this is what you'll always be, forever and an eternity. My father says God will battle the demons on Judgment Day, and send a Great Flood to save His people from our presence, but until that day, should it ever arrive, you, my darling, belong to us, and you would be wise not to anger me."

She leaned toward him, went to place her lips on his.

Was it a dream? It certainly felt surreal, unnatural, like I was remote and cold and watching from far, far away.

"Fuck you," Damien told her, jerking out of her reach.

And so I wasn't dreaming, as I could never have conceived of such a phrasing in my entire life.

Chapter Sixteen

I didn't die. But that is obvious, isn't it? I am laughing at myself, at how idiotic I am sometimes. I feel a bit hysterical, like everything is bubbling and boiling and spewing inside me, ready to rush forth in hot liquid anger.

Damien will be home soon and I feel frantic to finish my writing. I have been successful in concealing my ramblings from him by sliding the papers under the mattress of my bed every night before retiring. There are many things Damien will do on and around a mattress, but lift it up is not one of them, and thus my thoughts are safe from his prying eyes. What he would do if he read these letters, Angelique, I know not.

There are rules between us, some unspoken, others quite clearly verbalized. I am not allowed into town, or to visit the other plantations for social calls. It has been told to our neighbors that I am indisposed again due to losing our child, but that I am expected to have made a full recovery in time for Christmas festivities.

I am already recovered fully. The tales of illness are a ruse, a fabrication so Damien can watch me, keep me close. He does not trust me, since I have repeatedly told him how *offensive I find his pact with Rosa to be. That his unholy role he so willingly accepted is abhorrent and disgusting to me.*

Yet that is not all that is disgusting to me. What repulses, sickens, and horrifies me is that I still crave him, want him, physically and spiritually. My heart beats with love even yet, my body strums with anticipation at the sight and thought of him.

Night after night, day after day, I fight with my conscience, my willpower, and each time I fail miserably. I go to him, like the slut that I am, I simper and beg and flirt, display my breasts enticingly, lean over when no such action is necessary. I put my hands on his manhood and stroke it into hardness, then lift my skirts and climb on him like an enthusiastic rider does with his favorite stallion.

I despise myself, I loathe who I am and what I have become, and yet I cannot stop. I go to him, again and again, with legs spread and body wet, begging for the release that only he can give, and it aches, it hurts, a pleasure so acute that it acts like an opiate upon me, luring me back when I have barely been gone. Do you understand what I am saying? That I would beg and plead and disgrace myself if necessary, that I cannot go more than twenty-four hours without feeling his body inside mine, without being bedded hard or fast or slow or voyeuristically, whichever way Damien should choose that day, and that I am more than willing. I am the instigator, the catalyst, the utterly lost fallen woman. This we do not speak about, we don't put words to my shame, my utter abandonment of all that is good and proper and moral, and if I could be grateful for anything it is that my husband doesn't glory in my wretched state.

He holds me when I cry afterward, when my frustration and shock at my continued weakness overcome me. But it is only balm to the festering, gaping wound of my virtue, which has fled in large parts, slowly evaporated in others, and fights the bondage of desire wherever it still remains.

It will never go away, I shall never win, I cannot be

strong enough to beat it back, and the devil works in me, through me, every time I strip off my gown like a whore and dive into sin.

There is another babe on the way, and this time, Angelique, this time I cannot wait for God to take it from me. My husband is an unnatural being, immortal, enslaved to the powers of hell, a charming, handsome vessel of all that is evil. What sort of child could this possibly be, born of my weak licentiousness and Damien's empty, Godless soul?

I am not fit to raise a child, nor would this be a baby. It is an aberration, it is like when Rosa was born of the union of her father and a mortal mate, born directly into servitude. They would own this child and raise it in their world to be as they are.

Whatever sins I have committed, whatever becomes of me, this is something I cannot bear. I am not meant to be a mother, not with Damien. That is why I lost the first two, because it was a warning sign from God that I had fallen afoul of all that is right.

Martha, one of our house slaves, has been kind enough to procure for me a local herb that is said to ease the ailment I suffer from. She was startled by my questions, but I told her that the doctor has informed me carrying a child to term will kill me, and I choose to live. Not only did she give me the solution for my immediate concerns, she gave me some advice and options for preventing future incidents, for which I am most grateful. I do not believe I can endure this a second time.

I am not even sure I shall survive the first.

❧

Rosa has just left me. She has offered me a solution, a way to release both Damien and myself.

Not ten minutes past, she stood in my bedchamber, with its pretty lilac wallpapering, and ran her fingers idly over the rich silk of my window hangings. "Do you love him?" she asked.

"That is none of your concern," I said, afraid yet unwilling to give her what she desired. And if my insolence displeased her, how else could she hurt me, truthfully? I cannot suffer any more than I already have.

"Oh, do not be missish." She made an unpleasant face. "I am not a witch, you know, I do not enjoy other people's pain. I am more concerned with giving everyone pleasure, not causing suffering."

"It would give me great pleasure if you would leave."

That made her laugh. "You have a wit, Marie du Bourg. I can almost forgive you for being so pasty-faced and delicate. Men love that in a wife, you know. Proper, pale, a champion hostess, who looks the other way at a husband's indiscretions, bears an heir, and promptly takes herself to the grave. A perfect wife."

"I might have been that at one time, but your descriptives do not accurately portray me any longer." I was sitting at my writing desk, as I am now, and I sanded my latest efforts before slipping them in the drawer.

"No, you've become quite the mistress, haven't you? It's very clever, you know. Being a man's wife in public, his mistress in private. I'm quite impressed by your strategy. But you do know that Damien regrets the choice he has made with me."

"Yes."

"He is not a man who likes to serve. He will try to take his life, as he would rather die than continue powerless in this role. He will rail in anger and frustration. He will take it out on you, as you grow old and he stays the same, never changing. And eventually, while you wither and dry out with age, he will go mad, his mind collapsing in on itself. It does not seem a pleasing future for you or Damien."

I knew she was right. It was an accurate assessment of

Damien's character. The truth had me around the throat, like cold, strong hands squeezing with authority.

"I can offer a solution. It can save both your unborn child and Damien. You need simply exchange yourself for him. Then he will be free, released, repentant, and can raise your child. You, who understands the lure of sexual pleasure, can live out your days wallowing in it. My father, he will please you, and you'll know nothing but ecstasy in his company."

So the offer was simple. So simple after all this pain. Sacrifice myself, who is already so lost, for Damien and our babe.

I bade Rosa give me time to think it over, but my conclusions have not changed in ten minutes. I am simply too weak to resist. So very utterly fatigued. Better to throw myself into the fire and burn quickly than to simmer slowly in the sin of seduction.

Pray, Angelique, for my soul, and please post my enclosed confession to Father Montelier. I will not see you in heaven, but tell my God I am sorry.

Yours, most regretfully,
Marie Evangeline Theresa Bouvier du Bourg

⚜

Marley tucked the last letter back into the plastic bag and headed for the door. She was absolutely positive everything she had just read was a load of crap. It had to be. No matter that it was detailed, intriguing, even wrenching at times. She wasn't going to allow herself to emotionally connect to it because it was a work of fiction. There were no such things as demons, and the Damien in the story couldn't be immortal.

Because that would mean the previous coincidences would have to be reexamined and would lead her to conclusions she wouldn't tolerate, couldn't fathom.

Obviously Anna wasn't going to tell her the truth, but she needed to see that old woman, hear the lies she was going to spin to accompany the story of the letters.

Marley was getting adept at sneaking out of the house so Damien wouldn't see her. She had gotten surprisingly bold in the last ten days. She had also gotten flirtatious, selfish, sexual. Like Marie.

Damn it. She pushed through the back door with less care than she should have and it slammed into the wall. Cursing, she closed it and plowed her way through the garden, down the gravel path, and cut past the ramshackle slaves' cabins. She was not like Marie du Bourg. She had not succumbed to sin, to pleasure, given up pieces of herself, despised the choices she'd made, sank into her own weaknesses.

Marley's time at Rosa de Montana had been empowering. She had finally faced the truth about her sister, knew she was going to have to step back and let Lizzie make her own mistakes, especially since Sebastian was well cared for. She had allowed herself the indulgence of an affair with Damien. He hadn't talked or coaxed or lured her into that sexual relationship, but had offered and she'd taken.

But like Marie, she too had fallen in love with her Damien.

And somehow it felt like Anna knew and was laughing at her. A woman like Marley Turner could never keep a man like Damien du Bourg. That was what the little insecure, nasty bitch of a voice whispered in her head, and Marley hated it. Hated it that she hadn't grown past that yet, that she was still such a needy little girl who needed love.

Not that it mattered whether she could keep Damien or not, because she wasn't going to try.

He didn't want that, no matter what he said. Intellectually, neither did she. She had a life to go back to, such as it was, and she understood Marie's ache, her pain, her want for a child. Marley wanted a baby with every fiber of her being.

"Didn't take you long," Anna said from her chair on the porch.

"You knew I'd be back, because these are totally made up. You know this couldn't have happened." Marley held up the bag of letters, knowing she was being rude as hell, but unable to stop herself. "I believed everything up until the immortality thing slipped in. So were those just a woman's delusions when she was dying and her husband was cheating on her, or did someone at some point just make these letters up out of thin air?"

Marley waffled between both theories. Part of her felt that Marie had to be real, because her emotions, her pain touched Marley, as tragic as it was. She had died very unhappy, and that made Marley feel profoundly sad.

But somehow she'd rather that Marie had been real, known that suffering, than the idea that someone had manufactured those words, taken Marie's name and image and created a story for whatever purpose. Yet it was possible. The use of Rosa's name raised a red flag for her. It niggled at her and made her wonder if Rosa was the author.

"They are not made up, Marley, not one word. It's all true. All true."

Marley paced across the porch and scoffed. "You may believe in immortality, but I'm sorry, I don't. The first Damien sounds like a bit of a jerk, but he wasn't in cahoots with a demon."

"That Damien is the Damien you're in love with."

That brought her to a dead halt. Anna had just spoken the incomprehensible out loud. That she could possibly be in love with Damien. Forget the other thing. She didn't believe that for one lousy minute. But she was in love with Damien and she knew it in her heart, had just admitted it to herself not ten minutes earlier, but it was too special, too quiet, too unrequited to speak about out loud. Unspoken, it was her secret, like a gift to herself, a warm, wondrous feeling. Stated by Anna, it sounded hopeless, silly, naïve.

"I told you, I'm leaving on Sunday. None of this matters." Which didn't explain why she was standing on Anna's porch with her heart racing.

"He can't love you back, you know. He isn't capable of it. He loved that little wife of his, too late to save her, and it eats at him, rots him from the inside out. He thinks it is his nature, it is the demon curse that holds him, but it's guilt, his unwillingness to forgive himself that holds him in slavery. He didn't love Marissabelle, couldn't, and he can't love you."

Marley knew Damien felt guilt over his wife. He'd said that, admitted he'd cheated on her with Rosa. Marley was smart enough to know he couldn't care about her until he dealt with his past. Which was why she was leaving as planned. She couldn't fix him, was done helping people who didn't want to be helped.

"So what happened to Marissabelle?" Marley sank onto the front step, tired, shoulders aching. So Anna believed Damien was immortal. She was old, and she'd lived in this wild country her whole life, hearing the rumors, whispers. It was like a ghost story, about the mysterious owners of Rosa de Montana, and while Marley thought it was a little off, she figured everyone had their quirks, their superstitions. Or heck, maybe it was senility.

"Why should I waste my breath telling you when you're not going to believe me?"

Marley drew her knees to her chest and dropped her chin down. "I want to know. I would appreciate it, Anna." Maybe there were no answers as to why she'd found herself here, as to why she'd met Damien and fallen in love with a man she couldn't have, but she wanted to hear the story. The secret.

The plantation, Damien, both had a whole closetful of skeletons, and before she left Marley wanted to see them.

"So, you know then, that Death's Door was your Damien, but in those days he was wild, like we talked about earlier. He wanted to die, but he couldn't, so he took risks, and that was part of the appeal for Marissabelle. He was exciting, thrilling, he allowed her to forget about all her responsibilities and all her worries, and he took her with him into his lifestyle. Late nights, elegant sensual parties, fast carriage rides, and a sexual voracity that matched her own, that piqued and intoxicated, that spurred her to new daring, exploration. Nowadays you all would call it kinky, and maybe it was, but for Marissabelle it was just damn good sex. Feminists talk about liberation. Well, honey, let me tell you, this was liberating loving. She felt freedom for the first time ever in her life."

If Anna was inventing this story, she was doing an amazing job of touching on everything that had relevance to Marley. She heard Anna's words about Marissabelle and figured she might as well be talking about her. Her experience with Damien had been the same. She had done things sexually she'd never dreamt of before, but it had been liberating, powerful, freeing.

But she didn't want to talk about it with Anna, not now.

"I can understand that."

"But she didn't know the truth, didn't know about Damien and the demon until Rosa appeared."

There it was again. That name she was growing to despise. "The same Rosa? The one who had long black hair and was Spanish the first time around, or the now Rosa with curly hair and an African heritage?"

"Same one. But in those days Rosa had the creamy white skin of the Irish, and rich auburn hair. It is her talent, you know, to take on the personality, the appearance of a city. And in those days New Orleans was bursting with European immigrants and for a while she was white.

Marissabelle was jealous of that, envious of the purity of Rosa's skin, her dusting of pretty freckles, the way she could walk into a room and turn every man's eye. The security of a mistress lies in ensuring that she is a man's carnal desire, that she satisfies his every licentious need, his every urge to misbehave. If his eye is turned by yet another woman, her control is lost completely. It was obvious to her that Rosa already knew Damien, that they'd had a relationship, and it bothered her."

That sounded familiar. While Marley didn't think it bothered her that Damien had a past with Rosa, given the annoyance he clearly felt when she was around, it did get on her nerves that Rosa popped in whenever she felt like it. And she had a whole new perspective regarding Rosa's friendly overtures the morning after the last party. At the time it had seemed so nice, but now Marley could only remember that Rosa told her that Damien never stayed over with the women he slept with. Like she was trying to hurt Marley's feelings. Out of jealousy.

"What did she do?"

"She tried not to show her worry, her fear, but he was pulling away from her and she was starting to get desperate. So when he suggested it might be rather amusing to bed both her and Rosa together, she agreed."

Marley gasped. Well.

"Shocked you, did I?"

Uh, yeah. Marley nodded. Anna looked downright pleased by that. She leaned closer to Marley.

"But what shocked Marissabelle was how much she enjoyed those random nights, how she liked the soft feel of a woman's lips, how she liked to taste between her thighs while Rosa did the same to her. And in one of those pleasure-drenched moments they told her the truth about Damien, about Rosa, about the father and his quest for human servants. Marissabelle thought about the power of immortality, thought about the fragility of her life, and wondered what would happen to her son if she died or wasn't able to sell her charms any longer as she aged. She thought about endless life and endless pleasure and the strange attraction Damien held for her. She would gain that devotion from men, all men, that instant longing, that drooling, desperate desire, and that appealed to her vanity, her pride. Four men had used her body and left her, and she wanted to do that herself, hurt the way she had been hurt. So she asked for a place in the demon world, requested the same bargain that Damien had—immortality in return for sexual servitude."

Marley was starting to feel a little ill. There was something about the gleam in Anna's eye that was disturbing. This story wasn't real, couldn't be real, but Anna spoke with such passion that Marley was starting to feel uncomfortable. Scared. "Did they give it to her?"

"Yes, only she didn't understand they were playing her off against each other. That Damien had in mind to switch himself for her, to gain his freedom by promising her. Or that Rosa had guessed Damien's intentions and was maneuvering so that she would gain Marissabelle, but not lose him. Rosa won that little game, and when Damien found out, he left Louisiana and didn't return for fifty years. Marissabelle did what was required of her, and she became quite the favored whore of men throughout the city, and many of their wives as well. And when that son, who she did it all for, grew up, he left, casting her aside in shame and disdain for what she was, turning his nose up at her love, and making his way north to where he could be a free man of color and pretend his mother had never existed."

"Another betrayal."

"Yes, another betrayal, and another hard lesson about men and their selfishness. And yet when he died in a fire, she mourned the loss all over again."

"You know this story well." It was surreal, eerie, how Anna was looking at her.

"That's because this is my story, Miss Marley. Don't tell me you haven't figured that out yet. I'm Marissabelle, and this house was given to me by my rich white lover, Damien du Bourg."

She hadn't seen that one coming, and a shiver raced through her. Anna seemed so together the first few times she'd met her, not at all delusional, but she was different today, wilder, unrestrained. "But you said 1833 . . . there's no way . . ."

"Oh, yes, there is. I served Rosa and the father for a hundred years until I gained my freedom and started aging, changing my name to avoid questions. Damien wants to know how I broke free, he burns with the need to escape his immortality, but I'll never tell him. The hell with him. He set me up, manipulated me, and left me high and dry, and now he can want answers, but I'll never give them." Her nostrils flared in anger, spittle appearing in the corner of her mouth. "Not when I sit here rotting year after miserable year, too old to do a goddamn thing, unable to die. This isn't escape, this is worse than servitude ever was."

Marley stood up quickly. "I, uh, should get back to the house." Anna was scaring the crap out of her. She looked fierce, feral, and her words were jumbled, made no sense to Marley. She could not be over 170 years old for obvious reasons, and she'd clearly lost her grip on reality.

But Anna grabbed her arm in a steely grip that was way too strong for a such an old woman. "They want *you*, you know. Not your sister. You, because of your goodness and innocence. They love that you've gotten Damien to break his vow, and they love that he's leading you from right to wrong. It doesn't feel wrong, does it, not when it's one small step at a time, easing you in so you hardly notice, until in two years you'll find yourself fucking anything that walks for him, and you'll love it at the same time you hate yourself."

Heart pounding, adrenaline rushing, Marley yanked her arm back. "I don't know what you're talking about."

"No? Then you won't see it until it's too late. And I hope you sink fast and hard because then I get my body back all that much quicker."

Marley stumbled down the steps. "Sorry to have bothered you."

"Go on, go to your sex party. See how it makes you feel, see if you've already gotten used to it. See what a dirty little whore you are, just like I was." Anna cackled in laughter, voice high and unnatural.

Giving in to her urge to run, Marley jogged over the grass, the gravel, feet flying, that horrible sound ringing in her ears.

"It's too late to run, you know," Anna screamed after her. "You're too late. You've already served yourself up on a platter."

Chapter Seventeen

⌘

The guests had already arrived. Marley saw the cars with dismay and veered off to the back of the house. She didn't want to see anyone except Damien. She needed to talk to him, have him hold her, assure her Anna was crazy. Not that she believed any of Anna's ramblings, but it had made her feel unsafe, unprotected, unsure that she knew what was going on, ashamed that Anna had guessed at her lustful relationship with Damien and smirked at it.

While Marley had been feeling empowered, Anna had told her she was being used, and it scared and worried her, made her wonder who was right. Especially since she was living in Damien's house and wearing a skirt, tank top, and shrug sweater that he had bought for her in the French Quarter, including a very expensive coral necklace and earrings. Everything on her body had been purchased by him, right down to the mango-colored seamless bra and matching thong.

Before it had felt thrilling, romantic to have him giving her gifts, but now she felt . . . kept.

Determined to find Damien, see him smile at her, reassure her, whisper words of affection and banish all the uncomfortable, icky feelings she was having, Marley went in the back door and quickly ran through the rooms on the ground floor. No one was down there, so she went up the stairs to the main floor.

This party was even more crowded than the last, and Marley squeezed past people gathered in the center hall, moved through laughing couples, into the salon that Marie had called the morning room. She scanned quickly, ignoring a few glances in her direction, turning away quickly when she realized there was a man standing in front of the French antique mirror she'd always admired, watching Marley in the reflection as a blonde gave him oral sex. Her gaze shifted, landed on a woman who was sitting on a dark-haired man's lap, her skirt lifted to her thighs as she rode him, head back. Another turn, another set of bodies, flashes of skin, sounds of moaning, hot breathing, candles and sex scents floating through the air, and Marley felt panic rise like bile in her throat.

This was wrong. This was wrong, and this was all done by a man she said, thought, felt she loved. How could she have ignored this, convinced herself that Damien was removed from these parties? He created them, nurtured them, encouraged them. Must enjoy them.

She turned quickly, needing out, and her arm brushed a man's bare ass as he thrust into his partner, who was bent over the antique Sheraton desk, its hand-carved cherry legs shaking from the jarring motion.

"Sorry," she murmured.

Instead of being annoyed, he smiled at her, hips still moving. "No problem." He looked down at her chest. "Hey, stick around for a second. She's almost done here."

Marley realized the bent woman was moaning quite vigorously, her voice rising.

"Then I'd like to get to know you."

They were having this conversation while he was having sex with another woman, and Marley didn't know whether to laugh or throw up. "Oh, uh, no thanks, I'm looking for someone . . ." She trailed off as the woman went into frantic mewls.

On that note, Marley turned and left the room. She just couldn't do this. Trying not to make eye contact with anyone, touch anyone, or see any more body parts, Marley moved past through the opposite salon, the dusky room quieter than the last, conversations, intimacies more muted, couples tucked into corners, on couches, but no Damien.

Deciding she just wanted to go upstairs and get the hell away from all of this, Marley eased toward the door. And nearly bumped into her sister.

"Lizzie!" Her sister was leaning against the wall, a man bent over her breasts.

Her eyes popped opened. "Hey, Mar." Her voice was languid, aroused. "Great party, huh?"

No. In fact, she didn't think she could stand one more minute and she'd only been there for five. "I'm so glad to see you! Come upstairs with me so we can talk."

Lizzie looked down at the man. "Alex, can I go upstairs with my sister to say hi?"

His head lifted. "No."

Lizzie shrugged. "Sorry, Mar, Alex says no. Maybe later."

Marley stared at her sister. "Lizzie." She hadn't seen her in almost three months, and she wanted to talk to her. And who the hell was this guy?

He turned and Marley instantly disliked him. His expression was amused, arrogant, disdainful. He didn't say anything to her, just raised an eyebrow. Then pulled Lizzie's shirt back over her breasts.

"Elizabeth, I want you to give that man oral sex."

"Which one?"

"The short one next to the fireplace, looking lonely. Go now."

Lizzie started to walk toward him, then turned and asked, "For how long, sweetie?"

"Until I tell you to stop or until he comes in your mouth."

"Okay." Lizzie blew him a kiss, went up to the guy standing by himself, said a word or two, than went down on her knees.

Marley watched in disbelief. What the hell was Lizzie doing?

Alex smiled at her, like this was perfectly normal. "She likes being told what to do. It makes her feel safe."

Marley gasped in disgust. Horror, panic all had her choking on a gag. She couldn't look at Lizzie or this guy, and she pushed past him, tears in her eyes, through the archway, down the hall, out the front door. She ran down the two dozen steps, her sandals slipping, nearly sending her face-forward down the stairs.

Where was Damien? She'd left her phone in her room, so she couldn't call him on her cell. Nothing could induce her to go back into that house until every last human being was gone. Heading toward the *garçonnier*, she wiped her eyes and took deep, shuddering breaths to get ahold of herself.

Maybe if she asked, Damien would cut the entertainment short and ask everyone to go home. But that wouldn't fix what had her feeling shattered, pummeled, disillusioned. What the hell was the matter with her sister? Marley didn't understand how anyone could possibly be happy doing what she had just seen her sister do. And Damien. What did Marley do with Damien in her mind, her intellect, her heart, and all her feelings for him?

She knocked on the door, then pushed it open. With a huge sense of relief, she saw Damien immediately, sitting on top of his kitchen table, of all places, bare feet on a wooden chair. His shoulders were slumped and he had a piece of paper wadded in his hand.

"Damien. What's the matter?" He didn't look right,

and for a split second she thought he was dead. But he was sitting up, he couldn't possibly be dead.

His head lifted and she saw his eyes were red, swollen, bleary. "I thought it couldn't hurt anymore," he said. "It's been so long, but then I read what she wrote, and God, Marley, I can't take it. Marie was this sweet, innocent wisp of a woman when I married her, and I didn't appreciate that."

"What are you talking about?" His wife's name had been Marie? The panic was rising again, like a furious hot air balloon inside her chest, pushing up, shoving, threatening to take her head right off her shoulders.

"I didn't know about this confession she wrote. I can't believe that she thought any of that was her fault . . . it was me, all me. And it's my fault she died."

"How did she die?" He stared at her for so long she thought he wasn't going to answer. And when he finally did, she almost wished he hadn't.

"She killed herself." Damien spoke the words for the first time in two hundred years, forced them past his teeth, out into the air, knowing he was ruining his relationship with Marley, but certain the truth had to be told. Marie deserved the truth.

"Oh, God," Marley said, tears in her eyes. "I'm so sorry."

Her compassion always got to him, touched pieces deep inside he thought were gone, obliterated. "I'm sorry. I'm sorry that I talked you into staying here, Marley. Sorry that I pulled you into the mess that I am. You deserve better."

"I stayed because I wanted to stay. I care deeply about you. But I think you need to tell me everything . . . for both of our sakes. Anna was, well, she was acting crazy tonight, Damien. She said all these insane things about immortality and you and how she is really someone named Marissabelle."

Marley looked worried, and she clearly wanted him to tell her that Anna was indeed a lunatic. But his old mistress and nemesis had actually perfectly paved the way for him to tell Marley the truth about himself. "Anna isn't crazy, *ma cherie*. She is Marissabelle, and I am the first Damien du Bourg, the *only* Damien du Bourg. I am over two hundred and forty years old, and I cannot die."

Her head went back and forth. "Don't . . . don't say those kinds of things. It doesn't make any sense."

Watching her eyes dart wildly back and forth, running up and down over him, her expression horrified, Damien was sorry for what he had to do, what he was about to put her through. But Marley had the right to the truth, and part of him understood that he wanted Marley, wanted to keep her and the future she represented, take the love she offered and return his own. He wanted to let go of the past, move forward like she had asked him to.

He wanted out one way or another, once and for all.

She clearly hadn't noticed the gun sitting behind him on the table until he lifted it up, because her eyes suddenly went wide with alarm. Damien settled it into his hand and spoke to her, hoping she could hear, could understand how earnest, how serious he was. "I just want you to know the truth, because I have fallen in love with you. I want you to understand that it is an honest feeling, even though I haven't been honest with you. I hope you can forgive me, and understand why I couldn't tell you about me before."

The color drained out of Marley's face. "No," she whispered, fingers lifting up.

Damien smiled at her. She was amazingly beautiful, so vital and good and sweet. "See you in ten minutes, *ma cherie*."

And he put the gun to his chest and pulled the trigger.

⚜

Marley screamed and screamed, feeling it rise up and out of her throat and mouth, wrap around her head, echo on all sides of her, smother out everything except for the terror and the hideous sound of her own agony.

It had happened so fast. Suddenly he had a gun, and before she could process what he meant to do, think how she could stop him, he had shot himself, the sound deafening, his body falling backward on the table.

She ran over to him, her shriek trailing off as she forced herself into action. There had to be a phone, his cell phone somewhere, maybe in his pocket, and she had to call for help. Blinking back tears, she fought the urge to give in to hysteria and tried to think, tried to figure out what to do. He was on his back, his left shoulder slumping over the side of the table.

As she scanned from head to toe, she couldn't see where he was injured, couldn't see any blood. There was a blackish dust on his hands, but no other obvious wound. That wasn't right. Didn't make sense.

"Damien," she said in frustration and helplessness. What the hell had he done to himself? Patting his pocket, she found his cell phone, was trying to pry it out of his jeans, her damp hands slipping and sliding across the plastic.

His chest was moving, so he was breathing. He wasn't dead and he wasn't bleeding. Getting the phone out, she paused for a second, staring hard at his shirt. There was a hole, a small jagged tear, in the center. Marley grabbed the bottom of it, gently eased it up. His chest was covered in blood, the room having been too dim for her to see it soaking through his dark-colored shirt. She could hear his labored breathing, see his chest rising up and down rapidly, like he was in pain. Yet she still didn't see an obvious wound.

"Marley."

Marley snapped her head up, found herself looking

into his green eyes, open and alert. "Damien? What the hell happened? I can't see where you're bleeding from . . . I saw you shoot yourself. God, you must be in so much pain."

Shaking his head, he pulled himself to a sitting position. "Listen to me. I'm fine. I cannot die, do you understand? I am immortal, servant to the Grigori demons."

"That's not possible . . . you shot yourself. I saw it." Marley touched his chest, smoothed her hands over his unblemished flesh, ran her touch across tendons and muscles and paused to feel his heartbeat. She was losing her mind. She had seen and heard that gun go off. Yet there was absolutely no evidence of that.

His arms came around her, his warm lips pressed to her forehead. "I shot myself so you would believe me when I tell you this. I was born in New Orleans in the year 1765, the Creole son of Phillipe du Bourg, a wealthy indigo planter, and his equally wealthy wife, Serena Beaumont du Bourg, the daughter of a French landowner. In 1789 I married my wife Marie Bouvier in France and brought her here to Rosa de Montana after the death of my father. In 1790—"

"That's enough!" Marley cut him off, yanking back out of his arms.

"Marley, it's the truth. You need to know who and what I am."

Thoughts colliding, Marley pressed her eyes closed, picturing the gun going off, seeing in her mind him falling backward, remembering the hideous laugh of Anna on her porch, Rosa's knowing, helpful smile . . . everyone knowing, knowing, while she knew nothing, while she stumbled around in the dark, falling in love with a man who was not, could not, be over two hundred years old.

But was. Backing up, she stared at him, knowing the truth, hearing it, feeling it, despising it. While her brain revolted, screamed that it was illogical, impossible, the core of her knew the truth. Believed. For if God existed, which she knew He did, so did demons. And for whatever reason, Damien had signed on to serve the side of evil, and his life was unnatural, without positive purpose.

"No, this isn't happening. This isn't real." She shook her head, stared again at his chest.

"It's real. I'm real. Immortal."

Marley felt a hot, sick taste in her mouth. The truth was before her, no matter how much she didn't want to believe it. And if he was immortal, if he had been the first, the only Damien du Bourg, those letters from Marie were real. All that pain, all that suffering had been endured.

And like Marie, Marley had fallen under the spell of the demon servant, had given her body, her heart to Damien, had let him strip her of her inhibitions and boost her up the ladder of sin one rung at a time.

He must have sensed her withdrawal, because he shook his head, reached out, and grabbed her hand. "Don't do this, don't pull back from me. Let me explain. You know who I am now, know the man I try so hard to be. If I could give it all back, if I could redeem myself, make right all the wrongs I've done, I would. I've learned from my mistakes. I was young, I was foolish, selfish. That is not who I am anymore."

Marley stumbled backward, the expensive new sandals he'd bought her sticking to the brick floor. She clutched his cell phone in one hand, turned and ran yet again, terrified of him, of her own feelings, of the sensation that her entire world was caving in upon her, heavy bricks of truths raining down, smacking and smarting.

"Where are you going? Marley, stop!"

But she couldn't stop. She ran down the path away from the house, through the lane of oak trees, past the slave cabins, shadowed and ominous and hushed in their dilapidation. It was dark, but the moon was high, and she wanted to disappear. Just run on and on into the night, until it was all gone and she was back home, just Marley Turner, family martyr, where none of this existed, and she and her sister were safe.

Damien was chasing her. She could hear the pounding of his feet, but he was barefoot and slower than usual, maybe an aftereffect of shooting himself. The sugarcane fields loomed in front of her, and to the right, the swamp. She had the overwhelming urge to run straight into the murky water, to just splash in to her chest and to let oblivion take over, sinking under the cold, dark curtain, where sound and time and reality stood still. Nearly there, she was startled when Damien reached out, grabbed her arm, yanked her back.

Off balance, she screamed, and they collided, dropping to the ground hard, the air shoved right out of her lungs. Stunned, she lay on her back, head, chest, and leg aching.

"Are you insane? You can't just stroll into the swamp! What if I lost sight of you? You just gave me a fucking heart attack," he said, leaning over her, resting on his hip, hands in his hair, breathing hard.

He sounded so damn indignant that Marley just stared up at him, hysteria bubbling up and out with a laugh. That he could speak as if the situation were normal, as if he were normal, struck her as ludicrous. He had just *shot* himself in front of her.

"Would it matter if you had a heart attack? You can't die." She choked back the laughter, but a sob burst forth. "Oh, God."

"Shhh, Marley, come on now. It's alright. Everything is alright. I know this is a shock."

"That's the understatement of the millennium." Marley turned, not wanting his face so close to hers, his mouth and breath hovering over her.

"I'm the same man I was yesterday. The same man you've been talking to, laughing with, making love to. You and I, that hasn't changed."

"Of course it has!" Tears were in her eyes again, and she tried to wiggle across the dirt away from him, but he pinned her down with his arms, his chest. "You're not the same man at all. I thought you were Damien du Bourg, a man who inherited this plantation from his ancestors, a man who lost his parents, his wife, and was an innocent victim of fate." Another sob crawled up her throat. "That's not who you are."

Damien looked away. "That's true. I am certainly not a victim. This is all my doing and I take responsibility for that." Then he swiveled back, locked eyes with her. "But I am the same man nonetheless. What I say, what I do, is real, is the truth, is the man I am today." He brushed her hair back, giving a shuddering sigh. "I have tried so hard to walk the line between what the Grigori demons want, and what I can live with as a man, and I have so much remorse for all of my mistakes, all those I've hurt. If I could undo the past I would, in a heartbeat."

He looked sincere. He looked very much in pain, dripping with regret. Her heart swelled, wanting to trust, wanting to believe. The torment on his face was familiar to her. She'd seen it a number of times since she'd met him.

Marley couldn't reconcile this Damien, the one she had thought she'd known, with the Damien that Marie had described. It seemed like they were two men, but if they were one and the same, then either she or Marie was wrong. And given her lack of experience with men and her naïve inclination to believe everyone was truly good no matter what mistakes they made, it would seem that Marie was a better judge of character than she was. Then again, maybe they were both right. Maybe Damien had changed. And while she desperately wished that was true, it seemed foolishly optimistic. Leopards didn't change their spots, and right now, still in viewing distance from them, one of his adult parties was in full sexual swing, and she had never seen Damien express any remorse for his part in producing them.

"Why do you do it?" she whispered. "The parties, the themes, the cocktails . . . I thought it was meant to be a sort of punishment for yourself for cheating on your wife, a sort of defiance, or coping mechanism to keep yourself distanced from women. Safety in sex, stay away from relationships . . . but if you're not the victim, not the suffering widower I thought you were, why do you do it?"

He shrugged. "Because I have to. It is my burden, my never-ending task, to promote sexual sin among mortals. That's what I agreed to do in exchange for eternal life. It was a very bad bargain on my part."

"Do you enjoy them?" she whispered, not exactly sure what she was asking. "The parties?"

"No. Not for a long time. I told you, I've changed." Then he sighed. "It amazed me how quickly I did change, how soon I was tired of my task. Within a month, maybe two, I already regretted the choice I had made. I already wanted nothing more than to live with my wife and pretend that night had never existed."

"You were married to Marie," Marley said stupidly, shocked all over again to realize that everything Marie had written was the truth, the brutal, pain-wracked truth. "You cheated on her, you were a cold, heartless husband when she was suffering."

"What are you talking about? What do you know about Marie?" Damien stared at her in censure. "What do you know of her suffering?"

Marley figured her promise to Anna was no longer valid now that she knew Anna had been toying with her, Anna's motives unclear but suspect. "The letters Marie wrote to her friend back in France. I read them all. I read

what she said about you, how you were cruel at the beginning of your marriage, impatient with her, how you took
her virginity on the ship when she was violently seasick."

"What letters? There are no letters." Damien sat back
in shock, horrified. "But if you know about the ship . . .
how could you know that? Let me have them, Marley. Let
me read her words."

"No. She didn't want you to see them." Marley didn't
know why she said that, why she felt the need to argue, to
protect Marie's memory, and to protect herself, her very
real and frightened self, who saw Damien and wanted to
believe in his goodness so very, very much even when
evidence to the contrary stared her in the face. "She hid
them from you because she was afraid of you." That
wasn't entirely truthful and she knew it. In the second
half of their marriage, Marie hadn't been afraid of him at
all, but Marley was so hurt, so disgusted with herself, so
afraid that she had no sense of character if she could fall
in love with a man who was a lecher, an aberration. No
matter who he was now, he had said those things to Marie,
done those things. Asked for immortality from a woman
he'd only known long enough to lift her dress and have
sex with her.

Marley felt foolish, felt naïve and embarrassed by her
own behavior. She'd come for her sister, and instead she'd
taken her clothes off for the first man to pay her a speck of
attention. She had fallen in love with him, or thought she
had. "You forced Marie, even when she was seasick," she
repeated, wondering if she was trying to convince herself
he was cruel so she'd feel less stupid, less ashamed of herself for succumbing to his practiced charm.

Damien just shook his head though, looking certain,
even if a little puzzled. "She was not seasick that night, I
would swear to it. She made that up because she hadn't
wanted to marry me. She was trying to prove a point, trying to torment me, to show me that I wasn't good enough

for her, and that the only reason she had deigned to marry me was because of my money. She was beautiful, delicate, petite, and she made me feel like a barbarous oaf, so that I couldn't forget that I was not of the aristocracy. But Marley, you have to understand, I have told you I was spoiled, I was selfish, I was young and stupid. Marie was young as well, and naïve, and later I came to realize she was shy and perhaps even insecure. We started poorly, that is true, but we came to an understanding, I thought, we came to enjoy each other, and share some happiness, love."

Marley closed her eyes, unable to think, to breathe, to reason, her emotions sporadic, random, vacillating. There were too many things to think about, to dissect, compartmentalize, and the most obvious place to begin was with Marie. "I know . . . I know. That's what she said, that she came to love you, but she also felt that you led her down a path of moral destruction. Ultimately she blamed herself."

"I know that she blamed herself and I can't stand that. It was my fault, it was all my fault. I made a bad bargain with Rosa when I was drunk and angry with Marie, upset that we were being denied a child, disgusted with myself for not being good enough for her, for not being the kind of man she wanted."

"Why did you do it? Ask Rosa for such a . . . thing?" His answer might scare her, but not knowing was worse. Marley stared up at him, wanting to understand, wanting to hear that his heart wasn't black and vile and irredeemable.

"I am not even exactly sure anymore," he said quietly. "But I remember how I felt that night, remember the rage I felt that Marie was disgusted with me, that Marie, my own wife, despised me. We had an argument, or rather, I yelled at her, and she gave me that wounded, terrified look she had perfected so well, the one that made me feel like a villain who had kicked his best hunter hound. I had women fawn over me every day, yet my own wife could not stand me. I was drunk, as I often was in those days, and I was frightened that I would pass from life the way my mother and father had, without warning, with little fanfare. I was afraid of death, angry that our child had died without ever living. Angry that with all my money, I could not buy Marie's respect or affection."

Damien shrugged. "They are not feelings I am proud of now. But I wanted to live forever, to control the world before it controlled me, and I suspect, if I am being completely honest, that I wanted Marie to desire me the way I desired her. Her honesty, her goodness, her morality, all nurtured my respect for her, at the same time I disdained her because of her disgust of me. I was jealous of who and what she was, even as I loved her." He gave a rueful sigh. "I did not choose the best way to express my feelings, did I? And I have lived with my stupid, egregious mistakes every day for over two hundred years."

"Damien." Marley felt her anger deflate, if that's what it had really been. She couldn't stay upset with him, not over Marie. She heard his sincerity, felt it, had known that he was suffering from guilt and pain and loss since the very first moment she'd met him. Whatever his mistakes in his long-ago youth had been, he had paid for them over and over. "Damn it, I'm sorry. I'm making it worse and I don't know what I'm saying. I know you're sorry . . . I'll give you the letters. Maybe if you read them, you can finally get closure. You both deserve it after all this time."

It seemed like she should say more, but her head was still swirling, her thoughts muddled and thick. But her panic was fading.

Damien stared down at her. "You're amazing, do you know that? Truly amazing, with a huge heart and a compassion that I admire, cherish. I have no idea how to even attempt closure. But thank you, for believing me. Believing in me, and for giving the letters to me. And please . . . I want you to know that you're the only woman I've loved since Marie. The first woman I've had sex with in a hundred years."

Marley blinked, the back of her head still in the dirt, stunned. "And I thought my dry spell was long."

He gave a startled laugh. "It was intentional. I knew that I had to fulfill my end of the bargain, but that didn't mean I had to take personal pleasure from what I knew was wrong. Maybe that doesn't make sense to you, but it was my defiance, my way to try and retain some sense of self, some bit of my humanity. The Grigori gave me power over women, to seduce and charm, but I've focused my attentions on the shy, the unattractive women, and I . . . I pleasure them, empower them with their sexuality."

This she didn't need to know. Her compassion bled out. "That's very flattering. I'm so glad you shared that with me, glad you empowered me, a shy, unattractive woman."

He made a sound of frustration. "I don't mean you. I mean other women. You have been a challenge to me from the start . . . a complete reversal of my experience with every other woman. You were able to resist me, and yet I couldn't resist you. I told myself no, but I had to have you, wanted to revel in the way you seemed to see me, the man, not the seducer. I thought maybe . . . maybe you were attracted to me for myself, my personality, not my appearance. Not the demon charm."

So in the end he wasn't so very different from her after all, wanting love, needing to hear he was worthy. Marley's heart softened. "I was. I am." She reached out, touched his cheek. "Yes, you are a very attractive man, but what I fell in love with was the inside."

He kissed her fingertips. "I couldn't tell you, you know. 'Hey, I'm a demon servant' isn't something you blurt out when you first meet someone."

"I guess not." And no matter how much she wished it

had never been said, wasn't real, it was, and she had no idea what to do with that skewer slashed into her beliefs, her life. "So can you tell me how Marie died?"

Looking away, he frowned, hesitated. But then he said, "She found out about me, the immortality, about Rosa, and she was so horrified, she killed herself. She took medicinal herbs, way too many, ten times more than the house slave told her to take, which convinced me it was intentional. She had requested an aid to incite menstrual bleeding . . . to prepare her womb to conceive again, she told the slave. That doesn't make any medical sense now, but in those days, it would have. But she took too much, and when I found her, she had bled to death. I have never seen that much blood in my life . . . it was unreal. The mattress was soaked, sagging with the weight of all that blood. It was everywhere, hot and wet, and sickly sweet in smell, and she was very much dead. And with Marie died my chance for happiness, for redemption." Damien turned back to her, brushing his finger along her cheek. "Or so I thought, until I met you."

What concerned Marley, maybe more than Damien's relationship with Marie, was what he had done, who he had been, in the two hundred years between Marie and her. She had a sense of him then, and she knew him now, but how had the one grown into the other? "What happened between you and Marissabelle?"

His voice hardened. The tenderness, the sorrow, the guilt that were always present when he mentioned his wife vanished. Marley thought in his expression she saw glimpses of a harder Damien, the one who earned the name Death's Door.

"She used me. I used her. I was in a destructive phase, risk-taking, trying to find the weakness, the way to end my life. It was not a good time for me, and Marissabelle was entirely too much like me. She craved the thrill, the danger, and she embraced anything licentious, eagerly explored all avenues of sexuality. I had the very appealing idea that she would want to take my role, that I could tell her the truth, ask if she would like immortality, to be young forever. But together she and Rosa backstabbed me, and I wound up the same as before, with Marissabelle immortal as well and triumphant. Sixty years ago somehow Marissabelle won her freedom, and very much enjoys that I don't know how she did it."

"So you would give up your immortality?" Somehow that question felt very important to Marley. If after everything he'd been through, he would still cling to his immortality, hold tight to that invincibility, she would have her answers.

"Yes, I would give it up, without hesitation. If I knew how, I would. I don't want this, I don't want to be this man. I want the chance to prove to myself that there is good inside of me."

"Anna . . . Marissabelle . . . she hates you."

"She is a bitter, vain woman and she always has been."

"She lost her daughters. Made degrading choices so she could better her son's life."

Damien scoffed. "It's a sympathetic picture she paints. But I never saw evidence of the loving mother. What Marissabelle had in spades was lust. Lust for money, power, sex. She was the mirror of me in my youth and the perfect partner when I was determined to destroy myself. Physically and emotionally."

Marley wanted to pass judgment, wanted to turn her nose up at Marissabelle's flaws, even at Marie's weaknesses, but she was no different. She too had succumbed to lust, to greed, to the lure of selfishness.

"I do feel responsible for introducing her to Rosa, though. Perhaps without our influence, she wouldn't have become the most notorious mistress in New Orleans."

"I think sometimes we overestimate our influence on other people." Sorry she'd steered the conversation back to Anna, Marley stared up at the dark sky, unsure what she was supposed to do now, and she felt stunned, numb, jumbled. "My sister, Lizzie, is here, Damien. With some creepy guy who seems to be ordering her around. I almost think there's some kind of dominant-submissive relationship going on between them. It was disgusting." Everything, everyone felt disgusting. Even she felt disgusting, out of control, all the worse for her sins and flaws because she had been so damn certain she was *better*.

"Given how you've described Lizzie's personality, I'm not surprised. Maybe we should go back to the house so you can talk to her."

"I can't talk to her. She's too busy giving total strangers blow jobs because her boyfriend told her to." Marley closed her eyes. God, this hurt so much.

"Ma cherie . . . I'm sorry."

"Will you stop having the parties, Damien?"

"It's part of my bargain. I have to, or the Grigori will punish me. I could survive that, I'm sure, but they'll also punish Rosa, which I can't live with. And they'll take Rosa de Montana, they'll burn it to the ground . . . all I have left of my family, my father, Marie, and in the end I'll still be in servitude, chained to them. I could survive all that, I know I could, but in the end, after destroying everything that I have, they would take my soul. I would be lost in their power . . . no longer me, just a vessel of their evil. I may hate what I am, how I have to live, but I'm still me this way. I am in control. I don't want to lose the essence of my soul . . . Does that make sense?"

"Yes." Better to lose pieces of himself than the whole.

"And these people at the parties, they live this way because they want to. I have no real influence on them, I'm just a setting they chose, and without me, they'd just go somewhere else."

It was a justification and they both knew it. But Marley knew he had no choice. On the other hand, she did, and she couldn't willingly take part in any of this. It had nothing to do with her feelings for Damien, and everything to do with her respect for herself. The truth changed everything. Before, when she had thought they were two lost souls searching for comfort, it had been different. Then again, they were still two lost souls. But she had always intended to leave. That hadn't changed. What had changed was the understanding that if she stayed now, knowing what she did about Damien's servitude, about Rosa, she would be allowing herself to hover near the edge of what she knew to be wrong. She needed to pull herself back before she tripped over.

"I can't stay, Damien, you know that. I have to go home."

He sighed. "So nothing has changed? You're still leaving?"

"Yes." Her heart pounded. "Unless you ask me to stay." She didn't mean to say that, but the words slipped out, illuminating how shaky her convictions were, how vulnerable.

Damien rubbed his jaw. Then he picked up the cell phone she'd dropped and hurled it out toward the swamp with a roar of frustration. Marley jumped a little, but just waited for him to say what he needed to say.

"Damn it. You know what I have to do, Marley. You know if I ask you to stay, it just starts all over again. Rosa and her father, they'll have me by the balls, and I will slowly do to you what I did to Marie, until you can't stand me or yourself any longer. No matter how much I love you, how much I want to keep you with me, pretending that everything is okay, it isn't. This is who I am." He stabbed a finger into his chest. "I am a demon servant. And if I want to be able to live with myself, to retain any piece of decency in me, I have to tell you to go home."

It wasn't what she wanted to hear, but it was what she needed to hear. She knew he was right, knew that she

would compromise herself, lose her hold on her princi-
ples for selfish happiness, pleasure. "Is there a way I
could help you? There has to be a way to break free."

"If there is, I don't know it."

Marley felt guilty, like she was abandoning him, like
she was just tossing him to his fate and running. It tore
at her heart. "I understand everything about the past,
Damien, and I can accept it, because I know what kind of
a man you are now . . . I could even get over my jealousy
at the thought of you in bed with Marissabelle and Rosa,
but I can't deal with the immortality, the Grigori. I'd feel
like I was turning my back on my faith, letting myself . . ."

He covered her mouth with his hand. "Shh. You don't
have to explain. It's the right thing and we both know it.
That doesn't mean I like it, but it's what I want for you.
For me."

Tears flooded her eyes. She was on her side, but had
never bothered to sit up. Now she did, reaching for him,
pulling him toward her, kissing him with all the frustration
and heartbreak she felt. Their mouths collided, tongues
thrusting, and Marley slid her hand down, yanked at the
button on his jeans, needing him.

Damien slowed her hand with his and ran his lips
along her jaw. "Marley. This has to be the last time then.
The absolute last time."

"I know." She brought his mouth back to hers and
buried her hands in his hair.

Damien pushed her back onto the ground and they
yanked at clothes, clawed at each other, hot, moist mouths
sliding together, bodies grinding.

Marley heard her panting, felt the warm air on her
skin, embraced the deep, wet ache between her legs. The
night was sharp and clear around them, the swamp humming with insects, and she felt bruised, smacked, but
alive, and appreciative of that fact. It amazed her that she
could feel anything any longer, yet she did, even more so,

everything stark and sharp and pricking, like she'd been dunked in ice water and pulled back out, dripping and shivering.

Damien's tongue moved over her, stretching the neck of her tank top down and tasting her breasts, his knees kicking and shoving and maneuvering her thighs apart while she worked his jeans down.

It wasn't pretty or tender or slow, but desperate, hard, demanding, her head pressed down in the hard-packed grass, expensive clothes shoved away brutally as an inconvenience. This was what she wanted, to feel him, ferocious and primal, their frustrations bursting out as they pounded their bodies together.

Damien was hot and possessive as he shoved her skirt up, yanked her thong to the side, and for the moment he was hers, only hers, regardless of the past, ignorant of the future. When he pushed inside her, she cried out, the power of his motion skidding her on the grass. Wrapping a leg around her, he rolled them, until he was on the ground, Marley on top of him.

She spread her thighs farther, eyes half closed, swarming in sensations, wants, the agony of knowing now was it, all there was ever going to be. Skirt caught between her leg and his hip, Marley yanked it out of her way, balanced her knees in the grass, and started to move on him. Each slide up was a delicious tease, each push down a soothing ecstasy.

Shoulders tense, hair falling in her face, damp with sweat, Marley took Damien into her over and over, until they were both panting, thrusting, slapping together with all the urgency they felt. Her teeth tore into her bottom lip, Damien's fingers dug into her waist, rubbing her flesh raw. When she forced her eyes open, looked down at him, she let herself go, sinking into the pleasure, wrapping it around her, holding on to her tight, agonizing orgasm as long as she could.

Damien gripped her forearms and flipped her onto her side with more ferocity than finesse. Marley blew her sticky hair out of her eyes, lightheaded and blissfully exhausted. Prepared to lay back and let him do all the work, Marley was shocked when he shifted her hip up, so one leg crossed the other. "How . . ."

The question died on her lips when he pushed forward into her, intense and determined, touching everywhere, tripping off a whole new buildup.

And as they climaxed together, Damien stared down at her in the dark and said, "I love you. I love you."

It was more than she had expected. Yet it could never be enough.

Chapter Eighteen

Marley leaned into Damien, his arm around her waist as they walked back down the path, her muscles sore, body satisfied, mind empty, heart full for now.

"Will you spend the night in the *garçonnier* with me?"

"I thought you said that was the last time." Not that she was going to object to a sleepover.

He nudged her hip. "It was. I just thought you'd be more comfortable with me than alone in the house."

"Yes, I would. Thanks." Marley smiled up at him, then stopped walking when she heard a snort of disdain.

Rosa was in front of them, hands on her hips. "I wondered where you were hiding tonight. Nice grass stains. Let me guess, you've been doing a little midnight gardening."

"How did you know?" Damien drawled. "Those oleander bushes needed trimming."

His answer clearly irritated Rosa. She crossed her arms over her chest, which was barely covered in a gold bikini top, body jewelry wrapping around her waist and attaching to her belly button ring. Her peasant skirt glowed white in the moonlight. "I want to talk to you, Damien. Now. Alone."

"I'm sorry, it will have to wait. Marley is leaving in the morning, and we're spending some time together." Damien pressed her waist, urging her forward, clearly intent on passing Rosa on the path.

Marley didn't like the look on Rosa's face. She thought Damien was making a mistake in disregarding her. "It's okay, I can go ahead."

"No."

"Listen to your little girlfriend, she's obviously smarter than you. I want to talk to you right now."

But Damien just strode on past her. "You sound like a three-year-old, Rosa. I'll speak to you tomorrow."

Marley heard Rosa gasp, glanced at her over her shoulder, and saw her screwing her hands into fists, saw the rage on Rosa's face. Then suddenly Marley felt a whoosh around her ankles, felt heat licking her legs.

"What the hell?" Startled, she jerked back, looked down, and saw the hem of her skirt was on fire. "Damien!"

She looked around frantically, not sure what to do. The heat from the flickering flames was stinging her skin, and she bent at the knees so the skirt would hit the ground and she could swat at it.

Damien swore and stomped on her hem with his bare foot. The fire died, and the fabric smoldered. "Rosa, that is not fucking funny."

"What?" Rosa sniffed, studying her fingernails.

As Marley stood back up, she felt the back of her skirt lift like a wind had caught it. "Oh, God!" Now the seat of her skirt was smoldering. There were no flames, but the fabric was darkening, making crackling sounds as it smoked and spread out in a circle. She felt the heat on her backside and froze in panic.

Damien smacked her hard, preventing a flame from springing up. Marley stumbled forward from the blow.

"Look, if you're into spanking, that is your business,

but I could do without seeing it." Rosa looked to be fighting a smug smile.

Marley was suddenly afraid of that smile. Rosa had
powers she didn't understand, and she clearly saw Marley
as the enemy. Skirt still hot to the touch, Marley started
to turn around when the whole hem burst into a colorful fire ring. She screamed, and Damien yanked her skirt
down to the ground and pulled her out of it.

"Damn it, it, that's enough," Damien told Rosa, seriously annoyed with her. She was scaring the hell out of
Marley and he really didn't like that.

She glared at him. "Don't mess with me. I'll set her on
fire like a human Molotov cocktail if you don't show me
some respect."

"You'd never do it." Damien tossed Marley's skirt a
few feet away from them and stared down Rosa. She
looked serious, but he had never known her to be truly
malicious. Mischievous, yes. But cruel, no.

"Want to try me?"

No, he didn't want to risk it. "Fine, you win. Does that
make you happy?"

Marley was clinging to his side in her tank top and
thong panties. Damien yanked his shirt off over his head
and handed it to her. "Here, put this on. Go ahead back
and wait for me in the *garçonnier*. Lock the door behind
you. I'll be there in five minutes."

She nodded, eyes huge with fear, and she took the shirt
from him, fingers trembling slightly. "You'll be okay?"

He smiled at her and kissed her lightly. "I'll be fine.
Rosa and I understand each other." He patted her backside gently. "Go on."

She nodded, pulled the shirt on, tugging it over her
butt, and walked quickly, glancing back over her shoulder. The bush to her left burst into flames and she skit-
tered away from it. Damien started toward her, but it
fizzled out and Marley kept going.

"Nice, real nice," he told Rosa.

She shot him a look of pure gleeful triumph as she twitched Marley's skirt around on the ground with the toe of her sandal. "Expensive label. That's too bad."

"Going to pay me back for it?"

"Oh, *you* bought the skirt. I should have guessed. That girl doesn't have the taste to buy something this nice. How sweet of you. But then you were always good to your whores."

She was trying to get a rise out of him, and damn it, it was working. Damien forced himself to take a deep breath. "What would you like to discuss, my dear? Obviously it's something urgent if you felt the need to play fire starter."

"Don't mock me. You're already on my shit-list. I'm serious. I'd love an excuse to burn this house to the ground."

Why did Damien suddenly feel like that wouldn't be a bad thing? It sometimes felt like Rosa de Montana held him captive as much as the Grigori did. "Don't be so damn sensitive. Since when do you take a little ribbing so seriously? I thought we were better friends than that." Rosa looked volatile enough that he felt the need to defuse her anger.

"Friends?" She laughed. "That may be stretching it. What we are is two sides of a coin, a mirror to the other, male and female versions of the same person. But the one huge difference between us is that I accept who I am, and you fight it over and over, and you exhaust the hell out of me."

"Then let me go. If I'm such a burden to you, just cut me loose, resign me to hell, let me return to the vulnerability of mortality." It was futile to ask, but he had to. He would give anything to be just a man again.

"You'd like that, I know, but the thing is I can't do that. But there is a way for you to gain your freedom."

"How?" She was toying with him, he was certain, but a small part of him still hoped, still ached to have an answer.

"Like I'm going to tell you. You have to work it out yourself."

"You mean by getting someone to take my place. That's what Anna did, isn't it?" At one time he had been desperate enough to try that, and had rationalized Anna wanted what he offered, which she had. But it hadn't been right, he knew that, and he wouldn't do it again, under any circumstances.

"Yes, that's what she did, but there is another way."

"How?"

"Come on, I can't spell it out for you. That would be too easy. You have to get enlightened and shit . . . you know, seek the answer in the obvious and you'll find peace." Her anger seemed to have dissipated, and she flicked his arm with her finger in amusement. "Look inside yourself, dummy. That's the way these things always work."

"You're joking." She sounded like a fucking fortune cookie.

"Dead serious." Rosa crossed her finger over her heart. "But that's not what I came to tell you."

"No?" This conversation was only frustrating him. Damien struggled for patience.

"Nope. I meant to tell you he's here, you know."

"Who?" It wasn't like Rosa to talk in obscurities. That was Anna's specialty.

"My father."

Damien had to admit, that shocked him. As far as he knew, he'd never met the demon to which he was enslaved. "Where? In the house? Who is he with?"

"You're cute when you're being stupid. He's with Marley's sister."

"With Lizzie?" Damien was astonished, but equally amazed he hadn't seen this coming before. "Oh, shit, Rosa. None of this was a coincidence, was it?"

"Now you're finally catching on."

His mind was racing, forcing the pieces into the puzzle. "You and Anna gave the letters to Marley, didn't you?"

Her eyes gleamed, black with shiny flecks of gold. "Duh."

"Why?"

"That's for me to know, and you to find out."

His temper flared. "Cut the cutesy shit. You're not a fifteen-year-old schoolgirl. What do you want? What does your father want with Lizzie?"

"I can't tell you! Not because I don't want to, but because I can't. Don't you get it? You'll have to figure it out yourself."

What he needed to do was go to Marley and then find her sister. "Fine, whatever. I wouldn't expect you to do something for someone other than yourself."

Her shoulders slumped and she took his hand, wiggled it back and forth. "Don't do that, don't be mad at me. I care about you. You know you're like family to me." She grinned. "Kissing cousins. But seriously, I care about you. I never meant to hurt you. I never meant for Marie to kill herself. I thought she'd say yes, not drink a bunch of poison."

Damien felt everything inside go ice cold. "What do you mean?" he asked in a steely voice, extracting his hand from Rosa's. "Yes to what?"

"I offered her the chance to save you and the baby. All she had to do was offer herself to my father. It was a good bargain, I thought she'd take it, and everyone would be happy."

"The *baby*? She was *enceinte*?" Pain ripped through him, tearing open wounds he'd thought were long since healed.

"You didn't know about the baby?" Rosa asked in astonishment. Then she said, "Oops. Sorry." She made a whoopsie face, like she'd just accidentally revealed a surprise party, not that his wife had been pregnant when she'd killed herself.

Everything made much more sense, though, why Marie had done what she had. She would have rejected the idea of sleeping with a demon, even if it meant death to escape it. In that regard, she had been a much stronger person than him.

He should have known, he should have protected Marie, his child. Like he needed to protect Marley now.

The truth came to him in a flash. This was his punishment, once again. The punishment of lust. He started to run.

❧

Marley knew the minute she clicked the lock on the door of the *garçonnier* that she wasn't alone. Whirling around, she saw Lizzie's boyfriend, Alex, sitting in a chair at the table.

"What are you doing here?" Too freaked out from Rosa's little display of fire power, she didn't bother to be polite. She was in a T-shirt and her underwear, her lover was immortal, and her sister had appalling taste in men. She had no interest in chatting with this creep. "Where's Lizzie?"

"In the house, naked. I put her on a couch and gave the room an open invitation to do whatever they'd like with her."

Marley's stomach churned. "You're disgusting. You should be ashamed of yourself for taking advantage of someone as needy and insecure as Lizzie is." And for the first time, Marley realized that truly was what drove her sister.

"That's not how I'd describe Lizzie. More like how I'd describe you."

She wasn't going to rise to that bait. "Did you need something? Because this part of the plantation is off-limits to partygoers. I need to ask you to go back to the big house."

"Waiting for your lover?" Alex had long legs and he stretched them out casually, his elegant fingers tapping a rhythm on the chair arm. "I confess I had hoped Damien would appreciate your unique charms, but even I am surprised at how taken he is with you. It seems our boy fancies himself in love. I find that amusing in the extreme."

Marley's irritation turned to fear, and she gripped the hem of Damien's T-shirt. "What are you talking about?"

"I keep forgetting you don't know who I am. I am Rosa's father and a Grigori demon." He stood up and bowed to her. "It is a pleasure to make your acquaintance, my dear."

For a split second, Marley thought she was going to faint. Her fear clawed up and down her back, her throat, ringing in her head, and she swallowed hard, pushing back bile. "What do you want?" she whispered. God, this man, this demon, this walking evil, was with her sister. Had Lizzie completely under his control.

"I should have thought it was obvious." His eyes raked up and down her body. "I want you."

Marley fought the urge to take a step back. "For what?" Not that she thought he was looking for a good cook or a teacher for his children. She knew what he wanted, but the very concept made her feel ill, raw terror rising like vomit inside her.

"Let me explain myself. You look a bit concerned. I want you as my lover, perhaps eventually my wife if we are both so inclined."

His voice was smooth, cultured, low and coaxing, and he smiled, his manner neither threatening nor intimidating. He looked like a wine connoisseur, a piano virtuoso, a patron of the arts. He had none of the wildness Damien possessed, that instinctive edge of danger that surrounded him. This man was physically attractive, his features smooth, cheekbones high, hair neatly trimmed. But Marley could see that the intense look in his eyes didn't match the casual tone.

"I'm not so inclined."

He laughed, and the sound sent a shiver down her spine.

"And you already have my sister. What do you want me for?"

Alex, if that was really his name, shrugged. "Sure, Lizzie has been fun, but there's just no challenge there, Marley. I am a demon. I love to promote sin. A woman like Lizzie will sin with or without me. I only encouraged her to dive fully into her base nature. Maybe when I was younger, that would have satisfied me. But now it's just not enough. I want you. I want the thrill of turning a good girl bad. Now that would be very satisfying indeed."

There was no way, ever, that Marley would willingly have sex with that man, creature, whatever he was. She wondered if she could run for the house, or if she should stay and talk to him, waiting for Damien. Not that she really wanted to force a confrontation between the two. If Rosa could set things on fire, Marley could only imagine what Alex could do. But no matter what he was capable of, she was not going to sleep with him.

"If you want me, you'll have to rape me."

Alex made a sound, obviously offended by her frank speaking. "My dear, I have never forced a woman. Ever. What would be the point in that? The whole point is a woman's capitulation, don't you see? The moment that she throws over her values, what she thinks is right, her inhibitions and ridiculous prudery, and embraces what I'm offering, that is when I win. That is the glorious moment I desire, the moment I crave with you."

Marley could see his logic in a sick sort of way. "You're never going to get me to agree to walk over to a total stranger and give him oral sex because you asked me to. That's just never going to happen, not in my lifetime, not while I'm sober or drunk or anything else."

"I can see I haven't explained myself well. My relationship with you will be different than mine with Lizzie. I give her what she wants, needs, and that is a firm hand, guiding her, telling her what to do. She enjoys the crudity of my dominance. That isn't what you need or want, though, and I recognize that. You crave loyalty, stability, a nice home, and a faithful partner who worships you in bed. I can give you that, I can give you pleasure. I want more children, you want children." He ran his thumb across her cheek, making her shudder. "I have only been married once, to Rosa and Marguerite's mother, and I don't take the institution lightly. You wouldn't want for anything."

Did he really expect her to just say yes? She was waiting for the moment his pleasant, rational coaxing turned ugly, because surely he didn't expect her to just fling herself into his arms, even if he had managed to hit on exactly what she did want from a relationship. She shifted her face away from his touch, voice shaky, heart pounding wildly, but conviction as strong as ever. "You can't give me what I want."

He leaned forward, brushed his lips along the corner of her mouth, up her jaw, to her ear. "But I can take away that which you love the most."

Here it came. She steeled herself, tried not to beg. "Leave Lizzie alone."

"It's so simple, Marley." He pulled back, cupped her face with both of his smooth hands. "You come to me, willingly, and I release both Lizzie and Damien. A phone call and we can trot Lizzie off to rehab back home, and one word from me and Damien is released back to his mortality, free to do as he chooses. And you get everything you've ever wanted. A husband, children, a beautiful home, respect and love, sexual freedom."

Marley tried to pull away, but her legs felt frozen, cemented to the floor, and her thoughts tumbled and turned in her mind. She managed to shake her head. "You mean sacrifice myself for Lizzie and Damien." Isn't that what she'd always done? Was this really so different?

"Sacrifice? What sacrifice?" He smiled, a gentle, passive smile, brushing her hair off her face. "Am I really so horrible to look at? Women usually respond well to me."

His lips touched her, barely there, then gone again. His hands stroked her hair, and Marley shifted uneasily. It felt like his fingers were also sliding up her thighs, even though they were clearly buried in her hair, holding her head. Yet she felt it again, a soft caress across the front of her panties, and her body responded positively, sending forth a welcoming warmth.

Horrified, she shoved at the hands that weren't there, trying to knock the sensation of the touch off her legs, her thighs, her sex.

"It's not so different then, is it?" he said. "You can have with me what you have with Damien du Bourg."

Marley wrenched herself back, rubbing at her temples, her arms, crossing her legs tightly. "Stop it!"

Visions leaped into her head, clear and sunny. Flashes of her in front of a large Dutch Colonial, planting fat, lush geraniums, three small kids playing in the yard. "Mommy, watch me!" the little girl called, before attempting a wobbly cartwheel. Marley felt the joy in her heart in the scene, smelled the freshly cut grass, knew the pride and love for the children, her children. Then she saw Lizzie, sitting on the porch of a tiny bungalow, her hair shorter, cheeks fuller, a little girl in her lap, a kind-looking older man leaning over and kissing Lizzie on the head. "How are my girls?" he asked, and Lizzie smiled, a happy, sane smile. Tears popped into Marley's eyes, seeing her sister so content, and she raised her hand, thinking she could touch her, when she disappeared, and in her place, Marley

saw Damien in front of Rosa de Montana. The house had
been painted, the yard cleaned up, and there was a petite
and very pretty Hispanic woman on his arm, both smiling
as they watched two rough-and-tumble little boys run
pell-mell down the path toward a playset.

Marley felt invisible arms wrap around her, holding her,
stroking and soothing, as she watched the man she loved
have everything he wanted, her sister well taken care of,
happy. "No," she said, but it was a whisper, lacking in fire
and strength. "They can both have that with me."

"No," Alex said, his voice soft and sad. "No, they can't,
and you know that, Marley. They can only have it if you
let them go, if you take what I offer. Don't you see how
happy everyone is? That's within your power to give."

She didn't know how he did that, holding her, the very
weight of his arms around her, yet he stood five feet away.
And she hated that it felt comforting to have that feeling
there, like a deep-seated relief to give up all her responsibilities, to let herself have happiness. Rubbing her temples, she saw Sebastian, a boy of ten, playing basketball
with Rachel's children, looking happy and well-adjusted.
Watched Lizzie painting on a large canvas, her baby on
her back in a pack. Marley had forgotten that once upon a
time, in obliterated childhood dreams, Lizzie had wanted
to be an artist.

And she saw herself, in bed with Alex, snuggled up together, laughing, their children bouncing at the bottom of
the four-poster bed. They leaped off one by one, a girl,
two boys, all with auburn hair, so real, so alive as they ran
out of the bedroom door, and Marley saw herself reaching for Alex, saw herself whispering to him, stroking his
chest, below his waist, felt her arousal, her desire for him,
felt how she would never get tired of him, would never
stop wanting him, would always be grateful for what he'd
given her . . .

Marley snapped her head up, stared at the real Alex,

heart beating wildly, fingers and feet ice cold. "You're very cruel."

"Why? Because I show you what you want, what I'm willing to give you?"

Because he tempted her, even when she knew it was wrong. "Where is God in that pretty picture you paint?"

Alex shook his head. "He isn't there. There is only you, me, and bliss."

The tears rolled down her cheeks as she fought an overwhelming wave of sorrow, an ache that threatened to swallow her. "I . . . I . . ." His touch was there again, like twelve hands touching her, holding, invading her in places he had no right to go. "I need to leave." It was a trick, all just a horrible manipulation, she knew that, and she needed to get away from him.

"Okay," he said soothingly. "Why don't you go to the house, talk to your sister, take some time to think. Put these on before you go."

Marley felt fabric brush against her, and when she looked down, she was wearing jeans over her thong, Damien's T-shirt gone, replaced with a cute pink short-sleeved pointelle sweater. She reached up, felt her hair brushed and tidied into a bun.

"I'll find you when you're ready to talk," he said.

He didn't seem to require or expect anything else from her, so Marley backed out of the room, tripping over the door strip before she recovered herself, and slamming the door shut behind her.

She sucked in deep breaths and wiped her clammy forehead.

As she stumbled down the steps and headed toward the big house, she started to pray.

For her sister.

And for strength.

Chapter Nineteen

Damien made sure Marley went into the house before he jogged up the steps of the *garçonnier* and opened the door.

"What do you want with her?" he asked Rosa's father, without preamble.

Alex, who Damien knew was really the demon Azazel, turned from the window and lifted an eyebrow. "With who?"

"Marley."

"None of your damn business."

Damien wasn't that stupid. He had seen the look on Marley's face, had seen her wearing clothes he'd never seen before, remembered what Rosa had said about his need to be punished. The father was going to use Marley to punish him, and if he succeeded, it would be a brutal one.

He couldn't live with himself if this demon hurt Marley. But the very worst punishment would be that he *would* live, on and on and on, forever with his guilt and self-loathing, and Alex knew that.

"If this is about me, do whatever you need to do to me,

just leave Marley out of it. She's innocent in all of this. Leave her alone and you can do whatever you want to me. Kill me, steal my soul, make me a mindless slave, give me to Rosa as a sex servant, just please, let her go."

"Well, that was very dramatic. Are we in an opera?" Alex rolled his eyes. "Though I imagine Rosa would have liked to have heard that bit about the sex servant offer. She has an adolescent crush on you and always has."

Damien fought anger. He didn't like Alex on principle, but he also didn't like the way he stood, his posture arrogant yet effeminate. He reminded Damien of his drawing master in the late eighteenth century. Alex was a prig, just like Master Colbert. He just couldn't bring himself to fear this man.

"Adolescent is a good word to describe Rosa."

"You insult my daughter, after all she has done for you?"

Damien shrugged. He wasn't sure Rosa had ever done him any favors.

"You're still angry because she betrayed you with Marissabelle. That was over a hundred and seventy years ago. You need to learn forgiveness."

"So what does Marissabelle have to do with any of this?"

"Oh, I promised her she could have her old body back, that luscious, youthful body she used to such advantage with lustful men, both young and old. All she had to do was help keep Marley here long enough for you to succumb to her charms and give up your asinine vow of celibacy. She did her part well, playing the sweet old lady and gaining Marley's trust. I think she blew it tonight, though, letting her rage get the better of her." He shook his head. "I'm rather annoyed about that. I think maybe I should take her back to sixty years old and let her age from there to ninety all over again. That would really infuriate her, wouldn't it?"

Damien thought not even Anna deserved to relive her latter life over and over. "What do you want with Marley?"

"I want a loving wife, more children. Marley suits my requirements."

Damien's vision blurred, his hands twitched. The thought of Marley with this demon for eternity, serving him, made Damien dizzy with anger. His fist shot out, landed right on Alex's elegant nose, cracking it. Raising his hands in front of his face, Damien waited for retaliation, waited for the provocation to throw another punch and pummel out all of his anger onto this man, this demon, who held his life in his hands.

But Alex just rubbed his nose carefully and said, "That was entirely unnecessary. And ridiculous, since it did not hurt in the least. I can't feel human pain."

But it had felt good nonetheless. Damien forced his anger into check. He needed to negotiate, not provoke. "What do you want? I'll do anything. Just leave Marley alone. I'm serious. Please."

"You'd do anything if I let Marley go? Would you bark like a dog?"

"Yes," Damien said through gritted teeth. He honestly would do whatever it took, would swallow all of his pride and dignity. He couldn't let Marley fall into Alex's clutches, not Marley, who was better than the rest of them combined. Marley deserved her life, her choices, her loving husband and children that she wanted.

"Would you lick my boot?"

"Yes."

"Would you die for her? Permanent, never to return, death?"

Damien didn't even hesitate. "Yes."

Alex frowned. "I should have known you were going to say that. You've been a gigantic pain in the ass since the day Rosa made you. I'm glad to finally be rid of you."

And suddenly Damien was in the room alone.

Marley went into the house through the first floor and ran up in the interior steps, shoved and pushed her way through rooms, and found her sister splayed out on a couch, just like Alex had told her, a man between her legs. Lizzie's eyes looked unfocused, and without her clothes on, Marley could see how gaunt she looked, how her tan had faded and her arms had lost muscle tone.

Frightened by Alex, hovering on the edge of hysteria, Marley reached out and yanked the guy off of Lizzie by the back of his hair. He let out a surprised "Hey" and turned as if to protest. But he took one look at her and clamped his mouth shut.

"Find someone else," she told him, tugging on his hair to make her point clear. Never in her life had she resorted to violence, but if he didn't take himself off somewhere far away from her, she was going to lose it.

Lizzie made sounds of protest, prying her eyes open. "Marley, what are you doing? He was just getting it right."

Fortunately, the guy recognized she was on the edge, and he scooted around her and left the room without another word.

Marley pulled Lizzie up by her arm. "Come on. You're coming with me."

Lizzie made all sorts of protests, yanking at her arm, but she was too drunk or drugged to resist Marley's iron grip, and she stumbled along behind. Marley pulled her into the hallway, and up the stairs to the room she'd been using. She let go of her sister, who made a big show of rubbing her arm.

"What the fuck is your problem?" Lizzie asked.

"We have to leave here, Lizzie, do you understand me? Alex is dangerous. We need to go home. Where's your stuff?" She pulled her own suitcase out of the armoire and flicked it open. "You can wear something of mine, and we can stop for your stuff, or we can just forget about it. I'll buy you new clothes."

"What are you talking about?" Lizzie sat down on the bed, obviously not the least bit bothered by her nudity, and crossed her legs. "I'm not going anywhere. Alex is my soul mate. I love him, and he loves me. We're getting married."

Marley started folding her jeans and stacking them in her suitcase. "I'm not going to let you marry him. He's not a nice guy."

"You have no say in who I marry! You're just jealous because you can't get a guy to marry you." Lizzie smirked. "Oh, I get it. Damien dumped you, didn't he? He said all the right things, made you think he cared about you so you'd screw him, and now he's dropped you. That's why you're in such a hurry to get out of here, and that's why you're jealous of my relationship with Alex."

That would be the day. Marley strove for patience, knowing she needed Lizzie to cooperate. "I am not jealous, honestly, and if Alex was a nice guy, I'd be totally happy for you. I want you happy more than anything. And Damien did not dump me. We mutually decided it was best to go our separate ways. This has nothing to do with Damien. You're in love with Alex and you're not seeing the truth, sweetie."

Lizzie snorted. "What truth is that?"

"That Alex is a jerk." She couldn't exactly say he was a demon, or Lizzie would think Marley had more of their mother in her than they'd realized.

Lizzie looked sullen, her legs swinging. "No, he's not. You don't know him like I do."

"He hit on me twenty minutes ago, Lizzie. He said if I hooked up with him, he'd dump you." A modified version of the truth, but the truth nonetheless. "I'm going to tell him no, and I think he'll be angry. I really think he's dangerous."

Marley wasn't prepared for Lizzie to hit her, and when she did, it was such a shock that Marley didn't even block the blow. She took the full force of Lizzie's hand across her cheek and temple, and stumbled, dropping the shirt she'd been folding. Pain burst out from her cheekbone, her eyes watering, her teeth slicing into her tongue from the jarring motion.

"Lizzie!" Marley gasped, the tinny taste of her own blood in her mouth. "What's the matter with you?"

"I hate you!" Lizzie said, crying. "Everyone thinks you're so goddamned perfect, Marley who never does anything wrong, who everyone likes, who everyone always told me I should be more like, and it's all a big fat lie. You're just a selfish, jealous bitch who can't get a man and resents that I can. I don't believe for one minute that Alex said anything more than hi to you and I'm sick to death that I'm the only one who ever sees what a manipulator you are. You fool everyone with that stupid helpless good girl act, but not me."

"Lizzie . . ." Marley wasn't sure what to say, was shocked to the core that her sister had such hateful feelings toward her. "I'm only trying to protect you."

"I don't need protecting. I can take care of myself, way better than you can, because you never see the obvious. You walk around all shy and insecure and you never seem to get that people adore you, they admire you, they think you're a fucking angel, and while everyone thinks I'm fun, it's you they really like. And you never even know it. Remember John Schwartz, your friend from college? When you'd bring him to our house for the weekend, I used to sneak into the family room where he slept and go down on him. Why do you think he always loved coming to our house? It wasn't because Mom and Dad were such great company. But the ironic thing was that he never liked me, he just wanted the blow job. It was you he liked, you he wanted to spend time with, but your virgin act finally turned him off."

Marley held her throbbing cheek and listened to her sister rant, felt her twist the knife inside her heart just a little more. She had loved John as a friend, wished he could have been more, but thought he wasn't interested. "You did that to hurt me?"

Lizzie shrugged. "Yes. And because you never got that sex is what makes the world go around. Everyone thinks you're so smart, but I'm the one who knows the score. You could have had John wrapped around your finger if you'd thrown a little pussy his way. You'll never get ahead unless you figure out how to use that."

"If I have to use sex, then I'll gladly stay right where I am and never get ahead." Marley started shoving T-shirts into the suitcase.

"Hey, guess who Sebastian's father is?" Lizzie's anger seemed to have abated and she was holding on to the bed post, swinging back and forth, her hair streaming around her.

Marley was really sure the answer wasn't going to please her, but this might be the only opportunity to learn the truth, and for Sebastian's sake, she needed to hear it. At some point, he had the right to know who his father was. "Who?" she managed to say, despite the fact that her tongue felt three sizes too big.

Lizzie gave her a perky smile. "Alan Daniels."

Now that hurt. Marley blinked hard. Alan had been a lawyer she'd gone out with twice, an older guy, in his forties, who she had really, really liked. They'd been friends for several months, introduced through a criminal case he'd been prosecuting that involved one of her students as a witness. She had thought their dinners had gone well, but he'd stopped calling her, and had been extremely un- comfortable around her the next time she'd bumped into him. "Before or after I went out with him?" she asked, even though she already knew the answer.

"After your second date, of course. I was at your place and he dropped by to see if you wanted coffee. I invited him in, and an hour later, I was fucking his brains out. I knew it would bug you, and I was curious how an old guy would be with stamina and stuff. He loved it, believe me, but he pissed me off by talking about you afterward. How it had been a mistake, that he really liked you, thought you were smart and funny and sweet." Lizzie made gagging motions. "Please. I told him to leave you alone or I'd tell him about us. I didn't mean to get pregnant, that really was an accident."

"You never told him about Sebastian, did you?"

"Hell, no. I don't want a lawyer of all people screwing around in my life or my kid's life."

"But he's entitled to know he has a child."

Lizzie scoffed. "No, he isn't. Serves him right for having sex with a woman he only knew for an hour."

It was logic that made no sense to Marley. Lizzie had set out to entrap Alan . . . then somehow blamed him. Marley couldn't listen anymore. Her sister was beyond being rational, and she couldn't fix that, couldn't change that standing in a room at Rosa de Montana at midnight.

"Okay, you've succeeded. You've hurt me. Though I don't know why you felt like you had to compete with me. You're the one who was always popular, with guys and girls."

Lizzie sat back down on the bed, her expression indignant. "You are so in denial. You compete with me all the time. Always making me feel bad about Sebastian. And now you've gone and slept with a guy I told you I liked, and you've thrown yourself at the man I'm in love with. You don't want me to be happy."

Marley sighed, her heart shattered, her will gone. She couldn't fight this, couldn't change Lizzie. "Believe what you want. Stay here and do whatever you want, Lizzie. But tell me why you sent me Marie's letter in that e-mail. What was the point in that?"

"Who's Marie?" Lizzie shrugged. "I don't know what you're talking about."

Which made Marley wonder if it had been Rosa who'd attached the letter. But she didn't see how that was possible.

"It was a confession, from Marie du Bourg. It was attached to your e-mail to me."

"Oh, that." Lizzie leaned back on the bed, bouncing again, tossing her head side to side, looking utterly disinterested. "Rosa thought it would help get you down here to visit. And she was right, wasn't she?"

"How do you know Rosa?"

"She's at all of Damien's parties. Duh. You know, I never thought I could get into the girl-on-girl thing until she talked me into it." Lizzie grinned. "Now I can't believe what I've been missing out on. You should try it, Mar."

Marley closed her eyes. Rosa had known all along. Had planned for Marley to come to Rosa de Montana. Had used Lizzie. Marley felt ill, her fingers clamped onto her suitcase.

"Going somewhere?" a voice asked from the doorway.

Spinning around, eyes flying open, Marley felt her heart rate ratchet up again. It was Alex, looking refined and in control.

"Alex!" Lizzie ran over to him and kissed him, wrapping her naked body around him.

He tolerated the embrace, but no more. "Seeing your sister off?" he asked. "It looks like she's leaving in the morning."

Actually, she'd been intending to leave right then, and hoped like hell she could find a hotel room at one in the morning in New Orleans. In retrospect, it didn't sound like a great plan. Maybe Damien would let her spend the night in his town house on Esplanade.

"Yeah, Marley has some bug up her butt, as usual. She said the most awful things to me."

Marley turned back to her packing, figuring Alex already knew what she was doing, and she wasn't about to stand there and argue in a circle with her sister. They would just have to patch things up later, when Marley was gone from this place, when Alex ditched Lizzie and she wanted her big sister again, like she always did. Marley would be there, of course, like she always was.

Alex's offer to her was a false one, and she couldn't accept it, no matter what the consequences. Damien wouldn't want her to, and freeing Lizzie from Alex still wouldn't fix what was wrong with her. And no matter how pretty it was in pictures, Marley didn't want a life that was based on falsehoods, weakness, the seduction of sin.

I sensed you had an answer ready for me, Marley heard Alex say. She whipped around and stared at him. He was letting Lizzie kiss along his shoulder, bump her hips against him. Lizzie gave no appearance that she'd heard him speak.

So your packing is your answer? You're leaving, refusing my offer? His lips weren't moving. But she could hear his voice, clear and hypnotic, in her head.

Marley shivered. She wet her lips with her tongue and nodded. "I can't. I won't."

You're certain? Absolutely certain? Not even for Damien and Lizzie?

"No." Down that path lay destruction for all of them.

"I'm sorry you're leaving," he said out loud. "We were just getting to know each other so well."

Lizzie pulled her head back and looked at him, instantly suspicious. "What does that mean? You've never even said two words to Marley."

"Actually we might have said more than two words

when we were fucking in the guest house a little while ago."

Marley felt the blood drain from her face. So this was her punishment for refusing him. "Lizzie, he's lying, we didn't . . ."

But Lizzie was already weeping, big wet tears. "Alex? Tell me you didn't."

"I didn't think you'd mind," he said, all honest astonishment. "We have an open relationship. And Marley was so tempting. She came to me, in tears, with an adorable pouting lip, upset because Damien used her badly. I felt so sorry for her heartbreak that I thought it would be in bad taste to refuse her overtures. Besides, I enjoyed how shy she was with me. A sweet, innocent good girl is so arousing sometimes."

It was exactly the right thing to say to revive Lizzie's anger. She pushed away from Alex. "Don't sleep with my sister again, Alex. I'm serious."

"Since when do you give orders in this relationship? If I want a sister act, you'll do it." He grabbed her elbow when she would have stomped away from him. "But truthfully, I'd rather have Marley alone. She intrigues me, the way she was such a quiet, shy lover, yet so quick to come."

Marley gasped, a sick feeling spreading in her gut.

"But . . . but I thought you loved me." Lizzie's voice sounded whiny, pleading. "I thought we were getting married."

"Elizabeth, there are girls you marry and girls you don't. You're fun, but Marley is the kind of woman a man wants to marry, not you."

Marley closed her eyes. He was so very good at this.

Lizzie let out a little gasp. Then she turned to Marley and said, "Don't you ever speak to me again. I despise you. And don't go near my son, either."

She ran out of the room, hands covering her face, her nakedness never a concern.

Marley looked at Alex, resigned, tears in her eyes. She had done the right thing, but she had just lost her sister, completely and forever.

Alex smiled and gave her a shrug. "I'm sorry, my dear, but for every action there is a reaction. You had to know there would be consequences for your refusal."

She nodded, not trusting herself to speak.

"I'm disappointed, I must say. I was greatly anticipating my success with you."

"We don't always get what we want," she said, voice and emotions raw.

"True." His touch caressed her cheek, her lips. "Enjoy your lonely, barren life, Marley Turner."

When he left, Marley stared into her suitcase, the jeans and shirts she'd already packed blurring and shifting.

That had sounded like an ominous prediction, one she really feared was going to come true.

❧

"Oh, thank God, there you are," Damien said from the doorway. "When you weren't in the *garçonnier*, I . . ."

Marley looked up when Damien stopped speaking.

"What are you doing? Are you alright?"

No, she wasn't, not in the least, but she was going to have to be. Marley finished stepping out of the jeans Alex had put on her and flung them into the corner of the room. "I'm as good as can be expected. I just told the demon that I will not do what he wants me to do, and in return, he told my sister I had sex with him. Lizzie hates me."

Though it seemed Lizzie had been angry with her even before Alex had lied about them. Marley was still shocked to realize that her sister had manipulated men Marley had been interested in. Obviously, she was totally stupid, just like Lizzie always said, because she had never seen that. Not once had it even occurred to her to suspect Lizzie of that kind of betrayal.

"What did he ask you to do?" Damien asked, coming into the room and closing the door behind him.

"Nothing." She blushed as she reached for her own jeans out of her suitcase. It was embarrassing the way Alex had so easily picked up on her wants and desires, and the image of Damien with that woman, with his children, played again in her head.

"What did he ask you to do?" Damien repeated, and he sounded so angry, so jealous, that she turned around, shook her head.

For the first time, she saw the traces of the Damien that Marie had known.

"What sick thing did he suggest? Tell me, Marley."

That almost made her laugh. What the demon had suggested hadn't sounded sick at all, not the way he surrounded her sexual compliance with everything she'd ever wanted. "It's not what you're thinking. He asked me to live with him, have his children."

"What?" Damien had been moving toward her, but he recoiled at her words. "And you said no, right?"

She nodded, wanting to cry, but afraid she was out of tears. There were just none left in her.

"I'm so sorry . . . that was meant for me, Marley. Meant to be my punishment—to have to watch you with him, as a family, having the children I want so desperately, with the woman I love." He wrapped his arms around her. "But obviously he didn't understand how strong you are. The strongest woman I've ever known."

Marley let herself lean on his chest, just one more time. Breathe in his scent, take comfort in his strength. "Even though he offered to free you if I did, I couldn't, Damien, I just couldn't. It's so vile, so wrong, what he is, and I didn't think you'd want me to give myself up for you. And no matter how enticing he tried to make it sound, what he doesn't understand is the vast difference between lust and love. He can only offer me lust. You can offer me love, and that is trump every time in my book."

"I would have never wanted you to sacrifice yourself. That would have destroyed me, knowing I'm not worth it, knowing you're worth so much more than that. Because nothing has really changed. I can love you, do love you, but I'm no better than Alex."

"The very fact that you can love makes you better than him." Marley wiped her eyes on his T-shirt and drew in a breath. She could do this. Even though she felt cold and tired and sick, her heart splintering like dried wood. She would do this. "But you're right, nothing has changed in circumstance. I still have to leave. It's the right thing for both of us, I think. At least for now. I need some time to think."

Damien didn't say anything, but his arms tightened around her.

"Can I spend the night at your place on Esplanade? I can leave the keys with the manager or ship them back to you."

"Of course," he said, voice hoarse. "I'll drive you there."

"No, I can't . . . really. I need to be alone. Please. I'm afraid I've used up all my resistance tonight, and neither one of us needs to drag this out." What she really needed was a soft, safe bed, and the oblivion of a few hours' sleep. As it was, she wasn't sure how she was actually still standing. Her body felt numb, frozen from the inside out.

"Okay." Then he gave a muffled laugh into her hair. "God, I can't believe I'm just letting you walk away. I'm either a complete fool or I've actually grown up."

"I'm going with the latter."

"And it only took me two hundred and thirty years," he said. Then he pulled back and gave her a kiss, soft and devotional. "*Au revoir,* Marley. May you get everything you deserve."

"Good-bye, Damien." She touched his cheek, stroked that long, masculine cheekbone. "I'm proud of you."

For a minute, she thought he was going to say something else, but he just reached into his pocket, pulled a key from his key ring, and pressed it into her hand. He closed her fingers around it, his green eyes boring into her, then he nodded and left.

Marley turned and clicked her suitcase closed.

Chapter Twenty

Damien was walking across the yard, heading toward the road, and the river, wanting to get away, wanting silence, when he heard someone calling his name. He turned and saw Marissabelle striding toward him in jeans and a tank top. She wasn't the lush twenty-five-year-old Damien had known, but more like a woman of forty. Alex had obviously decided to show her mercy.

But gone was Anna. It was all Marissabelle, from the saucy sway of her hips to the triumph on her face. "I'm leaving," she said. "Just wanted to tell you that I hope you rot in hell."

The timbre of her voice was more like what he remembered, before age had ravaged it, and the sound raked through the stores of his memory, drew up unpleasant associations. Marissabelle had been part of his past, the violent decade when he'd been intent on driving himself to the grave, defiant and miserable. "Thanks. You too."

She laughed. "You can do whatever you want with the house. I'm heading to New Orleans. I'm not sure what I'll do, but maybe I'll get a job in a club or something. I might as well use this body again, though I should probably spend a month or two doing some Pilates. The last time I was forty, women were expected to be soft and curvy, not tight and bony like they all are now."

"Well, good luck." What the hell else was he supposed to say? And did she think she was going to make him jealous if she took up stripping? He had finally come to terms with the fact that he hadn't been responsible for her downfall—she had ordered that fate for herself. He had merely been witness.

"She wasn't right for you," Marissabelle said. "Come on, you know that. People like us, Damien, we never change. We'll always walk on the dark side, and a girl like Marley, she walks the straight and narrow."

He wasn't going to have this conversation with her. Damien started walking again, giving her a wave as he turned his back on her.

She called him an absolutely atrocious curse word, but he ignored her and walked to the road, crossing it in the dark, climbing the levee. He sat down on the grass and watched the Mississippi roll by, moonlight reflected off the water, the small waves lapping against the shore.

He wasn't sure where he'd go from there, if he had the ability to go on as he had before. Nothing had changed. He was still a Grigori servant, and they still had the power to destroy everything, everyone that mattered to him, to take his soul, if he refused to serve.

Yet everything felt different. He was different.

And whatever the consequence, he suddenly knew he could no longer serve as an accomplice to the demon. He was done even if it meant death.

He was the first Damien du Bourg, and the last.

And he was going to will his plantation, his town house in the French Quarter, everything he owned, to Marley. She would take care of his legacy, tend the houses, appreciate his history.

Lying on his back, he stared up at the sky, grateful for everything he'd been given, regretful that he'd wasted so much. Rosa floated in front of him, doing that hovering thing that he couldn't stand. She only did it when she wanted to remind him she was a demon-child. Like he ever forgot.

"You're blocking my view," he told her, too tired to play games with her.

She landed on the grass with a soft thump, sitting beside him. "You look so pitiful I actually feel sorry for you." Wrapping her arms around her knees, she nudged his leg with her foot. "You hate me, don't you?"

He sighed. "No, I don't hate you."

"But I gave you this, and it makes you miserable."

"I asked for it. You warned me you couldn't undo it. I take responsibility for my own actions."

"I wanted you to be sorry you'd asked, you know, and I wanted you to love me. But I didn't really understand what love is. I'm not sure I ever will. I think the demon in me overrules the human."

Damien glanced over at Rosa. She had her chin on her knees. "I don't know, Rosa. I wouldn't be surprised if you met a man and found yourself head over heels. Sometimes I think you're a pretty big softie for a demon. Look at how many times you've watched my back or warned me about something."

"I set you up this time. I knew you'd fall for Marley."

He shrugged. "I don't regret that. Not at all. And you did what you had to do."

"Damien . . ."

"Yeah?" He plucked at the grass blades with his fingers, waiting for her to continue.

"I was with Marie when she died," she said in a rush. "I tried . . . I tried to help her. I felt . . . guilty. I didn't know I could feel guilty, but I did, that night. But it was too late. The only way to save her was to change her, and she wouldn't accept that. I'm sorry. I truly am."

Damien sighed. "As am I."

"She held my hand, wanting comfort, I think." Rosa made a sound in her throat. "It was terrifying, the idea that someone was looking to me for comfort instead or sex or recklessness. But I think that I actually did it, I comforted her, because before she died, she smiled. It was beautiful, Damien, to see her at peace."

In the dark, he closed his eyes tightly, fighting back the emotion that crashed over him in big, violent waves. It didn't take the pain away, but it helped. It did. Reaching out, he touched Rosa's hand, threaded his fingers through hers. "Neither of us is as terrible as we fear, are we? I think there's hope for us yet."

"Shit." She sighed. "I'm totally going to regret doing this, I just know, but then when have I ever done anything smart when it came to you?"

He glanced over at her. "What are you talking about?"

"I'm leaving Louisiana, heading north, but I wanted to tell you one last thing before I go." She leaned over, stared straight down at him. "Damien, you're free. You're mortal again."

It took him thirty seconds to process what she was saying. "Don't fuck with me."

"No, I'm serious. I'm not supposed to tell you, because, well, my father finds it amusing to free servants and not tell them. Then when they do something, take a risk assuming they're immortal, and die never knowing what hit them, he enjoys the irony."

Damien went up on his elbows. "You're serious?" She looked serious. And for all the complexities of their relationship, he did trust her. Rosa had human compassion in her. Yet he didn't feel any different.

She nodded. "Yes. So don't kiss a cottonmouth, okay?

You'll be six feet under, and that would really upset me, I think."

"Did you do this for me?" He was suddenly touched beyond belief.

But she shook her head. "No, you did it for yourself. When you offered to sacrifice yourself for Marley, you showed yourself unworthy of the gift."

So that was that. The elusive answer.

Damien fell back on the grass and started laughing.

⁂

Sunday night Marley parked her car in Mt. Adams and picked her way through the parking lot of the church, glancing back at the monastery hovering precariously on the steep hill. She stood at the edge of the grass, where the railing separated the parking lot and pathway from the sudden decline, spilling the hillside straight down to the river.

She stared at the Ohio River in the dusk, at the landscape she'd known her entire life. This was home, yet she had returned different. Pensive and thoughtful, heart aching, but no longer feeling the hysteria she had at Rosa de Montana the night before. Alex wasn't here, or Rosa, or Anna. Neither were Lizzie or Damien. It was just her and a future that was hers to determine.

A barge glided by, silent and large, rusty and weatherworn.

It had been the right thing to do, to leave. But it hurt, great slicing jabs of agony, and she felt raw, though determined. She would take the confidence she'd gained, the strength she'd honed, the convictions she'd sharpened, and she would live her life. On her terms. Her way.

Clutching the railing, she whispered, "Please forgive him," not sure if she was beseeching God or Marie or the whole of humanity. She just knew that Damien didn't deserve to suffer anymore, and that he had paid for his mistakes ten times over.

That the punishment of lust should be followed by the redemption of love.

Marley stared at the water, seeing her answer. Then walked away.

Chapter Twenty-one

After he left Our Lady of Guadalupe Church, Damien felt satisfied. Giving Marie's confession to the priest, requesting she be granted absolution posthumously, had been the right thing to do. It was what Marie deserved, even though he didn't feel she actually needed forgiveness. She hadn't been at fault. But forgiveness was what she had wanted. He couldn't turn back the clock, couldn't undo his mistakes or let her know that he had loved her, though badly and without maturity. This he could do, though, and hopefully she was at peace.

It had taken him over two hundred years, but he had found pieces of that for himself. Stepping into St. Louis Cemetery #1, Damien walked the crowded rows of the cemetery and pulled out his cell phone. Since she'd left eight weeks earlier, Damien had had Marley's number programmed into his cell. He'd been waiting for the right moment, for the courage, to call her. To tell her the change in his circumstances. To tell her he loved her.

He pushed send and hoped he would actually figure out *how* to say that when she answered.

"Hello?"

She sounded breathless, like she was rushing somewhere.

"Marley?" he said, his heart in his throat. God, he missed her.

The phone crackled, like she had propped it on her shoulder. "Who's this?"

"It's Damien. Du Bourg. In Louisiana." He rolled his eyes at himself. Like she knew twelve Damiens. He hoped she didn't know twelve Damiens.

"Damien. Hi."

Was that pleasure in her voice or awkwardness? He couldn't tell. "So, how are you?" He silently cursed himself for sounding like an idiot.

"I'm okay. You?"

"Yeah, about the same. Listen, um . . ." He smoothed his eyebrows and paused in the path. He had to do this. "I'm calling because I miss you, Marley. I want to talk to you. I was hoping I could come and see you in Cincinnati."

She said something, but there was a background noise, some kind of speaker voice on her end, and it drowned out her reply. It figured. Anything to prolong his torture.

"I'm sorry, I couldn't hear you. Could you repeat that?"

She made a small sound. "I said I want to talk to you too. I'm actually at the airport right now."

"You're coming to see me?" Well, alright. That was very promising. "What time does your flight get here? I'll pick you up."

"It's already here. I'm in the New Orleans airport. And I just got the keys to my rental car. Can I meet you at Rosa de Montana?"

"Of course. Sure. I'd love that. But why didn't you tell me you were coming? I could have made arrangements." Bought a diamond ring.

She gave a nervous laugh. "I figured if I just showed up you couldn't tell me not to come."

His nervousness all abated. He'd spent eight weeks

worrying that she would no longer be attracted to him without the charm of the Grigori, but so far, things were sounding good. "I never would have told you not to come here. I want to see you."

"Good. I'll see you in a couple of hours then, okay?"

"Perfect. And Marley?"

"Yes?"

"I love you." He'd never played it safe, and he wasn't about to now. Might as well lay all his cards on the table.

"I love you too." Her voice was soft, but confident, comfortable.

Damien grinned. That was it then. Now that he knew she still loved him, he wasn't taking no for an answer. She was going to be his, happily ever after, damn it.

⁂

Marley had driven the rental car faster than she should have, but she was anxious to see Damien. He had called her. He had said he loved her without a prompt from her, hadn't suggested she was a lunatic for flying down to see him unannounced.

She was hopeful, but worried that she was reading too much into it. And it had been a long plane ride, then drive out to Rosa de Montana, feeling like her entire future rested on Damien's reaction to what she had to tell him.

There were two vans pulling out of the plantation as she pulled in. Both drivers waved cheerfully to her, and Marley automatically lifted her hand in return, confused by their presence. But then she saw Damien, sitting midway up the front steps, hands on his knees, legs spread, watching her arrival.

In the two months since she'd left, her feelings for him hadn't changed one bit. If anything, they'd grown stronger as she'd had time to reflect on what Damien had endured, the bad choices he had made and the consequences he'd suffered for those mistakes, how he had chosen to continually fight against the reality of his servitude, and find good for himself in that which was inherently evil.

She had come to tell him she respected that, and let him know that circumstances had changed, that she was no longer afraid, that she trusted both him and herself, and to offer him the opportunity to discuss their future, together or separate, in a rational manner with no outside influences. Or just fling herself at him, one or the other.

Parking the car, she got out and met him at the bottom of the stairs. "Hi," she said nervously, feeling a goofy little smile cover her face.

"It's so good to see you," he said, taking her hand, kissing the back of it. "You look beautiful, *ma cherie*."

Actually, she probably looked ragged out from the traveling, but he was definitely looking at her with admiration. She'd take it. "Thanks. So, what were those vans doing here?" she said, just to say something. He looked good. Different somehow. Content.

"It was a tour group. Now that I'm no longer, uh, entertaining, I decided to allow tours here on Fridays. The admission fees go into a foundation I started in Marie's name. We'll be giving scholarships to a university for disadvantaged high school students. Marie enjoyed her years at the convent school and I think she would have approved."

Marley knew she was touch and go with her emotions, but that made tears pop into her eyes. She blinked hard. "That's wonderful, absolutely wonderful. And you're not entertaining?"

"No." He smiled at her. "No more parties. Are you disappointed?"

She gave a laugh. "Hardly. If I wear a bikini ever again, it will be too soon. But . . ." She was wondering about the Grigori, his servitude, but she couldn't force the words out. Tucking her hair behind her ear, she cleared her throat. "So you don't mind that I'm here? I had a three-day weekend and I thought . . . maybe . . ."

"I'm very pleased. Can you stay here, with me? No hotel?"

"Sure."

"Good. Can I get you a drink or some refreshments? Do you want to sit on the gallery?"

Marley laughed. "Wow. We're being awfully polite, aren't we?"

He nodded. "Yes. And it's absolutely killing me."

"So if you didn't have to be polite . . . what would you really say or do?" Marley asked, her heart thumping with love, desire. He looked so handsome, so delicious, so masculine, and she loved him. She wanted to know that she was entitled to a place in his arms, wanted to claim it and own it, but was scared to make the first step.

It had been her choice to leave.

But it had also been her choice to come back.

Despite the demons, or maybe actually because of them, Damien had become a good, moral man, and she needed to tell him the truth. Wanted a life with him if he was interested.

"If I wasn't being polite, I would do this." And he leaned forward, buried his hand in her hair, dragged her mouth to his.

With hot, urgent passion he kissed her, and Marley grabbed on to his T-shirt, overwhelmed, dragged under. She had missed him so much, and he felt so strong, so real.

"I called you," he said between kisses, "to tell you that I am free to love you, free to live my life, free to marry you."

Marley tried to pull back, startled, her hope swelling to irrational proportions, confused and needing to see him, but Damien wouldn't let her go. "What do you mean?" she whispered.

He nuzzled along her ear. "I mean that Rosa's father freed me from my immortal servitude. I am very much mortal now, and I very much want to marry you if you'll have me."

"Are you sure?"

"That I want to marry you?" he teased. "For the most part."

"No!" Marley yanked back, stared into his eyes. "How do you know you're mortal?"

"Rosa told me I am, and I have to trust her on this one. I can't go and shoot myself to prove it." He gave her a wry smile. "But I haven't done anything sinful in the last two months and neither Rosa nor Alex has said a word of censure to me. I've been practically monklike, Marley. It feels fantastic. I feel different too . . . vulnerable, yet stronger. That makes no sense, but it's true. I feel separate, like my own man."

She wasn't sure what to say, couldn't believe that it was going to be so easy. Then she realized that while she had been living in agonies of indecision, missing him, he hadn't bothered to share the news with her. "Why on earth didn't you tell me?"

Damien grimaced. "Well, you said you needed time to think. I didn't want to infringe on that. And to be totally honest, I wasn't sure if you had fallen in love with me, or fallen for the lure of the demon. I was afraid I'd tell you the truth, you'd take one look at me, as I am now, and wonder what you ever saw in me. I tested it, you know, by flirting with some women on Bourbon Street. Some responded, but others just completely blew me off. That's never happened before, not since I took the curse. I was a little . . . concerned that you might not be attracted to me any longer."

Marley felt a grin split her face. He was worried, shoulders tense, eyes narrowed. She uncrossed his arms from his chest and squeezed his hands. "You are so adorable."

He winced.

"I fell in love with you, the man, Damien, not the charms of the demon. I am attracted to you, and I absolutely want to marry you and make a life with you."

"Really?"

"Really."

"That is a good answer." He wrapped his arms around her, kissed again and again.

When he let her up for air, she laughed. "And you know, I'm relieved there won't be women drooling over you everywhere we go. That can get old fast."

He feigned indignation. "You don't think any women will drool over me? I didn't become ugly, you know."

"No, you didn't." Caressing his lower back, Marley stared up at him, marveled at all he had been through, all he had seen and done. Wondered that of all women, he could choose her to be with. Grateful that she had the courage, the confidence, to reach for her own happiness with her very attractive and masculine man. "Not ugly at all."

"Let's go in the house and I'll prove to you I still have certain charms." Damien scooped her up into his arms and held her tightly. "Oh, *ma cherie*, I don't deserve this."

"Hey." Marley touched his cheek, tears filling her eyes. "Yes, you do. You are a good man, Damien du Bourg, and fortunate that you were given two hundred years to prove it."

He nodded, swallowing hard, then smiled again. "Where will we live? I don't want you to have to give up your life in Cincinnati if you don't want to."

"We'll live here. I love this house, this plantation. I can teach here just as easily."

"What about your family? Your sister?"

Marley wrapped her arms around his neck. She wasn't going to let her sister spoil her perfect moment. "She's not speaking to me. She checked into rehab after Alex dumped her, but the minute she got out, she ran off to Chicago this time. Sebastian is doing great with Rachel, and Lizzie gave her full custody. I told his biological father about him, since Lizzie finally told me his name, and he has visitation now. That was the last nail in the coffin of our relationship, the fact that I went and contacted Alan, but I thought he deserved to know he has a son."

"I'm sorry," he said. "And you know you did the right thing."

"I know, but I'm sorry it had to be this way. But, Sebastian is fine, that's what's important. And I'm free to live here, with you, to make my own life with you and our baby." She dropped that in, wondered if he'd pick up on it.

He paused with his foot on the first step, his arms snugly under her back and legs. "You mean with me and the hypothetical children we might have in the future."

"No. I mean you and me and the baby that's going to be born in seven months."

Damien nearly dropped her. "Holy shit, are you serious?"

"Yes." This wasn't exactly the reaction she had hoped for. "Is that okay? It wasn't intentional, Damien, I swear. I wasn't trying to get pregnant, and I honestly thought it was the wrong time . . ."

Damien just set her down on the step, went down on one knee, and started speaking in French, clenched fist resting on his forehead. Marley looked at him, stunned. What the hell was he saying? Was that happy French or get-away-from-me French? She had always been lousy at understanding spoken French. Between her fear and panic, and his very traditional accent, she had no clue what he was saying.

"Damien, what are you doing? Is this okay . . ."

"Amen," he said, eyes still closed.

Unsure, Marley just watched as Damien stopped speaking, took a deep breath, and stood up. He pulled her to him. "I was giving a prayer of gratitude to Mary, the mother of God. For the gift of our child."

Marley closed her eyes, let out the breath she'd been holding. "So you're happy?"

"Are you kidding?" Damien pulled back and grinned at her. "This is *fantastique*. Perfect."

"I thought so." She laughed when he ran his hands through his hair, forcing it straight up in the air.

"You're feeling okay? Everything is okay?"

She nodded.

"Then we have to call the contractor. We have to wire the house for electricity and plumbing. We have to paint it. We have to buy a crib."

Marley laughed, loving his enthusiasm. "We have seven months. And in the meantime, I can think of other things to do." She leaned closer. "You know, I've been a bit lonely for the last two months."

That changed the look in his eye. He ran his finger over her bottom lip. "I'm so sorry to hear that. But I promise you I'll make up for lost time. I may have lost the lure of the demon, but not the experience I've gained."

That sent a shiver rolling up her spine. "That sounds promising."

"Yes, it does." Damien kissed her softly, passionately. "For the first time in two centuries when I look into the future it's not empty, but full of happiness. Can you see that too?"

"Yes." And Marley pictured a playset in the yard, right where Alex had placed it in her vision, to remind them of where they'd been, what they had, and what they'd refused to submit to.

"I definitely can see it, Damien, and it's beautiful."

༺❦༻

Rosa had missed New Orleans, missed the heat and the laid-back attitude, the river, and the crowded French

Quarter. So when she returned, she strolled through Jackson Square, took great amusement in getting her palm read by a grizzly haired fortune teller, and treated herself to dinner at Muriel's.

Then she went to Bourbon Street, bored and restless, and walked, not sure what she was looking for, but feeling that hunger rise inside her, that burbling need for satisfaction, for a man.

The October air was getting crisp, but the doors to the bars were still thrown open in welcome, and Rosa caught the eye of a good-looking guy sitting alone at a round table, two empty shot glasses in front of him, a third full glass raised to his lips. She went in as he tossed it back and saluted her with the empty, a welcoming, suggestive smile on his face.

"What are you drinking?" she asked, sliding onto the stool across from him.

"Absolut and Baileys."

"Together? Disgusting. But it will get you suitably shitfaced if that's the goal."

"Yep. Might as well enjoy life while I can." He flagged down the bartender. "Nobody lives forever."

Rosa smiled. He had very nice teeth, and his eyes crinkled at the edges when he spoke. She leaned forward, her leg brushing against his. "Would you like to live forever?"

. Penguin Group (USA) Inc.
is proud to present

GREAT READS—GUARANTEED

**We are so confident you will love
this book that we are offering a
100% money-back guarantee!**

If you are not 100% satisfied with
this publication, Penguin Group (USA) Inc.
will refund your money!
Simply return the book before
November 1, 2007 for a full refund.